I0681306

DREAMER

Also by Richard L. Miller

Under The Cloud
The Atomic Express

DREAMER

A Novel By
Richard L. Miller

Two-Sixty Press

Copyright March 2000 by Richard L. Miller, All rights reserved.

No part of this book may be reproduced or transmitted in any form by any means, electronic or mechanical, including photocopying, recording, or by any information storage and retrieval system, without permission in writing from the publisher.

For information address:
Two-Sixty Press
P.O. Box 7888
The Woodlands, TX 77380

Page layout & typography:
BiblioPress.com

····· ◆ ·····

The author gratefully acknowledges permission
for use of lyrics from the following songs:

Respectable
Words and Music by Kelly Isley, Ronnie Isley and Rudolph Isley © 1960 Ronnie
Runs Tunes; By Permission, Isley Management

Baby, I Need Your Lovin'
Words and Music by Eddie Holland, Lamont Dozier and Brian Holland. © 1964
(Renewed 1992) JOBETTE MUSIC CO, INC. All Rights Controlled And Adminis-
tered by EMI BLACKWOOD MUSIC INC. on behalf of STONE AGATE MUSIC,
INC. (A Division of JOBETE MUSIC CO., INC.) All Rights Reserved International
Copyright Secured. Used By Permission

Can't Help Falling In Love
by George David Weiss, Hugo Peretti and Luigi Creatore. © 1961 by Gladys Music,
Inc Copyright Renewed and Assigned to Gladys Music (Administered by
Williamson Music) International Copyright Secured. All Rights Reserved.
Reprinted By Permission.

The Thrill Is Gone
Words and Music by Rick Ravon Darnell and Roy Hawkins ©1951, 1979
Powerforce Music (BMI)

It's Now Winter's Day
Words and Music by Tommy Roe. © 1966 by Low-Twi Music.

Sister Love
Words and Music by Curtis Mayfield. © 1963 by Warner/Tamerlane 1963.

For Ava

Always Remember.

Part I

"Just as there is an infinity of actual pasts which have led to the present state, so there is an infinity of really existing futures which evolve from the present state."

— Frank Tipler, *The Physics of Immortality*

1

Signal

Nine p.m. Lab 14 is absolutely quiet. I sit in the black leather induction chair for a moment, reclined to horizontal, waiting for the drug to take effect. It should be about thirty seconds. Sure enough, the room is getting cottony and, despite the chill of the ventilation system, becoming quite warm. Like someone turned up the heat. I attach the throat microphone, then strap on the helmet. Suddenly Leonard's voice crackles over the headset.

"Mike. Can you hear me? Give me a count."

Without moving my lips, without opening my mouth, I breathe, *think* the numbers one through ten.

"I hear you loud and clear. You can stretch out for a minute. I have to key in your vox signature."

I take a deep breath, look up and do what I usually do just before induction: count the holes in the ceiling tile. I get to fifty-nine when Leonard's voice returns. "Okay, Mike. You comfortable?"

"Yeah. I'm fine." I hear my own voice echo in the headset—a metallic, robotic strip of noise that sounds like the whine of an automatic bank teller machine. I hate it.

"Give me a full-body signal."

I take a deep breath and *will* movement through the left side of my body, feel the buzz ripple down my spine then back up, reaching a point at the top of my head. Another deep breath. In my headset I hear Leonard's steady drone: "Lessee—everything looks fine. EEG's good. Surprisingly, everything is up and running...okay, Mike, think of a blue square…thank you. You may close the visor, now."

I reach up and slide down the metal shield. Now the world is dark. The last thing I'll see are twin green dots floating in the darkness—an effort by the machine to track my eye movement while I'm down there.

"Look up. Down. Sideways. Now, think of your Aunt Nancy naked. Heh. Just kidding. Hm. Looks like the pupillometer is tracking okay. We're almost ready."

"Good." My own voice echoes in the headset. It sounds metallic, lifeless.

"Remember, it's lock, then scan. Then unlock. Always lock before you call."

"Right."

"If it's night, try to get a shot of the television. Outside, try to notice the stars and the position of the moon. Remember, twilight ends when the sun is 18 degrees below the horizon."

Amid Leonard's words I hear the whirring of the machine and a dissonant chirping emanating in the headset. And now there is another sound, like an elevator switching on.

"—If you happen to hear a radio playing, let me have the song title. And always try to get the time and weather. If there's precipitation, that's significant—"

As the elevator sound increases in pitch and volume, I feel my body grow lighter, probably the result of the preinduction hypnosis. I imagine myself floating off the chair. Up and into another dimension.

"Now let's take a look at your math coprocessor. Give me the sum of twelve and ninety-one…thank you. Visualize wherever it is you hope to visit. Thank you. *Very* good signals in both frontal and occipital lobes…now, recite the Gettysburg Address."

"I don't know the Gettysburg Address."

"Okay. I'll take anything. How about the Beatles? You're a Beatle's fan, aren't you?"

I hear the music in my mind. A song from the spring of 1967 flows around me like a river.

Nothing is real.

"Got it. We have theta…and…entrainment.

Good afternoon, Mr. Mitchell, have a nice dream."

I sink into the pulsating circuits of my cortex, down past the great pyramids of Betz, past the great curved fornix. Like liquid, I dissolve through my skin, through the black chair and fall into the clear sky below.

It's Tuesday, 10:00 a.m., exactly fourteen hours after my induction. I'm embedded in a thick leather chair watching the Lab Director, David Poundstone, rummage through his desk. Every few minutes, he pauses to brush his thin brown hair from his eyes or to push his round, rimless spectacles back up the bridge of his nose. With his ragged beard, short-sleeved oxford shirt and khaki slacks, he resembles an Oxford University paleontologist on a dinosaur dig.

I glance behind him through the window to the skyline of summertime San Antonio, Texas—a brown landscape of brick and glass and the occasional mesquite tree. Even though we're not allowed newscasts, I'm sure the outside temp is pushing one hundred. Probably could fry an egg on your forehead. No way I would step out into that furnace, even if the Lab allowed it.

"Forgive me, Michael, I always manage to misplace exactly what I'm looking for—ah! Here's your file!" Poundstone chuckles apologetically. "Was on the desk. Heh."

"Heh." I echo the laugh and flash my most genial smile. I don't want to get on Poundstone's wrong side—it would be bad for my personal history.

"There. Yes." He opens the file and adjusts his glasses. "You've been here two weeks now—and last evening was your tenth induction." He looks up. "Did you remember anything about it?"

"Not much." I shake my head. "But after I went to bed I dreamed like crazy—very vivid images—a lot of it from my grade school years."

"Yes, that's a fairly common occurrence," he nods. "The brain's initial response to the induction techniques is through lucid dreaming. Were you able to control it at all?"

"No." I pause, afraid to ask the question. But what the hell. "Do you think I'll ever be able to control where I go? Say, for example, I want to visit a certain day in 1966—will I be able to do it?"

Poundstone's eyebrows rise in one of his Oxford shrugs. "Well—the chances are against it. As I told you early on, it's theoretically possible—some subjects have excellent control—Otto Pleer and that Coltrane fellow come to mind. But the vast majority aren't so fortunate. We explained that to you on the first day."

"I know." I can imagine what's coming next. I'm in the fat part of the bell curve. In there with all the average guys who have *no* choice over where they go. One minute sitting through a second grade arithmetic lesson, the next puking up a bad school lunch. "I was hoping—" I let the words trail away into a barely audible whine.

Poundstone smiles. "Yes, I realize most people want to control where they go. But very few ever do. Like most of the others, Michael, you will doubtless fall into your memory banks on a purely random basis."

Great. Just great. Fourteen thousand dollars and three months out of my life—to visit my first sandbox. I should have booked that one-way flight to Vladivostok.

Poundstone pauses to scribble a note to himself. "Why not schedule another hypnosis session for you. This afternoon okay? At our regular time?"

"Sure. Fine." I watch him write down the time in his notebook, a little black job with some sort of latching cover. Probably a Japanese design. Professionals like Poundstone are suckers for Japanese design. Retro-sixties. Do you suppose they're ahead of us in memory-travel too?

"I'll do a regression to loosen things up," Poundstone is telling me. "After that, you should begin to retain at least some information." He looks up at me over the top of his spectacles. "You understand, of course, not all the memories back there are pleasant—"

"I understand that."

"Actually, I suspect the existence of unpleasant material is the most common reason for recall failure. The subconscious simply doesn't *want* to remember." He pauses, a tentative smile on his face. "Perhaps that's the case with you, Michael."

"I seriously doubt it." I rise to leave. "This afternoon, then?"

"This afternoon." Poundstone says, shaking my hand. "At four."

Walking down the empty hallway to the elevator, I wonder whether I should stay with the program at all. Why waste all this time and money if I can't recall where I go?

I press the "19" button on the elevator and ride to the window-rimmed top-floor lounge. As the doors slide open, I see that it's empty. Just a big gray, carpeted room overlooking the brown, strangely baroque San Antonio skyline.

I walk across the carpet and collapse on a couch next to the window. Outside, maybe eye-level with the nine-foot-tall window, are three scruffy white clouds. Directly beneath them is a clump of about a hundred automobiles—all motionless in a Texas-style freeway traffic jam. As I watch, the clouds disappear, dissolved by the heat from the altercation below.

Now, all that's left is a dusty blue sky.

My thoughts drift back to my first day here, listening to Poundstone address the group of time-travelers, his voice resonating through the auditorium, telling us that despite the restrictions—no current news, no television, no radio, no leaving the building, no anything—the journey would be worth it. He congratulated us for our courage, called us "pioneers in the truest sense of the word, embarking on the most remarkable journey since the leap to space—the leap into *memory*."

Wedged in that tense audience, I mentally catalogued all I would see, hear, feel, *experience*: the CBS Evening News, November 19, 1963 when Cronkite showed the clip of the Beatles at the Palladium—that day in 1964 when the very first Ford Mustang rolled into town. I'd take notes, then jump back a few years earlier to see cars with grille bombs, bat-wings, push-button transmissions and wrap-around windshields. Cars that grinned chrome teeth like Dick Tracy villains.

Back a little further, I'd enter another world entirely—a world cluttered with drawings of boomerangs, starburst patterns, asterisks, delta shapes and rockets. There would be flying saucer lamps, Calder mobiles, sensitive lines and handles on everything, no matter how heavy.

And radios with tubes. Radios that played songs in the night: Sam Cooke, The Platters and the very first record by Little Stevie Wonder—"Fingertips Part 2."

Real American history. A damn good place to run back to.

And even if I couldn't stay, I could at least make a few bucks on the trip.

I look at the buildings of San Antonio, giant rectangular crystals sticking up out of the concrete. It's an even bet someone—*someone* out there—is calling my ad agency in Boston right now, wanting help to sell their product. And they all say the same thing: "We'd like a *sixties* feel to this—the baby boomers have all the purchasing power, you know—"

"Yes, sir. It's a very popular and effective tool. Perhaps we can place it with an early soul song—have you heard of *The Four Tops*? No? How about *Tommy James and the Shondells*—"

There might be another client like that twenty-something Hollywood producer, the one with the green silk suit and no hair except for a ponytail. The one who wanted to make a movie based on a song from 1968—*any* song from 1968. "Listen," he said, "you find the song, I'll find the story—I heard there was a lotta *serious stuff* goin' on back then."

I never saw the final movie, but my partner Jerry did. He said it was "confused." Just like the sixties. But like everything else about the sixties, it made a lot of money.

So, if I can't run away and hide in my own attic maybe I can at least inventory the damn place. Maybe there's something valuable, you never know.

"Your band wants to remake a 1960's song? Try 'Drivin' Wheel' by Little Junior Parker. Charted in May, 1961. Want a more urban sound? How about 'Village of Love' by Nathaniel Mayer and The Fabulous Twilights, 1962. Detroit band. Very obscure, but excellent. The public will think it's a current original."

I remember the dark February night I heard that song for the first time, roaring out of my old RCA tube-radio set like a runaway freight train. I turned the radio up so loud it woke my brother, Earl. "Good song, Scout," he'd said. "Guess ya got some class after all."

Well, Earl, you were wrong, but that's okay. At least I got the songs down. And maybe with some luck, I'll get to hear you say that again.

Maybe Poundstone's wrong, too. Maybe Mike Mitchell isn't in the big part of the bell curve—maybe I'll really be able to pick the time. I'd see my folks again, and like virtually every other guy in the program, take side trips to visit the loves in my life.

Brenda Lacey would be first. Green eyes, soft blonde hair, compact body, quick temper, a recognized expert in innovative kissing. I'd visit that perfect snowy prom night in March when she wore a low-cut yellow formal and played "Moon River" on her mother's Steinway. Oh, yes, Brenda would be number one—and probably two and three.

But maybe I'd appreciate Jill Jackson more. Pretty—a little too tall—but with penetrating blue eyes and long brown hair always tied in a ponytail. The only girl ever to pull a switchblade on me in public—I never knew why, but all my friends were impressed. I would probably go back to the time we biked to her father's cabin on Elk Fork, then lay on that little cot with the striped mattress and listened to the sounds in the night.

Or maybe I would travel all the way back to my freshman year in high school to see Pam Carswell. Pam with the heart-shaped face, hazel eyes and full, almond lips. I would go back to the night we both sat shirtless on the diagonal supports of the railroad bridge, talking about God and looking for shooting stars. Dressed only in cutoffs, high above the rails, she was an angel in the moonlight.

But after Pam I'd return to Brenda Lacey again. Incomparable Brenda—with her brilliant smile and smooth, perfect legs. Why on earth did we ever break up? Did it have to do with—what?

I draw a blank.

At the orientation session, we were told men and women tend to remember different things from their past—and generally travel back to different events. Given the choice, women in the program usually opt for the high road, visiting family and friends—while men immediately head for the underside of the cerebral cortex—searching through the heated little memory packets where their favorite girlfriends reside.

I came here looking for that, I'll admit it. I wrote the check, packed my suitcase, said goodbye to everybody, boarded the plane and came down here—with all that in mind. I had planned to spend an hour and a half each night touring the enjoyable part of my life. No cares, no responsibilities. Just nice warm, friendly memories. Jump on the cerebral highway and travel to the best places—bright little spots on the neural roadmap.

Now—after the checks were cashed, of course—Poundstone tells us there *is* no roadmap. Not even a signpost along the way.

The memory banks are nearly impossible to navigate.

Sorry.

I look out the window at the cloudless sky. In my mind I hear Poundstone's voice. "Take heart. At the end of the course you should be able to retrieve at least *some* information..."

Some isn't good enough.

I'm here to get it *all*.

2

Memory Channel

Noon. I'm in the cafeteria trying to work my way through a bowl of five-alarm chili and some suspicious material the cook calls *migas nachos*.

Across the table from me, rotund Otto Pleer, attacking his second helping of the mixture, is smiling and talking. Otto, like me, is assigned to Lab 14. He's a retired physician—a neuropsychiatrist—so I take his enthusiasm for the food as a sign it's probably not toxic. At least in small quantities.

Next to him, the bluff, friendly Jim Keller is carefully polishing off a Greek Salad. Like Otto, he is in his late sixties and probably packing twenty extra pounds, but unlike Doc Pleer, Keller hasn't visited the past for any great lengths of time. He's scheduled for his first long run this week.

Despite that, he doesn't seem particularly nervous. Half the time he's tossing out gibes and jokes based on arcane chemical concepts from his years teaching at Texas A&M. "Here, Ott, lemme borrow your pen, 'cause I wanna show you the chemical structure for my latest patent— *amino-world*. Get it? A mean-old-world—?"

Right. Everyone's seen the little diagram before, but we chuckle politely, even the normally acid-tongued Gail Banks, seated next to me. Gail is picking at a small bowl of fruit salad—kiwis, honeydew chunks, grapes. Keller told me last week Gail was once a clinical psychologist—or a nurse. Or maybe a newspaper reporter. Something like that, he wasn't sure.

"Hey, Otto," Gail says, giving us her best sneer. "You know what 'migas' means in Spanish? It means *ants*."

"Ants huh?" Otto raises his bushy eyebrows. "Well, I think they're delicious!"

"Anybody hear how Russell Coltrane's doing?" I ask.

"He isn't." Gail forks out another grape. "Twenty-two hours into the run, Leonard had to scram him. Said the trace was going flatline."

"You're kidding," Keller says. "Coltrane is the best there is."

"I saw the printout," Gail says. "You could barely see a wave pattern. Looked like static. Leonard thought ol' Russ was heading for an eclipse, so he hit the red switch. Brought him right back."

"Leonard scrammed me a month ago," Keller says. "I was in 1952, it was summer and I was walking along Pennsylvania Avenue in D.C. Beautiful night. I heard Leonard's voice. He asked me where I was."

Gail glances at me. We've heard the story.

"Well," Keller chuckles, "I decided this was *my* night, so I didn't answer him. I guess I went another five or ten minutes—then the lightning hit. When I came back I threw up all over the induction chair."

"I'm not surprised," Otto says. "That scram is an electroshock straight to the cortex. I try to avoid it whenever possible. How's Mr. Coltrane doing?"

"All right, I guess," Gail says. "Leonard says it didn't really seem to bother him. Just got up off the chair, shook his head and went to his dorm room."

"Coltrane's a tough old bird," Keller says.

"He's a *strange* old bird." Gail stabs a chunk of a green-tinged cantaloupe. "I heard he could do long runs the second week he was here—two days in the chair."

"He's good," Otto smiles. "It took me a month to work up to the long run."

"It must be strange to spend all that time in the past," Gail says.

"*Eh*," Otto shrugs. "It's no different than your standard one-hour session—you're just in the movie for a longer period of time. You can still only observe."

"That's the only part I mind," Gail says, glancing up at me.

"After you spend more time in the past," Otto glances at me, "you'll hear this talking in the background—it will sound like a radio."

"Radio?" I ask. "You're tuned to a *radio*?"

"It's your mind," Keller interjects, aiming a long finger at my forehead. "You've got a memory record of your own thoughts too, y'know. If you listen real close you can hear them. Whatever they were at the time."

"So I was only a tape recorder back then, huh?" I lean back in my chair. The lunch has lost its appeal.

"That's right, Michael. A tape recorder," Otto smiles. "That's what we humans do—we make tape recordings of our lives. Heaven knows why, but that's what happens. And with hypnosis and the chair, we can go back to any part of the tape—and stay there as long as the IV fluids hold out."

"Hey, Ott," Keller says, "tell 'em about Gus Giordano."

"Oh, yeah," Otto nods, "Gus was the best. Stayed down the longest and brought back the best information. I heard he could tell you what was playing on the radio on some Tuesday in 1941. Could even tell you what the radio looked like down to the nick on the dials. Zey said Gus had the best peripheral vision of anybody he's ever seen. A natural. King of the navigators."

"I can't imagine going back that far," I mumble. But it's a lie. I *can* imagine it.

"You know," Otto says, "you can only go back to a time after your birth. None of this past-life mumbo-jumbo."

"The time distance isn't important," Keller says, retrieving a cheese wedge from his salad. "It's how the brain arranges the memories. You might have the memory of your first birthday stuck next to something that happened to you a month ago. That's what makes this whole thing interesting. When you travel back there, you don't know *where* you're gonna end up."

"Especially during the long runs," Otto nods.

"Yeah?" Gail stabs the final melon chunk. "I think staying in the chair for more than two days at a time is *weird*. I've had a little psychology training myself and I know there's all kinds of things that can happen to you down there—dissociation—appearance of multiple personalities. Leonard says he's seen some dreamers come back shredded like an old newspaper."

"That sounds like Leonard, all right," Otto chuckles. "Listen. Every normal personality is composed of multiple intelligences. Otherwise, you couldn't drive a car, carry on a conversation and listen to the radio at the same time—"

"I don't want any of mine splitting off to start their own band, okay?" Gail interrupts. "This shredding stuff gives me the creeps."

"Well, the multiple personality stuff doesn't bother me," I say, looking around the table. "I just don't think I'd like a needle stuck in my arm for two days."

"Hey," Keller gives me a Texas grin. "Ya gotta *take in fluids* while you're down there. Th' thing *I* don't like is the catheter they—" he glances at Gail. "Well, *you know.*"

"Boys, just remember this physiological principle—" Gail gets up from the table, "if yer gonna drink, yer gonna pee."

We watch her straight-arm the cafeteria door, her polka-dot skirt a flurry of activity.

"I sure do like that woman," Keller says after a minute. "I bet she'd be fun to run a double-time with."

"Double-time?" I look at him.

"Jim's favorite fantasy," Otto says. "It's when you send down two people who knew each other to their shared past—and then have them talk to each other using the larynx mikes. The two people can experience the past together and comment on it."

"*Comment,* huh." I laugh.

"Well, yeah!" Keller turns back to me. "Leonard told me there was a couple in here two months ago that tried to do that. I guess *something* worked pretty good. The got outta the chairs and went straight to their room—an' it was the middle of the afternoon."

"Leonard told me about them," Otto says, turning to Keller. "They were both about our age, Jim." He slaps the Texan on the back. "Maybe you should bring your wife down here."

"Louise wouldn't do it." Keller shakes his head. "She doesn't buy into any of this booshwa. Real practical woman."

"My wife's the same way," I tell them.

"That's too bad," Keller shrugs.

"Yeah," I say, getting up from the table, "it is."

"Henderson, Cobham, Mitchell, Lambert."

"Hi, Kazy? This is Mike Mitchell."

"Oh. Hi, Mr. Mitchell. You want to speak to Mrs. Mitchell?"

"Is she in?"

"She was just leaving. I'll see if I can catch her."

There is a click and I'm listening to a traffic report for the high-ways around Boston. A mid-day jam in the tunnel, a fender-bender on Mass Ave and an auto-pedestrian on Boylston. Then another click followed by a familiar voice. "Linda Mitchell."

"Hello…Linda?" It sounds tentative. Like a question. Maybe it *is* a question.

"Mike! How are things in Texas?"

"Boring. The food's not bad, though—"

"Well, have you *found yourself* yet?"

"No. Have *you*?" I shoot back.

"Hey, Pal. You're the one running away from everything," she says. "Last time I looked I was still earning a living."

"Give me a break. I'm down here on business. I'm getting sixties material for the ad campaigns—"

"Oh, please, Michael. Spare me. The only business concern you have down there is of the backseat variety. What was her name?"

"Who?"

"The chubby little blonde who ditched you in high school or when-ever. What was it—Brenda Lucie—"

"Lacey. Brenda Lacey. And if I happen to see her, I'll tell her you said hi."

"I'm sure you will."

"Look. To be honest, I've been through ten sessions in the chair and I still can't remember anything."

"Right. Michael, you're starting to sound like one of our criminal clients—'that's not the real reason I did it—and besides, I don't re-member anything—'"

"Come on, Linda."

"Justaminute. Can I put you on hold?"

The traffic report comes on again. The auto-pedestrian accident on Boylston has cleared, but the tunnel is still jammed.

"Okay. I'm back. Had to take a call from our office in DC. I think our client's going to be indicted. Seventeen counts."

"That's too bad."

"For him. Lots of billable hours for us. Uh—so tell me—how's the food down there? Have you found any good Mexican restaurants?"

"I haven't seen them." Just like Linda. Push the opponent to the edge of the ledge, then change the subject.

"One of the senior partners will be in San Antonio next month.

He wants to know some good restaurants. Van has a book on restaurants around the country and San Antonio isn't on the list. I thought you might know of some good ones."

"The dreamers aren't allowed to leave the building."

"You spent fourteen or fifteen grand or something on this little getaway and they won't let you leave the building. What is that place, a fat farm?"

"Dammit, Linda, being sequestered in the building is part of the deal."

"Yeah, I knew that, but I couldn't resist. Sorry. It just sounds so weird—like you're in some kind of high-rent pokey. Do they lock you up at night? Do you have to wear a little electronic leash or something?"

"No."

"Oh, don't sound so sullen. I'm just having a little fun with you. So tell me about the rations. Do you get three square meals a day?"

"The food in the cafeteria is pretty good. It's been tough to lose weight."

"You should really do that, Mike. That's getting to be some spare tire you have." She pauses, allowing me to stare momentarily at the front of my shirt before launching another mortar round. "Hey. When you go back to see Brenda, are you going to tell her how much weight you've put on over the years?"

"If she asks." I'm looking down at the roll of fat around my waist. My size 32 belt is out to the last hole. Thinning hair, flecks of gray, and now getting fat. Unidentified middle-aged man. If you know this man or have seen him, please contact—

"Michael? You still there?—Mike?"

"Yeah. I'm here."

"Stay away from the Mexican food, okay? I hear it's loaded with fat. I don't want you to have a heart attack. I saw on television that a single cheese enchilada has over a thousand calories."

"You're watching television again?"

"There's some good things on TV. Besides, Van has a book that shows the calorie count of every damn food under the sun—"

"Is Van your private librarian now?"

"No, but he reads books. Not biz mags, but real books. Do they let you read books down there, Mike?"

"Look, Linda, I gotta go—"

Silence. I can almost hear her shift gears, changing subjects, backing away from the ledge. I glance at my watch. Five minutes with Linda is like going fifteen rounds with a pro boxer.

"Paul called last night. He said they're reading his script."

"They're reading Paul's script? That's great news!" I pull the phone closer. Thankfully, conversations about the kids are in the demilitarized zone.

"Someone at some agency said it had great potential for a sitcom. And the reader's fee is only three grand."

"Three thousand dollars? To read a script?"

"That's the way things are out there. You know that. You deal with those people all the time."

"*Three* thousand dollars? Hell, Linda, I would've read his script for free."

"You make television commercials, not sitcoms. You have zero clout with the studios. Besides, you're down there in Texas—trying to find your—"

"You didn't actually send the money, did you?" I interject.

"Of course I did. He's our son. Besides, what's a measly three grand?" Her voice picks up the edge again. I hear the big guns roll out, hear the shells drop into the chamber. "Listen, Michael. Three grand is chicken feed compared to what you've spent on your *little vacation in Dreamland.*"

An impressive performance

"Mike? Mike, are you there?"

"I'm just cleaning the venom out of my ear."

"Nice try, but I heard it already. Look, Mike, I gotta go. Gotta make some money. When you get back we still have these things to talk about."

"Yeah, like who gets the house?"

"Hey. I told you. You can *have* the house. I just want what it's worth. *Sweet Dreams, 'Lil Nemo.*"

Click.

I stare at the dead receiver. All I hear is the hiss of the ventilation system.

····· ◆ ·····

4:00 p.m. My stomach still churning from my encounter with Linda, I open the door to Poundstone's office. Maybe a dark room and a little hypnosis will help me relax.

And maybe not. For some strange reason, Poundstone has the blinds open: I'm met with the bright yellow glare of the afternoon sun.

"Please have a seat." Poundstone motions to a chair in front of his desk. "Enjoy lunch?"

"I had the nachos." I blink my eyes: the sun is directly behind Poundstone, giving him the appearance of some fiery, glowing being of light.

"Nachos, eh?" Poundstone says, his spectacles flashing like little halogen beacons. "Well, it's been four hours, so it's probably okay. Most psychiatrists won't admit it, but straight-on hypnosis can make some people a little queasy." He glances at something on his desk and a ray of sunlight ricochets from the bald spot on the top of his head, hitting me squarely in the eye. "Leonard claims it's the cafeteria food here, not the hypnosis that makes people nauseated. Sure you're feeling okay?"

"I'm fine." In truth, I want to leave. Leave the Institute, leave Texas. Leave this part of the world.

"I'll darken the room a bit," Poundstone says, rising from his desk. "And while I'm doing that, I'd like to ask you to focus your attention on the little statue on my desk."

As Poundstone walks around the room closing the blinds, I concentrate on the object: a green copper angel holding a sundial. The angel's wings curve gently out and down around her sides as though she's landing. Or taking off, I'm not sure which. As the room darkens, slivers of light seem to advance up the angel's wings, followed by rivulets of shadow. In a moment, the angel is in shadow, a mere outline in the darkened room.

"Michael," Poundstone returns to his desk, "if I were to ask you to return to any specific year in your life—and made sure you could remember it later—would you go?"

"Of course."

"Even if there was loss?"

"Yeah. I'd still go."

"Then you will."

The couch is similar to the leather induction chair—soft and smooth with an almost liquid texture. In my first week here, I learned all about hypnosis. What it is, what it isn't, how it works, and how to help it along.

Calling on what I learned that first week, I send waves of tension and relaxation up from my feet through my center and finally out my head. Then, as the last wave leaves, my body becomes heavier, a solid, leaden weight, sinking into the couch.

I focus on Poundstone's voice, locking it in like a radio station amid the stray signals of my own thoughts. Soon he'll introduce the metaphors for the trance state. Here's where he calls on my beliefs, experiences and background to help coax me into the dark center of my midbrain.

The elevator. He'll probably use the elevator.

"...You will relive all the experiences of that time in your life. You will enjoy what is there with all of your five senses. You will hear what is there to be heard, see what is there to be seen..."

As I listen almost absentmindedly, somewhere deep in my thalamus, some part of me is watching, listening—checking off the phrases as they come—the authoritative "you will," the sensory commands, the assurance of a pleasant experience. The standard stuff. If it was to be a deep trance, Poundstone would try other techniques—affect bridge, pyramiding, pressure, confusion—perhaps all of them at once.

"Michael, you will remember the feelings of the year 1963. The sights, the sounds, the music. The smell and sensations of 1963. Concentrate on that feeling and experience it again...and while you are experiencing it, I want you to picture yourself in an elevator."

The elevator again. Hypnotists must like elevators.

"...It is now the present and you are on the top floor, while 1963 is the ground floor. As the elevator descends, you are going into a deep, peaceful sleep. You will see the images of your life as you descend to your home in 1963, all the while feeling safe and protected, feeling the sights and sounds of 1963 more and more...and you will be able to tell me what you see—"

And now, there is silence. It occurs to me I'm lying on my stomach and holding on to something flat and metallic. Though it is dark, I can tell I'm at a slight angle with the horizon.

"Hey, Mitchell." I hear a child's voice call my name. "What time is it?" The voice belongs to my best friend from eons ago. His name was—*is*—Evan Carswell.

"I can't see my watch. It's too dark." My own voice, high-pitched, reedy and choked with fear.

"Yeah? I thought you said it had radium in it, so you could see it at night."

"I guess it doesn't work." I look around inside the darkness, watch the shapes from background—outlines of a superstructure.

I'm on a bridge. I'm on top of a railroad bridge sometime in the late fifties or early sixties.

There is a bright light near the periphery of my vision: a crescent moon with a background of stars. In the distance, I hear the distinctive nasal wail of a train horn.

"He's passin' the first crossing," Carswell says. "There should be two longs, a short and a long."

He's right.

"It's around the bend," he says. "Just before the trestle." I hear his voice, but I can't see him. Of course. My eyes are squeezed shut. There's a click. Then another. My heart is trying to hammer its way through my chest.

Evan laughs. "I asked my dumb brother to come ride the bridge with us when the train came through. He said he had better things to do than get killed. Big pansy-ass."

I open my eyes for a second. The steel girder I'm on is about two feet wide. My hands are gripping the edges so hard my arms ache. Thirty empty feet below me is the vibrating train track. Another sixty feet below that is the dark, flat surface of the Salt River.

Without warning, a blinding white light arcs across the horizon, searing the trees in its path. Now I hear the low thrum of the diesel locomotive.

The bridge begins to shake.

"This is cool," Evan says. "Better than the water tower."

I try to breathe, but can't. All my muscles are locked.

The beam of light swings around, skimming the nearby trees, then aims in our direction. I see the nose light is actually a rotating beacon, swinging the beam in a counterclockwise fashion, a cyclone of light.

The bridge superstructure begins to flash, alternating between pitch dark and a blinding, searing white. I see my hands, covered with grime, gripping the edges of the girder, welded to the metal, flashing in unison with it.

The diesel starts across the bridge, horn howling.

The girder rattles violently, then unexpectedly moves from side to side. To my left, on the opposite truss, I see Evan roll back and forth, one leg dangling down from the girder. I squeeze my eyes shut.

Minutes later, the rumble subsides and I look around. Across from me, I see Evan's outline on the bridge, sitting on the girder, his legs dangling into empty space. The scene shifts to follow the train—the beacon now illuminating the buildings at the outskirts of town. And finally, the last car, the caboose, follows the train down the track, a dot of glowing red, receding into the distance. I feel the breeze on my face. Someday Evan will be gone and his younger sister will come here with me to cry over him.

I slide down the black bridge girder, toward the present moment. Then stop.

I'm in my upstairs room back in Corinth. It's late evening and I'm in bed reading *The Mystery of Marr's Hill*. Across the room, lying on his bed next to the window, is my older brother, Earl. He looks like I've always remembered him—an eternal 17-year-old with a crooked, amused grin and dark brown hair growing out from a butch flattop. He's in his pajamas, the stupid ones with the diamond pattern. And he's wearing socks—the only person I've ever known who wears socks to bed—even in the summer. His rationale: he wants to be ready in case one of his cigarettes burns the house down. Sensible.

My gaze wanders to the dresser, reddish-brown in the glow of a small lamp. Outside, I hear the steady drone of summer locusts. The alarm clock on my bedstand reads ten after one. It all seems real.

Earl looks up from the magazine. "Hey Scout. I'm gonna raid the icebox. Get a Pepsi and maybe fix a cheese sandwich. With chips. Want me to bring you something?"

"I can get it." I hear my voice, still high-pitched. A child's voice.

"You sure?" Earl flashes the crooked grin. "I don't wanna take you away from that book."

"That's all right. I've read it once already. Besides, I'm starving to death."

"Don't wake the folks."

I'm downstairs now, rummaging through the refrigerator—mayonnaise, hamburger buns, Kraft sliced caraway cheese, some tall bottles of Pepsi. And a bag of Guy's potato chips. So greasy they're *translucent*.

Waitaminute. My family kept potato chips in the refrigerator? Must have been a sixties thing.

I pack it all on a tray and head back upstairs. It occurs to me Earl must have done okay on his date with Sally. Making out with her always makes him hungry afterward. "It'll happen to you too, Scout," he told me once. "Wait and see."

I doubt it. But I have to admit, his girlfriend *is* cute.

Back upstairs, I hand him the tray, grab a sandwich and return to my book.

The clock ticks forward.

I watch Earl take a huge bite of sandwich and switch on his little wooden radio. From the brown fabric speaker I hear a chorus singing *double-you-ell-esssss—Chicaaago—*."

I close my book and set it on the nightstand. I *am* eleven years old. That really *is* my big brother over there, reading his magazine. Down the hall, my mom and dad really *are* in their room asleep. And across town, my best friend Evan Carswell probably has his radio on too, listening to WLS or KAAY or whatever it is he has tuned to in this world. I close my eyes and the darkness reaches out.

Fragments drift in from the periphery of my vision—from somewhere else. They overtake the scene, coalescing into an image of my mother's eyes, red from crying. She looks impossibly young, younger than I am now.

"How come we didn't get any cards from them?" she asks. "We've known them ever since Earl was a child. He once dated their daughter, for god's sake."

A blur. Things seem to be moving too fast. I see a man. My father, dead these twenty-odd years, also young. He shrugs. It's eloquent, perfect, and so very familiar.

Then, his voice, deep: "Some people can understand what another person feels. Some people can't. It's not that they're bad, they just don't have the equipment. I'm not gonna hold it against 'em."

"We sent them flowers when Joel was in the hospital."

"And we'd do it again." Dad is grim. "Come on. We have to get to the cemetery. Mike, you okay?"

"Sure, Dad." Everything is blurry. My throat hurts. I see the cold, gray November day, the flowers, the row of bright gladiolus—the worn rug at the funeral home, the organ music. The townspeople crowded around. Filing past the closed casket. The bronze coffin where my brother is lying.

Not long ago I watched the evening news with him. There was a

British rock band on. All I can think of is that song, it goes over and over in my mind—*From me to you*—

The future and the past are the spokes of a huge wheel. And the wheel has rotated. What is future is now past. And is fading from view. Gone.

Abruptly, I'm in Poundstone's office again, my face wet with tears, my throat constricted from the pain of what I'd seen. Of where I'd been.

"Here," Poundstone hands me a tissue, "use this."

"Sorry. I thought—I mean, this is really stupid—"

"Don't worry about it," Poundstone pats me on the shoulder. "I thought maybe you were trying to do too much."

I blow my nose, then collapse into a helpless wash of tears—a whimpering, drizzling idiot.

It's night in San Antonio, and the scenes remain. Dark, wet, cold. Menacing. Is this what it's like to remember? I hear Poundstone's voice, vivid amid the soft hiss of the ventilation system: "the retrieval of verifiable information through simple memory channels—"

Channels? Is my memory tuned to that night on the railroad bridge? To my brother's death? Where are the nights with my mom and dad, like that evening we watched a satellite drift across the black summer sky?

Simple memory channels, *right*. At least I remembered.

That's something.

I look out the window, at the expansive city sparkling orange and yellow under a low, wet cloud deck. Though it's summer now, the scene doesn't look much different than it did that army autumn thirty years ago.

I search for the channel, find it. Change it.

There's a Frontier Jet landing with a hundred shaved-head recruits fresh from basic training in cold November Missouri. We step from the plane into humid air, walk across the flat concrete tarmac, climb the corrugated metal steps into the waiting green buses. Some stop to admire the St. Augustine grass, dense as living-room carpet.

San Antonio is a city from science fiction: trees green in winter, shirtsleeve weather that could drop forty degrees in a half-hour, downtown spotlights shining against billowing orange clouds, a huge tower that rises from the city like some Albanian minaret.

And then there is the River, winding through the city like a memory, a long, sinuous stream of translucent green water escorted by a wide cement walkway. It has no beginning or end, only an endless loop of water and grass and trees and sidewalk and sun.

I change the channel to San Antonio 1970—to that Friday in February when the drizzle made the city look like a watercolor in the rain. Out of the Post, board the Kelly Street bus and then to the River. There, at one of the restaurants, I write a long letter, the words coming in confident blue strokes. Another beer, another page, and I write until the words become blurry as the windowpanes. Then the restaurant closes and I return to the barracks along with letters I can never mail.

And they always begin the same: Lightning-wife.

I smile at the thought, turn the channel back to the starting point. Here and now.

I've got to call home.

"Michael? Is that you? What time is it?"

"It's ten thirty. I thought you'd be up still."

"Well, I'm not. I'm in bed with a 300-page deposition."

I hear something.

"Is there someone on the downstairs phone?"

"No."

"You sure?"

"There's no one here except me. Look, if there was someone here with me, I'd *tell* you."

"I only wanted to call. To see if everything is going okay."

"Well, it is."

Standard Linda. The best defense is a good offense. Besides, if there *was* anyone there, she *would* admit it. Just for the hell of it.

"I just wanted to know what's going on in the real world. Fill me in."

"If you mean about what's going on in the news, you know I can't do that. It's part of the agreement."

"Tell me about your job then. Any of your clients go to prison?"

"Only the ones that can't afford us. In fact, we have a client who suddenly discovered he's got four toxic waste dumps on his property. Actually, the feds discovered it and pointed it out to him. I was reading his depo when you called—hey, did I tell you Paul's got a new girlfriend?"

"No."

"Yeah. Our son's got him a California girl. Blonde hair, blue eyes. Has a pair of in-line skates. But I think he's getting fed up with her demands. She wants him to write her master's thesis: *Deconstructing Babette's Feast*."

"She wants him to *write* it for her?"

"That's what he said. *And*…she doesn't want to pay him anything to do it. She said that if he wrote it it would be good experience for when he has to write his own thesis. I told him, I said—Paul, you should get paid *something*. It's only fair. It's not easy writing a master's thesis for somebody."

"*Deconstructing Babette's Feast*? What's he supposed to do—analyze recipes?"

"How should I know? I thought it was a Norwegian cook book."

I hear a shuffling noise, like paper rattling, then another click. I press my ear to the phone. "Linda, are you sure—is there a way to see if our phone is tapped?"

"Mike, our phone is *not* tapped. It is illegal to tap a phone without a person's knowledge. There's a bad thunderstorm here tonight. Maybe the lightning is doing it."

"That's probably it."

"Look, we're not supposed to talk more than a few minutes each time, that's part of the agreement."

"Yeah, I know. I wanted to hear your voice. I just wanted a taste of civilization. This place is starting to close in."

"I'm sorry. But you signed up for it."

"I know."

"Look. I gotta get back to work. I'm deposing this toxic waste expert tomorrow and I don't know a damn thing about the specialty. Okay?"

"Sure."

"See you, kiddo. Bye."

"Bye."

I put the phone down and walk to the window.

Outside, the old buildings glow gold under a burnt orange cloud cover. Not far away, the Tower of the Hemispheres still reaches 600 feet into the mist, just as it did in 1969. And of course the River is still here, only now there are more restaurants and bars lining its length. More lights, more tourist boats, more concrete, more of everything. And much less than I remember.

I draw the curtain, remove my shirt and shoes and collapse on the bed. No television in this place—Poundstone and his staff won't allow us access to outside broadcasts. There's only a beige metal speaker in the wall near my bed, pouring out a spare, barely audible version of what I think is the Gayne Ballet Suite. The first time I heard it was in the movie 2001—while watching a lonely spaceship float past Jupiter.

I take off my slacks, pull up the covers and turn out the light. In the background, against the ethereal space music, I hear the soft woosh of the ventilation system. Across the darkened room, the last thing I see tonight is the window curtain glowing orange from the sodium lights of San Antonio.

The Gayne overflows into the hazy brown world behind my eyes, conjuring up random images—my first meeting with Linda, the woman who would be my wife. A wisecracking transfer student from the east coast, she knew the right things to say, the right places to go. Hamburgers at the Village, then all-night lovemaking in that Kansas City hotel. Later, her law school in Boston, *my* flights to Logan International, the final move away from the midwest. Sayonara, Kansas City.

I see my first job as an ad agency intern, the rented ranch-style house in Lexington, not far from Walden Pond. The day we brought Paul home from the hospital. Linda's first big defense case, the celebration, then our first real home—painted battleship gray. Paul with the video camera, following the big white ducks. Five white "Donalds" and they all looked the same. They all came when called.

I like the Boston area. Fair amount of woods and expansive fields, not the bleak, rocky edge of civilization I had once thought the east coast would be. After a few years I even got used to the subways, old dark libraries, brilliant autumn days, bone-chilling winters, and long, bleak commutes to New York City. Well, actually, I guess I never got used to it—any more than Linda and I got used to each other.

Static.

Guess I gotta switch the mind channel to a friendlier station, like maybe a nice New England winter sunset—driving along the pike in our beat-up Chevy Suburban—Paul asleep in the back, Debbie chewing on her Mr. Bear. A song comes on and Linda turns the volume down. "Okay Mike. Name it."

"Good Vibrations. Beach Boys. First hit the charts in the third week of October, 1966. Went to number one. Charted about fourteen weeks."

"I can't *believe* you know that stuff."

"It's my job." I turn the volume up and see someone else. Someone far away. Now the sunset is gone and with it the Suburban and my family—I watch them as they drive north toward Lexington. But as I float away toward the music, I hear another voice—Poundstone's. It is from his initial address in the Institute's auditorium, welcoming the new dreamers.

"Of course, we have our own program goals to consider—namely the retrieval of verifiable information. It's a goal we share with our funding agencies who are interested in how much the mind can retain over the years."

"Here," she says. "Here is where spring starts. Right on this spot."

The weeds have given way to an expanse of dense grass. Ahead of us is a small gray pond, its surface corrugated by the wind. Her sweatshirt is gray, the color of an overcast sky. I feel the earth beneath us, hear the soft rustle of grass.

"Spring'll be here any minute." I hear her voice, young, familiar. I know her. And now I feel her fingers interlocked with mine.

The sun breaks from behind a veil of high cirrus, and a quick burst of wind rattles the reeds, ripples across the grass and across my body, a cold breath from the blue sky.

High above us, tiny dots of silk drift by, spiders in their parachutes, riding the wind.

"Tell me," she says, "tell me about Evan."

"The subjects will learn to access their own information through simple memory channels. The data will be evaluated and scored by an independent laboratory. In this way, we can improve our techniques for memory retrieval. Currently, we're close to the magic 95 percentile confidence interval..."

"I tell you, Mitchell, we can sell these things. Maybe get good money." Evan turns over a rock with his tennis shoe. "You'd think there'd be a bunch of them here."

"There are no lizards here," I tell him.

"Sure there are. They're all over the place. Listen. We can put them in a box. Keep them as pets for awhile. *Then* sell 'em."

"My dog would eat them."

"Then *stop* your damn dog from eating them." He aims his flashlight at the ground and nudges another rock. There is nothing there. He removes his ratty baseball cap and wipes his forehead with his sleeve.

"Hey. Whatcha doing?" The voice is pitched high like a child's.

Evan turns and aims his flashlight at the voice, illuminating two little girls—probably no more than ten or eleven—warily watching us. The taller one has long blonde hair and a pretty smile. The shorter girl has a small oval face and a serious, no-nonsense look. She's wearing a red knit sleeveless top and jeans with tennis shoes. I notice her thick, dark hair is pulled straight back into a ponytail.

"We're looking for lizards," Evan says evenly. "So get outta here. You'll scare 'em away."

"Lizards?" the smaller girl says. "That's a stupid thing to be doing in the dark. Bet you didn't find too many, didja?"

"We're too busy to be talking to little kids," Evan growls.

"Oh, you're *real busy*," the smaller girl snaps back. "*Real* hard at work, you and that little flashlight of yours. Looks to me like it needs batteries. The light's already yellow. Probably go out any minute—"

"You know, the band is gonna play at the pavilion in a few minutes," the taller girl says. "You two want to come down and dance with us?"

"We're too busy to dance," Evan says, nudging a rock loose.

"Okay." The smaller girl folds her arms. "Anybody see Davy Crockett at the Alamo?"

Evan and I look at each other.

"Didn't think so," she smiles, picking up a long stick. "So I'll tell ya about it."

"Look—" Evan says.

"Shutup and listen," the girl continues. "This is important: When the Mexicans were getting ready to *charge*, Travis called everybody together and he said, 'okay—there's a lot of Mexicans out there, so ya gotta either fish or get off the pot.'"

The taller girl gives her a puzzled look. "Rachael, did Travis say that? Or was it Davy Crockett?"

"Doesn't matter," the smaller girl says, "—because *then*, he took out his sword and drew a line on the ground. And he said—if you're gonna stay, cross the line. If you're not, then *beat it*."

Evan gives me a confused look. "What the hell is she talking about, Mitchell?"

"Now, if you guys would like to escort two *very personable young ladies* to the dance—all ya gotta do—" she drags the stick across the gravel walkway, "—is step across this line. Simple, huh?"

"Forget it," I tell her. "We don't dance with little girls."

"Bad decision," she says, "I won't hold you to it—I mean, everybody deserves a second chance—even guys like you. Right, Connie?"

"*These* guys?" The blonde curls her upper lip, Elvis-style. "I really don't think so, Rache."

"The band's gonna start any minute now," the smaller girl says. "What's it gonna be?"

Evan gives her his best scowl. "Get lost."

"Okay. Y'had your chance," she tosses the stick aside. "C'mon, Connie. Let's leave these jerks to their lizards."

The lights come on and the dome of sky changes from black to blue. Evan's here, wearing his brown baseball cap and a striped orlon shirt. I know he isn't real, yet I see him now, Scout backpack, canteen. Same orlon shirt as always.

It's early afternoon, I know it's a Saturday, and we're walking along a gravel road, near the railroad tracks. Evan is talking.

"You know that guy who plays Chester in *Gunsmoke*? Anyway, he'd done something and they were going to execute him for it. Put him in the electric chair. And he told them it wouldn't do any good because he was dreaming the whole world. But they executed him anyway."

"What happened?"

"The lights went out. Then the whole thing started all over again."

"The whole show?"

"Nah. But you knew that was going to happen." He flashes a lopsided grin, his right eye squinting in the sun. "Did I ever tell you about the guy who jumped from the train?"

In the distance there is the sound of a locomotive.

Poundstone's voice again: "*Some researchers have said that the past is a dangerous place to be. That it's inaccessible for a reason. We at the Institute, of course, don't agree with that philosophy——*"

My brother Earl is looking at me, shaking his head. He's wearing his only suit, his only tie. "Scout, it's all a film. That's all it is."

I can't cry. I'm not *supposed* to cry.

"It's all up here in your head. Like on a big reel. It goes through a projector or somethin' and that's what you see."

"But where does it go? I mean when it's done?"

"It goes onto another reel. And when you die, you get to see it again. It's a movie of your life."

"Is that what Evan's doing now? Watching his movie?"

"That's what he's doing, Scout." Earl nods his head slowly. "He's sitting in his own theater, with his own personal guardian angel. And they're watching his movie."

"What happens when he gets to the end? I look up, all blurred. "To when he got killed?"

"Then they get up and the guardian angel takes him out of the theater," Earl says, his dark eyes glistening under the rainy sky.

"And then they go to heaven?" It's a demand.

"Yeah," Earl puts his arm on my shoulder. "They go straight on to heaven."

I open my eyes. Evan and Earl are gone, but the rain is still falling. I can hear it.

It's falling from the sky, outside my window. Falling onto the empty streets of the world.

𝟑

Magnetic Tide

I t's finally morning.
Outside the rain-spattered window the sky is an angry indigo.
A rumble of thunder sends a nervous rattle through the venetian blinds.
Standing slump-shouldered and sleepy in the energy-conserving, luke-
warm shower, I realize I probably shouldn't be taking a shower during
a thunderstorm. I envision a lightning bolt hitting the building, traveling through the pipes into my shower stall, turning my naked ass to
steam. I quickly turn off the water only to hear the phone. Sliding into
the bedroom, I catch it on the third ring.

"Mike? This is Linda. Did I get you up?"

"No."

"Look, I'm sorry I was so short with you last night when you called.
I've been overloaded with work—it wasn't a good time. You're not
mad, are you?"

"Not anymore. How was the deposition?"

"Which one are you talking about?"

"Didn't you tell me you were studying for a deposition?"

A minute of silence, then, "Oh, that one. It was reset for next week
sometime."

"Oh."

"But I wasn't actually going to take the depo, one of the junior
partners was going to do that."

"That right? For some reason I thought you were studying for it."
Here I am, sitting soaked and naked on the bed, quizzing my wife long

distance. There *must* be more to life than this.

"Michael, June is always a bad month for the firm, and we're short-handed after Tom quit. I've had to work morning, noon and night. And on top of it, there's this *thing* you're doing down there in—in—*Texas*. Why Texas?"

"San Antonio is a big military town. This thing probably had some funding by—"

"Texas—San Antonio—I don't know how to make sense of it. I'm under a lot of pressure, and you're not helping."

"Probably not," I pause for a moment. Why not be honest with her? "I was thinking about quitting the program and coming back home."

There's a long silence. She wasn't expecting something like *that*. "Michael, you want to *quit the program*? After all the money you spent?"

"Yeah. You've convinced me that it's a waste of time. So, I'm going to quit and ask for a refund."

"What if they don't want to give you a refund?"

"You're a lawyer. You can get the money back."

"I saw the contract. It's bulletproof. You quit and you can kiss that money goodbye. What was it, fourteen thousand plus ninety bucks a day for the room?"

"Something like that."

"You've spent the money, you may as well go through with it. After all, it's *your* mid-life crisis."

"At least I didn't run away to Russia. I was really thinking about doing that. I was going to get a ticket to Vladivostok."

"That was *last* month's plan. The month before that you talked about opening an office in Seattle. And before that, you were going to sell out and move to upstate New York to what—work on bicycles? At least with this *brain thing* in Texas, you're actually going through with it. That's something, anyway. And didn't you say it might be good for your business?"

"Oh, I'll probably find an old song or two back there, but—"

"Look, there's a call coming in from our Mexico office. I gotta run. We can talk about this later."

There's a click and I find myself sitting on my bed, staring at a dead hotel phone.

Suddenly, there's a flash—and now it's raining outside.

······✦······

Breakfast this morning is as dreary as the weather—a choice of corn flakes, shredded wheat or oatmeal. Lowell Anderson, a tall, taciturn dark-haired kid in his mid-twenties, refuses to even consider the stuff. Instead, he has somehow managed to round up a plateful of melon cubes.

"The neuros threw a party last night," he says in a slack, Southern California drawl. "Catering forgot to send down the snacks."

Gail Banks eyes him critically, then glances over at me. This morning she's going casual—tank top and baggy shorts, her long honey-blonde hair tied in a ponytail. Though she's probably in her mid-thirties, this morning she could pass for a trim twenty-six.

"Hey," Lowell continues, "I have some smoked oysters and fajita nachos in my room. You guys can have some if you like."

"I know I'll be there." Keller looks up. "Usually, I stay away from oysters, but I'll eat a *cooked* one. Don't have to contend with the *vibrio*."

"Let's have a picnic on the roof." Gail glances at me. "We can sit in the elevator house and watch the rain."

"We'll get *soaked* out there," Otto says, stirring his oatmeal. "Besides, they haven't mowed the grass up there in a week."

"Any *other* wet blankets in the audience?" Gail looks around the table. "Or is Otto the only one?"

"You could ask Coltrane," Keller says. "He'd probably go."

"Come to think of it—" Gail looks around the table, "where *is* Coltrane?"

"He's still in his room," Keller says. "With his scram migraine."

The table erupts in laughter, while I smile and eat my cereal. Years ago, one of my college professors told me that, psychologically, women never age past sixteen, while men are lucky to get past twelve—and generally stop at nine. I don't know where he got the idea, but surrounding me this morning is the hard evidence.

"Y'know," Keller says, "Leonard's got a quick trigger finger all right, but he sure knows how to run that jukebox. Yesterday, I was passing through the seventies and caught a show on the tube—'Hawaii Five-O'—and I wanted to see if Leonard knew where I was. So I told him what the show was about—a physicist was threatening to blow up Honolulu with a nuclear bomb—"

"I remember that show," I nod. "Spring of '69, right?"

"Not even close," Keller shakes his head. "November 27, 1973. Took Leonard a minute and a half. *Then*, he told me that it was a

Tuesday night and if I was in Georgetown—which I was— it's raining outside." Keller's eyes are wide. "I locked the scene and checked my peripheral vision—and sure enough. It was raining to beat the band."

"Yeah," Gail nods. "When I was a kid I used to watch 'Mannix' all the time. Now I tell Leonard the plot and he tells me the date."

"I have a story for you," Otto says. "My wife used to be interested in astronomy. One night, I think it was 1951, I heard her mention that Jupiter was directly overhead—and some such star was on the eastern horizon. I locked the scene and told Leonard. You know, it took him no more than a minute to pin the date, the time and the weather. He's truly amazing."

"Leonard's good all right." Gail looks at Otto. "But it's still kind of weird, when you're down there talking to this goofy-sounding electronic voice in your head. And you know it's coming from this big computer nerd with long, greasy hair and little round glasses. It's still hard getting used to."

"You know—" Otto leans forward conspiratorially. "I've been thinking of some way to fool him—and I think I've found it. If I can get to the right place and time, I'll be able to send him data that will be nearly impossible to verify. He won't even get the year right."

"What are you gonna do, Otto?" Gail asks.

"I'm not telling. But you can come and watch." Otto gets up from the table. "I'm going under at ten this morning for a group of visiting neuros. You can sit in the gallery above the lab."

"So you're gonna fool Leonard," I say. "From down there."

"From down there," Otto taps his forehead. "Stop by and watch."

It's 9:45 when Keller, Gail and I step through the thick, smoked-glass door into the dream lab. Other than Leonard, hunched over the computer "vox box," we're the only ones here.

"Hey, guys." Leonard looks up and adjusts his wireframes. In the half-light from the instruments, he resembles a denim-shirted, pimple-flecked graduate student. "You here for Otto's trip?"

"Yes," Gail says. "He invited us."

"Otto's excellent." Leonard pushes his glasses up and returns to the task of attaching a cable to an electronic switchbox. "Gives a performance completely indistinguishable from a rigged demo."

We walk up the carpeted stairs surrounding the lab and take seats in the front row of the gallery. Twenty feet below us is the empty leather induction chair, the black plastic helmet resting on a gleaming metal cart. As Leonard putters about, I visually trace the medusa of cables sprouting from the helmet back to the gray plastic manifold connected to the machine. The Big Iron. The Engine. The *Cray-ola*. I've heard Leonard call it all those things. To me, it's an irritating signal, a chirping sound in the speakers of my headset that grabs my brain waves and holds them until my body goes to sleep.

"What are you working on, Leonard?" Gail asks.

"Replacing some memory boards. One of the dreamers from the B group nearly pulled an eclipse this morning, then did a fandango on the core. Absolutely smashed the stack. Had no idea where we were."

"Sorry."

"It happens. Every time this guy gets in the chair, he hoses the system." He taps his head. "I think he's got a misfeature up there somewhere that lets him slide off into hyperspace."

"Oh, come on, Leonard—" Gail says.

"You see it with computers too, like that bletcherous old dinosaur in Lab 10. Have to watch it all the time, otherwise it'll lose the vertical and go flat. Chugging away in its own little universe. Just have to throw the red switch and start over."

"Leonard," Gail shakes her head, "you are truly a geek."

"Be nice to me, Banks." Leonard pushes up his glasses. "When you're down there, I'm your only link to reality. In fact, it was me who talked them out of using the Penfield probes."

Gail rolls her eyes.

Leonard looks at me and smiles. "Penfield probes. Named after Wilder Penfield—neurosurgeon who operated in the thirties and forties. During surgery he'd use an electric probe to touch the patient's brain—and the patient would relive some particular event in his life."

I glance over at Gail, who's shaking her head in disgust.

"One of the neuros here was trying to figure out a way to actually touch the patient's cortex." Leonard grins. "The effect would be the same—instant memory. I guess the idea was to attach a video board and see what's going on. He probably saw too many sci-fi movies. Brain pirates from the future."

"They were actually going to do this?" I ask.

"Oh, yeah!" Leonard laughs. "They were heads-down serious. Wanted to use a photon gun or microwave or something. Pinpoint precision. Same principle as a disk drive and probably as reliable." He shrugs. "I told them it wouldn't sell. Who wants their neurons toasted? Besides, it would have put me out of a job."

"Thanks, Leonard," Gail says.

"Of course, the approach was elegant," Leonard says. "Anyhow, the neuro who came up with the idea left the Institute."

"Where did he go?" Gail asks. "The CIA?"

"Nah," Leonard shrugs. "I think he was hired by one of the cable networks."

At ten sharp, the door opens and Otto shuffles in, wearing the standard surgical green shirt, pants and booties. After a few words with Leonard, he waves at us, removes his spectacles and slides onto The Chair. After getting into position, Otto puts the helmet on and slaps down the smoked glass visor.

Leonard pulls on a microphone headset and throws a switch. "Can you hear me, Dr. Pleer?"

"I can hear you fine, Leonard," Otto replies, folding his hands over his chest. "Mind if I catch a few winks?"

"Try to appear alert until show time, okay?"

"Where would you like me to go this morning? Early fifties?"

"That's up to you," Leonard shrugs. "Surprise us."

"Maybe I'll go back to Manhattan in November, 1940. That's a good time. My wife Gina and I take a little vacation in the Catskills on October 16. Crisp autumn air. Trees turning colors. You should see it. It's delightful."

"I *can't* see it, Otto." Leonard flips on a set of switches. "Only you can see it."

"Yes, and that's too bad. It's really beautiful."

"Maybe we should glue a television cathode onto your occipital cortex. Then everybody can see how nice the trees are in there." Leonard grins at us, then lowers the lab lights to a soft red glow.

There is the muffled thump-thump-thump of people coming up the stairs. In the dim light a group of figures appears at the stairway entrance—neuros, here to watch Otto's session. Silently they file past and take their seats in the row of chairs circling the lab.

The door swings open and Poundstone enters the room, followed by short, stern-faced Dr. Tom Zey. As Poundstone whispers to Leonard, Zey carefully attaches a long black glove to Otto's right arm and adjusts a strap near his elbow. From experience I know it will be used to measure respiration, heart rate, blood pressure and partial pressure of oxygen. If necessary, it will also be used to deliver some sort of anesthetic into a wrist artery. Liquid sleep.

I've had it myself: a brief tap from the glove needle and then the sensation of ice water coursing up toward my neck.

And all the while, there's the chirping from the headsets.

We watch Zey attach the sensor apparatus to Otto's throat and place the thick ceramic cylinder over it. The super-sensitive throat microphone.

"All right, Otto," Leonard says. "Think for me. Count to five."

"One—two—three—four—five." The voice coming from the vox box is flat and tinny, but unmistakably belongs to Otto.

A few seats away from us, one of the neuros switches on a chair lamp, illuminating a small oval of red light on his notebook. A second later, there is another light. Then another. Everyone's taking notes.

Poundstone looks up at the balcony surrounding the lab floor. "Gentlemen, it will be only a few more minutes. We're making some final adjustments."

I look up at the acoustic-tiled ceiling glowing red from the writing lamps.

"We're ready," Poundstone says. "Leonard, start the tape." The reels on the tape machine snap into action. High above, chilled air begins to rush through the ventilation ducts and the temperature in the room drops. At the same time, I see the glove on Otto's arm puff up. Is Zey injecting something already?

"Tape rolling," Leonard says. "Induction ninety-six. Subject 1802. Ten-oh-five a.m." Leonard's delivery is crisp and professional.

"Introducing liquid nitrogen into the system."

"It's to keep the electronic detectors cool," Poundstone tells the audience. I look at the body on the chair. A faint crust of ice forms on a small metal cylinder attached to the throat mike.

"We're getting a good signal," Zey says. "Fast fourier transform engaged. Sodium pentothal ready."

There's an electrical whine, like an elevator starting up. I glance at the glove. It's inflated. No doubt: Otto is being helped into the arms of Morpheus courtesy of a general anesthetic.

The whirring sound increases in pitch. The computer engine is scanning, searching through the brain waves for one particular pattern.

"Theta detected," Zey says, his voice tense.

"Signal introduction," Leonard responds.

"The signals are introduced through the headset and serve to keep the conscious mind awake while allowing the body to go to sleep." Poundstone's voice is soft, like an announcer at a golf game. "The subject, of course, has been preconditioned using standard hypnotic techniques—"

"Entrainment," Leonard says.

"Here," Poundstone continues, "the signals from the computer match the brain wave pattern. Some of our subjects claim to be able to actually sense this. We'll give him a few seconds—"

The body in the chair is absolutely still.

"Otto," Poundstone breathes into the microphone. "Otto, can you hear me?"

"I can hear you."

I feel the goose bumps rise. Distant, flat and melancholy, the voice is one of the *eeriest* sounds I've ever heard. Do we *all* sound like that from down there?

"The signal," Poundstone turns to the gallery, "originated in the subject's larynx, was amplified over a million times, then digitized and filtered to remove the associated neural and thermal noise. From there the data is sent to a four-way parallel processor where it is time-adjusted and analyzed to preserve sentence context. The result is a 95 percent accurate transcription of messages from deep sleep—and from the realm of lucid memory."

There is a murmur from the audience. Whatever it was Poundstone said, it got the attention of the neuros.

"I'm going down now."

Listening to the metallic voice, an image forms in my mind of a robot descending into a pool of liquid mercury.

"I'm in."

"What do you see, Otto?"

"Street. Cars in the street." Static. I see Zey glance nervously at Leonard, who in turn fidgets with the control panel, apparently trying to tune in the signal. A pair of nervous Frankensteins with their pudgy little monster. I saw a movie like this once.

"Where are you, Otto? Tell us where you are."

Silence.

"We broke contact." Zey says, his voice tense.

"Nah." Leonard peers at the computer monitor. "He's still down there. I can see him thinking. He's probably just hiding."

"Hiding?" Poundstone looks both perplexed and embarrassed.

"Yeah, he's done it before," Leonard says breezily. "No prob, though—I've got his theta wave in a hammerlock. Give him another call."

"Otto?" Zey taps his microphone. "Do you hear us? Please come in. You have us worried up here."

Gail leans over and whispers to me. "Otto got away from 'em—whatcha wanna bet?"

After a long, tense moment, the metallic voice fills the room. "I'm still here, Tom. I was just floating around in the ether. I can see my whole life from up there. It's very interesting."

Leonard smiles and reaches for a can of Jolt cola.

"I'm on a city street," Otto continues. "It's Manhattan. Cars look like—yes, 1949. Just a minute. I see—I see a newsstand. It's—it's February 12, 1949. There's rain. It's been raining."

Leonard quickly leans forward and types something on his keyboard. The computer screen responds with a spreadsheet and a map.

"Can you tell us the temperature, Otto?" Poundstone asks.

"I'm wearing a wool coat. I see snow. There must have been snow…"

"Okay," Leonard says. "We know the afternoon temp that day reached 41° F. Cloudy with drizzle over parts of the city."

"Where are you, Otto?" Poundstone asks.

"Walking through Central Park with my wife Gina. She's carrying a package from Macy's. It's a blouse. A blouse with a little blue ribbon…"

"Well, Otto, I can't really verify *that*," Leonard shrugs. I turn to catch the expression on the faces of the neuropsychiatrists. No one is taking notes: They're all staring, some with their mouths open.

"Can you examine your peripheral vision, Otto?" Poundstone asks.

"Yes. Can see almost to the edges. I'm wearing glasses, so it gets a little distorted. Beyond the edges, the usual things. The gray zone, sparks—ah. Drat. I seem to have made a time shift."

"Where are you now, Otto?" Poundstone asks.

"I'm not sure—"

Gail nudges me with her elbow. Is this the beginning of Otto's cat-and-mouse game?

"I'm looking at a movie theater—I don't know the city—"

Leonard, his eyebrows bunched, taps something on the keyboard.

"What is the name of the theater, Otto?" Poundstone asks.

"The Paramount."

Leonard shakes his head. "Otto, *all* the movie theaters back then were named 'Paramount.' What's the film?"

"It's—uh—looks like 'Storm Warning'—"

"With Steve Cochran, Doris Day and—ahem—Ronald Reagan," Leonard says. "That narrows it down to early 1951. And now the weather data please."

"I can't tell—I'm downtown in a city, but everything seems dark."

"Blackout, huh? Thought so." Leonard types on the keyboard, then peers at the computer monitor. "What are you doing out so late?"

"I'm walking back to my hotel."

"Watch your step. You're probably in Boston, and the visibility there is only ten feet. There was an ice storm the day before and some power lines are down." Leonard glances at Poundstone. "I'd say near midnight, February 2nd, 1951."

"Otto?" Poundstone asks. "Leonard says you're in Boston. Is that about right?"

"I—it could be—"

"You've really got some interesting weather down there, Otto," Leonard says. "The jukebox says it snowed the night before, then rained, then froze. Huh. Two degrees. That's cold!" He pauses to type on the keyboard. "And look at this— electrical blackouts in Savin Hill, Cambridge, Revere, Wellesley. I'd stay at the hotel if I were you—"

"I guess I will."

"Want the television schedule?" Leonard asks.

"No."

"Okay. How about sports—" Leonard peers at the screen. "Hm. Looks like Holy Cross defeated Loyola 81-56."

"Thank you."

"If you get a chance, you might hike over to the Astor theater tomorrow and catch 'The Magnetic Tide.' Watch your step. It'll be icy."

Silence.

"Otto?" Poundstone asks.

"I'm back in New York."

"Good move," Leonard says. "How about some data?"

"I'm on the sidewalk. Gina—my wife—is with me. It's raining and we're, uh, waiting for a taxi. I can't feel it, of course, but I can tell it's cool out. There are little mounds of dark snow here and there. And Gina is wearing a coat, a tan camel hair. Black gloves, nylons. Black shoes. I'm looking up at the street signs now—it looks like Fifth Avenue at Sixty-Third. Yes, there's Central Park—ah, the taxi just went by. Drat!"

I glance at the neuros. They're all leaning forward in their chairs, stunned at the performance.

"Do you have the date?" Poundstone asks.

"No. There's no newspaper stands. But I hear a car radio playing—just a moment."

Except for the swoosh of the ventilation system, the lab is silent.

"It's someone singing 'McNamara's Band'—"

"One minute." Leonard types, then scans the screen. "That song was recorded by Bing Crosby on December 6, 1945 and was a million-seller. He's probably in February or March of 1946. If he gives us a time and temp I can pin it down exactly."

"Did you hear that Otto?" Zey asks. "Do you have the time and temperature?"

"I'm sorry. I'm watching the street. It's raining and the traffic is really terrible. And Gina just now stepped in a puddle. Ah. I hate that."

"Shall I bring you back now?" Zey reaches for a switch on the control panel.

Silence. I stare at the body in the chair. Immobile, asleep. Not a part of this world.

"Otto?"

The room is absolutely still.

"Otto, are you there?"

"Yes. I'm ready."

Among the neuros there is an audible sigh of relief.

"All right, Leonard," Poundstone signals to the technician. "Bring him up. Slowly."

There is a whirring sound, like an electrical motor speeding up. Then a click, followed by an extended rash of static from the vox box. The body on the table jumps as a ripple of electricity passes through.

Leonard shuts off the tape machine. Down below Otto slowly reaches up to lift the helmet from his head.

The show's over.

4

Highway

Otto pokes at the roast beef with his fork and shakes his head. "I don't know how he does it!"

"I was watching the computer," Gail says. "First he listed the Paramount theaters, then narrowed it to the ones showing that particular movie."

"But how did he know I was in Boston?" Otto says. "Tell me that?"

"After you told him it was dark, he called up a list of electrical grid blackouts." Gail shrugs. "He can find anybody anyplace."

"Unless it's Wyoming," someone says. I look up to see tall, Russell Coltrane, dressed as usual in work boots, jeans, blue plaid shirt and round, wire-rimmed glasses.

"Have a seat, Russell." I pull out a chair for him. "I understand Leonard gave you a little headache."

"Yeah." Coltrane folds his lanky frame onto the chair. "I was cruisin' along route 20 south of Thermopolis and forgot to check in, so he yanked my chain." He smiles sheepishly, his grey eyes wide. "It was my own fault."

"I've never been scrammed." Gail leans forward. "Did it hurt?"

"It didn't feel good." Coltrane wraps his huge hands around a cheeseburger. "The fillings about jumped outta my mouth. There for a minute, I thought I could smell *smoke*."

"Like bein' in the middle of a thunderstorm!" Keller says, nodding vigoriously.

Gail glances at Keller with a look of unease.

"Well—" I get up from the table, "I've got a session in the chair this afternoon, and I hope Leonard keeps his finger off the switch."

"All you gotta remember is one thing," Coltrane says between bites of the burger.

"What's that?"

"Never *ever* lose your t-4 wave."

"My *what?*"

"Your t-4," Coltrane says. "It's a little wave signal coming from the right side of your head. Leonard watches it like a hawk. He'd let almost all the other lines go flat before he hits the scram. But if that t-4 starts to look the least bit funny, he throws the switch and pulls you outta there. Boom. Just like that." Coltrane nods solemnly. "Then you wake up with a headache and seein' double."

"So how do I keep my t-4 wave from—uh, getting lost?"

"Ya got me," Coltrane shrugs. "Wish I knew."

"Thanks," I smile. "Thanks a lot."

"You're welcome," he says, returning to the cheeseburger.

·····◆·····

"Henderson, Cobham, Mitchell, Lambert."

"Hello. This is Mike Mitchell. Is—"

"One moment please." Music. An easy-listening version of "Hey Jude." I press the receiver hook and try again.

"Henderson, Cobham, Mitchell, Lambert, can you hold?"

"This is Mike Mitchell. Is my wife in? She's—" It occurs to me that I'm listening to "Hey Jude" again.

And finally, a voice: "Linda Mitchell's office."

"Hi, this is Mike Mitchell—"

"Oh, hi, Mr. Mitchell. This is Kazy. Mrs. Mitchell isn't going to be in the office until next Wednesday."

"She isn't? I talked to her this morning—"

"Oh really? She left to go home at noon. I think the conference in Mexico is supposed to start tomorrow and they wanted to leave tonight—"

"She's going to a conference in Mexico?"

"Oh, didn't she tell you? It's the—oh, excuse me—" The line clicks and I hear the tail end of "Hey Jude." Then, merciful silence—

then a dial tone. The connection failed.

I redial, my fingers furiously punching the keys.

"Henderson, Cobham, Mitchell, Lambert."

"Hi. This is Mike Mitchell and I'm calling long-distance from San Antonio and—"

"One moment please." Now I hear an easy-listening version of "Light My Fire." An excruciating minute later, the receptionist returns. "I'm sorry, Mrs. Mitchell isn't in this afternoon and her secretary is out to lunch."

"Kazy's out to lunch? But I just talked to her!"

"You did? Well, her voice mail is turned on. Would you like to leave a message?"

"No. Is my wife going to be in this afternoon?"

"No."

"Tomorrow?"

"You'll have to talk to Kazy."

"But she's not there."

"I know. She's out to lunch. Would you like to leave a voice message?"

"No. I'll call later." I slam the phone onto the hook.

4:05 p.m. The visor snaps over my face, blocking out the lab. The cuff on my right arm expands to a snug fit. I wonder if they'll use the needle this time.

"Everything okay in there?" The nurse taps on the side of the helmet. "If you need a little muscle relaxant, let me know."

"Uh, I don't think I'll need it." I open my eyes to see the twin dots of green light staring back at me, like the eyes of a cyborg cat. Or something.

"...Blood pressure is a relatively relaxed 120 over 70—"

Leonard's voice in the headset is reassuring, but I'm still a little nervous. Will I remember anything this time? I'm beginning to wonder if Linda was right. Maybe I *should* have spent my money running away to Russia. At least I'd have memories *and* photos.

"...Pulse is a smooth, even seventy-eight. Partial pressure of oxygen is a nice, perfect 100 percent. Heart activity extremely boring. Good QRS. No PVCs. Electroencephalograph is...nice and squiggly with all sorts of questionable spikes and subdeltas—only kidding. If you can hear me, raise your pinkie..."

I raise my hand and speak into the microphone. "Keep away from the scram switch, okay, Leonard?"

"How come you're worried about the scram switch?" Leonard asks. "Don't you plan to come back today, Mike?"

"I heard being scrammed hurts."

"Think of it as tough love."

"Don't do it, Leonard. *No scrams.*"

"You've been listening to Jim Keller," Leonard shrugs. "Keller has a very tender scalp. Gets blotchy just after a volt or two."

"Leonard—"

"I *refuse* to believe the scram is that bad—all you feel is a little tingle. You barely notice it. There's more static electricity in a hard rubber comb."

"Ever have it done to you?" I ask.

"No time-surfing for me. I leave the high weirdness and transient scalp pain to you guys."

I realize it's a losing battle. "Just tell me before you throw the switch okay?"

"Try not to misplace your t-4 wave," Leonard responds.

"I'll do my best." I try to get comfortable. Before I came here I didn't even know I had a t-4 wave. Now I'm making deals over it.

"Ohhh-kayyyy, Mike. If you would like music piped in, raise your other hand. One finger for metal, two fingers for psychedelic, middle finger for middle-of-the-road. I've got a great CD here from 'Shonen Knife'—"

I hear the chirping sound, first in one ear, then the other, then both. It picks up speed until it is almost a buzz. Outside, Leonard is watching the monitor, adjusting the rate to match my brainwave pattern.

I close my eyes and the green dots vanish.

"Okay. Roll your eyes up please. Thank you—very nice alpha. Look straight ahead and think of a green square...thank you. Now, a yellow circle...very good. Count backwards from a hundred by threes...thank you. Nice activity in your math coprocessor...now let's see if our expensive theta grabber can catch your wave. Listen to the music..."

The buzz intensifies. In the background I hear a whine.

"...Looks like we have a match. Your escort to the netherworld this evening will be Guy Lombardo. Please hold on to your pants and remember—the memory that is real is not the true memory."

The buzz overtakes me like a swarm of bees. It's happening: my entire body feels out of alignment with itself, like a window slipping on its frame. Then the trap door opens and I fall through.

I *must* remember.

The darkness becomes clouds, and the clouds dissolve to reveal a filigree of lights stretching away to some distant point. A brilliant, glowing highway into the past. There is the sensation of forward movement, of entrainment by some internal jetstream pulling me along. The dark landscape below me is abstract, strange, yet I seem to recognize each glowing light. An intuition, really, like knowing exactly where to turn on an unfamiliar street.

Suddenly I know: I've been here before. I know what everything I see represents. This time, I'll try to go to the part of the web that reminds me of my early childhood. I allow my intuition to pull me along until I see it. The right place.

The lights surround me in a swirling field of color. As I draw closer, memories and emotions well up and encircle me. And now, I hear a siren.

There is a distinct click, like something fitting into place. I'm here, a disembodied presence in front of a screen. Watching. I hear breathing, the soft thump-thump-thump of a heartbeat and the rhythmic hiss of blood through arteries. I tune them out, and the sounds vanish.

The visual field clears to form a forest of chair legs. All around are children huddled on the floor in orderly rows, their hands covering their heads. The field of vision shifts and I'm looking at the underside of a metal desk where someone has scrawled the letters *FUK*.

A pair of slim legs supported by black high heels moves through the scene. *Click. Click. Click. Click.* "Now, children, if war were to break out and a bomb were to drop on Corinth, we would all hear the siren and get under our desks. Isn't that right?"

"Yes, Mrs. Kinnesman."

The boy in front of me has holes in his shoes and a patch on the bottom of his pants. In the next row, a little girl dressed in a green plaid dress is giggling furiously.

"Jill-shhhh. No laughing, please—"

Click. Click. Click. Click. The shoes move away and the little girl peeks out and continues laughing, tears rolling down her face.

Some pencils have fallen from my pocket and are in the aisle next to a crushed piece of hard candy.

"Hey, Mitchell. The Russians are gonna bomb the grade school. Think we'll get a vacation outta this?" I turn to focus on a small, square face—a close-cut flattop and a crooked grin displaying two large front teeth. The right eye squinted almost shut, like a movie tough guy. It's Evan Carswell.

"Did I tell you my big brother found a cable for the hand pulley? He strung it from our treehouse over to the creek this afternoon—and now, he's gonna ride on it. It's about a hundred feet off the ground—I bet he falls and busts his butt. You wanna watch?"

"Yeah!"

The scene dissolves and I'm back, floating over the web of lights.

"Hey, Mike. How is it going down there?"

"Fine, Leonard. I think I was in grade school."

"Already? You've only been under for a minute."

"Seems like it's been longer. I'm up above the lights now—"

"Don't stay out in hyperspace too long. We need something on the tape and there's only an hour left on the clock."

"Okay. I'll get something."

"And don't overflow your buffer."

"Right." I fall toward the lights again.

I open a door and step onto a dark wooden porch. Though I can't feel it, the night air seems cold and thin. About a hundred feet away, a streetlamp spreads a harsh blue glare across the dry, leaf-covered lawn. At the end of the sidewalk is an automobile, a brown 1964 Ford Fairlane—the same car I sold nearly 25 years ago.

I walk down the concrete steps and out to the car, open the door, throw a gym bag into the back seat, get inside. I insert a silver key into the ignition and after a moment of grinding, the engine kicks in with a roar. No muffler.

And no seat belts. This *has* to be in the mid-1960's.

Something clicks, like a slide in a projector, and a darkened hallway comes up to meet me. A dormitory. I recognize this place—I'm heading back from class during my freshman year in college. Nothing here. I recall a technique Poundstone suggested: "Whenever you want to leave a place or time, just fall *up*."

I rise up. In response, the walls, ceiling, floor—all implode into a bright point of light in a black background. In the darkness of my memory, I want to move sideways a week, and—it works. Maybe I *can* navigate this place.

"*Mike. Are you there?*" The words seem to be coming from a stack of books on a long wooden table. "*Give me some info.*"

I scan the visual field. Near the edge of the scene, near the border of my vision is a newspaper. Freezing the frame, I make out the words: Frost Warnings Issued for Missouri Tonight.

"I think I'm in the college library. And there's supposed to be frost tonight."

"*So we know it's not the middle of the summer. Hear any music down there?*"

"It's a library, remember?"

"*Oh. That's right. Sorry. Look, I have to change the tape, why don't you take five?*"

Leonard clicks out and I'm left alone inside my own film. Something drifts fluidly by: It's a girl, walking between the heavy wooden tables, her green-and-white checkerboard shift reaching past her knees—no socks and plain leather flats. I look at her hair: black, teased into a helmet with a flip at the ends.

Definitely the mid-sixties.

I get a glimpse of a wristwatch, *my* wristwatch, one with a cream-colored dial and luminous hands.

Three-thirty in the afternoon.

I remember losing that watch in army basic training. It seems strange to look at it now. I wonder where it is in the real world? Probably part of some landfill somewhere.

There's a sound like a distant radio: *Great. Time for my last class of the day. Tuesday. Three days to go...*

My own thoughts thirty years removed.

Poundstone said they can be experienced only rarely—a ghost train of words rumbling through and then gone.

The screen blinks and shifts. Two arms appear wearing a long-sleeved striped blue shirt. On the left hand is a class ring. I see a book: *Background of the Modern World.*

Now I detect something forming in the space in front of me. Something else.

"*Hey, Mike, you all right?*"

"I'm fine, Leonard."

"*The detectors are picking up a fast theta from your right temporal lobe. What's going on down there?*"

"I'll let you know when I figure it out."

Initially, the image has a brown and white quality, like a grainy film clip projected on a sheet. As I watch, it gradually takes over the scene of the library—almost, but not quite replacing it. With a start I realize I'm looking at a thought within a thought. A mental image from my past: a girl moving inside a mosaic of pastels. No lines, only an impressionistic canvas of blue and gold and yellow and green. A girl, standing in a grassy field, her black hair blowing behind her. In the background I see dark clouds with lightning flashes.

"Anything yet?"

"I'm taking a commercial break."

"Your t-4 signal is acting a little strange. I think maybe you should Control-C whatever you're doing down there and come up for air."

The girl turns to face me.

"Mike, your heart rate's increasing. If it crosses ninety I'm hitting the scram switch."

"No. Not yet." The image dissolves into the pages of the newspaper. Into the lines and words. Something about a party at the lake.

I remember the instructions on how to stop the motion. Lock.

Instantly the movie becomes a photograph, fixed and motionless in time. I carefully scan the scene, looking for artifacts, clues. Eventually, I find it, the top right corner of the campus newspaper: "October 4, 1966." So *that's* where I am.

Unlock. And the scene moves again.

"How much time do I have?"

"I'll let you know."

Two places in my past so far this trip. Will I remember them?

I rise up and the library walls collapse into two dimensions, then one.

I'm looking down on my time spent there. In one direction, I see the line of the past—the first day of college, the summer, the nights at the drive-in, the days at the factory—then, high school. All are part of a three-dimensional cylinder of light receding into the distance.

Looking the other way, I see my time in the military, my wedding, my life with Linda and our kids. Stretching away toward a distant point of light.

Inside space, yet outside time. It's no wonder I can't remember this—my waking mind would never understand or accept it.

"Mike, it looks like you shifted into paradoxical sleep for a minute there. Is everything okay?"

"I'm fine. I'm going in for another pass."

"Keep me posted."

I fall toward another scene, an image that becomes more and more real the closer it gets. One instant, it's like a billboard, then there is motion. The frames snap faster—24 frames a second, then 50, then double that until the image becomes perfectly clear. The third dimension appears, subtle at first, then pronounced. No longer a back-then.

A back-*now*.

And I'm here—standing at a window in the dim half-light of nearly-dusk. The sky is muted, with pale coal-smoke haze obscuring the setting sun. In the middle distance is a long line of scattered clouds that have broken away from a shelf of stratus. Beneath them, a thin, barely perceptible line of haze across the horizon, punctuated by the faint metallic glint of my hometown water tower. On the side, I can barely make out the words: CORINTH. A veil of dark grey haze—probably from burning grass—drifts across the road leading toward town.

A car passes, driven by a man in a dark coat. It occurs to me I'm looking at a past that doesn't exist anymore. The person who was in that car is thirty years older, maybe dead and the car a pile of rust. Or, like my old wristwatch, in some landfill somewhere.

I scan across the street, look at the gray rows of houses beneath the darkening sky. How many still exist? How many of the people living in them are alive today?

From the houses I scan to the street, over the cracks in the asphalt pavement to the crumbling chunks of gravel and tar at the side of the road. Where is this material now, thirty years later? Buried under more asphalt? Or has it been dug up and replaced by concrete?

Another car goes by, a 1961 Mercury Comet, its rear bumper curled down in a sneer by some minor traffic accident. It's driven by a young, dark-haired girl. Thirty years later does she even remember the car? I watch the car disappear over the hill, smoke trailing from the exhaust pipe, red tail lights staring back like two round, bloodshot eyes.

I recall something Keller said once, "You have to make sure not to breathe too deep when you go back—there's so much lead in the air, it'll make you sick *today*."

Everyone laughed at the absurdity of the comment. Yet, looking at the trail of black smoke hanging in the air, it's hard to realize all of this isn't really happening right now. But it's only memory—electrical impulses exciting phosphors in my brain.

I hear static, then a reverse arpeggio in liquid darkness. Barely audible, the notes float from the radio amid jagged bolts of static. And I know *exactly* where I am—5:20 p.m. on a Saturday in early March, 1963.

I'm hearing the song "Pipeline" for the first time. New notes and new circuits. Floating here behind the screen, I can still feel that strange year—dark and angular; stormy and sad. Abruptly, I hear Leonard's voice in my mind: *"Mike, I'm back. How's the view?"*

"It looks like I'm in the first week of March, 1963. Probably a Saturday."

"That right? Justaminute. Fire up the old Jukebox search engine here. And we enter M-a-r-c-h, 1963. Song titles—question mark. Enter. There. History note coming up—next Tuesday the Beatles will record 'From Me To You' at 11:00 a.m. your time."

"Thanks."

"No prob. I'm here to help. Call me if you need me."

A car pulls into the drive—a blue 1956 Ford. It rattles for a minute and stops. A few seconds later, my father climbs out, closes the door and walks around to where my brother's Chevy Streamliner is parked. He pauses to look at something on the left front fender. Probably a new dent.

I move ahead an inch—a half hour?—and now my mother has dinner ready. Swedish hamburger, salad, new potatoes, broccoli, Pepsi. My brother Earl comes downstairs in his blue jeans, cuffs rolled up. I turn off the radio and pull up a chair to join the family.

As I sit down at the table, I see that my mother and father both look younger than I do now. My brother Earl sits down. A quick prayer, then everyone reaches for the food.

From this perspective, I notice more than anything else the pack of cigarettes in my father's shirt pocket. I want to reach out and tell him where I'm from and what I know—that those cigarettes will eventually take his life from us.

But I can't. If I said anything only Leonard would be able to hear me. And, since there is no sense of touch where I am, all I can do is watch. Helpless.

The downside to this experience is profound—seeing loved ones and not being able to touch them. Not being able to make contact. Because this place is gone—it no longer exists, except in my memory. Yet I'm here. Floating among the dead.

I watch myself reach for hamburger, watch my hands carefully place it on the bread, pour on ketchup. A bite. I grab for the glass of cola.

When a photographer takes a picture, he tries not to cast his own shadow. The shadow not only intrudes upon the scene, but also shows someone else is there. Artistically, the photographer shouldn't be there—only the subject.

As I look around the table, I know I'm part of the scene—I can't be here without having first taken part. My shadow preceded me, and now, floating behind my eyes, I'm truly invisible.

I reach for the broccoli. Did I like this stuff then? Guess so. The proof is before me.

"Don't take so much, Mike," my mother says. "Maybe the rest of us would like some, too."

"He can have mine," Earl says.

"Yeah, go ahead Mike," my dad says. "I'm fine."

I know this year—it will be hazardous to us all. My family will suffer. I roll the thought in my mind, then set it free.

Suddenly, I rise up again.

Can I navigate this strange river of memory? Perhaps it would help if I first picked a time—July, 1961 for example—then tried to match my disposition to its own unique structure. First I imagine July, 1961—thin and bright—waiting like a pool of stratus just inside the sixties. I think it, match it, become one with it.

And now I'm down again—this time in a room. It's the one I share with my brother. The window is open and Earl is on his bed, t-shirt, jeans, white socks. On the dresser is his old radio with the brown cloth speaker.

"Listen, Earl, I got this problem—"

"Yeah, what is it, Scout?" He pulls a pack of Pall Malls from his shirt pocket. Stuck inside the cellophane is his Zippo lighter. Decades later it will be in a dresser drawer in Lexington, Massachusetts.

"Earl, it's about Brenda. I think she wants to break up with me."

"That right?" He pauses to light the cigarette. "How do you know that?"

"It's the word around school. She told one of her friends she's getting bored with me."

"Isn't she a year older than you?"

"Yeah. She talks about stuff and I don't know what she's talking about. Like all her music classes."

"That's no good." He takes a drag from cigarette and blows a thin stream of blue smoke toward the window.

"No. She's the only girl I can't fully understand. I'm pretty sure I love her."

"Um-hm." He carefully balances the cigarette on the lip of the ashtray. I watch the smoke drift up and out the window. "So how long you two been going steady?"

"It's been a week now."

"Have you kissed her yet?"

"Are you kidding?"

"Sorry," he shrugs, picking up the cigarette from the ashtray. "Think that might be why she wants to break up?"

"'Course not."

"Okay. So how come you didn't take her to the ball game tonight?"

"I didn't know there was a ball game."

"Scout, if you're gonna date women, you have to pay more attention to—certain things."

"Like what?"

"Like—well, *things*." He takes a drag, blows a quick series of smoke rings, then returns the cigarette to the ashtray. "Listen, Sally and I have a date tomorrow night. I bet we could scratch up someone for you—"

"Can't. I'm going steady with Brenda."

"Did you give her a ring?"

"Earl, you know I don't *have* a ring—"

"Well, my friend, you're not really going steady then." He stubs out the cigarette. "Look. We'll make it a double date. It's the last drive-in movie of the season. And her little sis is a lot of fun."

"Oh, God, not Karen Barrett. She's in high school! And she's *taller* than I am."

"Come on, Mike—"

"Earl, Karen Barrett is almost as tall as you! Doesn't she have any other sisters?"

"None you'd want to date," Earl grins. "Besides, their husbands might complain."

"Mike, you've got about six minutes."

"Thanks, Leonard."

Up. I drift here for a minute, inside the framework of 1961. Searching. Maybe I can navigate this place. Wherever this place *is*.

"Five minutes."

"Okay."

I fall into the light, hoping I can finish the conversation with Earl. But instead of the light forming my own room back home, it becomes something else—my dorm room in college. Somehow, I've slipped ahead five years. A sullen-looking young man is handing me a phone.

"Mike, it's for you. It's a girl."

"Hi, this is me." I hear the voice, but don't recognize it. It's young, impossibly young.

"Hi. Uh, how are you?"

"Mom and Dad said it was okay to call you. Are you coming down here this weekend?"

"I don't think so. I've got a test Tuesday—"

"Hey, guess what? I asked if I could just wear the nightshirt you bought me to bed—that is, if you still promised to wear your cutoffs—and they said yes. I had to promise to keep it on all night, of course. But isn't that something? I mean, they know you're gonna be part of the family."

My vision is suffused with a kaleidoscope of images—glowing, translucent—like the ones I saw earlier while in the library. Memories of thoughts. Memories of memories.

"Three minutes."

I pull the covers over someone—a girl. The window next to the bed is blurry with rain, the light from the streetlamp shimmering against the wall. I sit up and look outside. On the street below, I see my car—a brown 1964 Ford Fairlane.

I look around. I know this place, this year. There is a realness about it. I brush the sheets with my hand as the rain outside the window intensifies. Thunder rumbles in the distance. Is there a storm outside?

"Mike, you're amplitude is dropping. You okay down there?"

In the yellow light from the streetlamp I can make out the room—dresser with a mirror, an old chest of drawers. The half-opened closet door. Clothes on the floor. The diamond pattern on the wallpaper. I've been here before. I'm here *now*.

"Mike, I'm bringing you back."

Suddenly, the scene implodes, evaporating everything in a pure, searing white haze. I scream, but there's no sound. No air. Nothing.

"Hey." The visor lifts and I see four pale blue eyes peering at me through wireframe glasses. "You okay in there?"

"I'm seeing two of everything—!"

"Sorry about that." Leonard lifts the helmet from my head. "Normally, I'd ask you not to speak or clear your throat or anything until I remove the squid mikes. But I think I toasted the circuit with that little scram so you can talk if you like—"

"*Little* scram?!" I grab my head. "You hit me with a sledgehammer!"

"Yeah. It *will* fork-bomb the wetware on occasion." Leonard helps me up. "Would you like an aspirin?"

"How the hell many volts did you hit me with?" I rasp.

"I dunno. Couple thousand. But absolutely no amperage." Leonard unsnaps the microphone and sets it on the table. "The voltage isn't important. It's the amperage that will kill you…your eyes uncross yet?"

"Yeah. I think so. God. My scalp is on fire."

"Really? Lemme see." He runs finger along my forehead. "Yeah—bummer of a burn mark, Mike—"

I try to stand up inside a spinning room. "This is so *painful*. Why didn't they tell me this would be so damn painful?"

"Hey, look. I wasn't getting a response—you had your interrupts locked out and your t-4 was going very nonlinear." Leonard looks like a huge offended housecat. "Seemed like you were ready to wedge."

"Wedge? What are you talking about?"

"Wedge. Eclipse. Lights out. Halt and catch fire. Activating the out-of-body circuit. That's what the theta detectors are for. To keep you from doing that."

"Speak English, dammit." I close my eyes to stop the spinning. It doesn't work.

"Look. This is really not a difficult concept. Your right temporal lobe produces an important little wave called the t-4. If your t-4 goes, *you* go. As in Flatline City. And letting you go to that bad place on my shift would be very evil and rude of me—not to mention *extremely* career-limiting for both of us. Comprende?"

"I think you gave me a stroke."

"Nah, you wouldn't be able to talk. Lemme look at your pupils." Leonard pushes his fat, sweaty face into mine and aims a tiny flashlight at my eyes. "Yeah. You're okay. Maybe popped a few capillaries is all. Probably a misfeature of electroshock. I can call one of the docs if you like…"

"No!"

"Okay. Want some day-old pizza? ANSI standard—pepperoni and

mushroom."

"I think I'm about to throw up——"

"You know, a cola would settle your stomach." He grabs a can from his desk. "All I have is Jolt. Sorry, there's no ice."

"I'll drink it anyway." I take the can. Slowly, the nausea begins to ease. "How many volts did you hit me with?"

"I dunno, I'll have to look—uh—" Leonard squints at me, then hands me a square of gauze. "Better take this——"

"Huh?"

"I think you bit your tongue."

I'm lying on my bed with a wet towel over my face, trying—and failing—to allay my massive, throbbing, scram-induced headache. To add to my misery, the angry red spots on my temples have blossomed into dime-sized blisters. I feel like that time I was caught up in a drinking match with a couple of Russians on the night train between Milan and Zurich. Jagermeister and Slivovitz and God-knows-what. I woke up feeling like I had a spike driven through my head.

I feel like that now—except for two things—one, my billfold is still with me and two, I'm elated.

That's right. *Elated.* Because, despite the excess electrons Leonard poured into my brain, despite being forcibly returned to the present—

For the first time, I can *remember.*

I close my eyes, reliving the scenes—a few minutes under a desk in my childhood, then up to my college years, back again to visit my brother Earl. Was he setting me up for that horrible date with Karen Barrett? Yes, that was it. I almost never forgave him, but she was cute. Tall, but cute.

Where else did I go? Maybe nowhere—the rest is a blank.

I slowly get up from the bed to retrieve another three aspirin.

Returning, I see that my wet towel has made a dark circle on the pillow. I look at my watch—seven o'clock—still early.

I replace the wet pillow with a dry one and fall back onto the bed. I can actually visit my past! Go to places I've been, see the people I've missed—my family, my friends. My girlfriends.

Brenda Lacey.

My head hurts but I don't care. It was worth it.

In fact, I might even be able to bring something back for my business—observe close-up the minutiae of an entire age and get it perfect. Right down to the paperclips. I could turn a middle-age crisis into a—well, a business opportunity. That's what I told my partner Jerry when I came down here—now, maybe, I can actually produce something.

I can imagine how he would sell it to our clients: "Want something from 1958? Hey, we got it! Pushbuttons, orbits and atoms, you name it. Stuff you heard about, stuff you didn't even know was back there..."

"Oh, you like 1962 instead? Great year. Very commercial, very successful. Bullet lamps and parabolic curves. Oh, yes—and big, square hand-held transistor radios. That year works with automobiles and small household items."

"You're selling pickup trucks? Then we recommend 1966. Square lines and metal dashboards. And for everything else we recommend compass roses and cork...how do we know all this? Because we were there. *Just this morning.*"

No, no, no, no, *no*. The past isn't just a warehouse of psychological icons, it's a place with some importance—some depth. Before grabbing for everything, I should just cruise the territory first—get the feel of the place. Maybe listen for some obscure but ahead-of-its time song that no one remembers today.

Yeah, that would be nice. I could be there to watch the reactions when it comes on the radio that very first time. I'll be *there*, riding along with my 16-year-old buddies—all of us making comments. And all I'd have to do is *listen*. And if we use the song in a commercial selling trucks or something—well, at least the public is getting a chance to hear a song they would otherwise miss completely.

I could live with that—riding around with my pals in the sixties just listening to the car radio.

Nice.

Of course, when I go *way* back for music, I won't be in a car at all. Instead, I'll be home in bed with the covers forming a little glowing tent—only me and my tube radio. I'd twist the dial carefully, listening for music amid the static. There'd be the signals from space—Kearny, Nebraska—a station in Baton Rouge—a night baseball game from some place in Florida. Another twist of the dial, and there it is—Arthur Alexander singing "You Better Move On."

And then I would no longer be in a house on the plains of eastern

Missouri—I'd be in Chicago, caught in the currents of a dark, roiling river of sound. Another twist and I'm in yet another fifty-thousand watt universe—this one with Roy Orbison's "Dream Baby" or Sam Cook's "Twisting The Night Away." Liquid music, uncomplicated romance, a glowing yellow dial.

I pull the towel down over my eyes, taking care not to break my new blisters. Perfect.

Perfect, perfect, perfect.

The phone rings.

"Hey Mike. It's Gail. I'm with Keller and Lowell and we're down here at the bar waiting to buy you a drink."

"A drink? No thanks, I've already got a splitting headache."

"*We know—that's why.* All new members of the scram club get a free margarita. Offer expires in fifteen minutes."

"Okay. You talked me into it. I'll be there."

5

Static

It's night, but you'd never know it. Like most bars, this one has no windows. Still, as saloons go, it's not a bad one—Spanish Inquisition-style red lampshades, lots of dark wood-paneled walls and a fake brick floor. The bar as dungeon. It reminds me of half the roadside watering holes between Bar Harbour, Maine and Providence, Rhode Island.

After four rounds of Corona Extra and fifteen or so chemistry jokes, Keller folded his tent and rode into the sunset. Now the rest of the party—Lowell, Gail and me—hover over black coffees and greasy nachos and woozily discuss our reasons for being here. After enough alcohol and coffee, I finally admit why I'm here. Not what's on the application form—that snappy booshwa about looking for "historical and cultural icons"—but the real reason.

"What it all comes down to is," I tell the others in my most dolorous voice, "I'm tired."

"Tired?" Gail echoes, her eyes severely bloodshot.

"Tired. Tired of hassles."

"Right." Lowell smacks the table with his fork.

"Tired of arguments—"

"Amen, bro," Lowell nods sagely.

"—I'm tired of arguing with clients and lawyers and my wife and my kids. I try to take a vacation somewhere, and I'm arguing with a travel agent who forgot to get my tickets."

"And when you get on the plane," Gail says, "the idiot in front of you wants to lean the seat all the way back in your lap."

"Yeah, right. Those guys," Lowell nods vigorously. "They want to take your space on the plane. I just spill my Coke on 'em. Or get up to go to the restroom a hundred times. They're greedheads. I'll do anything to make their flight miserable."

The normally taciturn Lowell now appears momentarily annoyed. Guess I've touched a nerve.

"And listen—" Gail says in a raspy voice. "When you—when you *get*—to where you're going—" she looks around the table. "The bags aren't there. They're in Montana or some place."

"Or the hotel has lost the reservation," I shake my head.

"Yeah," Lowell says. "That *always* happens to me."

"That happens to all adults," I respond. "That's why I came here— I want to be a kid again for awhile. No responsibilities. Nobody giving you serious trouble."

"Yeah?" Gail says. "That's 'cause you grew up *male*. Males get to do what they want when they're kids, get to roam around with their little buddies—like packs of wild dogs."

"Hey, girls do that too," Lowell says. "You should see my little sister and her pals."

"It wasn't that way when I was growing up," Gail says. "My folks had me under lock and key—practically handcuffed to the house. In high school, any boy who wanted to visit me had to pass a lie detector test. 'Have you ever been in trouble with the law—have you ever gotten any grade lower than C—have you ever had your hand down a girl's blouse—'"

"Aw, Gail," Lowell looks at her skeptically. "Your folks really didn't have a polygraph, did they? I mean, isn't that *illegal* or something?"

"Listen," Gail says. "My father would stare at the kid over the top of his glasses—really bore into his brain with these beady eyes. They were like ray guns or something. And at the same time he'd just really *torture* him with all these questions." She laughs. "And if the kid flinched—or even *blinked*, Pop figured he wasn't telling the truth. It was really pretty terrible, but kind of funny too. The only boys I finally got to date were these pathological criminal types who could lie perfectly under pressure. I could never trust them, 'cause I knew they'd lie to me too. But my pop always thought they were great."

"So how come you go back?" I ask her. "If you didn't have a good time—"

"Oh, I did okay—" she smiles. "It wasn't *all* bad. I guess going back to my past is like a vacation for me too. Parts of it anyway."

"How about you, Lowell?" I ask him. "What's your reason for being here? I can't imagine *you* running away from anything."

"To tell the truth," Lowell says with a sheepish grin, "my graduate advisor was *supposed* to be here, but she had a conference in Paris. Quite a choice, huh? Visit your past or visit the Louvre."

"So you came in her place," Gail says.

"The school had already paid the money, and I needed some graduate credit for my doctorate. So here I am."

"So how do you like visiting your past?" Gail asks.

"Oh, it's interesting. Of course, I don't have to travel as far as some of the dreamers here—" he looks up slyly.

"Thanks, Lowell," Gail says. "We really appreciate that."

"But, sure, I like to go back—usually to when I was about fifteen." Lowell immerses himself in the memory. "That was a pretty happy time for me. Last time I was in the chair, my dad took me in his sailboat on the Columbia River at Astoria. Then we went out to watch the whales. It was fun. When I get out of here, I'm gonna give him a call. Tell him all about it." He polishes off the coffee and gets up from the table.

"You leaving already?" Gail asks.

"Got to get some sleep." Lowell stretches. "I got a session in the morning right before breakfast."

"Before breakfast?" Gail asks. "Is Leonard gonna take you down?"

"Leonard?" Lowell laughs. "No way! He's too quick on the scram switch. I like Dr. Zey a lot better. With him it's set and forget. I've heard he doesn't even stay in the lab."

"I'll stick with Leonard," Gail says. "He keeps me out of trouble down there."

"I can't imagine what kind of trouble you can get into," Lowell shrugs. "It's only your memory. See you guys tomorrow."

"The kid's got the right attitude," I tell Gail.

"That's because he's still young," she says. "Wait until he's our age. Then he'll be complaining about the same kinds of things we are— idiots on the freeway, telemarketers trying to get you to invest in something, commercials that make you think you're the only one in the country still driving an old car—"

"Hey, be nice," I tell her. "If it wasn't for commercials, you wouldn't get such great television."

"Great?" Gail laughs. "You call television *great?*"

"Well, it would be worse without commercials." I finish my cup of cold black coffee. "Believe me."

"'Cause you make them, huh?" Gail says.

"Yeah, sort of," I nod. "I own a service agency for advertisers."

"So what kind of—services— do you *perform*—" Gail leans closer, "—for these *ad-ver-tisers?*"

I stare at the empty cup. "Ever heard the Four Tops sing 'Reach Out—And I'll Be There?'"

"Sure. It was a little before my time—"

"Do you watch television?"

"Only when I have to," she grins. "Is this a trick question?"

"No. When you hear The Four Tops sing 'Reach Out,' what do you think of? What's the *very first thing* that comes to mind?"

"Long-distance service."

"See? Okay. How about 'Wouldn't It Be Nice?'"

"Well—that's another song that was before my time—"

"Think of the *very* first thing," I tell her.

Her eyes roll up in thought. "Okay. Buying a house."

"'Up and Away.'"

"That's an easy one," she says. "Taking a picture—with those little green cardboard vacation cameras. With funny lenses that *seem* panoramic, but really aren't."

"See?" I shrug. "That's the kind of thing I do for a living. I mean, how many people remember the Fifth Dimension?"

"You mean, those songs weren't written *especially for the commercial?*" she deadpans.

"You asked what I do. Well, I'll tell you what I do—I stripmine the past. I'm the guy who steals old songs and uses them to sell cars."

"So you're the perpetrator, huh?"

"My partner and I send a dragline through the swamp of the fifties, sixties and seventies. We go after glass milk bottles, metal toys, original Barbie dolls, streamlined appliances, old sewing machines… the actors in the commercials tell us after a day on the set they think they're in a time warp."

"And this *works?*" She seems incredulous.

"It works. A big chunk of the consumer demographic grew up during the sixties. And these consumers tend to remember that past with a certain fondness."

"So you supply nostalgia for the commercials," she nods.

"That's what I do," I slump in my chair. "I replace personal memories with those of pickup trucks and real estate offices."

Gail looks at me sternly. "You came here to get material for your business?"

I shake my head. "That's what I'm telling everybody back home. But earlier when I said I was running away—well, that was the truth."

"That's a relief." Gail leans back in her chair. "I was worried for a minute."

"I guess I'm just like most everybody here."

"Well," Gail says after a moment. "I have to confess I *am* interested in the science and psychology aspects. I really like being a pioneer in something that has to do with the mind. It's a whole new dimension of human experience."

"You lifted that quote from Poundstone's speech."

"Yeah, but he was right," Gail says. "This is a neat thing we're taking part in."

"So you're here for totally altruistic reasons?" I ask her accusingly. "None of this going back to frisk some boyfriend in high school, none of this searching out nice memories just to make you feel good—"

"Well, *sure*, I spend more time in some places than in others," she allows a smile. "But think about it—this whole thing of being able to walk around in your memory banks is—well, it's—it's revolutionary."

"You're drunk," I say evenly.

"Or course I am," she says. "But it doesn't change my opinion about the program."

"What if there's trouble?" I ask her. "What if there's something about this that they're not telling us? I mean, we did have to sign a hold-harmless agreement before we signed up—"

"Nah." Gail shakes her head. "If there was the potential for real harm, I don't think Poundstone would let us do it. I mean, we're only fooling around in the place where our memory is stored. It's not like we're gonna get *lost* down there or anything—"

"Okay, then," I lean forward. "What about that thing that happened to Coltrane? That—what did you call it—an *eclipse*?"

"Oh, *that*," Gail shrugs. "Coltrane was on a long run when that happened. Besides, it wasn't a real eclipse, because his brainwaves didn't really go flatline. I mean, when you have a flat trace, *that's it*. You don't come back."

"So you think this thing *is* safe, huh?" I look at her warily. "I mean, I don't want to spend fourteen grand on anything that might kill me—I don't care *how* neat it is."

"As long as you stay away from the weird stuff, I wouldn't worry about it," she says. "The only hazard is to our fragile little *egos*."

"Well, lately, mine's pretty fragile." I stare at the empty coffee cup.

"You seem pretty solid to me," Gail says. "Besides, it takes a lot of courage to look down at the ribbon of your own life—stretching back into the past. Seeing your whole life in one instant takes it out of you. And when you get down into that ribbon—" she pauses for a moment, as if searching for the right words. "All those pictures and feelings and people are *right there*, and you can't really look away. It's like the life-review you get when you die."

"See," I tell her triumphantly. "It *is* like dying."

"So what?" She shrugs. "And who cares? Whether it's in the induction chair or at the end of your life—it all takes place in that little-bitty movie projector between your ears. When you lock the scene, you're just stopping the projector. So what if the same thing happens when you die? It doesn't mean you're going to code out in the chair. After all, you're not seeing the last big movie of your life—you're only looking at the previews."

"Who told you that?"

"Came up with it myself," she says. "You're not the only one who thinks about this stuff. I'll bet all the dreamers have a theory. Otto thinks everything you see down there takes place inside the brain. Keller thinks the brain is actually sampling the past and your consciousness follows some kind of memory wave. Lowell hasn't said, but he's probably got his own ideas, too. Everybody tries to make sense of what they're seeing when they go back."

"And you think it's a little movie projector in the brain, huh? What happens if you lock the scene too long? Will the film catch fire?"

"That's right. Smoke'll come out your ears." She bites into the nacho. "And I can say that, because I'm a nurse."

An hour later, I'm wobbling with Gail through the door and into the elevator. As the doors slide open, the saloon jukebox—a real one—begins to play "Who'll Stop The Rain." For a moment, we consider dancing to the music, but think better of it.

As the elevator takes us to our floor, Gail turns to me. "What does your wife think of all this?"

"She thinks I'm having a midlife crisis and refusing to face reality. As for the Institute itself, I don't believe she has much of an opinion one way or the other."

"Is that right? My husband really hates me being here. He wants me to come home. Guess he's tired of fixing his own meals and taking out the trash."

For the first time, I glance at her left hand. Sure enough, she's wearing a wedding band studded with rows of tiny diamonds.

As the elevator takes us up, I watch through the glass as the lights of San Antonio drop away below. The complex of streets and thoroughfares shimmers in a blurry network of silver and gold. On the horizon, I can barely make out the outline of the crescent moon. In the distance, a flash of orange illuminates the cloud deck. Another storm on the way?

The elevator arrives at our floor and I walk Gail to her room. She presses her hand against the security plate on the door and then steps inside. "You know, if there's too much alcohol in your system, the door won't open. I heard Keller got locked out last week and had to sleep in the hall. The maid found him curled up on the floor next to the fake potted plant. Want some water?"

"Sure." I wait as she kicks off her shoes and walks into the kitchen. Her room is the picture of entropy—clothes scattered about, a desk covered in notebooks, a bottle of red nail polish left open on the window sill.

"Here." She hands me a glass. "This stuff is supposed to come from the Guadalupe River or some such thing. Probably get it from the tap…"

"Thanks. Guess I'll go to my room now."

I close Gail's door behind me and walk down the corridor to my room. The hallway smells like a college dormitory—a combination of Right Guard, varnish and formaldehyde. Maybe the maintenance crew has shut off the air conditioner.

I place my hand on the security plate, hear the click, push the door open and step inside my dark room. Through the window, I see the crescent moon is now partially obscured by a thin layer of black cloud. Definitely rain.

After undressing, I turn out the light and fall into bed. After a moment, I hear the soft music from the wall speaker. For tonight, they've replaced classical with blues and soft jazz. Wes Montgomery's "Road Song," then something by B.B. King. Linda would like this one, she's a big blues fan.

I look at the phone, my link with home.

After a few false starts, I finally get the numbers right. After four rings the phone picks up and I hear Linda's voice.

"Hello. You have reached the Mitchell residence. No one is home to take your call, so if you will leave your name—"

I hang up the phone and look at my watch. Midnight—1:00 a.m. in Lexington. Where the hell is she—*Mexico?*

Wait a minute. She *is* in Mexico. With that other lawyer.

But maybe not. Maybe she changed her mind. Maybe she decided to stay in Lexington.

I try again.

"Hello. You have reached the Mitchell residence. No one—"

I place the phone back on the hook. In the darkness, I listen to the dark currents of the number, an old hit from early 1970: "The Thrill Is Gone."

Looking out the window, I see another flash. The storm is closer. I close the curtains and listen to the notes ripple through the matrix of my mind: The thrill is gone.

The thrill is gone away.

The dream comes slowly, drifting in from the edge of my vision like hazy autumn smoke from burning leaves.

"We're not completely sure of how the process works. While it is obviously an activity taking place entirely within the confines of the brain—"

The sun breaks through, forming leaning gray columns between the trees. In the yard, Earl, dressed in his red plaid work shirt, tinkers with the white Chevy. My father, never without his green baseball cap, rakes the remaining lawn scrap into a small pile near the smoldering fire. Inside our white clapboard house, my mother is finishing the dishes.

I marvel at the color, the reality of the scene. Has my time here sharpened my senses? Or has it merely allowed the film to be played again—one more time? It doesn't matter. I enter the image, follow its current away from the present. To another place entirely.

"It may also be the result of a simple standing wave pattern—"

I look up and watch the sky go dark, as if turning out a light. It's early morning, well before sunrise. A full moon hovers over the frost-covered landscape. In the distance, I see the bright red lights from some arcane tower, eleven long miles away to the horizon.

My hands numb from cold, I switch on my transistor and hear a song from three years before, "Walk Don't Run." Five kids heading west on the deserted pavement. A fifty-mile hike into spring.

I hear the sound of an engine revving. It's Earl, inching along in his '48 Chevy, holding a handful of lunchbags out the window. "Mom wants ya'll to take these. She's afraid you're gonna starve out here."

Then he drives off.

"Your big brother is really cool." One of the boys digs into his brown paper bag.

"Yeah," I smile. "He's all right." I turn up my transistor radio and hear the guitar sounds ripple across the frozen highway.

"Some of these trips back can be quite traumatic. It's certainly taking a chance..."

The scene glides away, and in the darkness I hear a silky voice:

"I think you look wonderful in a suit. It matches your personality—so formal—"

Yes. It's Brenda Lacey at last, even if it's only a dream. She's standing before me, dressed in a strapless yellow chiffon gown, her blonde hair piled high. "Here, let me pin this corsage on you—" She slides a carnation through the buttonhole in my lapel.

The band begins to play an unsteady version of "Moon River" and the kids file onto the starch-sprinkled floor of the gymnasium. It seems the entire building has been decorated in crepe, glitter. There are at least three cardboard wishing wells and four gazebos, each decorated in various well-known celestial objects, including stars, moons, comets and the planet Saturn. On the brick wall someone has constructed the outline of a city in white poster board and magic marker.

I swing Brenda around and the band comes into view—a six-piece group wearing black suits and patent-leather shoes. At each side of the band are two rotating Christmas tree lights. As the guitarist begins his solo, the lights rotate to red and green, now yellow and orange, now blue and green. The guitar player misses a note, makes a face and looks back at a diminutive woman playing an electric piano. The song stops cold and everyone stops dancing, frozen in place on the wooden dance floor. Then abruptly, the song starts over again and the crowd continues dancing as if nothing happened.

Brenda moves closer. "I don't have to be in until four tomorrow morning."

"Four? I've got the car until two-thirty."

She looks up at me, her eyes wide, "*Just* two-thirty?"

The scene flickers, then fails totally, going to black as if some unseen hand changed the channel.

"Whattaya want? The W's or the K's? We can get WLS in Chicago or KAAY in Little Rock." This voice is different, not silky at all. Instead it comes at me clipped and fast, like a staccato burst from a machine gun.

The girl brushes black hair from her eyes and twists the car radio dial. "Or maybe KOMA in Oklahoma City. Did you hear they had flying saucers down there last week? Landed on somebody's car. That's what my mom heard anyway. She's a phone operator so she gets all the news—here it is—KOMA."

Static.

I steer the car out onto the highway. Somehow, my prom night has vanished—perhaps floating out there in the stratosphere with the UFOs.

Another twist of the dial.

"Did I tell you what Daddy did last year? Somehow he rigged up some kite sticks, a candle and a plastic dry cleaning bag to make a little hot air balloon. And it worked—it floated over town and then the bag caught fire and exploded. The drunks at Dubs tavern thought a UFO was shooting at them. One guy hid in the restroom and wouldn't come out. I laughed so hard I wet my pants. Had to actually go home and change."

Somehow I've fallen into a sideroom attic of my memory, some dating purgatory. *Where* is Brenda? Where is my prom night?

"*The mechanism for choice is still elusive...*"

"I'm only here because I have to be here." It's Brenda's voice, barely discernable in the din of a band playing *Louie Louie*. "It's the campus-wide mixer."

I press the phone to my ear. "Are you *with* anybody?"

"I can't hear you, Michael. There's too much noise."

"Did you get my letters?"

"Yes, but I haven't had a chance to read them yet. I've been real busy. Water—"

"What?"

"Watercolor class—I'll be a minute—look, somebody wants to use the phone so I'm going. Write me. 'Bye." I hang up the phone, just as lights appear in the window—my ride to work. "Only a month to go and she'll be back—"

"We're exploring a dimension of human existence..."

The rain blows against the bedroom window like sand against glass. I hear the faint scratch of a tree limb against the house. Then, a whisper in the darkness, soft and slow. "The way I see it—when a soul comes down from heaven and starts up a baby, everybody knows. Deep down. It's like when a leaf drops into a pond and makes ripples. You know what I mean?"

"Yeah, I know what you mean."

"...we had never known existed—of course, it was there all along—"

I sit up, scanning the haze of brown darkness. Am I back in San Antonio? Am I awake yet? Then I see it—a door, open only a crack. Beyond it is the hallway, the bathroom light left on. To my left, at shoulder height, is the window, with its blurry streetlight. I hear it, the soft hiss of rain with the steady clink of water streaming down the roof and through the gutter.

What time is it? No watch.

There must be a clock around here somewhere.

Has to be.

The door opens and an expanding wedge of light travels across the floor toward the bed.

"Linda?—Is that you?"

"Michael—?"

I open my eyes, and the scene vanishes into darkness. From across the room, the partially obscured window is a lantern of lightning flashes. I hear a wash of rain hit the building.

The clock next to the bed reads 5:51.

I rub the sleep from my eyes, watch as the digits proceed to 5:52. Then 5:53.

Almost six—seven in Boston. Linda should be getting up right about now. Should I call?

Yes.

I punch in the numbers and wait, listening to the static from the thunderstorm outside. After two rings, someone picks up.

"—I got it. *Hello.*"

"Linda, this is Mike."

"Mike, what's wrong. Where are you?"

"I'm in San Antonio. I think I was dreaming about you."

"Sure it wasn't a nightmare?"

"No, it was—only a dream. And I wanted to call. I couldn't get you yesterday and you didn't answer last night—were you—?"

"Look, I really can't talk. The taxi's here—"

"Taxi? Is something wrong with the car?"

"Didn't Kazy tell you? We're opening an office in Mexico City and it's been chaotic. Van and I are flying down again to meet with our new partners and I don't know a word of Spanish."

"Again? You're flying down *again?*"

"It's been like this for two weeks. It's really hectic and I didn't want to bother you."

"Van's going along?"

"He has to. He's in charge of international trade and he's fluent in Spanish. Listen, I'll probably be back tonight, but in case we have to stay over, Deb and Paul will have the number of the hotel. Look, the cab's here—I gotta run. 'Bye."

I stare at the dead phone, a weak, uneasy feeling in the pit of my stomach. I don't like this. I don't like this *at all.*

9:45 a.m. The rain has tapered off and now San Antonio is resting beneath a thick blanket of low nimbus. I wonder if it is raining in Boston.

"Henderson, Cobham, Mitchell, Lambert."

"Hi. This is Mike Mitchell. I'd like to speak to my wife's secretary."

"This is Kazy."

"Kazy, this is Mike. Do you happen to have the phone number for Linda's hotel?"

"You mean in Mexico? Let's see—I think maybe Van's secretary might have that. Hold on—" The phone switches to an easy-listening version of "Marrakesh Express." After an eternity, Kazy returns. "Mike, I'm sorry but Donna doesn't have it. I don't even know if they've got a hotel yet. But you know, I think our Mexican partners are arranging the lodgings."

"What's *their* number?"

"You mean in Mexico City? Oh, it's around here somewhere—

they have an office in Cancun, too. Anyway, it's *one* of those islands down there. Hm. I really can't find it—and she never takes her beeper with her. It's only for tonight—"

"Are you *sure* you don't know where they're staying?"

"I have your number in San Antonio—when I get the number of the hotel, I'll call you back."

"Okay. Thanks."

I hang up the phone. Dead end on the east coast. I'll try Paul. It's 8:00 a.m. in Los Angeles. He probably hasn't left for school yet.

I dial the number.

"Hellooo." It's a girl's voice, sleepy. What was her name—Lois? Lucy?

"Hello, uh, is Paul there?"

"Uh. Whom may I say is calling?"

"This is his father. I'm calling from San Antonio."

"Is this, like—an *emergency* or something?"

"Yes. Tell him I'm calling long-distance—I'm in a Mexican jail on a weapons charge."

"Oh."

Silence. Was I disconnected?

"Hello?"

"Um…can he get back with you—? 'Cause he's kind of—um—*involved* with something right now and—"

"Hey, Dad. *Whew!* How're ya doin'? What do you think of Lisa? Isn't she great?"

"Who?"

"Lisa. You were just talking to her."

"She's a wonderful girl. Have you heard from your mother?"

"Yeah. She's flying to Mexico this morning."

"*Where* in Mexico?"

"Somewhere. There's some kind of meeting or something, I dunno, I didn't pay that much attention. I think it's for the company bigwigs. She won some kind of case and they're, you know, celebrating. I think they made a lot of money."

"They *did?*"

"I guess. But maybe not. Say, do you know if they have 'Babette's Feast' on video down there in Texas? Like in Dallas, maybe? You're not that far from Dallas are you?"

"Has your mother *called* you?"

"Oh, sure. She talked to me last week. Say, did I tell you about my script? My agent says it's good but needs a little more work—"

"Did she give you her phone number down there?"

"Yeah. But I think she's gonna be somewhere else. It's Mexico, you know? But everything's cool. Mom works real hard, so I think you should let her have a good time. I mean, she explained it to me—and it's *okay*...Dad? Are you still there?"

"I'm still here."

"When I hear from Mom, I'll tell her to call you. Okay?"

"Good. Ask her give me a call."

"Absolutely. I'll bring it up the *very first thing*. Bye."

Wonderful.

6

Juke Box

Ten a.m.

I'm sitting at the very back of the room, but it's not far enough. In the dim light, a little guy at a lectern is talking about a thing called the right temporal sulcus. Welcome to gross anatomy. Part of the deal.

Amid the horde of attentive neuros and bored dreamers I see a few familiar faces: Gail, near the opposite wall, squinting at the blackboard. Keller, two rows down, his head on his chest, fast asleep. Coltrane, four seats away, sitting with his arms folded, head erect but eyes closed.

On the pull-down screen is a diagram of a human brain. I learned enough from my psychology courses to know what the main parts are—the cortex, the cerebellum, the thalamus. But it *still* looks like a sponge. Or maybe a chambered nautilus. I'm glad I settled on history as a profession—I would have made a terrible surgeon.

"Okay, nurse, let's put the clamp on that little whatchamacallit in there next to that *tube-looking* sort of thing."

Down front, the speaker tugs at his tie and taps the brain diagram with a long wooden stick. "The right temporal area is clearly the seat of hypnagogic projection and, perhaps for this reason, has been erroneously associated with the famous near-death experiences…"

I have no idea what he's talking about, but the line gets a chuckle from the neuros in the audience. The guy next to me, a standard bald man wearing a tweed coat, smiles knowingly and jots something on his clipboard.

My gloom from talking with my wife this morning has hardened into a bona-fide depression. First my wife runs off to Mexico, then my own son stonewalls me. And after all that, I'm forced to sit in a room full of brain mechanics determined to remove the word *soul* from the dictionary.

I notice the speaker has only a fringe of red hair around his head, floating above his ears. It's the kind of halo you used to see with big thermonuclear detonations. H-Bomb hair. My partner Jerry should be here—he would push it as the next big fad. He probably would suggest adding sparkles to signify all the nifty radiation.

Now the speaker is talking about activity levels in the various parts of the brain, and the tweed guy next to me nods and jots down another note. I see now that he's not really bald—as in comb-the-last-five-strands-over-your-head bald—in fact, he has a full head of hair. But it's mowed down to within a quarter-inch of his scalp. The last time I saw hair this short was on a jazz musician.

No. It was yesterday, in my brief journey to grade school.

The room blinks and a slide appears on the screen. Another view of the brain, this time in color, with a little red curlique in the exact center.

"We know the short-term memory is processed here, in the hippocampus."

The hippocampus? It looks more like an ear. Or a question mark. A question mark in the center of the brain.

It figures.

"Now, the amygdala here on the right temporal area...processes the *emotional* information. It is associated with norepinephrine receptors and is the reason we more easily remember events which hold a certain excitement for us. It's generally unreachable by hypnosis. It operates well beneath the realm of consciousness."

I wonder what Leonard would call the amygdala. Bare metal?

Perhaps some kind of coprocessor. Maybe what I saw yesterday wasn't a ribbon of light after all, but some internal circuit throbbing with overheated electrons.

I rub my ear—probably a few inches away from some internal filing cabinet.

"Hypnosis, of course, can retrieve most of the information, but the brain, particularly the hippocampus, does most of the work." The lecturer pauses to scratch his halo. "Think of hypnosis as the softwear, the brain as hardware, and machines such as the one Dr. Poundstone and his colleagues use as peripheral communications equipment."

Perfectly clear. I stifle a yawn.

The halo-man tugs at his tie—a chartreuse number that extends way past his belt. Then he runs his long fingers through the halo again.

I look at my watch. A few more hours and I'll be in the chair again, traveling back to the past. Where will I go this time? Maybe to that time the family sat in the yard and watched the newly launched ECHO satellite. Or maybe I'll go back further, to those cold, bright Sundays reading the funnies in front of the gas stove.

Then I'll try to do some work—check out the fads, locate a few artifacts, catch a movie at the drive-in. Warm Cokes and endless bags of stale popcorn and millions of June bugs popping against the windshield. Then maybe I'll turn on the radio and listen to the absolute latest song by the Beach Boys or the Beatles.

Rummaging around in the attic—right above the question mark.

·····◆·····

One p.m.

"Hey, Mike. Come in." Leonard buzzes the unlock button, and I open the heavy glass door to the lab. Instead of walking the short distance to the empty leather chair, I turn right toward the maze of computer terminals, panels and tape drives.

"I'm a little early. I had a question, and I—"

"I'll have to be in geek mode for another moment here, but I'll be with you real soon now. Make yourself comfortable." He motions toward a row of wooden chairs lined up against the wall. All are covered with stacks of paper. I carefully remove one stack—an EEG trace for someone initialled C.R.—and sit down.

"We had a little storm action last night. The lightning strikes hosed the main transformer upstairs." Leonard adjusts his glasses. "So the system started routing things around. In the shuffle, the Big Iron lost a few cycles, probably some nontrivial problems lurking in the system—"

"Right." I look at the stack of paper beside me. It's covered with numbers. I have no idea what they mean. "Did the Juke Box get hit?"

"Nah. It's bulletproof. Has its own port. Pardon me while I bang on the machine for a moment. He slides back a case and peers into the heart of the box. "Oh, great. This circuit's toast—goodbye throat modem."

"Excuse me?"

"The lightning nailed the communications box…which means it may have got the theta bus, too," Leonard says, resignation in his voice. "Unless I can patch in a sacrificial cow, you dreamers are on your own." He pauses and strokes his chin. "Or maybe not. I suppose I could hack the workstation—"

"Leonard—"

He looks up. "Sorry. I paged out for a minute. What was the question?"

"I only wanted to see how the Juke Box works."

"Oh. Sure. Okay. No prob. I'll do it right now." He steps through the maze of wires and computer cases and sits down at a keyboard in front of a large monitor. "Okay. High bit, please?"

"Say for example, when I tell you I'm listening to a song—"

"Song. Okay." He scratches his ear and adjusts his glasses. "The Juke is connected to some really neat music databases. They don't show everything, but they come close." He types on the keyboard and a list appears on the screen. "There's the database—"

Another few taps on the keyboard.

"—I use the Robert Mitchum criteria," Leonard says. "Any record database that includes 'Thunder Road' will probably have everything else. Here's a good regional one from the Seattle area—Fleetwoods, Kingsmen, Paul Revere and the Raiders, Ventures, Wailers—now, here's one from the midwest—"

I look at the screen. Leonard enters what appears to be *loc, MDW2* and the screen explodes into multiple windows, each with its own list. He expands one window slightly and reads from it.

"Lessee—" Leonard mumbles. "Chessmen Square, Bob Kuban, The Red Blazers—*Friar Tuck and His Merry Men*? *Saturdays Children*? Performance tapes only. Whoa. These guys include every little dink band that ever played anywhere."

"Suppose I heard a song on a particular station—"

"Then I could find you real easy," Leonard shrugs. "We'd call up the station, get the playlist and cross-check it with the song."

"I have no idea what you're talking about."

"Look," Leonard spins around to face me. "This is real simple. The big stations all used pre-taped playlists. They'd study Billboard's top hundred songs, then they'd record the top forty or so on tape. It was only forty, 'cause I think that's all the ten-inch reel would hold. Anyway, there's a database that purports to show the lineup for *each* big station across the country. For example—"

He points to the screen.

"From your file, I see that you grew up in north-central Missouri. Okay. Missouri radio in the sixties was dominated in the daytime by two stations—WHB in Kansas City and KXOK in St. Louis. Here, for example, is WHB's playlist for, say—" he types on the keyboard, "November 11, 1966."

A list appears on the screen.

"See? Here's 'Respectable' by the Outsiders, then 'Cherish,'—on up to 'Devil With The Blue Dress,' '96 Tears,' 'Poor Side of Town' and 'Good Vibrations.' Then comes the news and then they start over." He rolls his eyes. "And over and over and over until that song list is inscribed on every little teen-aged cortex in the listening area. Thus were hits made."

"Well, some of the songs back then were never hits."

"Of course not, but it doesn't matter. A teen-ager's brain will remember not only the good, but the bad, the ugly and the truly stupid." Leonard smiles. "With a slight statistical emphasis on the truly stupid."

"I suppose."

"Anyway, you tell me the station and the last two songs you heard, I can tell you approximately where you are, precisely when, about what time of day it is, and what the next song will be. It's all in the playlist. And the playlist for a given station is usually good for a solid week."

"So that's how you do that."

"That's how I do that," Leonard nods. "Let's say you're down there blindfolded, locked in the trunk of your girlfriend's Buick, whatever. You don't know the month, year, where you are. Anything. You can only hear the radio. And you tell me that the last sequence you heard was 'I'm Your Puppet,' 'Psychotic Reaction' and 'Rain On The Roof.' No prob. I run a cross-check and find out that's the November 26, 1966 sequence for the St. Louis station, KXOK. *And*…since that station only broadcast at 10,000 watts, I know you're in Missouri or Illinois and it's sometime between sunrise and sunset. If you can give me the name of the announcer, I could place you within two hours. Stupefyingly simple."

I nod my head. "I'm impressed."

"Look. If you don't tell Poundstone, I'll make you a printout.

Memorize some of these song sequences and it'll save the Jukebox time in getting your location."

"Can you do the weather, too?"

"Don't be silly." Leonard smiles. "*Of course* I can do the weather. I can also do planets, stars, asteroids and the hundred major satellites."

"How about the weather for this past week—in Lexington, Massachusetts? I want to know if there was a thunderstorm there—say about four nights ago. At about midnight, Boston time."

"Lexington Massachusetts, huh?" He looks at me warily, then shrugs. "Sure. Why not?" He turns to the monitor and types something on the keyboard. The screen immediately displays a radar map. "There we are. Cozy little town just outside Boston. Four nights ago, huh? Lessee—" The screen blinks for a moment, then displays a weather map overlay. "Clear."

"Is there a storm anywhere? Lightning? Rain? Anything?"

"Nope. Perfectly clear."

"You're sure?"

"See for yourself." Leonard backs away from the screen.

"Were there any electrical blackouts?"

"That's a second question. You're only allowed one—"

"Come on!"

"Okay—" more keystrokes and a list appears on the screen. "I've just mined the service interruption and police event list for New England. See? No major service interruptions anywhere near Lexington. Nothing. It was a very quiet week. Except for the usual burglaries, of course. And some guy flashed a bus load of tourists." He squints at the screen. "No, that was in Newton."

I stare at the screen. Linda said there was a *storm* causing the clicks on the line.

"Okay. Can you tell if there were any problem with phone lines? Say, at around 10:30 our time?"

"Ah, phones." Leonard smiles. "When you called did you hear an echo?"

"No."

"Then you weren't on a satellite. So the router algorithms must have trunked it through. Let's take a look. I have an auto-ping set up on the network—"

"A what?"

"A ping—it's a softwear packet that can probe the phone network.

Look—" A few more taps on the keyboard and a network of glowing green lines appears on the map. "Okay. That night was pretty quiet. The call originated here—that's your room number—and it was trunked up to Dallas—

"From there it went to a hub in Atlanta—no surprise—and then around to Philly and finally in to the main hub outside Boston. Then, of course, through the local to your house in Lexington. No outages, no hangups, no reroutes. The web should be so simple. Want to see the entire web? Looks like a big bow tie with IBM as the knot."

"No thanks. I'll stick with the phones. Can you get me information on hotels in Mexico City?"

"Mexico City?" Leonard stares at me. "Mike, life is hard. The technology *does* have its limits."

"Sorry."

"No prob." Leonard closes the program. "Just don't tell anyone about the demo, or we'll both be out of here. You still gonna go under today?"

"Yeah, I guess so."

"Well, I should have the replacement theta bus linked up in about an hour, so I guess I'll see you then."

"Fine."

Walking from the lab, I picture the radar screen of Lexington. Clear. No storm. No outages. What the hell is going *on* back there?

I lie on the chair, visor down, staring at the twin green lights, one for each eye. I'm ready for the trip, but mostly, I'm still thinking about Linda. Why would she lie to me about something as minor as a storm? Was it because I heard the clicks on the phone? Was there someone on the downstairs line?

For a brief moment, I consider going back four days, to that instant she told me. Just to hear it again. But what if I did? I wouldn't be able to confront her about it—she's in Mexico. Maybe going to spend the night there. Just like that time *before*.

"Hey, Mike." It's Leonard. "Your pulse and blood pressure are getting into the nontrivial range. Lighten up."

"Okay. I'll try."

"Think of a blue circle."

All I can think about is Linda—in some Mexican hotel with her law partner. Did they get separate rooms? She didn't the *last* time this happened.

"Mike, both your frontal lobes are starting to look very *interesting*. You sure you don't want liquid sleep?"

"I'm *fine*."

"Not so loud, you'll bark the throat mike. Okay?"

She's probably staying at the Presidente—the big hotel near the Zona Rosa. Probably having dinner with that Van dweeb. Maybe even plans to spend the night with him—

"Big drive's locked and loaded...thetas up—hold it—w... have...*entrainment*."

I fall backward into the darkness.

Surprisingly, the anger I had in the chair was apparently left there— sloughed away like a shark losing its skin. I look down at the lights below, knowing they're only images produced by some arcane circuit in my brain. Still, the view is beautiful, like floating above a river of fireflies.

As I ease into one of the lights, I try to take note of the transition from up there to—down here?

The first thing I notice is the sound of my own footsteps. Amazing how I never thought to listen to them before—but apparently, they were there. I hear my own breathing. And the blood rushing though my ears. Now the heartbeat—and from here it spreads out to the wind, insects, birds, treefrogs—everything surrounding me in an ever-widening circle. As I get closer, the circle expands further. I hear cars on the road, their tires whining against the pavement. There is weather, a thunderstorm. People nearby.

The circle expands further.

I begin to see. In the center of my vision is color, perfect, absolute color. The sharp green of the grass, the corduroy brown of the earth. First the greens differentiate into a hundred different shades, then a thousand—blending into blues and grays. There is movement. Bright yellow movement.

Raincoats. I'm walking on a sidewalk, surrounded by yellow raincoats. I stop, look down at the wet sidewalk and flick the metal latch closed on one of my black rubber galoshes.

A voice: "Stupid shoe keeps coming loose."

If I could feel, I probably would discover my socks are soaked.

Locking the scene briefly, I notice tiny rocks in the glistening concrete—and dark puffs of moss at the edge of the walk. Closer, I see the bare outline of a heart carved in the cement.

A schoolbus approaches on the nearby blacktop, lights on, tires hissing in the rain. A spray of water splashes into the ditch.

Headlights are everywhere. The cars pass, their lights shimmering in the early morning rainstorm. All around, pools of stormwater reflect the dark gray sky. On the horizon, gray clouds hang near the ground, trailing dark curtains of rain.

The lights begin to dim as my perception begins to retract. The rainclouds on the horizon are first to turn to a gray haze, then the glistening brown trees, then the road. As I lift away from this place, all I hear are the footsteps.

Up, drifting toward another moving light in this stream, I feel a sense of freedom and anticipation. I'm inside the movie of my life.

Actually, I'm inside Audrey Hepburn's life. At least that's who it looks like from here in the back seat of my brother's Chevy. A beautiful, perfect Audrey Hepburn—twenty feet tall on the drive-in screen.

Across the back seat from me, on the other hand, is a wiry, tomboyish girl with short brown hair and suspicious eyes. The girl in the front seat turns around to face us: "Michael? Karen? Aren't you two going to *do* anything?"

"Doesn't look like it," the wiry girl says, folding her arms.

My brother Earl looks over his shoulder. "Maybe ya'll could take a walk or something—"

I scoot over to put my arm around her, then apparently give her my best shot at a kiss. I can't tell because I can't see from up here. Wherever it is, *when*ever it is, I've got my eyes closed.

Now they open again—and I'm peering into two *other* eyes—no more than six inches away. An absurd thought: is Karen close enough to actually *see* me up here—floating behind my own eyes—watching my own past?

My eyes close again—followed by a quick flash of yellow light. "Ow!"

"Stopit!" A girl's voice.

I open my eyes, still only inches from Karen's. Her eyebrows are bunched toward the center. She's angry.

Sally looks up over the seat. "*What?*"

"Mike got fresh."

"Did not."

"Did. He put his hand up under my blouse so I hit 'im."

"Don't be fresh, Scout," Earl mumbles from somewhere.

"You guys either calm down, or you'll walk home," Sally says. "Both of you. Think about it."

She and Earl disappear behind the seat. I glance at Karen, then move in again.

"No grabbing this time," she says. "Unless I say it's okay."

"Is it okay?"

"No."

On the huge drive-in screen, Audrey Hepburn is dancing with George Peppard. Then the movie slides away as Karen pushes me down into the seat.

"*Mike. Where are you?*" It's Leonard.

I lock the scene—which is pointless, since I have my eyes closed anyway.

"Leonard, I'm at a drive-in movie watching Audrey Hepburn and George Peppard—"

"*Breakfast At Tiffany's. Solid gold, 1961. Theme song is Moon River by Henry Mancini. But of course you knew that.*"

"Yeah, I knew that. Anything on the schedule at the Corinth, Missouri Drive-In?"

"*Sorry. As I've said earlier, there are limits to the technology. Do you have a car radio?*"

"Yeah, but my brother has it tuned to a ball game."

"*I don't do ball games. Junks up the drives. Call me when you get a song title.*"

As I unlock, the scene abruptly vanishes, like I've switched a channel to someplace else. Some *time* else.

Now it's morning. The sun is hiding behind a thin, bright overcast. Something is snapping in the wind—the sleeve of my blue nylon jacket—with my arm resting on a metal railing. I see two legs in cuffed new blue jeans dangling over empty space. I sense there is a massive object behind me—a wall of silver-painted metal.

I'm on the catwalk of the Corinth city water tower.

"I wouldn't fool with her if I were you," someone says. It's a familiar voice. "Tell her to get lost."

Far below is a flat landscape dotted with houses, roads, a set of railroad tracks. Seated a few feet away on a corrugated metal platform is Evan, wearing a brown windbreaker, corduroy jeans and green sweater. As usual, his Scout canteen is slung over his shoulder.

"I'm tellin' you, I *know* her. She *is* my sister."

"Well, yeah, but—"

"She's selfish—did you know that?" Evan says. "When the family goes camping, she squeals to Mom about all the mosquitos. So then she gets my Scout tent and I have to sleep outside. I really hate camping when Pammie's along."

I see a vision of Evan's freckled, taciturn little sister in lantern light—brushing her long dark blonde hair from her hazel eyes, sitting alone on a sleeping bag in her t-shirt and yellow-striped shorts.

Evan waves his hand dismissively. "She'll go on the railroad bridge, sure—but d'ya think she'd ever climb with us *up here*? Forget it. She'd get dizzy and fall off. Then my folks would *really* get mad—"

The scene changes, like a film on quick-edit. The tower is gone, replaced by gently swaying scenery. I'm sitting on a porch swing with someone.

"...My mom is a telephone operator and my dad works five jobs—"

I turn to look at her.

"...He's also going to school and he preaches on Sunday. I know you'll like my folks."

She's about five-feet-four with a slim build, jet black hair and intense ebony eyes. Fifteen years old.

It's *her*—Rachael Sarah Dominic. The drawer in my file cabinet creaks out and stops: summer of 1966.

I *knew* this would happen. Sooner or later it had to. Now, if I can just get out—

"Leonard."

"Hello Mike. World here. I was going to call you."

"Is my blood pressure up?"

"Now that you mention it. And you're sending up a mixed theta trace. Anything special going on down there?"

"How do I get *out* of a particular memory?"

"I can call Terri in to nuke it. Little midazolam drip should send that year to the trash."

"Can you just erase a couple of months?"

"Sorry, Mike. The technology has its limits. What did you run into down there?"

"I'll get back with you." I try to think. Why this? Why *now*? If I can only find a way to jump—

Nothing happens.

Instead, the film continues traveling across the sprockets of my mind, frame by painful frame. A 1963 Pontiac pulls into the gravel driveway and shuts off the lights. The car door opens and a slender, medium-sized man wearing a white shirt and khaki pants steps out. I quickly lock the scene: his thick black hair is cut short and combed straight back. That, along with his five-o'clock shadow, gives him the appearance of a traveling salesman. Or perhaps a 1920's gangster.

"Hi. I'm Bob Dominic. Are you the guy who's been taking up so much of my daughter's time?"

"Uh, yeah, I guess—"

"Rachael's told us a lot about you. I hope none of it is true, but it probably is. Do your friends call you Mike? You *do* have friends, don't you? Or are you spending all your time with my daughter?"

"Daddy—c'mon!" She turns to me. "He does that to everybody. Try to ignore him. His bark is worse than his bite."

I look at that quick smile—an image responding not to me now, but to one she sees—me at 19. And yet *she* doesn't exist except in my mind.

The image of her father looks at her, back at me, perhaps seeing what she sees. "Bet she's already chased all your friends away. Her mother did that to me—that's why I don't have any friends anymore. Is that how you want to end up?"

"Oh, Bob, what are you telling that boy?" A tall, handsome woman with a round face and short, brown hair emerges from the passenger side of the car. She's wearing a sweatshirt over a pair of plaid coulots. Scanning my lower peripheral vision, I see she's also wearing tennis shoes. She's young—impossibly young—early thirties perhaps.

"I'm Wanda Dominic, Rachael's mother." She smiles and shakes my hand. "Rachael told us how you met." She turns to Rachael. "Hon, you dropped the Sunday paper and he helped you pick it up?"

"Yeah-huh," Rachael glances at me. "Something like that."

Yeah-huh. Like an acknowledgement combined with a sort of non-committal shrug. Is this when I heard that expression first? I thought I got it from Brenda. No, Brenda would never have said something like that. She was way too precise.

I turn to Mrs. Dominic. "I think I met Rachael five years ago. At the Indian Springs picnic. I was with Evan Carswell—"

"Oh, did you know him?" Wanda draws closer. "Isn't that terrible what happened?"

"Yeah. He was my best friend—"

The scene locks in place, a sepia photograph. I see Mrs. Dominic, her lips tight, her eyebrows arched in an expression of sadness. Then, particle by particle, the scene dissolves to brown.

I lock the darkness. My mind is preparing to fall another few millimeters into my past—but where? Does an inch down into the cerebral cortex equal a year? Maybe. And for that matter, where is that ridge or fold in my cortex that contains the Brenda Lacey movies? The night of the prom, for example. It's recorded in here somewhere—I'll just have to find it.

I scan the darkness for a clue. Nothing—only an expanse of grainy brown. It will be like looking for one picture in a million, yet I know it's there. And somehow, I'll find it.

I unlock the scene and the brown begins to lighten. I'm coming up on another memory. Will this be the one?

No such luck.

Instead of being with Brenda, I'm on a gravel road, my brown suede boots kicking up white puffs of dust with each step. My shirt is tied around my waist, and an arm keeps appearing to brush sweat away from my eyes. Amid the trill of locusts I hear a dull rumble. In the distance, I see a slowly moving light approaching a crossing two miles away.

Someone is talking to me.

"So, the guy's dreaming he's on a train that's going through a town where all his old friends are. And he wants to get off, but the train doesn't stop. So he opens the door and jumps. And he gets up and he's really there with all his old friends. Only they're dead. Get it?"

I turn. It's Evan—shirtless, with a bandanna tied around his head. He's not wearing his cap, but the canteen is still there. The one I saw on the water tower the last time I was here.

"Yeah, Carswell, I get it. He was on the train to the fourth dimension."

"Nah," Evan says. "The way I figure it, when he jumped out the door he jumped *into* the fourth dimension. Either that, or part of him went into the town. And part of him got killed."

"Think that's what happens when you die? Only part of you gets killed, and the other part is still alive somewhere?"

"Yeah, maybe," he nods. "In the fourth dimension. Either that or time slows down. Look, here comes the train. You wanna get up on the bridge?"

I look up. Amid the hazy greenery of September, 1961, just outside of Corinth, Missouri, is the tiny white dot of light on an approaching Norfolk and Western locomotive.

"You think we got time?"

"Yeah. The train always stops in town." Evan breaks into a run.

"Evan, wait——"

I watch the chunky twelve-year old scramble ahead of me up the cinder hill toward the railroad bridge. I follow him, but time seems to slow. Now I see the little puffs of brown dust rising behind his shoes as he scales the cinder railbed to the tracks. Now he's on the track and running toward the bridge. The light ahead gets brighter. Something is about to happen, but I can't recall what it is. I *won't* recall what it is.

I lock the scene, scan it for details. A kid and a bridge and a train. I know I've been here before, yet it's happening for the first time. I unlock and the train inches closer. I lock the scene again.

"Leonard."

"Hey. Your heart rate's getting a little high. What's going on down there?"

"I need a railroad timetable for Corinth, Missouri—September 1, 1961. Norfolk and Western. I want to know—did the train stop?"

"Whoa. What a question. Give me a minute."

I unlock the scene and watch Evan begin to climb up the side of the bridge.

"Mike? I've got the transportation archives up. Justaminute...Missouri, September, '61. For the entire month there was a work train that came through each morning at 11:34. No stops at Corinth. Max speed 54 miles per hour. You want me to check the cross-files?"

The train is halfway across the bridge, its diesel horn hammering my ears. I see the rotating light, bright even under the midday sun. *Lock!*

"Leonard. Bring me up."

"Sure. Only takes a microfortnight. Hang on."

I'm still in 1961. Yet not in 1961 either. Instead, I seem to be somewhere in between. *All* places in between.

"Leonard?"

"There you are. Sorry about the misfire."

"What happened."

"I had a little problem with the scram voltage. I thought you slipped off the edge of your cortex. Ha, ha, only serious. Give me a minute, okay? You're exhibiting a very interesting trace in your right temporal—"

"Hurry up. It's a little chaotic down here."

"Mike, if you yell down there, it just clogs up the signal processors and comes out sounding like a bark. Clarity is a virtue, especially where you are right now, so try to enunciate."

I see multiples of Evan, a dense cloud of them, locked in place, some leading toward the railroad bridge, some standing with me. Others walking behind—all blending into one another. And disturbingly, there is another cloud—a cloud composed of a thin, dark-haired boy wearing jeans, boots and a white t-shirt. That cloud also extends to the tracks.

It's the cloud of me.

"Leonard. Get me out of here."

Silence.

"Leonard!"

Nothing.

Somehow the sky above has turned a dark blue, almost black, and I'm drifting toward it. Up. Below I see the road fill with a haze of vehicles, the tracks with trains—all different, all blending with the clouds of Evan and Michael. I drift up, and watch the trees move, blend. In the distance, the town of Corinth is a haze of shapes: buildings, trees, open prairie, forest.

Suddenly, I'm somewhere I've never been.

Part II

7

Rachael

I drift higher into the sky, up through the cirrus, toward the vault of the heavens. Below me, the earth has become a blur—a dense cloud of superimposed possibilities frozen in time. Yet each layer is real. Somewhere down there, in that haze, the train didn't appear; somewhere we both were on the tracks. And somewhere in that blur my own life came to an end.

How can I see this? Am I outside time—wedged between a pair of instants so small the term "now" has no meaning?

"Leonard. Can you hear me?"

Silence.

I rise above the haze, up through the layers of cirrus. A ghost on the wind. Or a radio wave lost between stations.

"Leonard!"

I see a flicker of light in the dark. Heat lightning on some distant shore. Is Leonard trying to reach me? Or is it something else?

As I drift higher, I sense something above me, drawing me to it. At the same time I'm losing density somehow, like sea fog dissipating under a warm sun.

"Leonard—"

No response. Only a dim hiss—like the sound of waves on a distant beach. Above me, the light takes on a softer glow. Am I moving away from it? No.

"Michael." A voice in my mind.

"Leonard, is that you?"

"Hey, Mike, we're getting a signal breakup. You okay down there?"

"Michael, I'm here." That voice again.

Someone is here with me.

"Leonard, get me out of here."

"—I think the capacitors are behaving randomly—pardon me while I bang on this dinosaur—" The signal fades. Did I imagine it?

The light coalesces and the hiss becomes a whine, then a roar. A strange thought: if the house of time has a front door, I'm about to enter through the side window—just before it slams shut. And now, at the last minute, someone reaches out, pulls me through. It's someone I know. Or knew.

The scene snaps into motion and I lean to the side. I'm surrounded by warmth—soft, musty warmth. I'm sitting in the back seat of a car—and next to me in the back seat, wearing a white blouse, shorts and sandals, is a 15-year-old girl eating an ice cream cone.

Somehow, I've returned to a semblance of reality—inside a Pontiac. I hear the car radio. It's tuned to a song, "When A Man Loves A Woman."

"Mike, this is Leonard. Can you hear me now?"

I think: *Lock.* And the motion around me stops. A relief. I'm back where things work.

"Mike—?"

"I'm here."

"You went delta on us for a few minutes—must have had your interrupts locked out. Did you go to sleep down there?"

"Probably. It was a little confusing—"

"You want to come back now? I've got the capacitor charged up."

"No, that's okay. I recognize my surroundings now. Everything is fine."

"Well, everything looks good now. Your theta shows a few spikes, but that's probably from the software. Call me if you need me, I'm here to help."

I unlock with Mr. Dominic in mid-sentence.

"—Driving in Missouri isn't a challenge," he says. "There's a service station every ten miles. You get gas, get your oil changed, tires fixed. Whatever. Try driving in Mexico. There, you have to drive by your wits."

"Tell Michael about that drive to Monterrey, Hon," Mrs. Dominic says. I notice she is holding what appears to be a quart-sized milkshake.

Mr. Dominic leans back and smiles. "Y'see, Wanda was pregnant with Stacie and there was no hospital in Linares. So when Wanda started into labor, we jumped in the old Buick and headed for Monterrey. We were halfway there when the oil light came on. I stopped at this little roadside stand and picked up some cooking oil. Poured it into the crankcase and it worked great."

"But then we found out we didn't have any gas, remember, Bob?" Wanda says.

"A rock had knocked a hole in the tank," he continues. "All the gas leaked out and the car quit. Here we were, in the middle of the desert, middle of a Sunday afternoon. And I was desperate. And all we had was some of Bradley's baby stuff, rubbing alcohol, soap, that sort of thing."

"So what did you do?" I ask.

"After I found that hole in the tank, I prayed to the Lord for a minute. Then I got the soap and plugged the hole in the gas tank, and poured in the rubbing alcohol. Had to prime the carburetor, but it worked."

"The last time I heard this," Rachael hits me with her elbow, "the fan belt broke too. They fixed it with nylons or something. And the tires gave out and they drove on the rims. Then the headlights fell off."

"So did you make it to the hospital on time?" I ask.

"Yeah. With about a week to spare," Mr. Dominic says. "Turned out it was a false alarm. But that soap kept the hole in the gas tank plugged for a good week and a half." A pause. "You know, this family has had to do a lot to survive, but the Lord's always been there. Watching over us."

"That's right," Wanda says. "Even in Mexico."

"*Especially* in Mexico," Rachael says.

"*Okay, Mike. Capacitor's up. You ready?*"

"Just a minute." I lock the scene. Will I be able to find Brenda Lacey? Should I even try?

"*What do you mean, just a minute? Changed your mind?*"

"No. I'd just like to spend a few more minutes here—"

"*You've still got some time. Want me to protocol a pizza? ANSI standard. My treat.*"

"That's okay. I'm having an ice cream cone."

"*Suit yourself. See you in a millifortnight.*"

As Leonard signs off, I try to remember where I was just before this. I concentrate, trying to recall an image, but get nothing. It seems a door has closed. All I know is I'm riding around in a Pontiac listening to a 15-year-old tell me the story of her family.

"…When Stacie and Amy were born, Daddy started calling our house Rancho Conejo," Rachael is saying. "It means Rabbit Ranch. I think he got it from a movie or something."

"I thought it was appropriate under the circumstances," Mr. Dominic says, steering the Pontiac around a curve. "So, Michael, did you grow up in Corinth?"

I've heard this story before. I'm amazed I bothered to remember it the first time. I lock and scan the scene, looking at the passing cars for any sign of Brenda Lacey. Then it occurs to me—even if I found her, what would I be able to do?

Nothing, that's what. I'm Ahab strapped to the whale of the Dominics. Sighing mentally, I unlock the scene.

"—We used to live in Corinth—on Locust street," Mrs. Dominic says. "Rachael was born there."

"Born on a street named for an insect," Rachael says between licks of the cone. "Grandma still lives there—it's about two miles from your house. Walking distance."

That's right. Walking distance. And that particular walk took the 15-year-old Rachael right past Brenda's house. Every day. Every single day. I begin to remember why Brenda and I broke up.

"So I guess you're a senior in high school?" Mr. Dominic glances up in the rear view mirror.

"I graduated last month. In September I start college in Kirksville. It's about sixty miles north."

"That's convenient," Mrs. Dominic says. "You can visit your parents on weekends."

Rachael punches me with her elbow. "Michael, tell 'em about your summer job."

The universe blinks and I'm plunged into darkness.

"Here." The voice is a whisper.

"Here what?"

"Kiss me *here*. *Then* you can move down a little." In the darkness, I see the outline of a bare shoulder, then the hem of an unbuttoned blouse. Scanning down, I see a ridge of collarbone, then a border between tan and white, then the perfect, round areola surrounding a tiny bump of flesh.

I know this landscape, remember every square inch from thirty years before.

Somehow, *finally*, I've managed to locate Brenda. I watch as the nipple comes into view.

"Brenda, I'm gonna miss you this summer," I hear myself say.

"Mmmmm." It's a reply lost between a whisper and a growl. "Here," she says. "Do this."

The universe blinks again.

"—I work at the die-cast factory in Monroe." My voice. "I started there last week. The pay's pretty good. Dollar-ninety an hour on the eleven-to-seven shift."

I see Mrs. Dominic glance at her husband.

I'm back in the Pontiac.

"You know," Mr. Dominic says, "when I worked at the radio station, I *liked* the graveyard shift. It's quiet. Nobody to bother you."

"I'm trying to get Mom and Dad to move back to Corinth," Rachael says. "But they won't do it. I really like Corinth."

"Cherokee, Missouri is good enough for us," Mrs. Dominic says. "It has a nice school and it's only ten miles from the state college campus."

Another blink and I'm plunged into darkness. I hear a rustle of clothing. What's going on? Am I back with Brenda?

"Put your hand here—no, no—not there—*here*."

I open my eyes to see her other breast, a soft round orb in the moonlight. "Do you really have to go to that Art Camp?"

"Um-hm."

"Why?" I approach the nipple.

"So I can study watercolor—mmmm—don't stop."

I move down slowly past the tan line below her navel—

"Mmmmn. That's right—right along there—"

Blink.

"Cherokee is *such* a pit," Rachael says. "Last year I was on the pom-pon squad—that's like an almost-cheerleader, you know? Anyway, the school's so cheap they only gave us one pom each. We had to pretend we were waving these blue paper torches or something. Oh, and you can't wear miniskirts."

"Well, I'll go along with that," Mrs Dominic says. "Girls really don't look good in miniskirts. Isn't that right, Bob? *Bob*—?"

"I'm out of this," Mr. Dominic says. "I'm a married man. I have no opinions anymore, and certainly none about miniskirts."

"Well, you can't wear 'em in Cherokee High School," Rachael continues. "You have to go into the principal's office and kneel. *And if the skirt doesn't touch the floor*, the principal sends you home. It's really a bite. We can't wear miniskirts, can't bring mouthwash—"

"Yes, that's right," Mrs. Dominic turns to look me in the eye. "In Cherokee you can't bring mouthwash to school."

"And lemme tell you why," Rachael says. "It is *so* stupid. Some freshman girl got into a fight with her boyfriend and tried to commit suicide by drinking a whole bottle of Lavoris."

I scan the car. There is no sign of Brenda. Where did she go? I lock, but the scene remains the same. Absolutely the same. Mr. Dominic is tapping a cigarette into the ashtray, Rachael is pausing for a bite of ice cream cone, and Mrs. Dominic is apparently getting ready to interject something into the conversation.

I try again one more time. *Lock.* The scene shifts a little: the ash falls from Mr. Dominic's cigarette. Another lick on the cone from Rachael, and Mrs. Dominic turns another degree.

Belatedly, I give up and unlock the scene.

"—Not a whole bottle Rachael," Mrs. Dominic is saying, "It was one of those little bottles you keep in your purse."

"Anyway," Rachael continues, "when she threw it back up, it came out red and the teacher about *fainted*. Ambulance came and everything. No more mouthwash. At least no more *red* mouthwash."

Please, God.

Blink.

Suddenly, I'm back with Brenda! At least I *think* it's Brenda. Yes. It *has* to be. I lock the scene. Lock it so tight it will *never* move—ever.

And now, here I am—approximately three inches below her perfect round navel. I scan to each side, looking for the top hem of her underwear, but find only the smooth pelvic ridges and the soft border between tan skin and white. Down, only to find a line of shadow hiding everything.

I carefully unlock, hoping the image will begin scrolling north, but no such luck. Instead it moves down as the camera—my eyes—move *up*—past her breasts to her neck and now her face. While this movie was involved in more interesting activity, I was in some kind of weird commercial break—hearing about miniskirts and Lavoris and fainting teachers.

Is a replay possible? What button do I push?

The scene moves past full lips, past the pert turned-up nose, finally to the eyes slightly open, blonde hair in disarray. As I watch, she smiles and slowly slides down in the seat. Good. Finally.

Blink.

"Rachael's right. It's a hole-in-the-wall," Mr. Dominic says. "When somebody on the school board heard I was studying sociology at the college, they figured we were socialists. And from there, that went to nudists."

God help me, I've got to get out of this car. *Now.* I lock the scene and concentrate—and nothing happens. The picture remains—Mr. Dominic at the wheel, Mrs. Dominic with her arm over the top of the front seat and Rachael, her eyes closed, in mid-lick on the cone.

I'm trapped. I unlock the scene and Rachael finishes the lick, then begins talking. "Bradley—that's my little brother—used to run around naked," she says. "And I guess somebody saw 'im. Now they think the whole family's like that."

"If I knew who started that rumor," Mrs. Dominic says. "I'd just *shake* 'im."

Blink.

"It's for the whole summer?"

"Yeah." She opens her eyes. "It's for the whole summer. Michael, if you don't *want* me to go, say so."

"I don't want you to go. Please don't go! *Pleeeeese!* This summer won't mean anything without you here! I don't know what I'll do. I'll go crazy!"

"And I'll go crazy without you. But it's too late. My father's already paid for it and I told him I'm going. And I *want* to go." She sits up in the seat. I lock and scan the scene. Yes, I can barely detect the soft, dark triangle at the periphery of my vision. It *was* there after all.

"Maybe I can drive up to visit."

"I don't think it would be a good idea."

"Why not?"

"I'll have a roommate. Besides, there'll be a lot of college people there. You'd probably stand out."

"Huh?"

"Listen. You can write to me. You *will* write to me, won't you?"

"Absolutely."

"And you have a job this summer don't you? You won't get bored. And Art Camp only lasts two months."

"Brenda—"

"Look, I've got to finish packing tonight, so if you want to make out some more, we better hurry up."

"Sure." I look down on her, beautiful and perfect in the moonlight, an angel in the back seat of my Fairlane. No more blinks. Please, no more blinks.

Something flashes in my peripheral vision—a pair of lights.

Carlights.

Blink.

"Yeah," Mr. Dominic says wearily, "we'd really like to move to Weslayan but for now, we're stuck in Cherokee." He pulls the car to a stop in the driveway, then looks back over the seat at me. "Say, Michael. You know anything about *guns*?"

I lock the scene and concentrate. Out. Up...and...*out.*

The scene implodes like celluloid sucked into a vacuum.

The sun is shining.

It's late afternoon.

Blue and silver Greyhound busses are rattling away from a dusty gravel-strewn parking lot, leaving behind small groups of pale young men.

I know this place. It's called the assembly zone. There is chaos as soldiers wearing crisp olive drab uniforms charge through, glaring at the newcomers.

The air is thick with fear: One of the civilians, a young man in plaid slacks and short-sleeved white shirt, is doing pushups in a splotch of brown mud. A black sergeant in a green uniform is standing over him.

"Yer too *tired?*" the sergeant screams. "It's 'cause you been eatin' too good! Straighten up that back!"

The civilian, his huge pink forearms locked and shaking, tries to comply, then collapses into the mud.

Lock. The assailant, a large man with a football player's muscula- ture, is wearing a brown drill instructor's hat. On his shoulder are three stripes up, two down. Sergeant E-7. He's been here awhile.

"That's right! Too damn *fat!*" the sergeant snarls. "Get up and get outta here! I don't want to have to look at yer fat ass anymore! Git!"

The man scrambles away toward a row of parked cars.

"No! Gawdammit! *This* way!" The sergeant points in the opposite direction. "Think yer gonna run away from the fuckin' army, *boy?*"

The fat civilian turns and scrambles back to the relative safety of his peers, a gaggle of helpless, frightened young men.

There is no need to call out coordinates to Leonard. I know exactly where I am: August 28, 1969.

I shuffle with the rest of the rumpled civilians into a squat yellow clapboard building. Everyone is sweating profusely, either from fear or because there is no air conditioning. For once, I'm grateful I can't experience heat or cold.

"You know we're gettin' shots next," one of the young men is telling another. "For the black plague they use the square needle and they give it to you in the *balls*. Hurts like hell. I've seen guys pass out."

It occurs to me now this young man was lying. I try to survey my thoughts, but I hear only a jumble of static mixed with—improbably— the faint strains of a Beatles' song: "I Am The Walrus."

"College boy, huh?" The sergeant, his mouth bent into a deep frown, is looking at my induction papers. "Drafted?"

"Yes, sir."

"It's yes, *drill sergeant!*" He glares at me. "I gawddamn *work* for a living!"

I try again to read my thoughts but they're still mostly static. The Beatles' song, however, isn't playing anymore; it's been replaced by the distinct, rhythmic woosh of blood in my ears.

"It says here you're married. Put your wife's name on this line here. That's so we can send her yer belongings when you get yer ass shot off."

"Excuse me—"

He looks up from his papers. "What did you say to me?" He's looking directly at me, his eyes filled with rage.

"My wife—"

"What!?" The sergeant stands up from his desk. He's hovering over me. His face and uniform fill my field of vision.

"I—I'm not really married."

"Then why did you put it down that you were married, boy? Were you lying to Uncle Sam? Is *that* it?"

"I—mean I *was* married, but I'm not anymore. My wife died. Just this summer."

The sergeant's face softens immediately. "Man, I'm real sorry to hear that." I notice his huge hand is patting me on the shoulder. I can't feel it.

I decide to leave this place, let the elevator, pull me up. The army building, the sergeant, the surroundings stretch, fade, then dissolve, like a photo left in the sun. The browns and yellows and greens of August, 1969 coalesce into white and the white becomes a point in a network. The silver ribbon, sparkling like an icy highway under a full moon.

"Hello, Mike? Lampman Delivery Service. The pizza's on the way. You want a countdown?"

"No. That's fine."

"Want to surface on your own, huh? Understandable. I'll switch off the throat mikes—"

"—so you won't burn anything out."

As I raise the visor, the lab comes into view. And the scenes that were so clear minutes before are gone.

"You okay?" I hear Leonard's voice in the headset.

"I guess." I take off the helmet and remove the throat mikes.

"Sorry about the little problem earlier," Leonard says, walking over to the chair. "I pulled the chain and the capacitor went no-op. Probably anomalon flux."

I look at him.

"Mike," Leonard steps closer. "Didn't you ask me to bring you back? About twenty minutes ago?"

"I was at my first day of basic training—and before that—I was in a car with—uh—some people. And I think I lost them."

Leonard gives me a fishy look. "Lost them?"

"Stuff that happened years ago." I slide off the chair. I feel the cool tile of the lab floor through my socks. "My shoes around here somewhere?"

"They're under the chair," Leonard says warily. "You still want the pizza?"

"No. You can have it. I guess I'll see you tomorrow." I stumble out the door and head for the elevator.

8

Above The Stars

I breathe in the San Antonio night. For the first time since I've been here, there is no acoustic tile, no copper mesh, no girders above my head. Only sweet black sky, flecked with clouds and the occasional jet.

The management company that previously owned the building thoughtfully decked the roof out in something resembling a midwestern oasis: grass-covered hillocks, three small shade trees and in the center a large lighted pool lined with blue Italian tile. Along the perimeter of the roof is a single row of New Orleans-style streetlamps. I can only imagine what kinds of parties were thrown on this little square of property.

Tonight, though, everything is dark. Quiet, except for the dull roar of the fans in the mechanical room—our surreptitious method of entrance to this nifty place.

I'm lying on my back on the grass—or more precisely, on the quilt Gail brought for the occasion. She tells me she bought it in Hempstead, a little town near Houston. It's an original, maybe thirty years old and has a damp, quilt-like smell. It matches perfectly the essence of the newly cut grass, even the chlorine of the pool. In my old days I would try to distill this scent, turn the memories into chemicals and the chemicals into a marketing strategy. No more. At least, not right now.

"Want a potato chip?" Gail shakes the bag of chips. "Nice and fresh."

"Can't. My tongue still hurts from that scram a few days ago."

"Some wine? It'll sterilize the wound."

"Sure." I close my eyes and listen as the wine washes into the glass. Somewhere, maybe from the street far below, I hear the faint hint of song. Joni Mitchell? The Beatles? No. It's an accordion—a Mexican polka.

"Here." Gail hands me the glass and settles onto the quilt next to me. "Cabernet and potato chips make a great combination, don't you think?"

"Yeah." I open my eyes to watch another jet rumble overhead. "My brother would have appreciated wine with potato chips. We shared a room when I was growing up. He'd always bring in a sack of potato chips, a couple of Pepsi's and cheese sandwiches."

"Cheese sandwiches?" She looks at me. "Cheese? That's all?"

"More or less. Sliced caraway cheese on hamburger buns. He'd spread some mayonnaise on and add crushed potato chips. I guess it was kind of weird, but as far as I was concerned, if Earl came up with it, it was okay."

"I had an older sister," Gail says, stretching out on the quilt. "We fought all the time. Finally she got a job and moved out of the house."

"Earl and I got along. We were pals." I lie on my back, my hands behind my head. "Let me tell you what he was like. Back when I was fifteen, my girlfriend—who was a year older than I was—invited me to the junior-senior prom. I was real excited. Earl and his girlfriend Sally helped me pick out a corsage, sat me down, gave me advice on what to do—the whole nine yards. They had been the prom king and queen a couple of years before that, so they had some *authority* in those matters."

"That sounds like a fun time," Gail smiles.

"The fun didn't last long. Three days before the prom, my girlfriend broke up with me to date a senior. It destroyed me. When Earl and Sally heard about it, they talked Sally's cousin, Joyce, into asking me.

"She had a boyfriend, but he was in college and couldn't make it to the dance. I wasn't old enough to drive a car—so he probably wasn't too concerned."

"Did you have a good time?"

"I had a *great* time. The dance was held at the basketball gym and had all the standard things—a ton of balloons, confetti, wishing wells. They even had a dance band—all the musicians were in tuxedos. They looked like penguins. I had a suit and a clip-on tie. Sixties-style narrow—about two inches wide. All the girls were in these gigantic crepe dresses with low-cut tops. They looked like flowers. Carnations, maybe."

"They were *supposed* to," Gail says. "That's the idea."

"But of all the girls there, my ex-girlfriend included, Joyce Barrett was the prettiest. Really beautiful. And she even let me walk her to her door."

"You were a fast kid," Gail grins.

"Yeah. And I owed it to my brother. He always watched out for me."

"Did he and Sally ever get married?"

"No. He always wanted to fly. I recall him taking flight training at this little airfield near Corinth. He got his student license in the summer of '63—but then, a couple of months later, he was flying this little Piper Cub and he crashed. Just fell out of the sky. I remember when we got the phone call, telling us he didn't make it."

"I'm sorry."

"I don't think the family ever got over it. I know I never have. And the really bad thing about it, I still don't remember the last time I saw him alive. All I can remember about that day is the phone call. And the funeral." I take a deep breath.

Gail is silent for a moment, then hands me a glass of wine. "Here's to your brother."

"To Earl." As I raise my glass, a fat orange 737 thunders overhead on its way to the airport.

"See that?" Gail points. "Southwest Air. Probably coming in from Houston. It's the official bus of Texas."

"San Antonio must be a busy place."

"It's a tourist spot—and of course, the military's here too." She pauses to pour another glass of wine. "One Army base and three Air Force bases. You go far enough out of town you'll see the missile silos."

"Yeah, I know. I spent some time here in 1969 and '70—fresh out of college and into the army."

"Did you like it? The military, I mean?" She looks at me. A slight breeze ruffles her hair.

"I liked it *here*. It was freezing in Missouri when I left. And when I landed in San Antonio, it was warm and dry. Like being in paradise. They loaded us into a big green troop bus and drove us through the city and into the fort. I looked out the window and saw this huge grassy field, all lighted up. Somebody said Fort Sam's MacArthur Field was once the largest military aerodrome in the US."

"Aerodrome." Gail tries the word out. "I like that better than 'airport.'"

"I was assigned to Brooks Army Medical Center—it's where they sent all the burn cases from Vietnam."

She empties the wine bottle into my glass. "What was it like for you? During Vietnam, I mean."

"The army was okay—as long as you didn't get sent overseas."

"Yeah. I can imagine."

"But Fort Sam was an interesting place. The circle drive in front of the Brooks Army Medical Center happened to be connected at four points by a central set of sidewalks. Then somebody in a news helicopter noticed the whole arrangement formed the world's biggest peace sign. The brass immediately had the sidewalk torn out and replaced with the world's biggest *upside-down* peace sign."

She smiles. "That's a funny story. Is it true?"

"Sure. Don't you believe me?"

"Yeah. I guess." She looks at me skeptically.

"Well, you should."

"Okay. Then, I believe you."

For some reason, I wonder where my wife is right now. Best scenario: Hanging with a roving band of drunken women lawyers in Mexico City, pinching guys on the ass in the Zona Rosa. Worst scenario: In a hotel room somewhere in Mexico City, *getting* pinched on the ass by a drunken lawyer.

"So." Gail says after a moment. "What do you think of this place? The roof, I mean?"

"It's different—I mean, it's nice."

"Yeah and the skybox lounge is on the other side of the building, so it's secluded here," she smiles. "I come up every now and then, to get away from things. You have to watch out for the police helicopters. They know about this place and they're on the lookout for anyone on the roof. Guess they're afraid of jumpers."

"You're kidding."

"No, I'm not." She gets up and walks to the edge of the roof. "See the tower way over there? A little over a month ago, a guy from Lab 10 freaked out and jumped. He did it from *that* thing. Stepped out over six hundred feet of empty space."

"Did it kill him?"

She turns to look at me. "Kill him? What the hell do you think? They said it sounded like a car hitting a brick wall." She walks back to the quilt and retrieves the bag of potato chips. "I'd met the guy. He was one of the original dreamers—had been here when the Institute started up. The suicide scared everybody. After that, they restricted the dreamers to the building."

"What was he like?"

"He was nice. Pleasant. You remind me of him a lot." She reaches for another chip. "I heard he was from the State Department. He had an assignment in Moscow and they wanted him to recall it—in detail."

"They?"

"Whoever. The government. Somebody," she shrugs. "Anyway. He was doing fine. He'd completed his first long run—48 hours in the chair—and something went wrong. Nobody knows what. When he came out of it, he wasn't the same guy. Like part of him was gone. About a week later he killed himself. Shortly after that, the Lab 10 computer operator quit."

"Think the long run had anything to do with it?"

"Maybe. You spend too much time down there and your personality goes to shreds."

"*Goes to shreds.* Is that a psychology term?"

"It's a Leonard term," she says. "His way of describing the action when a dreamer goes multiple."

"Sounds interesting." I take a drink of wine. "I thought you said this deal was safe."

"Hey." She looks at me. "It's probably as safe as driving on the freeway."

"Good point." I reach for a chip. "So the government guy who went multiple—did he go down as one person and come up five?"

She gives me a disgusted look.

"How'd all those people fit in one chair?" I smile at her. "Was it crowded?"

"Wait 'til Poundstone hypnotizes you to ground," she says. "You'll probably see all the little Mikey's running around. You might even find yourself talking to them." She gives me a sugary smile. "Sure you don't want another chip?"

"All my little personalities are full, thanks."

"Uh-huh." She lies down on the quilt and stretches out. "Then tell me about your session with Leonard today—did you all have a nice trip?"

"It was okay. I was in the army. First day of basic. And before that, I recall some scenes from my home town. I think I saw this childhood friend of mine. Nothing special."

I empty the glass and set it aside.

"Tell me about your childhood friend."

"Sure. His name was Carswell. Real smart kid. Always getting into things. Rockets, molotov cocktails. When he was only nine he and his big brother made a three-story tree house—the biggest in town. It was like an apartment complex. Really amazing."

"His parents named him *Carswell?*"

"That was his last name. The kids I ran with always called each other by our last names. It was a tough-guy thing."

"Tell me some of the things you did when you were a kid." She rolls over on her stomach and props herself on her elbows. I notice her blouse has moved up, exposing an inch of bare skin.

"Well, okay—my mother was always canning stuff, so the place was full of mason jars. With gray metal lids."

"I remember those," Gail smiles. "I think I've still got some of them."

"Yeah. Carswell—*Evan*—figured out they were made of zinc. And he also knew that zinc mixed with sulfuric acid makes hydrogen gas."

"He knew chemistry when he was nine years old?"

"Maybe he was eleven. Anyway, we went around the neighborhood, rounding up all these zinc Mason jar lids. Then we went to the drug store and bought a jug of muriatic acid and some balloons. We'd chop up the lids, stuff them into a pop bottle, then pour in the acid. When the stuff started bubbling, we'd stretch a balloon over the neck of the bottle. Instant hydrogen balloon. It was kind of dangerous. The acid could have put our eyes out, and the hydrogen was explosive. No question we had a whole fleet of guardian angels watching over us."

"What'd you do with the balloons—play Hindenburg or something?"

"No, we attached tags with our names on them. Then we let them go. They'd fly up into the sky and travel east with the wind currents. Carswell calculated the balloons would sail around the world in exactly two weeks. I remember we'd stand watching, you know—*staring* at the western horizon, looking for those balloons. They never came back."

"That Carswell sounds like a pretty smart kid. Did he grow up to be a nuclear scientist or something?"

"He was killed in an accident. Not long after his twelfth birthday."

Gail is silent.

Looking out to the dark horizon, I see him now in my mind, filling balloons and releasing them into the cold March wind. I watch them go up and up, so far up I can't see the color anymore. Only dots. Finally, they're gone.

I pick up my wine glass. It's only half full so I decide to finish it off.

·····✦·····

Flat on the bed, arms and legs splayed out, I lie crucified by the alcohol. A few inches away, the phone is off the hook, ringing my house in Lexington. In a minute, the operator will come on and tell me no one is answering, would I care to try again some other time. Didn't Linda say she was coming back tonight?

Or was it tomorrow morning?

I forget.

The curtain is drawn back and the garish orange glow from the sodium vapor lamps fills the room. The fourth circle of hell. A perfect negative to this scene would be a cold blue mist falling from bright yellow sky. With a glaze of ice covering everything.

I strain to listen for the wall music. The selection is relentlessly smooth. It's a chorus of girls singing a copy of some shameless hit from the late sixties: "Love is all around..."

A little voice inside me: "The Troggs. February 24, 1968. The Fontana label."

Thanks, voice. You got me in trouble with my wife I don't know *how* many times. You would hear a song, identify it, then tell someone else in me to switch off the radio. Then ask Linda to guess who was playing it. And she never could. Voice, you helped ruin my marriage and at this minute she's probably in some Mexican hotel with a guy named Van—so I want you to please shut up now, thanks.

The music changes. It's a downbeat, heavily orchestrated version of—what? "Summer In The City."

Lovin' Spoonful. July 16, 1966.

I shouldn't complain. This part of me, the little circuit that can remember old songs, has made my agency a lot of money. "Mitchell, we want an ad that says '1971'...Mitchell, we want the alpha consumers who won't respond to old Beatle songs anymore…Mitchell, we want a playlist that includes the money demographic…"

Want, want, *want.*

The sound of a clarinet fills the room. It's an obscure tune from the early sixties, "Above the Stars." July, 1962.

I remember the first time I heard it, lying on the grass in my backyard in Corinth, listening to a Chicago radio station and watching for the newly launched ECHO satellite. Twelve midnight. My mom and dad were sitting in lawn chairs. Earl, his girlfriend and I were sprawled on the grass, looking at the sky. Dad saw it first, a tiny dot moving from west to east across the blackness of space.

Then the disk jockey, a guy named Dick Biondi, announced the song—and the name seemed perfect. It was all a coincidence, but I imagined being above the stars like that satellite, high above the houses and fields of Missouri.

No one wanted "Above The Stars." It never made it to the top ten. No one remembers the artist, Mr. Acker Bilk. And, of course, no one will remember me.

I close my eyes to the orange glare and imagine being in the machine, imagine Leonard attaching the helmet, throat microphone, injection cuff. I hear the elevator sounds from the computer, then the chirping.

"Entrainment…"

"We have cognition."

I drop down from above the stars onto a grassy plain. Into Corinth, Missouri.

I get up, walk to the back porch, and I know it's a dream. But I can get away. Away from Zey and Poundstone and Leonard with his electricity. Away.

I look over and see my father—my memories of him form his body, his shoulders, his face. He's sitting there, in his dark green slacks and work shirt, a baseball cap pulled down over his forehead. It's dark, but I know that he's smiling at something. Perhaps something nice happened to him today. I hope so.

I look at my mother. She's sitting in the lawn chair on the porch, her hands in her lap. She's wearing that familiar blue apron, still damp from the dishes. Did I help her dry them? I don't know.

It's twilight and the sounds of a ballgame drift across the yard. The Corinth Coyote ball team is playing somebody from another part of this ethereal place. The full maple trees rustle in the night breeze, dark shadows masking the light from the fairgrounds. In my eternal spring, this will always be my certain, true home.

In my dream, it becomes day. Clouds are drifting close to the ground, blocks of cotton hovering low over the earth. The morning warms into spring and the vapor dissolves into a blue sky. It's ten a.m. and only wisps of scud remain, hanging like ragged curtains from the tops of the hills.

A dishrag sky. Where did I hear that? Anyhow, it's a perfect description for the clouds today.

It's dark again. The lights from the fairgrounds draw near and the baseball game has been replaced with the pulse of music.

I kick back the covers and look. Sure enough. There is rain against the window. For some reason, I know there's supposed to be a crescent moon tonight, near Mars. But now there are clouds on the horizon and the storm is building.

And now I'm in my car, driving through a hard rain, watching streaks and rivulets race across my windshield between the beats of the wiperblades. I look ahead and see the gray texture of the rain, the trees, the glare of the pavement, the haze behind the trucks that pass on either side. Scenery without sharp margins.

A splash of water covers the windshield, momentarily obscuring my view of the road. In response, I feel the needle pricks of adrenaline stab my face, above the bridge of my nose. Is there fear in this world? Absolutely.

So why am I here? Why did my dreams bring me to this place?

I turn the switch to increase the wiper speed, then switch on the defroster. In response, a blast of air reflects against the foggy windshield, forming a four-inch circle of clear glass. A thick strip of gray cloud crosses the road ahead of the car, like a barracuda cruising for prey. I turn on my lights and see a yellow glimmer on the pavement.

Another car passes, spraying the windshield. Somehow I know I've been here before. Years before. I glance to my right.

Someone's here—sitting on the car seat next to me, her feet propped up against the windshield forming little vapor outlines against the glass.

It is Rachael Dominic. Fifteen-year-old Rachael Dominic.

A drawer in the mental filing cabinet opens and snaps free, spilling photos across the floor. Here is one of Rachael dropping her newspapers onto the sidewalk, another of her loading her father's

.45-caliber service automatic. Another of her throwing up on my shirt.

And here is a large glossy of me driving her down to see her parents in Cherokee, a village nestled in the rolling hills and plains of western Missouri. The picture moves. Of all the places I could have gone, all the people I could see—my brother, my folks, old girl-friends—of all the wonderful, interesting times I could visit, I drew this—a late, drizzling, miserable Friday afternoon in November, 1966. On my way to Cherokee, Missouri with 15-year-old Rachael Dominic.

The dream continues, frame by frame.

"Did I ever tell ya I can cook a meal on an engine?" She plants a foot on the dash board, leaving a distinct mark in the dust. "Daddy taught me how. First you wrap everything in tin foil and start the car, let it get warmed up. Then, lift the hood and put the food on the exhaust manifold. Tie it down with wire so it won't fall off when you're driving. You can cook something in about a half hour."

The scene moves up and down, apparently the result of my nodding in agreement. In the corner of my vision I see her pause to make more feet-tracks on the windshield, each imprint surrounded by a halo of vapor.

"It's *real* easy. Ya gotta be careful, though, 'cause if you don't seal the tin foil real tight, the food'll taste weird…like a garage *smells*. The potatoes especially."

Perhaps I can get information from this place, bring it back, send it to my business partner, Jerry. I examine the cars on the highway: mostly mid-sixties Fords and Chevies, the kind you see at classic car shows any day of the week.

"That kind of thing *ruins* the flavor, so you have to make sure the tin foil is real tight. I'll fix you a pot roast sometime. We'll get some carrots and potatoes, and the roast, of course. Are you gettin' hungry?"

"I am now."

"If we get in on time, Mom will have something for us. Otherwise, we'll have to get something at the Kuku. You like fish sandwiches? Or maybe we can eat the potato salad I brought. You want some?"

"I'll wait for the fish."

"Actually, potato salad isn't on my list of favorite foods. Did I tell you about my quest?"

"No."

"Everybody should go on a quest—for the one perfect thing they want. I have a quest for the perfect pie. And my favorite is coconut cream. I'm gonna learn to make it from scratch."

"I like cherry myself."

"I guess the thing to do is figure out the high point in your life and then find as much about it as you can."

The rain begins to let up, and the world becomes a palette of soft browns and glistening grays. An old green pickup truck hisses by us on the left, throwing a white spray of water onto my Ford. Ahead, I see the low, gray clouds hanging above the horizon—supported by the shelf of warm southern air. Closer, the trees with their wet leaves look like dark yellow patches of cloud against the light brown landscape.

My car accelerates and I hear a slight pinging sound from the engine. A voice from somewhere: "Damn. Probably water in the gas tank." My own thoughts.

And yet it's only a dream—a lucid dream, but a dream all the same.

More pictures from the filing cabinet, this one of Poundstone telling me I would have these images: "The brain is very tight with lucid memory—but once you unlock the process with the machine, everything becomes easier. You will probably find your dreams filled with memories of your past—some as real as those you encounter during regression—"

Apparently the locks have come off. But I'm still seeing the same things. The same places.

"Did you ever notice," Rachael says, "that cows in the rain look like black and white marbles?"

"Never noticed. I'm having too much fun trying to keep the car on the road."

I look around me, feel the warm air of the defroster and the cool wind from the door. And now, in my dream—I imagine what the smell would be—a damp wet-upholstery-and-oil odor of my car mixed with Rachael's essence of Heaven-Scent, Zest and hamburger. It would be perfect.

I realize, of course, it's only an image—everything I see is long since gone—no rain, no car, no Rachael Dominic. I'm here by myself—isolated within a real dream.

"Did I tell you I have class pictures Tuesday? That's the day my period starts, so my face is already breaking out. Ain't that a kick in the butt? I'll probably be doubled over in pain. They'll have to hold my face up to the camera."

Another truck passes, and the windshield goes gray with the splash-back.

I'd heard this before, or something similar, from my daughter. "Dad, they won't let us wear our nose rings. They say it disrupts the class."

"It might."

"But everybody has nose rings. Anyway, it's a free speech issue. Mom says we could sue."

"She's the lawsuit expert all right. I make commercials."

"Gawd, Dad. Thanks for all the *support!*"

The rain increases, turning the windshield into an opaque gray screen. "I can't believe this rain!" I turn the windshield wipers to full speed.

Rachael scoots over and puts her arm around me. "Michael, this weather is all your fault. And you know why? It's because you're a storm person. Before I met you I never saw a rainstorm this late in November and now look at it—raining and lightning and everything. And it happens every time you talk like that."

"Like what?"

"You know. About—"

The phone rings and the dream evaporates.

I open my eyes. It's morning and I'm back in my room in San Antonio. Through my window I can see the sky is a dull gray. But who knows what the temperature is out there?

The phone rings again and I turn to confront it. As I do, my stomach seems to expand a foot in circumference. Not good.

Another ring, then nothing.

Good. Whoever is calling gave up.

I roll over on my back and close my eyes. My heart is racing and my stomach is threatening to return its contents for an instant refund. I attempt to sit up.

Success.

But now my face feels like someone has taped twenty-pound weights to it. If I look down, my jowls will stretch to the floor. Did I go somewhere last night? I can't remember. Perhaps coffee will help. What was that dream about—Debbie's nose jewelry?

The phone rings *again*.

"Mr. Mitchell?"

"Yeah."

"You have a package at the front security desk."

"Who's it from?"

"I didn't ask."

"Okay. I'll be down to pick it up."

"And here's a note from Dr. Poundstone. He would like to see you at nine-thirty this morning."

"Thank you. Thank you very much." I hang up the phone and look at the clock. It's 9:29.

9

Core

I quickly shake Poundstone's hand, then collapse into the deep leather chair in front of his desk. "Sorry I'm late."

"Not a problem," Poundstone smiles broadly. "How are you doing? Able to remember things now?"

"Pretty much."

"Having a good time back there? Are you bringing back any *cultural artifacts* useful to your business?" He steeples his long fingers.

"I've seen a few things," I shrug. "Lots of 1960-model Fords and Chevies."

"Yes, I'd imagine so," Poundstone chuckles. He leans back in his chair. "You know, when we first explored this technique two years ago, I made all the trips myself. And I was amazed how different things look from year to year. Car models change. One year you'll see fins. The next year things might be flat and utilitarian, but with more plastic and less metal."

"That's what it seems like, all right."

"Have you experienced any problems with the regressions?" A grin lurks at the corners of his mouth. He probably heard about the scram.

"I guess you know Leonard had to bring me up once."

"He's fast on the trigger, isn't he?" The grin expands. "Has it caused you any problems? Headaches? Nausea?"

"No."

"I've been the recipient of Leonard's technique myself. It's painful but effective." He peers at my scalp. "If those little electrode burns cause you a problem, let me know."

"Sure."

"Any disappointments with the program?"

"No, why?"

"Some of the subjects aren't too happy when they find their sensations are limited to sight and sound. They want the whole experience—including touch, taste, smells. Does it bother you that the regressions don't offer that?"

"Yes, it's disappointing, I guess. But the sight and sound are still better than any dream—it's almost like the real thing."

"I suppose," Poundstone nods. "You know, in our hypnotic suggestions we always include the lines—'feel what there is to be felt—taste what there is to be tasted' and so forth. Yet no one seems to respond."

"Is that right?"

"I think the problem is a function of the way memory is stored in the brain—we're not able to access everything. But no one really knows. Maybe as we continue the research, we'll understand the process better."

Poundstone looks at the desk for a moment as if considering what to say next. "Michael—I've had a chance to go over the transcriptions from your last five regressions. And I've given this some serious thought—"

I feel my palms go damp. "Is there a problem?"

"Oh, no." He looks at me. "Quite to the contrary. You seem to have excellent control down there. Based on your tapes, it seems your navigation skills are better than anyone else here."

"They *are?*" I look at Poundstone and wonder what is on the tapes.

"I've talked this over with Tom Zey. We'd like to ask you to consider a long run."

"What?"

"You have a good psychological profile—you seem to handle stress unusually well. You're certainly motivated. I think you would make an excellent candidate for a long run." He smiles.

"I've heard multiple personalities can appear—"

"You mean compartmentalization?" He asks. "Yes, I suppose that can happen. After all, we're different people at different stages of our lives—"

"Yes, but—"

"Still, there's one core personality that guides the rest of them through," Poundstone smiles benignly. "And I'm sure the core is immune to harm from something like this."

"So if I do this, I'm not going to come back as somebody else, right? I mean, I have enough problems with the personality I have."

"I can *assure* you, Michael," he says, his smile broadening, "that nothing will go wrong. And we'll give you a close, careful hypnotic evaluation to make absolutely sure."

"Okay. Will it cost anything extra?"

"Of course not." Poundstone steeples his fingers. "We just ask that you sign an agreement that allows us to publish any results."

"Results of what?"

"Of our work. If we decide to write anything up, that is. And I'm sure we won't. It's just a formality. Something our lawyers make us do. Dot the 'i', cross all the 't's'." He pushes a form across the table.

"I don't know—" I stare at the page dense with legalese. At the bottom are places for my signature *and* initials. I've seen this kind of contract before. "Isn't this a *hold-harmless agreement?*"

There's a flash of irritation. "It's just a formality. You actually signed one as part of the initial agreement, but the funding agencies like to see that the patient has an ongoing understanding of the process and risks involved. I'm obligated to tell you that, but it's nothing we haven't discussed with you before."

"It just seems that if I've signed this when I came in—"

"Besides, for our longer runs we have to use somewhat more invasive support methods—IV fluids for example." He leans forward. "Michael, there is really no reason you can't begin the long runs next week."

"You really think so?"

"Well, medium run starting out. Perhaps no more than 48 hours. Of course, it might be longer or shorter in the memory banks. Otto, for example, routinely goes under for 10-hour runs, and he tells us that his perceived experience in lucid memory is considerably longer— days, sometimes."

"Days, huh?" I think about it: days spent with Brenda Lacey.

"You will be able to communicate with Leonard as you normally would. Just lock the scene before you talk. Otherwise, of course, the microtremors in your larynx," Poundstone taps his throat, "will come too fast for the detector to pick up. I understand we're getting faster computers that will help with the communication, but for right now we have to make do with the old, slow protocols—"

"*Days* down there, huh? I'll have to think about it." I lay the sheet of paper on the desk.

"Certainly," Poundstone nods. "And in case you decide to go ahead, perhaps we can schedule a brief session of hypnosis—to lower you to state."

"What's that mean?"

"Familiarize you with your consciousness structures. We want to make sure everything is integrated properly before we proceed. It will acquaint you with the various personalities that make up Michael Mitchell, and I hope will assure you that none of them will undergo dissociation."

"Dissociation?"

"Transient confusion." He says dismissively. "It's over in a few minutes. Nothing to worry about."

"I see."

"At any rate, this will be a routine hypnosis, very similar to the preinduction sessions you had when you first came here. And of course, you *will* have to sign the interim release agreement. Just a formality, but I can't proceed until you do."

"Of course." I shift in my chair. "Sure."

"Good," Poundstone nudges the legal form toward me. "Would you like a pen?"

Darkness. My eyes closed, I wait for the session to begin. In my mind I hear Leonard's voice, "Can Poundstone take 'em deep? You gotta be kidding. He takes them down to their *blood*."

I think of the first sessions with him—when I learned to navigate the inner space—learned the various techniques—locking the image; scanning the scenes all the way to the edge; zooming in. The techniques worked—my navigation skills are good. Otherwise they wouldn't be inviting me to do long runs.

Right?

"Michael." I hear Poundstone's voice, emanating from the gray screen behind my eyes. "*As before*, you are feeling your body getting heavier. And *as before*, you are becoming more and more relaxed— more relaxed than you have ever thought possible—"

His voice locks onto my mind, leading it to the edge of sleep as my body becomes leaden, then liquid mercury, and then vanishes altogether—leaving me behind. "You will descend to all of the parts that make up the complete you."

The voice is everywhere. Sonorous. *"You are inside the elevator going deeper and deeper, seeing each separate part of you without fear."*

I'm suspended inside the workshop of my mind, floating above the roaring superstructure, the thought factory. From here, I can see the many configurations of emotion and logic as they move across the vast network of my being—flickering clouds of mind-fabric, interacting with other clouds to create a vast glowing mental organization that is—me.

"You will travel deeper. Experience the place of your memories. You will experience no fear and no pain."

I look around. In an instant, I see a single note of my childhood, a summer of bright green grass and brilliant skies and white sidewalks. Turning, there is a compact bedroom with blue wallpaper. And now, an instant inside that rainy Friday. Walking to school, black galoshes on wet brown sidewalk in the glare of headlights.

"You will be able to go wherever you want to go. See what there is to be seen, hear what there is to be heard. If you hear me, raise your right index finger."

Somewhere around me, lighting flashes from cells sending signals down my spine and into my arm. Somewhere, some part of me complies with Poundstone's demand.

"You will go deeper. Deeper than you ever have before."

The elevator drops. I hear the steady beat of some internal clock, a fast, steady march. As the sound becomes louder, I realize it is composed of many separate patterns, all in perfect orchestration. Someone down here has left the radio playing.

I go deeper, and amid the din of signals, I hear the spark of my breathing, like the crackle of a distant thunder, twelve beats a minute. I hear its echo—the distinct *snap* and then the slow roar of air. Release. Snap. Release. The chest moves.

I see other rhythms of my body—nerves firing at the precise millisecond, the response in the auricles and ventricles and arteries of this liquid machine.

As I descend I feel myself splitting. In this cavern of waves, I am no longer I, but *we*. One of us is above at the surface, listening to Poundstone, responding to his monotonous, droning suggestions. Others are examining his words for clues, trying to determine what he means. And we sense the presence of the central being, watching the process as it unfolds.

"*Deeper.*"

Reality is gone—replaced by a haze of continuous, moving snapshots. The haze forms a ribbon of instants, a granular highway pushing into the future, retreating into the past. Spreading to all directions and places not found on any conventional road map. Places *perpendicular* to time.

The elevator stops—just short of the dark chaos at the bottom of the shaft. There is no reason to go deeper—there is no logic in this place, no sense, no love, no humanity. No questions, no answers—only swirling motion.

Gradually, I have become a singular again. The scene coalesces—someone or something is creating substance and form directly from the chaos. I'm standing on the underside of my own gleaming engine—a great humming, clanking factory of sparks and electrons and thoughts—all set in a field of rolling hills. And above, I see infinitely fine ripples of light radiate through a cloudless purple sky.

I step into the elevator, press the up button and ascend back toward the roof of this world—up through the chaos, up past the switching stations, past the portals to distant places, up. And as I ascend, I know I must remember this place—remember the road map here. Because I'll have to return here someday.

"*...You will awake, happy and relaxed...*Poundstone's voice, bringing me back. It's totally unnecessary.

I'm already here.

10

Peripheral Vision

The young lady at the security desk gives me a suspicious look. Her long hair flows down over her broad shoulders, barely concealing a small walkie-talkie. She's probably packing a .45 on her belt.

"Lemme see your ID."

I show her the plastic card on my lapel. She shrugs and pushes out a clipboard for me to sign. Then she hands me a small brown package, about the size of a shoe box. Special courier: no return address.

"You know what's in here?" I ask.

"It's a bottle," the girl says. "Probably some kind of booze. We x-rayed it…it's against the law to send that stuff through the mail, y'know."

"Thanks." I take the package and head for the elevator.

Back in my room, I remove the paper and open the box. The guard was right: it's booze—Mexican brandy. Napoleon Thirteenth. And taped to it is a card:

"Mike. Hope you like this. Bought it at the airport. Spent all day in DF, then caught the plane back. Probably have to go back next week, new partners are being horsey. Hope the brandy makes your stay bearable. Best, Linda."

"*Best?*" I look at the bottle. It's big and gaudy and the label shows a man on a horse with a sabre. The words are all in Spanish. I wonder what an entire bottle of Napoleon the Thirteenth would do for me—probably engrave Mr. Smiley Face on my cerebral cortex.

I place the bottle in the top dresser drawer and hope it doesn't leak on anything.

..... ✦ .....

"Anyone here with a hangover?" Gail smiles, carefully adding a sliced jalapeno pepper to her hamburger.

"Not me." I set my tray down next to hers and survey the meal: enchiladas, refried beans, french fries and a version of Caesar salad made with carrots.

Across the table, Lowell and Otto are discussing the finer points of auto racing, while nearby, a taciturn Coltrane carefully works his way through a huge plate of Mexican sausage and scrambled eggs.

"The cars of today are dreck," Otto says. "The best car ever made in the United States was the 1965 Ford Galaxy 500XL. It could do a hundred and fifty right out of the showroom."

"They were gas hogs," Lowell shrugs. "Those boats got no better than eight miles to the gallon."

"I used to own a Ford Galaxy," Coltrane nods at the memory. "Black, with a red interior. Big. Roomy."

"It was a whale on wheels." Lowell shakes his head. "A living room."

"That too," Coltrane nods.

"Ever notice," Gail says, "that males in captivity will turn on each other?"

"As a matter of fact," Otto grins through his beard, "we were originally discussing whether existence precedes essence."

"I think it's vice-versa," Lowell mutters, dipping a french fry into a pool of mayonnaise. "At least according to the transactional theory of quantum mechanics. In fact, it might even have relevance to what we're doing."

"Well, *maybe*," Otto chuckles.

Gail looks up suspiciously.

"Look," Lowell holds up two french fries. "For every physical interaction involving light, there have to be two waves—one traveling into the future and one traveling into the past." He pushes the fries together. "When they meet at the present they cancel each other out. So—" he pops the fries in his mouth, "if waves can travel backward in time, then essence precedes existence. Unless, of course—" he retrieves a curly fry, "—you have a *closed-time loop*."

"You gonna eat that too?" Gail asks.

"Yup." Lowell dips the fry into the mayonnaise.

"I have no idea what you're talking about," I confess. "I was okay with cars, but the philosophy stuff lost me."

"Come on, Mike," Lowell smiles. "We do it every time we get in the machine. Maybe every time we dream."

"What's your major in college, Lowell?" Gail asks, chewing on a french fry.

"Psych," Lowell says. "But I've also got a degree in philosophy with a minor in math."

"That's good. That's very good." I look at my plate. "Can anybody tell me what these little *seeds* are in this salad?"

"Pumpkin," Coltrane says. "They're good for you."

"You know, Lowell—" Otto says, "as a physician, I take issue with your contention that we regress in time during dreams. The science is clear. Dreams are the result of random activity in the deep areas. Probably neurons getting rid of excess calcium."

"Calcium, huh?" Gail mutters. "That's something my body needs anyway."

"And Otto—" Lowell says, "as a guy who keeps up with all this stuff—I'm sure *you've* heard Keller's theory that the brain doesn't dream at all—or store memory for that matter. It just scans space time to sample the actual event."

"Hogwash." Otto laughs. "As they say in Europe, that's a clear violation of the first principles."

"*Europe,* Otto?" Lowell replies. "It was a European physicist who first showed you can change the past!"

"Ah," Otto nods. "Schmidt's retro-pk experiments. Schmidt was employing a clever modification of simple delayed choice. And he has *never* claimed to have changed the past."

"Then how *else* can you explain what he does?" Lowell fires back.

"What," Gail looks at them, "are you guys *talking* about?"

Ignoring both questions, Otto turns to Coltrane.

"Russell, you've spent time with shamans and medicine men. What do you think they'd say about all this?"

"Well—" Coltrane looks at the table for a moment. "The Shoshone would probably say—if it works—use it." He shrugs. "The Shoshone are *real practical.*"

"Anybody heard how Keller is doing?" Lowell asks, cooling down somewhat. "I heard he started a long run in Lab 10."

"Nobody's heard," Otto says. "I assume he's doing fine. Probably walking around in some chemical company in 1951, knowing him."

"Sounds toxic," Lowell mumbles. "Hope he remembered to take his gas mask."

Gail checks her watch. "Folks, I'd love to listen to this discussion further, but I've got a trip scheduled this afternoon, and my hair's a mess."

As she walks out the door, Otto shakes his head. "She's got a regression this afternoon and she's worried about her hair? What's she got going on down there, a *party*?"

"Maybe she does." Coltrane watches her leave. "It'd beat *this* place all to pieces."

····· ◆ ·····

"Mike, can you give me a count?" I hear Zey's flat, calm voice in the headset. This afternoon, he rather than Leonard will do the induction. I open my eyes to the blackness of the helmet visor. I think backwards from ten to one.

"Thank you. Now, it'll be just another minute while I enter your voice signature—"

I hear a click, then another. Zey must be fooling with the communication controls.

"Michael, I understand you're planning a long run."

"I spoke with Dr. Poundstone about it this morning. I haven't made a decision yet."

"You show good navigation skills. I'm sure you'd find it interesting—how much time did you want to spend today?"

"I don't know. Twenty to thirty minutes is my usual."

"I see that from your record. We don't have anyone scheduled until eight this evening. Would you like to try for two hours?"

"Two hours?"

"I'll be watching your EKG closely. If you like, I can administer some labeled glucose and switch on the positron emission tomography. You won't feel a thing."

"Uh—"

"It'll keep track of activity in your temporal lobe. If you run into trouble, we'll bring you back. Ready?"

"Okay." I feel as though I'm about to leave for an extended journey in space.

After a few minutes of silence, I hear Zey's voice again. "All right.

We'll wait for that pulse rate to drop a little…there. Everything looks good. Remember not to hyperventilate and we'll get a good induction."

"Okay."

"Michael, you're on the larynx microphone now, so if you have anything to say, please think it—say the word to yourself. All right?"

Sure.

In the headset I hear a distant, metallic bark. Was that *my* voice?

"We've installed a newer device to capture theta rhythm, Mike," Zey says as the machine starts to rev. "It's specially designed to lock the right temporal lobe rhythm. I think you'll be able to see the difference."

An eerie sound emanates from the headsets, like a chorus of schoolchildren singing one note. It gets louder and I have trouble concentrating. My body is getting lighter and lighter. What are they doing? What are they doing to my temporal lobe?

The sound is louder, like an MD-80 jetliner aimed for the earth, filled with screaming passengers and singing angels.

Then, the sound of a bell—a deep, resonating chime that sends vibrations through my body, shaking it loose from my mind and allowing me to drop beneath it, into the shaft.

The lights appear. The ribbon of my life, stretching back to the past. I get closer. Is it real?

"Michael, can you hear me?" It's Zey again.

Yes.

"Good. We'll have you in theta lock. I'd like you to wait a few seconds above whatever it is you see until we can lock you in…thank you. Have a nice dream."

I drift down toward a dark summer night. The moon is a luminous sphere suspended behind feathery cirrus clouds in a pitch black sky. The lights of the nearby houses glow with a yellowish incandescence.

Rachael is holding on to the sleeve of my denim work shirt. "Brenda Lacey's coming back from summer camp next week. Are you going to see her? If you see her I'll just die."

"Look, my ride's here. I have to go to work."

We're standing in front of my house. It's dark, probably 10:15 p.m. I'm wearing jeans, and my blue long-sleeved denim shirt has oil stains all over it. Rachael, by contrast, is wearing light-colored shorts and a sleeveless top. The white rollers in her hair are covered by a thin scarf.

Perhaps to avoid answering her question, I'm now looking directly at the ground. In the light from the mercury vapor lamp, everything looks blue—my black engineer boots, the asphalt and gravel of the street. To my surprise, Rachael is not wearing shoes. Bare feet.

Lock. There are five or six small dots on her legs, probably from mosquitos or the ubiquitous chiggers found in this part of the country. I also notice we're standing outside her car, a light blue Mercury Comet. How could she drive? She just turned fifteen in May. Probably breaking the law.

So it was like this in the summer of 1966—I had to choose between a smart, sexy 17-year old with a perfect tan and great legs—and a loud 15-year-old illegal driver with rollers in her hair and mosquito bites on her legs.

Unlock.

A pair of lights appears and a red two-toned 1960 Chevy turns the corner. The arm resting on the door is huge.

"Look, Ronnie's here. I gotta go."

"Will I get to see you tomorrow?"

"Maybe."

"My folks want to take me back to Cherokee. If they make me go, I'll never get to see you again."

"Sure you will."

"Please don't talk to Brenda Lacey."

"I've got to go, Rachael."

"And be careful tonight. I don't want you to get hurt."

I get inside Ronnie's car and close the door. He is a huge genial guy with tight, curly blond hair. He steers the car by resting his massive hand on the hub of the steering wheel, turning the car with only a twist of his wrist.

"That your girl?" he asks as we pull away from the blue Comet.

"No. It's just a girl I know."

"You two havin' an argument?"

"Yeah. Brenda's coming back from summer camp tomorrow."

"Sounds like trouble."

"It is."

"You'll work it out." He switches on the radio. I notice there is no dial knob—it's permanently tuned to 890—WLS in Chicago. Guitar sounds reverberate into the car—it's a song I haven't heard before.

"Dr. Zey?"

"Yes, Michael."

"Fire up the Juke Box, I have some data. I'm hearing a song now, some group is singing something about, 'these are the ways of the girl you love.' And then there's a line about 'Who's got you holding hands, and what makes you understand——'"

"I'm really not very good with the Jukebox...I'll ask Leonard when he gets in. He can probably find it."

"Thanks."

I listen for the dit-ditditdit-daaah of the 10:25 news break. Continued trouble in Vietnam. Moderate losses.

Ronnie switches the radio off. "I hate hearing that. I just got my 1-A."

"You're kidding."

"Nope. I'll be in Vietnam this time next year. Turned eighteen last week—prob'ly never make it to nineteen."

We sit in silence as he turns the car onto the highway leading to Monroe. The window is rolled down, all I can hear is the wind.

A half-hour later, by my reckoning, I'm in the factory. A luminous white haze hangs near the ceiling, fumes from an enormous zinc pot. There is a constant high-pitched clanking of metal being cut, snapped, dropped, shredded.

I'm operating a trim press, a massive spinning iron wheel with a metal knife fixed to a steel block and a flat plate. I remember this, my summer job in 1966: Hit the foot switch and the block comes down, cutting into whatever is on the plate—a thick piece of aluminum, zinc, anything. No protective guards anywhere on the machine.

Didn't someone lose an arm here that summer? I remember the ambulance, the red lights. Someone rolling on the floor, screaming. An image forms of Brenda, smiling, her shirt unbuttoned, my ring hanging from the chain around her neck. It shimmers for an instant, then vanishes.

My hand reaches out to a stack of untrimmed Holley carburetors on a wooden pallet, grabs one, places it on the block. I watch my boot step on the shiny steel foot lever. I seem to be standing in a pool of black oil and metal shavings.

Click-ka*chunk*. The metal flashing falls into a bucket, leaving the carburetor. My hand grabs another carburetor, places it on the block.

Click-ka*chunk*.

Click-ka*chunk*.

Of all the places I could have visited on a two-hour trip, I end up in a factory working a trim press—white concrete walls, dirty cement floor littered with metal shavings and an assortment of discarded objects. The entire scene flickers under the hard glare of cheap fluorescent light.

To my left are wooden pallets stacked to the ceiling, filled with shiny aluminum and zinc items—automobile water pumps, fuel pumps, headlight housings. To my right are steel bins overflowing with detritus—flashings, shavings and oil-covered steel curlicues from beneath the drill press.

Not far away, a grimy steel hydraulic press slams shut, spraying the operator—a fat man smoking a cigarette—with a cloud of brown oil. At the far end of the building, a door swings open and a yellow forklift whines through with a tub of castings for the zinc pot.

The graveyard shift at Missouri Die Cast.

Click-ka*chunk*. A trimmed carburetor falls into the metal bin, and I reach around to the wooden pallet for the next one.

In the mind of my past I see more images of Brenda, this time playing Moon River on her piano. And now she's in her backyard pool, brushing water from her face, her blonde hair slicked straight back.

Click-ka*chunk*.

It occurs to me that, except for particular moments, most of life is probably like this: a boring, repetitive job. And sometimes, dangerous. The knife slams down, slicing the metal flashing only inches from my hands.

Click.

What the hell? The clutch has failed to trip the hammer. I check the metal wheel—still rotating. The machine is still armed. I kick the lever, and noticing a piece of metal jammed in the clutch mechanism, reach down to remove it.

For some reason, I'm looking up at the knife itself—a sharp-edged rectangular metal box attached to a flat metal plate. I lean closer and notice the edges of the box are shiny—probably from slicing through tons of zinc and aluminum. A rectangular guillotine.

Click. My boot pumps the foot switch. Nothing happens. The steel block hangs motionless. The machine is jammed.

Click. Click. Click. Click.

Bored, I lock the scene. Scanning past the metal guillotine, I see another young worker dressed in jeans and a plaid shirt, his hand motionless above a drill press. Nearby, another worker has just dropped a cigarette. The tiny white cylinder hangs motionless, half-way to the floor—a snapshot of a cigarette in the arc of descent.

In this frozen, motionless world I detect something strange and unexpected. Just beyond my field of vision, something is *moving*.

Kachunk.

Up here, behind this scene, I feel an ominous presence—something close by—

"Michael, this is Tom Zey. What's going on down there?"

"I'm not sure yet. I have this scene locked, but there's motion along the periphery. I want to check it out."

"You're displaying some unusual patterns in your right temporal lobe. Are you sure you're okay down there?"

"I'm fine." As I move my concentration toward the periphery of my vision, the colors fade to black and white. At the edge, the picture fragments into a haze.

The very edge of vision. The edge of my perception. Yet I still see movement. Beyond this border, something is definitely going on. I decide to scan further, rotating my virtual self farther into the edge— examining the darkness, following my intuition.

As my concentration continues through it, the haze begins to grow lighter, showing outlines of something. Something in motion

I see it: The metal knife is moving—falling toward me, slicing through denim, leather, skin, bone, all the way to the metal plate, leaving spurting blood and disconnected white sinew. In the haze, something drops to the floor. My arm.

"Zey!"

Then I remember, no screaming. The computers on the surface can't handle screams, they just come out as noise. But it doesn't matter. Somehow, I've fallen into some side-door to my past. Some place that never happened. I've stumbled into a nightmare!

Click—

I look for the border, find it, move through it.

The locked scene of the factory returns. Beyond the knife, everything remains motionless in time; the cigarette in mid-tumble still hasn't hit the floor. The rectangular steel guillotine is still suspended— inches from my face—and above my arm. Scanning down, I see the bare skin showing between the leather and blue denim. My arm is intact, alive, with blood still coursing through it. Nerves. Feeling. Touch. All there. But all still in the killing zone.

Move! Nothing happens—the arm remains fixed. A thought occurs: Have I returned to a time different than the one I left? Will I lose my arm in this place, too?

Unlock: Ka-CHUNK. My hand blurs into movement just as the knife slams into the plate. At the same instant, sparks explode from the machine's electrical box. The metal wheel locks in mid-spin.

A short red-faced man wearing a white coat approaches. "Gawdammit Mitchell. You kill *another* press? *Damn!* If it was up to me, I'd show you th' gate!"

"Yessir."

An echo. The scene—the supervisor, the press, the factory—all collapse into a flat image, into a point, and then are gone.

I'm sitting on the front porch. My dad and mom are in the porch swing. The sun has gone down and a few stars are starting to show through the soft summer twilight.

I hear my dad's voice. "Son, Mom and I are gonna take the car down to the Dairy Queen—maybe get some ice cream. Want to come along?"

"No, I'll stay here."

"You feelin' alright?"

"I'm okay, Dad. I'm fine." I stare at the concrete steps.

"The Dominic girl left that letter this morning," my mother says. "That's what's bothering him."

"You didn't see her?" Dad asks.

"I was out."

"We'll be back in a little while." My dad pats me on the shoulder. "Might bring you something."

After they leave, I unfold the letter. It's written on notebook paper in blue ink. Some of the ink is smeared.

"Mom and Dad came today. I decided it would be best if I went home with them. At least for awhile. They said they really wanted to see you again, and anyway, that's all I talk about. You. If I don't see you anymore this summer, you'll probably forget me, but please don't. Love always and I mean that, too. Rachael. P.S. In case you write, you spell Rachael with an 'e' and Cherokee like this."

"Michael, this is Tom Zey. I don't mean to bother you—"

"Yes?"

"You know that song you asked about an hour ago? Leonard just came in. He says the title is 'Sister Love' by some group called The Liverpool Five."

"Thanks, Dr. Zey."

"Moby Mike. This is fifty thousand watts of clear channel Leonard Lampman. How're things down where you are?"

"Fine. Thanks for looking up that song for me."

"It was kinda' obscure—had to net to the lyric database at Bowling Green. The song was written by the great Curtis Mayfield. Released in July, 1966. Is that where you are right now?"

"I guess so. Thanks."

"No prob. I'll turn you back over to the doc. Later."

I look at the letter, will myself up in an arc over the next few weeks, watching them flow beneath me in a colorful progression. And now, the trajectory takes me down into a bright afternoon in my car—just as I give the steering wheel a hard right turn. The car slides from the street into a wide cement driveway.

A minute later, pretty blonde Brenda slides into the seat next to me, leans forward to give me a quick kiss. She's wearing an expensive-looking knit shirt with extremely short shorts. I glance at her legs—perfectly smooth and perfectly tan.

"Mike! God, I really missed you this summer." Her voice sparkles. "Sorry I didn't get a chance to write, but I was so busy. Do you like your job?"

"Yeah." I back the car out of the driveway. "But I think it might be a little dangerous. I thought about you a lot. How was Art Camp?"

"Lots of fun. Learned watercolor technique." She scoots closer. "I hear you were kind of busy while I was gone. David Wetzell said you were dating his little cousin."

"David said that?"

"That's right. Pretty good source, huh?" She drapes her arm over my neck. "Where's she from? What's that town's name? Chickadee?"

I see an image of goofy, unpredictable David Wetzell. I look at Brenda's face, only inches from mine. Way too close. From my perspective it occurs to me I will never see her tan lines again. "What else did he tell you?"

"Well-l-l, he told me her name is Rachael Dominic, she'll be a sophomore this year—she's kind of a *brat*—and she's going around telling everybody that you two are going to be married someday." She wiggles closer. "Guess nobody bothered to tell her you're already going steady, did they?"

"I think I told her." My voice sounds tight, pinched, like a trapped animal.

"I'm sure you did," Brenda says. "But in case you forgot or something, I thought maybe you can give me her address and phone number so I can tell her."

"I don't have it. I really didn't date her. We only drove around."

"Drove around," she nods. "*I want her address.*"

"I don't have it."

"Too bad. Guess I can get it from David. I'd really like to meet her. Maybe we can compare notes."

"Okay."

"You can arrange that? Oh, good."

I drive along in silence, perhaps thinking of all the things I'll miss. The nights at her pool, the nights in the car—

"Mike, you're not saying much. Cat got your tongue?" She looks at me. Her pupils are tiny, like little black BBs. In the background I hear my mind rattling away, trying to organize a response, however pitiful or inappropriate.

"I bet you met some guys at Art Camp—"

"This counselor liked me—and would have asked me out. But I was wearing your ring. Wasn't that dumb of me? *I* think it was dumb of me, because he was really cute. Tall. Nice tan. Lifted weights." She shakes her head. "He's a junior in college and plans to go to medical school."

"Ahem. Sounds like a full schedule."

"He wanted to add me to it, Mike. And here I come back to find you're running around with some little *thing* just out of grade school. I guess I was stupid, huh?" I detect a change of tone in her voice— smooth and hard, like plate glass.

"She's gonna be a sophomore," I say finally, steering the car into the Dairy Queen parking lot. "Uh, you want an ice cream cone? Strawberry milkshake, maybe?"

"When is she coming back to Corinth?" Brenda asks, drumming her fingers on my chest.

"Who?"

"That little sophomore girl I-forgot-what-her-name-is. When is she coming back to Corinth?"

"I don't know." Looking down, I notice my high-school ring is missing from her hand. "Aren't you wearing my ring anymore?"

"I left it at home. I didn't want to lose it." She flashes a smile. "Now, about this little sophomore girl. Do you plan to see her again?"

"Doesn't look like it."

"Good. Because if she shows up around here again, I'm going to have a chat with her. I might anyway, if I can get her phone number. Why don't you get me a strawberry milkshake? I'm really starving. Then, after this we could—"

"Michael, this is Tom Zey. We've only got a few minutes left on this, so if you haven't taken any notes back there, now might be a good time."

"Thanks." I lock the scene, then scan the view for something interesting. In the parking lot nearby is a family in a wide-track 1962 Pontiac, similar to the Dominic's car—same split-grille, same huge horizontal headlights, same whitewall tires—but, thank God, it's a different color. Parked next to them is Chick Davis and Jeannie Willis in a birdlike Plymouth Valient. Brenda and I double-dated with them a few months back. Chick and Jeannie were immensely proud of the fact the seat back folded down to make a bed.

At the far end of the lot, I see Tom and Laurie Gennette in their 1961 Ford Falcon, a little blue bar of soap on wheels. Driving in from the street is someone in a rare 1956 DeSoto Firedome convertible. No DeSoto dealers in Corinth—the guy is probably from somewhere else.

My heart really isn't in this. All I can think about is Brenda. Was this how the breakup happened?

"Michael, Tom Zey here. You have about a minute left."

"Thanks."

Finally, I scan to Brenda, her eyes closed in mid-blink, her mouth open in mid-sentence. The yellow knit shirt she's wearing is probably a Bobbi Brooks, but there's no way to tell. The blue striped shorts are just that—shorts. The white sandals are also fairly standard. I see that the red color is chipping away from her toenails and there's a thin line of fuzz on her left leg where the razor missed.

"Thirty seconds, Michael."

What else? Any fillings in that front tooth? Can't tell. What kind of watch? A gold Bulova—yeah, I remember that. She'd always take it off and put it on the dash before we made out. Hm. Is she even wearing a bra today—?

Suddenly the scene dissolves in an ocean of light.

I open my eyes to darkness. Then I see the twin green points of light. The rapid-eye-movement monitors. I guess I'm back.

"Please refrain from talking until we can unhook your throat microphone—there. You can remove the headset now if you like."

"Thanks." I lift the visor, remove the helmet. "How long was I out?"

"Two hours," Zey says. "I think we caused you to miss dinner. Sorry."

"That's all right. I had lunch down there." I glance over at Zey. "At least I *think* I did."

11

Angel Radio

It's been two hours since my trip. I'm in my room, jotting down the thoughts, the memories, before they go away. Outside, clouds are building over San Antonio. According to Leonard, there is a tropical depression in the Gulf of Mexico. It's off the coast of Cuba and heading our way. I've never been inside a tropical depression—I assume it's not a pleasant experience.

I look across the city toward a particularly baroque building jutting up through the blue haze of twilight. It's a structure I recall from my days here in 1970. The roof is singularly impressive—covered completely in gold leaf. I once described this building in a letter to my folks.

I told them about the army—about how my hair was finally growing back out—how I had to walk patrol once a week and how we had to march in parades every Saturday.

As I watch, the spotlights come on and the roof of the building bursts into brilliant pure gold against the black sky. I step closer to the window, trying to record as much detail as possible. If I come back to this place someday, I want my guest from the future to be able to appreciate the view without having to lock the scene first. Are you there inside? Can you hear me? And if you can, what's it like where you're from?

No answer. Perhaps no one's here with me. At least not this evening.

Below, I watch the streetlamps wink on. Not far away, a lone stoplight turns red, then yellow. Finally green. The street is deserted, but the photons have traveled the distance to my eyes—exploded against my retinas to recreate the image. Or at least *an* image. Is it representative of what is really there? Probably not.

The sad fact is, these colors I see are ones I've created myself, produced by glucose and electrons flitting around inside my brain. None of it is real—only light-shadows of something that existed a millisecond before.

Of course, it's the same as in dreams.

The stoplight glows red again, a lonely dot of light hanging above a deserted street. I put aside the pen and close the book as the phone rings.

It's Gail.

·····✦·····

A few minutes later I'm outside her room. There's the sound of someone talking inside. Maybe she's getting a party together tonight. A roomful of dreamers discussing brainwaves and the meaning of life. Great. Just what I need now.

The door opens.

"Hey, Mike," she smiles broadly. "Come on in. The place is a wreck. Have a seat, I'll get you something. Cabernet okay? It's all I have." She's wearing a strapless cotton dress that reaches past her knees. No bra. It's very casual, very—relaxed. Compared to my standard getup of polo shirt and khaki slacks, she looks comfortable indeed.

I agree to the cabernet and take a seat on the couch. She's the only one here—the sound was coming from her television. "How come you get a TV and I don't?"

"You'll get one after you've been here awhile," she says, closing the refrigerator. "Don't get excited, though—it's closed circuit. All you can get are classical music and psychology lectures. Nothing from the outside world."

She returns with the wine and clicks off the television "Another hypnosis script. Seen it before." She settles onto the couch. "So. I hear Mike Mitchell is planning to spend some *serious time* in his past."

"Word gets around."

"Going to do a long run?"

I shift my weight on the sofa, trying to *look* comfortable. Like a kid on his first date. "Actually, I haven't decided to take the long run yet. I went down today for only two hours and I think I spent an evening in a factory."

"Lovely." She makes a face. "Did you have a good time?"

"Nope. Something weird happened. I can't explain it—it was like I was being divided up."

"Maybe you went multiple. I've heard that can happen on a long run. Maybe we *should* watch this psychology stuff." She turns the television back on.

"It's probably nothing," I tell her. "Didn't Coltrane go for 72 hours once—"

"That's like I told you about earlier—when he nearly flatlined on them. They thought he was headed for a full-bore eclipse—and they couldn't get to him. The consulting neuro freaked."

"How'd they finally get him back?"

"Zey rolled in the support equipment and waited until he finally came back. Didn't seem to have an effect on him. Guess he's got what they call a robust personality."

I turn to look at the television. The camera zooms to an outline of the brain filled with little cartoon characters.

"I've got this video memorized," Gail says. "This is the part about the hidden observer."

"The hidden observer? What's that?"

"Nobody knows," she shrugs. "It's like some hidden part of our selves. It was discovered back in '72 or '73, but it's difficult to study."

"*Difficult to study*? Is it shy or something?"

"It only shows up in the deepest hypnosis—where the subjects report that time is a meaningless concept." She smiles. "Or so I'm told."

"My kids feel that way—that time is meaningless."

"The guy who's done the most work with the hidden observer was a Finnish researcher named Reima Kampman," Gail continues. "In one study, he questioned the hidden observers of different people. Actually asked them who they were."

"Okay. And they said—?"

"All said the same thing," Gail says. " '*I am soul.*' Pretty fine, huh?"

"Pretty *weird*."

"Hey, if physicists can talk about ten dimensions and parallel universes, why can't psychologists talk about souls? Seems only fair."

"It might be fair, but it's *still* weird. Next you're going to tell me there are parallel me's out there, each with his own soul."

"What if all those parallel Michaels have just *one* soul—one that watches over all of them?"

"Mine would be bored with this particular life. Maybe I should have taken a job with the CIA. I could have brushed up on my Russian, learned to make black bread—"

"Maybe someplace you did." Gail gives me a thoroughly smug look.

"Hey, I've got enough problems without having to deal with *two* lives. Is my wife fooling around with a guy named Van in my other life too?"

"Ask your hidden observer."

"*I will,* the very next time I see him—it."

"You should," Gail raises her glass. "To your hidden observer—and your life in Russia."

"And, to yours." I lift my glass, then set it down. "Gail, you don't really *believe* this stuff, do you?"

"Oh, *of course not,*" she laughs. "But it's fun to talk about over a couple of drinks, don't you think?"

"You've had some psychology—"

"Some." She smiles. "A degree in clinical."

"What do you *really* believe?"

"About what? Religion? Politics?"

"The past. What do we really see when we get in the chair and go back?"

"Electrons. Sparks."

"That's *it?*"

"Well, electrons, sparks and chemicals. I mean, whatever it is your memory is made of, that's what we're seeing. Like a little television set in our heads. With a videotape running."

"That's it, huh?"

"What more can there be? I mean—when you watch an old John Wayne film, you don't really think you're back there on that stagecoach *with* the Duke, do you? It's just a film. That's all. And—" she taps her head, "that's the way it is up here. Disappointed?"

"No. Yes. Maybe I am a little." I take a drink. It's true. I'm both disappointed and embarrassed to admit that I'm disappointed.

"Well, Michael, mine is not exactly the *only* view." She gives an eloquent shrug, "But it *is* the standard neuropsych position—as taught at the University of Washington—be back in a second." In a quick motion, she gets up and walks into her bedroom. I watch her body move beneath the cotton dress. It occurs to me that there are other, equally important questions in the world.

A few minutes later she returns to the room. "Wanted to set my alarm. Have a short run tomorrow at eight with Zey."

"So, you went to school in Seattle, huh?"

"Sure did," she nods, returning to the couch. "In the great Pacific Northwest. Volcanoes and winter storms. Every time I turned on the radio—gale warnings on the Straits of Juan de Fuca. Sleet. Winter storms blowing in from Alaska. I've seen Interstate 5 completely ice-covered all the way down to Portland. Nobody could drive anywhere. I always managed to fall on my ass at least once month." She takes a sip of wine. "I went job hunting in the worst winter storm ever. That's when I found out you can't do much in psych unless you have a doctorate, so I kind of gave up and stayed home."

I only half-listen to her, at the same time wondering what my other self somewhere is doing—riding the train to Khabarovsk, maybe. No, probably just arguing with Linda. For a moment, I wonder about the man who jumped off the tower earlier. What is his other self doing now? Is he still here, at the Institute—and just like the rest of us, planning a trip to his own past?

"You know staying home was a real change," Gail is saying. "The kids were real supportive—they liked having me around the house for a change—but my husband didn't care for it *at all*. He thought the only prestige degree was a doctorate."

"Does he have one?"

"Nope. He's an investment advisor. Excuse me—" she reaches up to dim the floor lamp, then falls back onto the couch. "Yeah, Phil wants me to be a *contributing professional*, but he didn't want me working in the hospital. Guess he was afraid I'd bring home something." She laughs.

"So I took a job with a medical marketing firm—I mean, it made sense—I lived with the perfect consumer—Phil probably has twenty pairs of suspenders, and maybe a hundred power ties. All red. All look exactly the same. To me, anyway."

"I guess I'm kind of like that myself," I tell her. "In the ad business, either you dress to the nines or you go completely in the opposite direction—casual to the point of sloppy. I could never do sloppy, so I went for the nines. But after being here a few weeks, I feel like going back to a sweatshirt and jeans.”

“Yeah, this place’ll change you.” She takes a drink and stares at the blank television screen. “Phil came to visit about two weeks ago. He was dressed in a suit and tie—here it was, a hundred degrees in the shade and he’s in a dark suit. Can you imagine? I was in a t-shirt and cutoffs. And since I’ve been here, I’ve gotten used to walking around in sandals—or barefoot. And when I met him in the lobby—” She pauses with a half-smile. “He lost it. Just *lost* it. Wanted to know what had happened to his wife. Really read me out. I came back up to the room—changed into a conservative business suit, nice blouse, expensive shoes. The works. Then we had a *pleasant* meal in the cafeteria—up to the point where I politely told him to go straight to hell. That the next time he comes to San Antonio, he’ll have to spend his time at the Alamo.”

“What did he say?”

“Nothing. He just glared at me and left. That’s his way. The next day he went straight to Poundstone. *Demanded* that I be pulled from the program. Actually threatened legal action. Poundstone called me down to the office and I told Phil to leave me alone. So he left. He hasn’t called since.”

“Hey, at least he came to visit.”

“With Phil it wasn’t entirely altruistic. He was just checking up on me. He’s real possessive, likes control. It’s a relief to be away from him for three months. At least I can talk to other people now.” She gets up from the couch. “I’m gonna get a refill. You want one? Got some smoked oysters in the ‘fridge.”

A moment later she returns with the wine bottle and a small plate of smoked oysters and cheese cubes.

“Tell me what you like best—about going back.”

“I’ll tell you sometime,” she smiles, biting into an oyster. “Not now.”

“Come on.”

“Okay.” She smiles and closes her eyes. “I like it just after they turn on the headsets. You fall into this dark area and below you is the city—all lighted up…like New York City from the air—it goes on and on and on.”

“It looks like that to me, too. I wonder what it is?”

“Just the brain fooling the mind.” She pauses to bite into another oyster. “Before I started this, Otto told me about the city of lights. And

I will confess, there was a part of me—the kid part, I guess—that thought he meant there'd be an actual *place* down there. A real city."

"A real city in your brain?"

"Okay—a *fantasy* city—with streets named 1975, 1974, and so on. And there would be houses on the streets. Some painted with bright colors. Some with no paint at all. And I pretended someone would say, 'okay, Gail Lynn, this is 1973.' And there'll be disco music and hot summers with our old Wards window air conditioner. And I'll have my long hair and long cotton dresses. And other kids would be wearing *their* own brand of long hair—"

"And bell bottoms."

"—and bell bottoms and looking like little used-car salesmen." She laughs. "Vietnam would still be on the news, of course. Everything would be dry and flat and stupid." She reaches for a cheese cube. "But when I actually went back it wasn't like I'd imagined at all. I felt *different*. It was like I'd been to some other *me*. It was a whole lot more—I dunno, personal."

"Fantasy city in the mind, huh? I like that idea. I'd hate to think the mind was nothing more than a bunch of wires and sparks."

"Sorry, but that *is* probably all it is," she shrugs. "But, what's wrong with that?"

"I attended a lecture a while back and there was this little scientist pointing out all the parts of the brain. He was showing how memory is the result of certain signals coming together. Like a telephone switchboard sending signals to some kind of screen in the temporal lobes."

Gail nods. "Yep. That pretty well describes it."

"And he went on about the near-death experience being no more than so many neurons flashing in sequence. It seems life is just machinery grinding against itself."

"And death is when the grinding stops." Gail looks at the floor.

"Maybe that's why that dreamer jumped awhile back."

"Maybe," she nods. "Some say it was because he went into a long run and came back shredded—all these little personalities fighting for control."

"Well, I'm not sure I'd buy that," I tell her. "Of course, I guess it makes sense in a way."

"Of course it does," she brightens. "It's psychology. I'll bet there's all kinds of little personalities down there inside you."

"I know about one," I tell her. "He's my song trivia expert. I can turn on a radio and listen to some song and he'll tell me who did the song and when it came out. But before he does that, he takes me back to where it was when I first heard it."

"That's a nice personality to have."

"Sure is. One minute, I'm fighting traffic on Mass Avenue and the next I'm in Missouri, and it's March and there's frost on the ground and the radio is playing 'Our Winter Love.'"

"I never heard that song."

"February 2, 1963. Bill Purcell. Columbia label."

"Hey, that little guy is good," she taps me on the arm.

"Yeah. He made my company over two million dollars last year. Helped me snag half the oldies-format radio stations in the country, and he helped two of my clients sell their widgets. And, he probably was the one who talked me into coming down here."

"Your little guy talked you into this?"

"Sure. Have to blame it on somebody."

"Well," she says, "you can blame this on *me*." She pours the rest of the bottle, then reaches around and turns out the light.

The phone has been busy now through twenty-five tries. It's 1:00 a.m. here, 2:00 a.m. Boston time. Linda is obviously back from Mexico—the line is busy. I replace the receiver and stare at my shoes, then at the floor. Another attempt. Thanks to the wine, my fingers are hitting all the wrong keys. I reach someone in Michigan, then someone else in Carbondale, Illinois. I decide to let the operator do it. She's even-tempered. Probably handles these kinds of calls all the time.

"Mr. Mitchell, we've tried four times now. The line is busy."

"Get me the verification operator for Lexington, Massachusetts."

"We can't do that, Mr. Mitchell."

"Why the hell not?"

"They're on a different system. You'll have to contact them directly."

"How can I do that?"

"You can't. Not from that phone."

"*Thank* you!" I replace the receiver. Then dial again. Amazingly, the call rings through. And rings. And rings. Where is the answer machine? Probably another misdial. I replace the receiver and try again.

Busy.

I extract the bottle from the dresser drawer. Napoleon the Thirteenth, gift from my wife, attorney Linda Mitchell of the law firm of Something-Something-Something and Other. Where did she get this? I look for her note, but I can't find it.

I put the bottle back in the drawer. It's a gift, after all. I fall onto the bed, ceiling lamp blaring at me, laughing at my poor capacity for Gail's cabernet. In response, I thumb my nose.

There is no reply from the lamp. I rub the scram blisters on the side of my head. Burned, electrocuted—and now I can't reach home. I close my eyes and try to think of pleasant things: the drives up to Maine. The hikes in New Hampshire.

Nope. Sorry.

All I can think about is that phone. First busy, then no answer.

The scenarios flood my mind, all of them involving preening, arrogant lawyers with double-breasted suits and yellow power ties. And suspenders. That annoying damn 1940's Dashiell Hammett look. Was it one of my designers who came up with that? Probably. We billed *somebody* for it.

No. I can't think about that. It screws me up. I have to think of nice things. Pleasant things.

I take a deep breath, hold it, then let it out slowly.

Ducks. That's it. I'll think of ducks. The ducks that live behind our house. White fluffy ducks. They're asleep, but the sounds from the house are waking them up: heavy breathing and ringing telephones.

Nope. Ain't gonna work. I open the drawer and retrieve the brandy. After tearing the wax from the bottle, I extract the cork and take a drink. Napoleon the Thirteenth.

It's two o'clock. The hour of depression. I try the phone again. Linda, I'll say: I'm drinking your brandy. The one you got me as a gift, I'm drinking it now. Mixing it with wine courtesy of the girl next door.

The line is busy. Overcome by the sudden complexity of life, I stagger to the bathroom and throw up a colorful fresco of wine, smoked oysters and cheddar cheese. Some part of me, some hidden persuader-observer-whatever is shaking his head, commenting that the oysters were probably bad. Vibrio toxins or something and I'm going to die, right here on the floor of the bathroom. I examine the floor tile for imperfections. There are many.

The clock strikes three. The hour of failure. Big blue three. Cold blue-moon three. The hors d'oeuvres are long gone and now I'm thirsty. A glass of brandy would be perfect. It's 3:05. The Age of Enlightenment.

I stare at the wall and think of where I've been over the last few weeks—and especially the last few days. Inside beautiful movies? No, they have to be more than that. They *have* to be.

I simply refuse to believe the places I've been, the people I've seen, are sparks inside two pounds of gelatin no bigger than a *common bathroom sponge.*

The bottle gets lighter by another glass.

Of course, there's that guy in Seattle who claims there's a switch in the brain somewhere. Some sort of ejection seat of the soul.

Maybe that's where I'll go one of these days. Up through the roof.

I rub the blister on my scalp, from Leonard's attempt at execution. It breaks.

Maybe that's what memory is all about—dying.

Another glass of Napoleon. For some reason, I notice the wall speaker has shut up. Silence. No more blues in the night. Too bad, because I'm sick again. Another trip to the bathroom. More canapes into the john. I wonder if Gail is as miserable as I am. I hope not. Doesn't she have a session scheduled early this morning?

3:30 am. The Age of Rationalization. I carefully place the empty bottle on the nightstand, and like storm water searching out the drain, I fall face-first onto the bed.

Now I can go to sleep. Go back to some place where I'm doing something stupid and bad and painful. Of course, there's no pain back there because there's no sense of touch—no cold, no warm, no sharp edges, nothing—only soft cotton everywhere. Because it's only a movie. Only sight and sound allowed.

But I miss the sense of touch, I really miss it. Even if it's just a film in the mind, why isn't touch recorded along with everything else? It's not enough to I see and hear my memories—I want to *feel* them too. But maybe the brain doesn't work that way. There are some things that don't make it to tape. Maybe that part of my experience is truly gone forever.

Doctor, I get drunk and stupid sometimes and then I get in this machine and I visit my past.

Is it pleasant?

Yes and no. I was walking through a dead world—a world that didn't exist anymore—but I loved it. I was with those I loved and I was more alone than I've ever been. Can I go now? Can I go to the tower now and jump off?

No, instead, I'll jump inside. And float above the lights then dive right through them, into the wires and switches and diodes. Maybe I'll find that little printed circuit that stores my songs. And brought me here in the first place.

I open my eyes. The wall speakers are playing some horrible song from 1970. "My Baby Loves Love." Is this some kind of a *joke*? My stomach churns for a moment and then settles down. There is nothing left to throw up.

4:00 am. The Age of Decision. Thank you, Linda, your Napoleon has worked wonderfully. The room is spinning and the grass is blowing like a rippling green carpet. Above, the ceiling has turned dark blue and the clouds are rolling in.

Unexpectedly, a face appears, inches from mine. It is Evan, no more than 12 years old. "So, how do you know I'm not real, Mitchell?" he sneers.

"I don't."

"Right. And it all could be a memory. It's all up there." He points to my forehead. "All this is really inside your head. Somewhere, some time, I'm married with kids and inventing chairs that will take you back to the past."

Nice try, Carswell, but you don't make it to the future.

More clouds, and the room spins away.

I have to puke again and I really hate to puke. In defiance of my stomach, I curl my body into a fetal position. I hear the radio. I imagine that this bedroom, these walls are surrounded by a town, a 500-soul settlement on the plains of western Missouri. There is a church, a grocery store and a railroad track. Not far away, in the darkness, is a water tower. It will be my antenna to this place.

There's a highway before me and I'm driving silently across the brown flatness of November in Missouri. Out in the plains in the heart of the country. Sitting in the passenger's seat, a girl adjusts a strap hidden beneath her blouse. She seems so small and thin. The darkness surrounds us and we move inside a dream.

"Michael, I really want you. Do you know that?"

The lightning flash again.

Rain washes against the window. The rumble of thunder rattles the room and I open my eyes.

The tropical depression has arrived.

I see the bottle of Napoleon has fallen from the nightstand. The memory of the brandy sends an especially strong wave of nausea through me and I arise to weave my way to the bathroom.

Nothing. My stomach is finally bereft of oysters and, after a shot of mouthwash, I return to the sheets. Outside, the storm has picked up, with lightning flashes every few seconds or so.

I hear a car drive by, its tires like sandpaper on the wet street. How can that be?

"It's raining, isn't it?" A young girl's voice. *Her* voice.

"Yeah. Maybe it's the first day of spring."

"Spring in February? I think not. The first day of spring is in March. That's next month." She rolls over onto her back. "I like the rain. It never rained like this in Mexico. Did I tell you I lived in Mexico when I was four years old? Linares—south of Monterrey. My dad was working in a gas plant, don't ask me what that is. Anyway, it never rains in Mexico. Ever."

In the darkness I see Rachael. She's wearing a t-shirt and rollers in her black hair. Antenna. That's what's bringing me back to her across all these years. She's a radio, and I'm only a wave in spacetime. A standing wave from the future.

"Ha. Radio station. I've heard that joke, Michael."

There is a soft tap of rain against the window.

"You know, I've been thinking," she says. "I think you have something to do with this."

"What?"

"Every time you talk like this, it rains."

I sit up in bed. The room is empty. There is no one here. Through the window I can see the sky above San Antonio, still thick with clouds. I get out of bed and walk to the window. It's 8:15 a.m., well after dawn. The streets below are dense with morning traffic. I look for my favorite stoplight: Inexplicably, it is stuck on yellow. In the shadowy, rainy morning, it casts a steady, unyielding glow across the angry snarl of morning commuters.

I draw the blinds, remove my clothes and step into the bathroom. It smells of cabernet, brandy and smoked oysters.

I leave the light off and run the shower as hot as I can stand. The Institute had generously provided a standard flat square of hotel soap. I've replaced it with a bar of Zest, slippery with a sulfurous smell. Someone told me once Zest soap is like olives. Either you love it or you hate it.

In the darkness I feel the water flow over me, washing away the scent of brandy. I add some Prell and stick my head under the shower. Nirvana. It's an old brand that's been around for years. If I close my eyes I could be back in my college dorm.

Or somewhere in my past. It's a shame we can't detect scents and tastes while visiting the past. I think how great it would be to experience the taste of original Vess Cola. Kraft caraway cheese slices. Micrin mouthwash.

I wish I could experience the scent of whatever Brenda Lacey wore those nights in Corinth. For that matter, what about her kiss? Does a kiss actually have a taste, or is it more of a tug on the heart? It *seems* to have a taste.

I turn off the shower, wrap the towel around my waist and return to the window. I see the traffic on the street has come to a complete standstill. Two cars and a huge white truck have all gotten together in the exact center of the intersection, and three burly men are waving their arms and apparently yelling at each other. As a San Antonio police squad car joins the group, I close the blinds and return to the bathroom to brush my teeth. It occurs to me the ventilation system has stopped working and the room has become dark.

The electricity is out.

12

Leonard

It is a generally accepted axiom of this place that lab technicians and operators see the sun only under extreme conditions—such as lightning storms that damage the mainframe computers.

This morning, the cafeteria is packed with them; most are clumped at a table in the back of the cafeteria, arguing over stacks of printouts and sprinkling the air with what Leonard calls "geek flame."

Perhaps for that reason, Leonard is sitting with us, quietly eating a bowl of Frosted Flakes and reading a computer printout. Every now and then, he produces a mechanical pencil and makes a mark next to a line of numbers.

"It doesn't surprise me," Lowell says, stirring his coffee. "One lightning strike in the right place can knock out a whole city. There was a storm in '85 that brought Berkeley to its knees."

"Yeah, but the electrical storm last night wasn't much," Otto replies. "It lasted no more than a half-hour."

"It's not how long it lasts, it's how powerful it is," Keller says, digging into ham and eggs. "A single lightning bolt carries a lot of current."

"Does anybody know where the storm came from?" Gail looks around the table. "Leonard, didn't you say there's a tropical depression out there somewhere in the Gulf of Mexico?"

"The whole Gulf Coast is a tropical depression," Leonard shrugs, circling a line of code. "Always has been."

"Yeah," Lowell says. "We suspected that..."

"Hey, you two!" Gail looks hurt. "You ever been to Disneyland?

And isn't there a big aquarium in Texas somewhere?"

"The storm, Leonard." Otto persists. "What about last night's storm?"

"Well, it was *obviously* nontrivial," Leonard lays the pencil aside. "Real compact. There was no front or anything, it looked like it boiled up right over San Antonio. Cumulonimbus to forty thousand feet. Lots of columns, lots of downbursts, and lots of lightning in a real short time—most of it getting down from the standard source—freezing level. I came in early and firewalled the Lab 14 computer from the grid—diked the main boxes. Didn't want the storm to smoke anything." He takes a drink of milk.

"Did it damage our computer?" Otto asks.

"I hope not." Leonard points to the stack of paper. "If it did, I'd have to go through the code for the FFT circuits. It's evil *and* rude— of course, it was written in ADA. I mean, you would have thought *somebody* would have considered Visual Basic X."

"Job security," Lowell says.

"*Real* job security," Leonard nods. "If I had another year I'd dike and gun half this stuff. Forget the scripts and object code. I'd start over on the bare metal."

"Sounds awful," Otto says.

"Don't worry. I'll run another diagnostic before any of you climb into the chair."

"What could happen?" Otto looks at him. "We wouldn't get electrocuted, would we?"

"Well," Leonard pauses for a another drink of milk, "last year lightning got in and iced the bus in Lab 12 so bad the old theta detectors were crossed up with the modem lines. Every time somebody dialed information, the dreamers went to November 14, 1962. Heh, heh."

"So they can phone home," Lowell adds, "for their Captain Crunch whistle."

"Listen you two," Gail growls. "A joke's not funny if only a tiny percent of a group understands it."

"Okay," Leonard smiles, getting up from the table. "I was referring to the semi-famous issue of the *Bell Systems Technical Journal* that spilled the beans on multiplexing codes. The codes allowed hackers in the old days the ability to call anywhere in the world just by whistling into the phone."

"Yeah," Lowell adds. "Then some guy in the Air Force happened to discover that the toy whistle in a box of a certain type of breakfast cereal would produce a perfect 2600 cycle tone—the same exact frequency that would trigger Ma Bell's circuits. Before long the guy was phoning all over the world *for free*. The feds called him Captain Crunch."

Gail shakes her head in disgust. "How would anybody except geeks know that?"

"She's right, Leonard," Lowell shrugs. "That joke was *way* too inside."

"Back to the computer, Leonard," Otto interjects. "When will it be ready?"

"Who knows?" Leonard shrugs. "The thetas are probably off the trolley, the scanners are iffy. Of course, they never work anyway, so the difference is epsilon squared—" A pause. "I'd say the Big Iron isn't going to be ready for passengers until late tonight—if then. Sorry, Time Surfers."

As Leonard leaves the cafeteria, Gail whispers to Lowell. "*Free phone calls?*"

·····◆·····

Midnight. Gail and I are in Lab 14 with Leonard, watching as he tries to repair the damage the lightning caused. For the past hour and a half, he has replaced innumerable cables, monitors, power supplies and other, more arcane gadgets having to do with the communication system. Nothing seems to work.

"Oh, feep me harder—this is really bletcherous," he mumbles, shaking his head. Then turning, he smiles sheepishly. "Sorry for that outburst. *Everything* is no-op. Real collision in the hash tables."

"Don't worry, Leonard," Gail shrugs. "No one knows what you're saying."

"It looks like the lightning roached the software for the input filters—"

"What's an input filter?" Gail asks, taking a drink of warm Jolt cola. "Tell us. See if you can explain it in standard English."

"Okay," Leonard says, peering at the monitor. "The signals we receive when you're down there are real weak. The larynx mikes collect and amplify the signals, but they amplify the underflow—excuse me, *random noise*—along with it."

"Where's all this random noise coming from?"

"Teeny tiny electrons bumping into each other. Also, television signals—whistles from lightning strikes—meteors entering the stratosphere. We even pick up electrical storms on Jupiter. Jupiter is a non-trivial noise source. Much of the static you hear on an AM radio is from Jupiter. There's a lot we have to sift through just to hear you guys think. Technology may be pretty but it's not easy."

Listening to Leonard, I begin to feel like the Voyager spacecraft at one of the outer planets.

"Yeah," Leonard continues, "the throat mikes pick up all kinds of electrical noise—even voices—"

"Voices?" Gail asks.

"Citizens band radio, maybe, who knows? If they don't correspond to your particular electrical signature, the system filters them out. With any luck, we can hear what you're trying to say to us down there. Without the filter program, all we'd hear is the underflow, and the computer would drop it out. There would be just a blank place on the tape. You guys might have a great time, but Poundstone wouldn't be happy about it. Which means I have to reprogram the filters before you get into the chair."

"You got anything to eat around here?" Gail asks.

"I'll order a pizza as soon as I finish this," Leonard says. "There's a bag of *nishiki* in the top drawer—"

"What's that?"

"Japanese bean crackers. Very tasty if you don't mind the dried minnow annoyance."

"Forget it. I'll wait for the pizza."

"Yes!" Leonard points to the computer screen. "Zey made a copy of the filters. This is insanely great! I'll download the one we'll use tonight. Who wants to take a trip?"

"You go, Mike," Gail says. "I'll wait for the pizza."

"Okay," Leonard says. "We'll download Mike's electronic signature—bingo. We just have to plug the theta modules in. Wouldn't want you to go to sleep on us." He throws a switch and a hum fills the room. "The brain has an underlying network that is extremely fascist, but the theta module knows how do deal with it. Waits for a four to seven hertz theta signal to show up in the temporal lobes, then introduces a similar signal in the headset until it locks in—"

"Uh, Leonard," Gail interrupts. "Isn't it getting a little late to order a pizza?"

"They're open 'til one a.m. I'll protocol down to the desk in a microfortnight." He turns back to the monitor and types in my name and the date. "You know, in my humble opinion, the theta module is the most important thing in the system. If you slip through theta into delta trace, you go to standard, boring sleep. Or have a lucid dream. Used to happen all the time back when we started. People would drop into a high dream state and bypass the memory bank entirely. *Huge* waste of time."

"So how did you know it was only a dream?" I ask.

"Easy," Leonard shrugs. "They'd describe major geographical land-marks, like mountains and rivers okay, but they'd get the other stuff wrong. Buildings looked different, people would be wearing the wrong kind of clothes. Sometimes they'd see things that looked like highly evolved geckos—little gray lizards with big eyes. At that point we knew they were being kind of *unstructured* down there, so we'd pull their chains and make 'em start over."

"I see."

"There was some borderline strangeness though. I remember one week all the dreamers went lucid and somehow kept seeing the same thing. It was really tense. Zey mentioned it to one of his friends at Lackland Air Base and before you know it we had the military in here. Presto! Department of Defense blurted out all this funding for lucid dream research—real dogwash stuff. Naturally, Poundstone cashed their checks. But then he turned right around and put the money into theta locks. No more little gray lizards."

"What do you think they were?" I ask, wondering whether I want to hear the answer.

"It's an open switch. Bad cafeteria food, maybe—the catering was lousy that year. Could have been a misfeature in the induction software. Nobody really knows." He reaches for a bag of something with Japanese writing on it. "Nishiki anyone? Mucho tasty."

"Leonard," Gail says, "I will *not* eat bean crackers with little dried minnows. I want you to order a pizza. Not 'real soon now,' but *now!*"

"Sure. I can handle that." He picks up the phone. "Hello, Margaret? This is Leonardo. I'm waving a crisp twenty-dollar bill next to the receiver. Can you hear it? Good. Margaret, this bill is yours if you order us an ANSI standard pizza—that's right, giant pepperoni and mushrooms. You know the drill. Send it down with the guard and keep the change and a slice for yourself. Thanks in advance." He hangs up the phone and turns to Gail. "Happy?"

"Thanks. How much do I owe you?"

"Twenty bucks," he smiles.

"I'll pay you back someday." She pats him on the shoulder.

"No prob. I'll just have the maid service steal it from your room tonight while you're downstairs." He turns to me. "It looks like the Big Iron is ready to board passengers again. Tickets, please."

13

Respectable

I close the visor into darkness. Outside, the theta module, or what ever it is, has begun to whine like an elevator motor. From the head-set I hear Leonard's familiar voice.

"Mike, give me a count, please."

"Sure. One-two-three-"

"Fine. The filter has your signature. Hm. Looks like Lowell canceled his two-o'clock this morning—just a minute."

I open my eyes to the twin green dots of light.

"Mike, Gail's going over to Lab 10. Which means you have an extra two hours if you want it."

"Maybe. I'll let you know."

"You want the cuff?"

"No, I'll do self-hypnosis this time."

"Sure. Just don't hurt yourself, heh. Only serious. Ready?"

"Let's do it."

"Sayonara, time-surfer. Have a good dream."

My body turns to lead and sinks into the chair. Then the vibrations set in and I drop into the darkness, into the area above the starfield, above the highway to the past.

I fall forward into the time-stream. The light expands and forms sky, trees, rocks, river. Someone is sitting near me, cap sideways on his head, no shirt, cuffed jeans. Canteen lying on a nearby rock.

Evan.

He tosses a flat rock across the brown mottled surface of the river.

It bounces over a pair of black water striders, skips three times and sinks with a little gulp. "Mom let Pammie use my tent again last night. She put it up in the back yard and invited those stupid girls from her class in there."

"So?"

"They came in the house and got ketchup and crackers and all kinds of junk. About midnight they started laughing and then the dogs started barking. *Then* they got scared and came back into the house and got *more* chips and stuff. One of 'em even stole some of the old man's Falstaff." Another rock into sails into the water. "Girls eat when they're scared, did you ever notice that? That's why so many of 'em are bigger than guys."

"I guess."

"You know, Mitchell, my tent was a *wreck*. After they left, I had to hose it down. Ketchup everywhere. It looked like they had a food fight."

Floating here behind my ten-year-old eyes, watching this, I can't help wondering where Brenda Lacey is right now. Probably sitting at home in that great window-lined upstairs study practicing on her baby grand piano.

Brenda, oddly enough, was the only girl Carswell thought had any sense. "She's smart, I'll say that," he would tell me, the highest praise he ever had for girls.

Evan's sister Pammie, on the other hand, hated Brenda Lacey. Years later, when she heard I was dating her, she refused to speak to me.

For that matter, I wonder where Pammie is now? Probably at home watching television—Fury or Sky King, maybe.

And Rachael? Rachael is probably in Linares, Mexico. Or maybe in some small Missouri town. I can't imagine her at seven. That's so young. A baby, really.

The river abruptly turns white—and becomes a standard five-hole notebook. Red line down the left side.

"Mrs. Michael Mitchell. Hey, did you realize that was the first time I've tried writing that! Not bad! for a beginner. You. Be. Good! If possible. If not, be sneaky! Guess I'd better stop for now and study good old world history. Love "ya" forever, Rachael. Write me will "ya". PLEASE."

In the center is the huge "I LuV U." Then, at the bottom left corner, "Love again."

The phone rings. My mom makes it there first. "Michael, it's for you. Sounds like a little kid. Maybe it's somebody in your scout troop."

I pick up the phone.

"Hi. It's me." It *does* sound like a kid.

"Hi, Rachael."

"I just wanted to tell ya I got this call from Brenda whats-her-butt last week. She called me at home in Cherokee and then read me all your letters you mailed to her this summer. Read them to me word for word. I bet her parents are gonna be pissed when they see her phone bill."

"Are you in town?"

"Yeah. I'm at Grandma's. And guess what? I'm stayin'—Mom and Dad said I could go to school in Corinth. That is, if I could find a ride down to Cherokee once a month. So you know what that means."

"What?"

"*It means*—you gotta make up your mind. Are you gonna stay with Brenda or are you gonna step across that line and ask me out?"

"Guess I'll ask you out."

"Listen. Goin' with me might be a double handful. It means driving down from college to see me every weekend. It means taking me to see my folks. And most important—it means never lying to me. I'll put up with anything except lying."

"Want to go for a drive?"

"Sure—if we can drive by Brenda Lacey's."

"I'd rather not."

As I switch on the headlights and pull out of the driveway, Rachael kicks off her shoes and plants her bare feet on the windshield, then on the ceiling of the car. I'm surprised how long and muscular her legs appear.

"There," she says.

"Why'd you do *that*?"

"I'm real territorial." She reaches under her white blouse to adjust something. A bra strap? "If some other girl happens to look at the windshield, they'll know I've been here."

"Thanks."

"You're welcome." She scoots up in the seat, then quickly tugs at the cuffs of her blue cotton shorts. "I told Brenda I was *so* pleased for the opportunity to learn so much about you. I think it pissed her off."

"So she actually read you my letters. I can't believe she would do that."

"Better believe it. And I stayed on the line and said, 'uh-huh—hmmmm—really'—you know, to let her know I was still there. After she got through the last one, I thanked her for calling, hung up the phone and cried my eyes out. Then I was okay. *Sort* of okay anyway—"

She pauses to plant her feet on the windshield again. More footprints. I wonder what my Dad thought when he saw them the next morning.

"—Then, after I got back, I called her house, but she wasn't there. I figured she was with you. Guess I was wrong." Rachael sighs and looks out the window. "She's probably out with some other guy. If I were you, I'd ask her for your ring back."

"I didn't have to. She's mailing it to me."

"Good. If you don't get it in a week, let me know. I'll complain to the post office." She smiles at me. "We wouldn't want you to lose that ring—you might need it."

I steer the car out onto the main highway, then turn at a farm-to-market gravel road leading past a stretch of dense woods. Scanning to my peripheral vision I see a small house and barn. I recall it vanished sometime in the 1980's, replaced by a factory. Like these fragile images I see before me now, the past is never safe—it is plowed under, built over—or sold piece by piece.

I can almost feel the car slide on the loose rock. Without the benefit of seatbelts, Rachael and I both lean away from the turn. The speedometer keeps a steady 40 mph—insanely reckless for gravel driving. But then again, I'm eighteen years old—with the nerve and skill of the brand new driver.

The headlights illuminate a haze of gravel dust hanging over the road. Since we've met no other cars, it's a good bet that somewhere up ahead is another car, traveling in the same direction as we are. Apparently, my 18-year-old self comes to the same conclusion—I see the speedometer drop to 35 mph. My left hand hits the headlight switch and the world goes momentarily dark. Amazingly, Rachael says nothing.

Ahead, the white gravel road becomes a snowy ribbon stretching ahead of us in the darkness. After a very long minute, the lights return.

"Wanna park and watch the lightning?" she asks finally.

"There's no lightning tonight—" I hear myself say.

"Sure there is. There'll be some in the east, wait and see. I hate storms, but I'm real good with lightning. Did you know all animals and some people can tell when a storm is coming? I'm one of them."

"An animal?"

"Depends on who I'm with—okay, I'm only kidding, so don't get any ideas. Just tell me when you want to watch the lightning."

I shift into second and hear the soft kachunk of the transmission, followed by a distinct rattle. Did I ever figure out what caused that noise? Guess not. "Want to hear the radio instead?" I ask her.

"Suits me." She kicks off her shoes again and props her feet against the dashboard, then quickly walks them across the windshield. More footprints.

"Tell me about Cherokee." Perhaps I was trying to distract her from marking up my car.

"Okay. It's in the middle of nowhere and has the personality of a snail. Real cheap school. Guess I told you the pom-pon girls only get one pom each—"

"You told me. When your mom and dad took us out to the Dairy Queen, remember?"

"Oh, that's right. Anyway, if they let me stay in Corinth, I'm gonna try out for cheerleading squad. Or maybe twirler…My legs aren't fat. Do you think they're fat? Here, feel—" she grabs my hand and places it on her thigh.

"Not up *here*, down *there*. Right. See? Not an ounce of fat."

"You'd make a great cheerleader, Rache."

"Thank you. I think so, too." She returns her feet to the windshield. "I'm athletic. And I'm a night owl. I get most of my thinking done between ten and two in the morning. Just so you know, in case you decide to marry me."

I quickly lock and scan my peripheral vision. She has her feet on the dash again. It occurs to me her footprints were probably all over the car.

"Not only that," she continues, "I'm a perfectionist and demanding. My mama says I have sharp teeth. And I'll tell you something else—I'm real direct. If I want something, I'll tell you. And if I don't like something, I'll tell you that too."

"I'll try to remember that."

"I'd probably get on the cheerleading team except I'm ugly."

"What?" I look at her again.

"Oh, *c'mon*. I know what I look like—there are mirrors in this world. See these front teeth? I look like a chipmunk. And my butt's a little too big—"

"Listen, I think you're really—pretty." I look at Rachael and see an image of her in a strapless yellow evening dress—with a white corsage. I lock the image and study it—no question about it, this is the image of a reasonably pretty young woman. Not in the Brenda Lacey league, but certainly pretty.

"Pretty, huh?" She says. "Most people say cute. That's what my last boyfriend said. Of course, he also thinks rat terriers are cute—"

"Tell me more about Cherokee."

"Okay. Let me tell you about our house. It's at the side of Cherokee between the water tower and the church. It has two peaks and looks like a rabbit. It also has a burned place on the chimney, but it's the deacon's fault. You know why?" She looks at me.

"No. Why?"

"Last December the deacons at the church wanted to know why we didn't put up any Christmas decorations. So they gave Daddy a plastic Wise Man and put it on the chimney."

"A plastic wise man?" I look at Rachael. By now, she's moved again, leaning up against the door, the bottoms of her feet pressed against my leg.

"Plastic wise man," Rachael continues. "I guess they couldn't afford all three—and we didn't want to get a Santa Claus—they're really expensive."

"A plastic wise man."

"On the chimney. But after we put it up, we forgot about it. And when we started a fire, the wise man melted. The only thing left was his hat. The rest of him ran down the chimney. It's lucky we didn't have a fire."

"What did the deacons say?"

"Deacons? Who cares about them? *You* try explaining a melted wise man to three little kids." She reaches to turn up the radio. It's a Ronettes oldie from three years before: "Be My Baby."

"I really like this song," she says. "It has crickets."

"That's castanets," I tell her.

"Have you actually *seen* them?"

"No."

"Then, *you don't know, do you?*" She smiles sweetly.

As we drive south the radio static increases, threatening to drown out the music. Maybe she's right. Maybe there *is* a storm lurking out there somewhere. I lock the scene and peer into the darkness beyond the gravel haze. Nothing.

"Leonard."

"Yo, Mike. What's going on down there?"

"I'm in August or September, 1966. Somewhere south of Corinth, Missouri. Did any storms occur back then?"

"You give me a two-month-wide slot in the summer? Can you narrow it down?"

"Okay. I caught the tail end of 'Wouldn't It Be Nice' and when I locked, the radio was playing 'Bus Stop' by the Hollies—"

After a brief pause, Leonard comes back: *"You asked for it—you got it. The Juke says you're definitely in the first week of August, 1966. What station were you listening to, KAAY out of Little Rock?"*

"Looks like it."

"Well, better take this down, it'll be on the exam—KAAY's song rotation for the first week of August, 1966—is—: 'Bus Stop,' 'Drive My Car,' 'Summer In the City' commercial break for Sam's Record Shop in Shreveport, Louisiana, then back with 'Sunshine Superman,' news break, 'Black is Black,' 'Wouldn't It Be Nice,' commercial break for Sam's Record Shop— "

I scan the corner of my vision past the yellow light of the dashboard radio, down to the darkness of the floorboard, then to the outline of Rachael's feet planted against my leg. In this near-haze I can barely make them out.

"If you need the one for WLS or KOMA, just call."

"Thanks, Leonard."

"It's a slow night up here."

"I guess."

Unlock.

"Say, Rache. Want to guess what the next song is gonna be?"

"Sure. You go first."

"'Respectable' by the Outsiders—wait and see."

"The next one? Okay. I say it's gonna be—'Paperback Writer' by the Beatles. If you lose, you owe me another date—and you already owe me four."

"It's a deal." I reach over to shake her hand.

The news is over. I turn the volume all the way to the right. Abruptly, the air is hammered with a drum roll followed by the sound of guitars and horns. *"What kind of girl is this—that's never, ever come home late—"*

Rachael stares at me, her eyes wide. "Good guess! I *am* impressed." She folds her arms. "Tell me how ya did it."

"It was a good guess."

It *was* a good guess—and an extraordinary coincidence. Leonard had just read the station play list and suddenly my younger self blurts out a song title. I can vaguely recall the original event, over thirty years ago. It surprised me then, just as it does now.

Suddenly another image looms: that of Brenda in her prom dress playing her family's black grand piano. Now, she's in her striped swim suit—

"C'mon." Rachael prods me with her foot.

"What?" The images of Brenda vanish.

"C'mon, tell me how you did it. How'd you know that song was gonna be on?"

"Magic. I can see into the future."

"Oh, Michael—" she looks at me longingly. "You are *so* full of it. C'mon. Tell me how ya did it. And don't smile when you tell me. If you smile, it means you're lying." She edges closer. "See? You're getting ready to fib to me, 'cause you're smiling—"

"Did you love her—?
No, no no oh-oh—
Did you hug her—
No, no no no no no-o-o-o"

"You know," she says, "some Saturdays I used to sit outside on the front yard in Cherokee and watch the cars pass each other on the road. And I'm thinking, I bet in some of those passing cars there are people who know each other. But they never find out—they drive past and never look. I think about that a lot."

I glance over to see she's looking at me. I pause, probably to smile, then return my eyes to the road ahead. As I do so, the scene explodes in a flash of headlights. I steer to the right, nearly going into the ditch.

"Haytruck," I say, returning to the road. I scan to the speedometer—50 mph. On gravel.

Good reflexes, kid.

Rachael reaches to turn up the radio. "I wonder if we'll hear 'Summer in the City' tonight?"

"I've got an idea," I tell her. "We can go back to town—get some ginger ale and then go to the drive in." Would I see Brenda there? Of course, it wouldn't do any good if I did.

"It's too late," she says. "Let's drive by and see if there's any lights on in the jail."

Simultaneously the sky becomes brighter, as though someone turned on a light. The darkness surrounding the car is gone—replaced by a green, rolling landscape in a gauzy haze of twilight. The gravel road has also vanished. We're now on a concrete interstate.

Rachael is still here, but the shorts and the white blouse have been replaced by jeans and a dark sweatshirt turned inside out. She's in mid-sentence: "—Bradley, who is four years younger than me, and then there's Stacie who's seven and then there's Amy, who's four. You good with kids? "

"I guess so—"

"You better be, cause Amy's learning jokes, and when she tells you, you gotta laugh. Otherwise, you'll hurt her feelings. Her favorite joke is 'what did one dog say to the other dog?'"

"I don't know."

"*'Meet you at the bone-house.*' Isn't that *funny?*"

"Yeah. I don't know why, but it is. Kind of."

"Well, just remember to laugh when she tells it. Want me to drive?"

"No, I'm doing fine."

"I started driving when I was twelve. An Olds Eighty-eight. I figure if I can drive that when I'm twelve, the driving test next year will be a snap."

On the radio, I hear an old Rolling Stones hit, "Paint It, Black." She turns up the volume. "I like it where he talks about the seagull changing colors."

"I think he says something else."

"Nope. It's 'seagull.' In fact, thinkin' about it makes me hungry. Why don't you pretend you love me and buy me a fish sandwich with lots of tartar sauce?"

"*Mike, this is Leonard at the one hour mark. How's it going?*"

"So far so good. I'm listening to the Rolling Stones. It's twilight and—"

"*Control-C, Mike—your signal's coming in too fast.*

I lock the scene. "Any better?"

"*Yeah. Lock before you talk when you're in turbo mode, okay? The signal almost firehosed the translators.*"

"It doesn't seem fast down here."

"That's what Einstein said. You want another hour? You've got blanket authorization. Besides, the pizza's already cold."

"Sure. Why not?"

Unlock. And the scene evaporates. I'm in my room in Corinth flat on my back under a mountain of blankets. The light filtering through the window is frost gray. It's winter. I see that Earl's bed is unmade. He's still alive, so I must be in some time before 1963. I'll get to talk to my brother again. Early on, I was told that any elation I feel as an observer would be muted. The colors of emotion go from yellows and reds and blues to a sort of uniform beige. Poundstone said it was a ego-protective mechanism that helps to keep us in the present, in the real world. Still, I look forward to seeing my family again.

I scan the scene—a dark room in winter. It's too bad the sense of touch isn't available to dreamers—I might be able to scan my body, determine if I'm nine or twelve. Maybe check the distance my feet are from the end of the bed.

Unfortunately, all I have here in this strange world is sight and sound.

I pull the covers over my head and turn on my side. I must be cold. I hear a sniffle.

Aha. I must *have* a cold. Is this the horrible winter when I came down with the flu? Endless trips to the bathroom to throw up? Wonderful. Whoever is scheduling my trips is not doing such a great job.

A small hand darts from beneath the blanket to turn on the radio. The song is only vaguely familiar—"Catch A Falling Star." I lock the scene and the music stops.

"Leonard. Fire up the Jukebox. Do you have 'Catch a Falling Star?'"

"Just a minute. Yeah. Here it is—Perry Como—huh. The singing barber. Was on the charts 20 weeks starting January 11, 1958. How's it feel to have the musical tastes of a ten-year-old again?"

"Crummy. I've got the flu."

"Flu, huh? Hold on—yeah, that's possible. There was an interesting Asian strain rolling through the midwest that winter. Justaminute. I'm paging through the health archives—whoa! Bet you spend plenty of time in the bathroom—"

"Thanks for the information."

"No prob. Just ask Mr. Lampman, the answer guy for the rest of us."

I unlock the scene. I'm staring at the ceiling—a bored kid, in bed sick with the flu. My eyes close and I drift away. Suddenly the scene shifts and now I'm walking through the hallway of a house—it's not mine. I turn the corner and look down at the girl curled up on the couch, her black hair matted, her face pale.

"Rache—wake up!"

I see that she's wearing white cotton pajama tops covered with little red hearts. There is a yellow stain on her right sleeve. I turn to look at something in my hand—a small brown pill bottle. On the label: Seconal. Take one at bedtime.

The bottle is empty.

"Rache—"

Lock. I'm at the Dominic house in Cherokee. It's night—I see my heavy coat on a chair—it must be winter. November? December?

"Leonard."

"Man Behind The Curtain here. How's the surfing?"

"What can you tell me about a drug called Seconal?"

"Just a minute—okay, got it. Secobarbital. Red capsules...100 milligrams. Barbiturate. Street name—red devils. Definitely a bad thing. Where did you see that?"

"What are they used for?"

"Sleeping pills. It says here the docs were pretty loose with them until the late 70's. What's the deal?"

"I don't know. I've fallen into a problem down here."

"Then leave. No need to go through something twice."

"I don't know if I should."

"Your choice. But remember, all of this has already happened. Otherwise, you wouldn't be there again. Right?"

"I guess."

"Think about it. See you in the real world in fifty minutes."

I lift up from the scene and the room recedes into the darkness of December, 1966. Rachael falls away, helpless and alone.

I pass backwards from that time, through November, drift up through college classes in Kirksville, brown fall weekends with Rachael and my folks in Corinth. Up through drives with Rachael down to Cherokee—listening to the radio and the rain against the windshield.

Up toward the beginning of November now, and the last week of October.

The scene slows, then stops. I'm in the front seat of a car. It's a Pontiac. The trees outside are a mixture of green and orange. It's mid-fall. I see people in suits. It must be Sunday.

"He preaches a good sermon, wait and see," Rachael tells me, glancing at her father. "You're not gonna believe it."

I follow Rachael's eyes to Mr. Dominic, wedged in the back seat of the Pontiac between his bored black-haired son and two youngest daughters—both blonde. He's dressed in a dark blue suit, black shoes, blue tie. With Wayfarer sunglasses he would look like a saxophone player from some bar in Kansas City.

But Bob Dominic apparently *is* a preacher—an experienced one, judging by the way he is scribbling down notes into the margins of his Bible.

I remember this day. He will preach at some church in a little farming community called Huntsdale.

As Mrs. Dominic rockets the Pontiac around a steep curve, she informs me Mr. Dominic preached the Sunday before at a Community Methodist and the week before that at a reorganized community Presbyterian. Apparently there is a certain flexibility among Protestant denominations in rural Missouri.

Wanda cranks the wheel, guiding the Pontiac onto the Huntsdale turnoff. "Ten minutes to go, Hon," she says to her husband.

"Almost there," Mr. Dominic says, scribbling furiously. "How about something from John 14, verses one and two?"

"That's a good one, Bob," Wanda says from the driver's seat. "In my Father's house there are many mansions."

He looks up at me. "Think I should discuss the meaning of existence with the good congregation of Huntsdale this morning?"

"Oh, I'm *sure* they'd like that," Rachael says.

"Better stick to the King James version." Bob pauses to scribble something in the notebook, then looks up. "That's the first thing they always ask—what Bible do you preach out of? Up in this part of Missouri, it's the King James Version only. As dictated."

"To King James," Rachael's mom explains.

"Lessee—" Bob muses, "—many mansions. Maybe when you go on to your great reward, you stroll from one mansion to another—or maybe one room to another...of course, when that happens to *me*, I'll try to find where the coffeepot is. Then probably trip over the rug in the hallway."

"Don't tell them that," Rachael says. "They won't invite you back."

"You know, Michael," Bob says to me, "all the people in this congregation have great memories. You give a canned sermon and you find them mouthing the words along with you. It's embarrassing." He returns to the Bible to jot down another note. "Yeah, I'll go with the many-mansions. Any coffee left in that thermos?"

"Sure, Daddy, here." Rachael digs under the seat and hands him the thermos.

"Can't think without coffee," he says, unscrewing the top. "One year, I was down with the flu—*and* I'd been up all week studying for finals. Then I got a call—they wanted me to preach the Easter service. Mama fixed me two pots of Maxwell House and I went right in and did it."

"I remember that." Wanda nods. "He was green around the gills. Could hardly walk. I didn't think he was gonna make it. Then he just *straightened right up*—went in and preached a beautiful sermon. And you'd never know he was the least bit sick."

"Tell you what I did," Bob says. "I walked out there, and I saw that all walls were slanted to one side. I knew the walls were vertical, so it must have been *me* that was on an angle. So I kind of *lined myself up* with everything and walked in. Preached the sermon and left."

"After the service, I took him straight to the hospital," Wanda says, pulling the car into the church driveway. "He had double pneumonia. He was in the hospital a week."

Later, as Rachael's father meets with a group of church elders, Wanda, Rachael, the kids and I circle around to the front entrance of the red brick church. Glancing up, I notice that the stained glass windows are a light blue with white streaks. It happens to be the exact color of the October sky above. It's a remarkable coincidence, and one I'd missed the first time around.

Within minutes, we're seated in the back pew of the packed church. Despite the full house, the church interior looks light and airy, with sunbeams streaming through the narrow windows. Perhaps it's the blue in the stained glass, but the beams of morning light playing across the plaster and wood makes the ceiling seem impossibly high. I almost expect to see clouds drift through the windows. Why didn't I remember this before?

I hear a whisper. "Lemme show ya a trick."

"What?" I turn to look at Rachael. She's thumbing through the pages of the hymnal.

"If you get bored, look at the hymn titles—"

"Yeah?"

"And add—" she leans closer "'*in my bed.*'"

"What?"

"Here." She shows me a page. "'Glorious Things of Thee Are Spoken'—*in my bed*. Neat, huh?" She turns the page. "Here's another one: 'Yield Not To Temptation'—*in my bed*. Or how about, 'I've Found A Friend'—*in my bed*. *Ha!*"

"Rachael, shhhh." Her mother gives her a stern look.

"It's okay," Rachael says to her mother, "I was showing Michael something. In case he gets bored with Daddy's sermon." Without waiting for a response, she rifles through the pages. "Okay. *Here's* a good one—'Face To Face'—*in my bed*. Whoa!"

"That's a good one," I tell her. Glancing up I see a short, genial-looking deacon addressing the congregation. "The youth fellowship party scheduled for tomorrow night in the church basement has been moved to—"

"Michael!" Rachael bumps my arm with her elbow. "Here's a good one—'Why Not Now'—*in my bed*. Hahahahaha."

"—Flossie Green will be in charge of the bake sale next Saturday, we'd like a good turnout—"

"'When I See The Blood'—*in my bed*. Youch. For*get* it!" She turns the page. "'Nearer Still Nearer'—*in my bed*. 'Never alone'—*in my bed*. *Hmmmm*. Sounds like Brenda Lacey. Ha!"

"Rachael!" Wanda hisses. "Will you be *still*!"

"Sorry." Rachael closes the book for a moment.

A minute passes and I hear a snicker and a rustle of clothing as she bumps me with her elbow. Then I look down and see her white gloved finger pointing to the hymn title 'Will There Be Any Stars.'

"—We'd like to welcome Reverend Bob Dominic and his family again this Sunday…I see Bob's lovely family is seated in the back of the church—would you mind standing so we can all see you—?"

Wanda, Rachael and the kids stand briefly, smile, and sit back down. The deacon smiles beatifically at the congregation, then opens the hymnal. "Let us stand as we sing our opening hymn, number 48— 'Fill Me Now.'

As the choir begins to sing, I glance at Rachael, convulsed with laughter, tears rolling down her cheeks. An older lady sitting in a pew across the aisle turns and smiles. She's probably seen this before.

I return the smile and, as the music swells, I see beams of light form columns along the walls. Looking up, I can almost see the clouds race by overhead. It seems I know this place.

I turn to Rache. She's calm now, singing along with the congregation. She looks up and her eyes catch mine.

"You belong with me," I hear her say. "Do you know that?"

Then she smiles and returns to the hymn.

I begin to feel a slow acceleration of motion through time. The church falls away and I ascend to the sky. Where to next?

"Mike, Dr. Mbogo here. See any more drugs down there?"

"No. How much time have I got?"

"About a millifortnight—twenty minutes."

"Okay. I might want to come up sooner than that."

No response from Leonard. Probably back to his pizza.

The church is gone now. I'm walking through the rooms of a small house, escorted by Bob Dominic. He's wearing a dark blue long-sleeved shirt and blue jeans. In my peripheral vision, I see Rachael in the kitchen with her mother.

"We've got a great guest bedroom," he says. "Unfortunately, it's also the living room. You don't mind sleeping on the couch, do you?"

"No."

"Good. The first things you tell a house guest are the location of the refrigerator and the location of the bathroom. The fridge is in the kitchen, and the bathroom's in here."

I follow him through a narrow hallway into a small, pink-tiled bathroom.

"This spring we couldn't get into the house—somebody left his key at home—but Amy saved the day. We boosted her up from the basement through the clothes chute into the bathroom, and then she went in and unlocked the door."

"Good idea."

"But before she was able to do that, she got a little excited and knocked the mirror off the wall near the bathroom door. When Stacie, our second-youngest daughter, tried to fix it, she put the hammer through the other wall. Now there's a six-inch-square hole in the wall opposite the commode."

"Uh huh."

"The other side of the wall is the closet, and I doubt if anybody's going to be in there. But if you really want to make sure nobody sees you, just pull that towel over the hole."

"Doesn't sound like that would work too well."

"It doesn't," Bob laughs. "Sometimes you have to lean forward and hold the towel in place. Makes it kind of hard—you have to decide between your privacy and how bad you have to go to the bathroom."

I peer through the jagged hole in the wall. From here I can see the television set in the next room.

"I've been promising Wanda I'd get it fixed and I probably will, but there's no place in town with any sheet rock. I think I'll tack some cardboard over it. We're moving up the road to Weslayan in a few months anyway."

"Okay." I turn to look away and suddenly it's night again. Now I'm standing in the middle of gravel road somewhere.

"Watch this—" It's Rachael pointing at something in the night sky. *Lock.*

"Leonard."

"Back so soon?"

"I think I'm back to where—uh, *when*—I was a couple of hours ago. August or September of 1966."

"Probably stuck in a memory loop. Otto does that from time to time. If you want out, just yell. I'll call Terri in to dike it and nuke it. It'll never bother you again."

Unlock.

A sizzling flash branches across the sky directly ahead of the car, illuminating a massive line of thunderheads stacked atop the horizon.

I turn to Rachael. "How'd you do that?"

"I told you...I'm good with lightning. Always have been—so ya better watch out." She pauses for effect. "Okay. There's a trick to it. All you gotta do—" she lowers her voice to a whisper, "—is *talk* to the storm and ask where the next lightning'll be. If you just *believe* it, it'll *work*. Watch this—" She turns to the darkness. "Hey storm—left to right, okay?"

The storm responds with a burst of light, illuminating the dome of the towering cumulus, then sending a jagged yellow streamer in a breaking curve.

From left to right.

Lock. "Leonard, is there a storm near Corinth during the third week of August, 1966?"

"Interesting question. Justaminute. The Weather Folder please. Missouri, 1966—"

"Leonard?"

"I was just trying to find you on the map. I'm looking at a really bad copy up here, but there seems to be something sitting on Perry, Missouri on the night of August 21st, '66. Is that about where you are now?"

"It's probably close. Can you tell me if—if there's any lightning that night?"

"Mike, summer thunderstorms usually involve lightning."

"Thanks."

"Basic science 101."

"Okay, okay."

I unlock and the sky ahead of me erupts in another blaze of light— this one pushing me completely out of the frame. When the jumble of light and color finally settles into place, it's daylight and I'm still in my car.

The car is someplace else, but this time I know exactly where. I've somehow shifted 160 miles southwest of where I was before—to the small state college town of Weslayan, Missouri. It's the place were Rache and her family moved in January of 1967.

I lock the scene. Directly ahead of the car is a sign: *KuKu Burgers. Fish Stix Fries Orange 75¢.*

As I unlock, the car door opens and Rachael climbs inside, still wearing an apron emblazoned with the caricature of a smiling box of french fries.

"We were *so* busy this afternoon. I don't know what it is about Fridays—I was counting the seconds until you showed up—here, help me get this apron off." She turns her back to me and I fumble with the knot. Finally, it comes undone and the apron falls loose.

"Whew, thanks." She folds the apron into a little square and places it in her purse. "I smell like a burger, I know. Sorry. But I didn't think you'd mind—*c'mere*—" A quick kiss.

"*Slicker!*" I wipe my mouth on my sleeve. "*Argh!* Why do you *wear* that stuff?"

"Why did you smear it all over your shirt sleeve?" she asks, smiling. "How was your drive down from college?"

"It was all right. I took off early and stopped by to see Mom and Dad. They said to tell you hi."

"Tell them 'hi' for me. They still pissed 'cause we're gettin' married?"

"They're pretty much over it. Mom's more worried the army will get me."

"The army won't get you if you have a lot of kids. That's what my friend Melissa said, anyway. Tell your mom we plan to have five of 'em—I come from a very active family." She sets the purse in the back seat and scoots up next to me. "C'mon. I wanna get out of these clothes and take a shower. I smell like a cheeseburger."

"Okay." I start the car and drive west on a cobblestone street toward town.

"Did I tell ya Dad came in? Right after I started my shift. Had his usual. Fish sandwich, fries and Coke. Gave me a tip. He was on his way from school to his job at Safeway. He's working three jobs now."

"Three jobs?"

"Yeah." She counts on her fingers. "He instructs at the college, he stocks produce at Safeway, he had that job at the radio station—lessee, I can only think of *two...*"

"Does he sleep?"

"Sometimes. Oh, I know. He applied for a job with the sheriff's department. But they haven't hired him yet. Mom says it's because he teaches sociology, so they probably think he's a socialist—and that's an *almost* communist."

"I think your mom's pulling your leg." I steer the car onto Rachael's street.

"Listen," she says, "around here, everybody's for sending more troops to Vietnam. If you don't tape the flag on your forehead, they get suspicious."

"I'll probably get sent to Vietnam one of these days—"

"Not if we have five kids." She gives me a quick kiss on the cheek. "Wait—I know what job three is. Daddy preaches at the Methodist church this Sunday. That's job three."

"He's gonna preach? What time?"

"Early services. Which means we'll have to get up early. No staying up and talking, no fooling around. We'll have to go *right to sleep.*"

Did she say *no fooling around?* I steer the Ford up to the curb in front of the two-story house. It resembles a tall cube covered in white clapboard siding. Above the porch is a window, and across from the window is a street lamp. It all looks familiar.

There are no cars in the driveway: no one is home.

Rachael leans out the car window, "looks like Mom is still at work. She works on Fridays now. The kids are probably over at Melissa's. She had to take her cat to the vet for repairs. You want to come upstairs with me while I take my shower?”

“Are you kidding?”

“You can’t get in the shower *with me*. I just want somebody to talk to.”

I switch off the ignition, open the car door and step out into deep space. Directly ahead, I see a line of thunderclouds, gigantic gray columns rising into the night sky, their tops flickering and glowing with electricity.

“All right. Let’s have some lightning straight across the top.” It’s Rachael’s voice.

The thundercloud smolders for a moment—then I hear a *crack*, like a pine board splitting—and a fiery branch of jagged light slams into the earth.

“Guess I better quit,” she says. “The cloud is pissed at me for tellin’ it what to do.”

“Rache—” I turn to look, but her world is a already a photograph rotating sideways, now gone. I’m in the middle darkness again—floating above Rachael, the thunderstorm, my life in the past.

Unexpectedly, I have the overpowering feeling that I don’t belong in this place. I pull myself up from the scene, up from the image, up toward the induction chair in Lab 14. I hear an audible click as my mind fits back into my body. Am I here?

I open my eyes inside the visor.

“Back so soon?” I hear Leonard’s voice in the headset. *“Don’t say anything until I disconnect the throat microphone—*there. Okay. You can talk.”

“What happened?” I raise the visor and blink at the overhead fluorescent lights.

“You tell me.” Leonard gives me a hand. “You came up like the space shuttle. One minute you’re down there in heavy theta talking about meteorology and the next you’re up here blinking your eyes.”

“I was in 1966, then I jumped to 1967, then back to ’66 again. It was very strange.”

“Sounds like it.”

“You know, I think she could predict lightning. Funny. I’d forgotten that—”

“Predict lightning? Who?”

“This girl I knew once. When a storm came up she could guess where the lightning was going to be, don't ask me how." I look around the lab. "Is Gail still here?"

"She caught an empty chair at Lab 10," Leonard says. "Look, if this lightning prediction stuff becomes an annoying question for you, I'll try to find out if it's even possible—though I strongly doubt it. You want a caffeine fix?"

"No, what time is it?"

"Big two-oh," Leonard says. "By the way, while you were out, I got an e-mail from Poundstone. He wants to see you in his office tomorrow morning. Nine sharp."

"Thanks." I slide off the induction chair and slip back into my shoes.

Five minutes later, I reach my room and collapse on the bed. Will I dream tonight? I hope not. All I want is sleep. Blissful, empty sleep. Inside a big cavern with stars on the ceiling. And maybe a moon on the horizon. A crescent moon. That would be nice.

Very nice—

Yet all I see is Rachael—curled up on the couch in pajamas. Pale, her hair matted, her eyes closed. Did that happen? It must have happened, yet I can't remember. *I can't remember.*

I'll have to go back.

The phone rings.

I scramble to pick up the receiver, dropping it on the floor in the process. "Yeah?"

"Dr. Mbogo here—with an answer to your weather question."

"Huh? What?"

"It's Leonard."

"Leonard? Do you ever *sleep?*"

"Only when Banks is in the chair. Anyhow, I sent a spam query out to the usenet on your lightning question."

"Really?"

"Yes. And I got an immediate reply from some insomniac at the University of North Dakota."

"Oh. Good. Great." I rub my eyes. What'd they say?"

"He said a thunderstorm discharges electricity based on internal cloud dynamics—which makes the pattern fairly irregular. Though it's possible to statistically predict the strikes, he thinks your little girl-friend was merely lucky. That, or she had a computer plugged into the University of Oklahoma's lightning profiler—which I strongly doubt."

"Me too."

"Did she own a computer?"

"Leonard, it was in *1966*."

"Yeah, that's right. The cretaceous period. Heh. See you next time."

I hang up the phone and look around.

What *time* is it?

.....◆.....

It's nine o'clock.

I'm sitting in Poundstone's office with a terrific headache. By my calculations, over this past week, I've gotten only ten hours of sleep. I wonder if it's possible to sleep while I'm in the past. Maybe find some nice August night when I was nine or ten—throw open the window and let the cool evening breeze in. Of course, I'd have to make sure Earl kept the radio turned down. Yes, that's a good idea. I'd go back to get some sleep. Nice, peaceful—

"So, Michael, have you made your decision?" Poundstone's question jolts me awake. "About making longer runs?"

"I haven't completely decided yet."

"You haven't?" He seems to be surprised. "Are you experiencing any difficulties?"

"Not really. There were a few things that happened that seem strange—once it was like being in two places at once."

"We call that pseudo-bilocation. It's a normal response—the brain is just getting used to dealing with lucid dreaming." He pauses. "Are you still able to control where you go?"

"Lately, I've been spending most of my time in the mid sixties."

"That right?" Poundstone says. "Everyone has their favorite place they return to again and again. One of our subjects even goes back to the same five-week period—over and over. With all the years to choose from, she seems to be comfortable with just that one time period. Very interesting time loop. It's given us a chance to compare the particulars of each visit and helps us learn how memory actually works."

Listening to him, I begin to feel like the dreamers are nothing more than laboratory animals, wired up to a computer. For this I paid over fourteen thousand dollars?

"Well, Michael—" Poundstone smiles.

Should I tell him about the time at the factory? About losing my arm? "Dr. Poundstone, tell me what happens if I'm in a run and get caught in a place—and can't get back."

He appears taken aback by the question. "Can't get back? Oh, *that* can never happen. We have complete control. We just bring you up, wait a few days, then go back to find the problem. It might be a neural memory loop, could be a psychological manifestation—regardless, we just go back, identify it and ablate the loop itself. Very simple procedure."

"Ablate it?"

"We erase it from your memory—using hypnosis or other methods. None of them are hazardous or painful, I assure you." He smiles. "No surgery. All National Institute of Health–approved. And as for not being able to come back—we are always able to wake our subjects up. Always. *Every single time.*"

"What's the possibility of going flatline?"

"Negligible," Poundstone says. "Infinitesimal. Miniscule. The only way you can go flatline is if there's some prior underlying process totally unrelated to the regression."

"Didn't Russell Coltrane go flatline once?"

"Ah. You've heard that story, have you? While I obviously can't discuss his case in detail, I *can* tell you that Mr. Coltrane slipped into paradoxical sleep—and that is quite another thing from going flatline."

"I—"

"Let me assure you, Michael, paradoxical sleep is perfectly normal and natural and happens every night when you sleep. We don't understand much about it, but we know it's a normal process. Just to put your mind at rest about this, paradoxical sleep is not the same thing as going flatline. Totally different."

"Maybe it's like having a dream within a dream."

Poundstone smiles broadly. "Maybe so."

"Well," I take a deep breath. "I guess I'll continue with the program."

"And that would include a long run—?" He peers at me over his glasses.

"Sure."

"Good. Now, since you're going to be spending more time per session, we'll schedule fewer sessions—" Poundstone flips through his calender. "We don't want to wear you out, so instead of a regression every evening, how about twice a week—like we did at the beginning?"

"That would be fine."

"We'll do it that way, then." He scribbles on the calendar. "And Lab 14 is light this summer, so if you decide to take a heavier schedule, let us know."

"I'll do that." I stand to leave.

"You were a history major in college, weren't you Michael?"

"Yes."

"You're a natural for this, Michael," Poundstone says, patting my shoulder. "I know you'll find the long runs interesting."

14

Gail

The phone rings.

I open my eyes and scan the room. A bright light pours in between the curtains. It must still be daylight. After the chat with Poundstone, I came back and collapsed on the bed. And now—

Another ring.

Someone is trying to call me. I take a deep breath, rub my eyes, look at my watch: 2:35 in the afternoon. Wonderful. These late-night trips are screwing up my sleep cycle. I try to think. Did I dream of anything? If I did, I can't remember.

Another ring. This time I pick up the receiver.

"Mr. Mitchell? This is security. We have a call for you from Boston, Massachusetts. Go ahead."

"Mitch?" There is only one person who calls me Mitch. "Mitch, This is Jerry! How are things? Getting any info for us, Pal?"

"I've just started out. It takes a little time..."

"Yeah, yeah. I guess. Listen, you remember that proposal we sent to Hidaki? The one we thought went south? We got a call last week and some reps came in yesterday. We gave 'em a little song and dance. Showed them our video clips—and guess what—they loved it!"

"That's great, Jer. That's really great."

"These Japanese guys are amazing. They're into old jeans, vintage rock and roll, prom dresses, big boobs. They said the Japanese kids dress up like Elvis, get their boom boxes and dance to sixties guitar music. And they absolutely love surf. Remember The Ventures?"

"I wouldn't exactly call The Ventures *surf music*, Jerry."

"Hey, what do I know? The thing is, Hidaki wants us to manage their market campaign both in the states *and* Europe."

"You can handle it. Let me know how it goes."

"I can handle it? Mike, I was five years old when this shit was popular. I can't talk to 'em about this stuff! They'd know I'm bullshittin' em. The Japanese got a sixth sense for that stuff. We need the expert. We need *you!*"

"Look. I'll be back in a month and—"

"We need you next Friday. Ten days from now. Look, this isn't some Hollywood type wanting to make a movie of *Born To Be Wild*, this is the real thing! We are talking Japanese—the masters of the universe! We need our sixties expert!"

"I'll see what I can do, Jerry."

"And look, Mitch, my friend—I heard about you and Linda. Lexington's a small town y'know, word gets around. If you don't want to talk about it that's okay. But I gotta tell ya, the guy's a real dweeb. Combs his hair *straight back*. Wears those funny little concept shades that look like welder's glasses."

"That was one of *our* concepts, Jerry. You should be happy to see it on an alpha consumer."

"We did the welding glasses thing? We got money for that?"

"It was your account, Jerry."

"You know, Janine saw him up close. She says Linda's got ten years on him, easy."

"Who?"

"The dweeb. The guy with my concept glasses."

"Jerry—*c'mon*. I'll deal with this."

"Okay. But when you come back—and I hope it's soon—Janine and I have an extra bedroom. Got its own TV."

"I'll call you first thing Monday."

I hang up the phone and stare at the floor.

He combs his hair *straight back*?

·····◆·····

I stare at the phone. Should I call her office? Confront her about this guy? Or should I call the office and merely ask for the dweeb— the guy with the welder's goggles?

Maybe I should call home to see if she's there. I pick up the phone.

"Hello." It's her voice—she's home. I feel my heart begin to race.

"This is Mike."

"Hi, Mike." It's her little-girl voice. I've heard that impersonation before. It will probably be followed by a brief period of silence—and I'm right.

"Listen, I've been trying to get in touch with you."

"So I heard. Paul said you asked him for the hotel number in Mexico City."

"Are you seeing anyone?"

"Look. Why don't we talk about this when you get home, okay?"

"Who's the guy with the welder's glasses?"

"The *what*?"

"Combs his hair straight back."

"Half the guys in the office comb their hair back. What's the point in all this?"

"Does this Van guy comb his hair back?"

"Michael, this is really...I mean, you're sounding like some high school—"

"Just tell me who Van is."

"*Van?*" She repeats. Then, there's silence on the phone. I can't even hear her breathing. Did she hang up?

"Linda?"

"Well, if you're talking about Van Edwards, you met him at the New Year's Party. He was the new hire from London. You remember."

"Was I supposed to?"

"Michael, you are such a dope. Van is a colleague and a friend. And we talk. His wife is still in England and they're having some problems. And, yes, I'm helping him with some things. I am *not* going to stand here and give you a minute-by-minute accounting of my activities."

"Listen—"

"No, *you* listen, Mike. We've had these discussions before and they never get us anywhere. I'm on a very tight schedule and I really don't have the time or inclination to be put on the witness stand. So, I'll make it easy. Yes, he's a friend. Yes, we spend time together. And yes, we went to Mexico together. And if you want a play-by-play of what happened down there, what I said, what I did, how late I stayed awake each night, and what I did the first thing every morning, then you're just out of luck because I didn't take notes. Do you have a problem with that?"

"Linda—"

"Well, *do* you?"

Silence. I find myself staring at the phone.

"Mike?"

"Okay. But we'll talk about it when I get back home."

"If I were you I'd *call* first."

"Call? Why should I call—"

"It would just be better if you did."

"Linda—"

Silence. The phone is dead.

I hang it up, then check the clock again. I should be able to at least make it for dinner with—

The phone rings again. I stare at it through another ring. It's just like Linda to hang up and then call back for another round. After four rings I pick it up.

"Look, Linda—"

"Mike, this is Gail."

"Gail? I'm sorry, I thought—"

"I called to tell you. Something happened to Keller."

I take a seat in the cafeteria next to Gail. Across from us, Otto is discussing the incident with Gene Kapp, a burly lab supervisor.

"Gene, are they sure it was a flat trace?" Otto asks the supervisor. "The amplitude can be so low sometimes—"

"I know that, Doc," the man shakes his head. "I know. But it looked flat. They couldn't even pick up slow deltas."

"How'd it happen?" I ask, leaning forward.

Kapp glances at me, but doesn't reply.

"This is Mike Mitchell," Otto says, then tells Kapp. "He's okay. You can talk."

"Well—" Kapp eyes me suspiciously, then returns to Otto, "we don't know for sure what happened. It was on Joel Zanuk's shift and he's new. The trace record shows the amplitude first dropped in the high temporal leads—" He looks at Gail briefly, then returns to Otto. "—*including* the t-4, and then, *nothing*. The signals just disappeared. All we got was static. Now, like I said, Zanuk is new on the job, but Zey's techs attached the leads, and medical was monitoring vitals. And they've been doing this for as long as—well, as long as I've been here."

"Did Zanuk apply electroshock?" Otto asks.

"Oh, sure. But the trace showed his signal had been gone for more than two minutes."

"So he was flat for two minutes," Otto narrows his eyes. "Why did Zanuk wait so long?"

"Nobody knows. Either the alarms weren't working or Zanuk just went to sleep. It's a long shift. They're looking into it."

And now Keller's *back*? And alert?"

"Well, I'll tell you what it looks like." Kapp looks around the table, worry etched in the lines on his face. "Keller's awake but just kind of *out of it*. I hear that Poundstone's really bouncing off the walls about this one."

"Hm. I'd imagine so." Otto's eyes narrow. I can almost see the wheels turning behind his eyes. "Any evidence of demyelination?"

"Don't know." Kapp says. "I think they have a CT scheduled."

"Waste of time," Otto says. "Damage won't show on the CT for up to 72 hours. If it was me, I'd send him straight to the MRI." A pause. "Do they want me to look at him?"

"They haven't said anything yet, Doc." Kapp shakes his head. "But I thought you should know about it—in case they ask."

"Sure," Otto looks at Gail and me. "Let's keep this quiet until we know a little more, okay?"

I nod. "Wonder what he'll remember of his experience."

"Most likely, nothing," Otto shrugs. "He'll be lucky if he remembers how he got here."

Gail gets up from her chair. "Mike, let's go for a walk."

After a long, silent stroll through the empty corridors, Gail and I near the door marked Lab 14. As we reach it, Gail looks at her watch. "I really hate that about Keller. He was such a nice old guy."

"Was? Didn't Kapp say he was alert?"

"Kapp said he was *awake*. Awake is not the same as alert." Gail pauses, staring at the floor. "If Keller really went flatline for two minutes—well, that sounds pretty significant. I can't believe he brought back everything that he left with."

"Think they'll stop the long runs? I have one coming up."

"Are you kidding? They stop the long runs, and the grant money will vanish quicker than Keller's t-4 wave." She shakes her head. "I really don't want to talk about it."

"Maybe he fork-bombed something."

"Fork-bombed?" She gives me a hard glance. "*Fork*-bombed? God, you sound just like Leonard."

"Well, maybe that's what happened. It was a fork-bomb." I suddenly realize I have no idea what I'm talking about.

"Yeah, that's it, I'm sure," Gail says sourly. "Keller's software just got a little mixed up. All the docs have to do is just *reinstall his programs,* reboot and he'll be fine. Like we're all plug and play or something."

"Well, you have a medical background. You think there's some kind of serious risk here?"

She pauses, as if searching for the right words. "Medically, yes. There's a risk. Anytime you put somebody to sleep for two or three days, you have a risk. Your electrolytes could get out of whack, for example. You could throw a clot."

"A clot?"

"Yeah. That's why they put the little pressure booties on your feet—to keep the blood circulating."

"I didn't know that...say, didn't you say this was *safe?*"

"Maybe I was wrong," she says. "None of the staff will even get in the chair—except Poundstone. They leave the dangerous stuff to people like us. Poundstone gets his grant money and we take the risks. I assure you they have no idea why Keller went flatline. And even if they do find out, they'll keep quiet about it."

"Maybe he had a heart attack," I suggest. "Something got him excited down there and he—"

She stops and puts her hand on my chest. "Hey, Mike. You're talking to a nurse, remember? They had him on a heart monitor and an IV. If he had a coronary down there the EKG would have picked it up—and we would have heard about it."

"Yes, but—"

"Listen, Michael," she looks at me. "They don't know *what* happened to Keller. Flatlines aren't supposed to happen but it did happen. And it's probably not the first."

"Do you think we should quit this stuff? Is it really that dangerous?"

"Maybe." A pause. "I really don't know what's worse—knowing all the medical risks with all this, or knowing that I'm too hooked on my past to care about the danger."

"Kind of like cigarettes, huh?"

"Worse," she says. "I was able to quit cigarettes. In the chair I always go back to the same place. It's the only place worth going to." We walk in silence for a minute, both of us staring at the floor. I watch my Rockports keep pace with her bare feet.

"Michael, " she says after a moment, holding her notebook to her chest, "maybe I *should* leave this place."

"Afraid of flatlining?"

"No. It's something else. I'm starting to resent having to come back." She takes a deep breath, then releases it slowly. "Down there—in my dream—I see all those beautiful summer days, see that teenage girl in the mirror, and catch myself counting the seconds that I'll have left before the film ends, the point where I have to come back. Back to all these problems." She takes a deep breath and stops. "No. *No.* That's not right. The truth is, I really miss home, miss my teenagers, my big dumb cat. I even miss my twelve-hour workdays. And Connecticut's pretty in the fall." She forces a smile and resumes walking. "You ought to see it sometime."

"I'd like to."

"How about you? Don't you miss your kids, your work?"

"Oh, sure. Let's see—" I count on my fingers. "I miss my kids—but one's in college and the other recently got married again—so I haven't seen much of them lately...I miss my job, but I hate my job as much as I hate Boston traffic, so that doesn't count either. I miss my wife, but I don't miss all the arguments we've been having lately—so *that* doesn't count."

We stop across from the lab entrance and look out the window at the city's northwest skyline. For a moment, we silently watch soft cumulus clouds drift gently over the expanse of mesquite and thoroughfares. In the distance, there is the brief glint of an airliner descending toward the horizon.

"Do you like the places you go?" Gail asks.

"Some of them, but not all," I tell her. "I sometimes wind up in places I'd rather not be."

"Do like I do." She turns to face me. "Find a place you like and stick with it."

"Guess that makes sense."

"You know what Coltrane told me once?" She folds her arms. "He said you don't find your past, *it finds you.*"

"Stalked by your past," I nod. "Kidnapped and held for ransom by your senior prom."

"Michael—" she shakes her head. "I was being serious."

"It could happen to anyone," I tell her in my best 1950s radio voice. "It could happen to *you*."

She brightens. "You know, that's *funny*. Have you always been funny?"

"Up until I got married." It occurs to me that I'm telling her an absolute truth. And there's something else: I notice she's wearing lipstick—and perfume. Chanel? Yes, definitely Chanel.

"You know," I shake my head. "This really feels strange. I'm like a schoolboy walking his girl to class—"

"Yeah," she nods. "It's a little like that, isn't it?"

"I wanted to say I have a really good time when I'm with you—especially that night on the roof."

"There's no roof in Boston?" She smiles.

"Not like the one here. I wondered—if you're not busy tonight, would you want to do it again? Say, around midnight? That is, if you're not down there in your past."

"No," she smiles. "I'll be here tonight."

Two-thirty a.m. Gail and I are lying on her quilt, on our backs, watching the sky from twenty stories up. Somewhere east of the city, for some unknown reason, there were fireworks and now the diaphanous salmon-colored clouds are drifting overhead. Was it a celebration? Maybe someone invaded—perhaps Mexico decided that San Antonio should be taken back. Whatever the reason, the clouds are spectacular—slowly folding and reforming as they float no more than fifty feet above our heads.

Gail kicks her shoes almost to the edge of the pool. The maintenance crew left it lighted tonight, a clear blue-green dot to guide the various police helicopters in their rounds above the city. For all I know, we may be lying sixteen feet from the highest swimming pool in town.

"Do you remember where you went the last time?" she asks.

"I think I was in a church. And then I was driving somewhere. And after that, I was sick with flu—I don't remember much. It's been a few days." I turn to her. "Real exciting, huh?"

"Your memory will get better. All it takes is practice—unless you go flatline like Keller."

"Hey," I tell her, "you said you didn't want to talk about the medical stuff."

She laughs. "You're right. No flatline. Let's start over. Ask me something noncontroversial."

"Okay. How's your recall for the past?" I ask her. "Is it pretty good?"

"Mike, it's *great*. No hazy stuff, no drop-outs." She stretches and smiles. "As Leonard might say, it's as good as digital."

"Tell me about it."

"Ahhh, I don't think I'd better. You'd get the wrong impression of me."

"C'mon."

"You know the rules. Dreamers shouldn't discuss their trips with each other. Especially within a few hours of a regression. It might corrupt the data."

"*C'mon.*"

She appraises me for a moment, then sits up and crosses her legs. "Okay. I'll tell you. But you have to promise not to tell anyone. And don't use it in any of your damn ads!"

"Promise."

"Okay." She takes a deep breath. "It was the summer before I started high school. We lived in this community east of Glen Falls, New York. Not far from the Vermont border. It was a little cluster of five houses. Used to be a rail stop and it was about fifteen minutes from the nearest big town. All the other families were old. I mean, like in their sixties and seventies old. No kids. I was it. The only kid in town. My parents worked in Troy, so they would be gone all day from dawn to dusk."

"Sounds kind of boring."

"It was horrible. Here I was, bored, anxious, no car, too young to work and nothing to do that summer but watch soaps and game shows. Then the most amazing thing happened.

"One morning I heard this loud sound coming from next door. So I got up, looked out my upstairs window and saw this *boy*. He was mowing the lawn. He had long blond hair and he was about a head taller than me. When I first saw him he had his shirt off and his skin was nice and tan." She laughs. "Tan was a big thing with me then. As long as they had a tan I'd look at 'em."

"So you introduced yourself?"

"It took about a minute. Splashed around in the bath, brushed my hair, put on a dress. The works. He probably thought I was an idiot—but it was perfect. He had big blue eyes and a real nice smile. He was from Ferndale, Michigan and was spending the summer with his grandparents. And this was his third day there. I was asking myself—'Gail Lynn, how could you have missed this?' I couldn't believe it."

"What happened?"

"For one thing, he didn't know anything about the country. First I showed him all the channels we got on television—I think there were two. That took about a minute. Then, I showed him the barn. Then the tractor. Then the pond. Then, I showed him *me*." She smiles, wiggling her toes in the grass.

"After about a week, we were playing this game called 'too hot.' We'd go to my room and then I'd immediately complain how hot it was and I'd take off my shirt. Then, he'd take off his shirt. And it was *still* too hot. So I'd shuck off my shorts and he'd take off his jeans and then we'd be on the bed in just our underwear." She chuckles. "Of course, that only made things worse. Before long, we were lying there naked, kissing and making out like crazy. It was the first—the first for everything. And it all happened for me that summer."

"Everything?"

"*Everything,*" she nods slowly. "The works. We'd wait until my folks left, and then he'd come over. I'd fix him Wheaties and toast and orange juice. Then I'd take his hand and we'd go upstairs. We'd get out of our clothes and fool around in bed until the sun heated the room up—remember, there was no air conditioning. Then we'd go down to the pond and cool off. Or spray each other with the water hose. It was idyllic. Perfect."

"Did your folks ever suspect?"

She laughs. "I don't think so. My mom saw the big dresser mirror tilted down toward the bed once, but never said anything. Anyway, I always made the bed before they got home. It probably never occurred to her there was anything *intense* going on."

"I doubt if I'd catch something like that, myself."

"Yeah, adults see the world differently. Before that summer, I'd always been a bratty kid. Now, when my folks came home in the evening the grass would be mowed. Garden weeded. Fried chicken on the table. Nice salad. Pitcher of iced tea. Instead of being a morose teenager, I'd become kind of perfect little homemaker. Just so *bright and cheerful*. I'd get the giggles all the time over nothing at all."

"And they never figured it out, huh?"

"Well, of course, it scared my folks to death. They thought I was on drugs, you know, smoking nutmeg or something. My mom wanted to send me to some shrink at the college, but my dad said no. He was afraid I'd revert back to my little punk self again. So they just kept quiet and enjoyed the new improved Gail. Of course, I think the grass finally died from getting mowed everyday."

"What did his grandparents have to say about all this?"

"That was the most amazing thing. They didn't seem to mind. They sort of ignored the whole thing, and they never told my folks. Nobody in town ever did. I guess they were waiting for me to get knocked up. The funny thing is, I didn't really care. It was so perfect. I pretended I was a little frontier farm wife—we'd get naked and make out, then I'd go down and wash the dishes or weed the garden or fix dinner for him. And we'd sit out on the front porch swing and watch the train go by. It was like growing from little kid to adult in two months. It was really a stupid, delirious, erotic time for me."

"And when you go back—that's where you go?"

"That's where I go. To that day I first saw him. Mowing the lawn. I lock the scene and study it—the lace curtains blowing in the wind, the bright green grass, the yellow lawn mower, summer flowers in the garden, and him in these new, incredibly sexy Sears Roebuck overalls. Then I jump to about a week after that. Straight to the *romance*."

"Does Leonard know?"

"Leonard? Nah. He doesn't care what I do down there. He's more interested in the computer. We argue a lot, but Leonard's my big buddy. Lets me go off and play."

"What about Dr. Zey?"

"I have to be careful when Zey's on the board. He knows what to look for. I mean, with some things it's kind of hard to hide. Your body gives you away. For example, when you dream you're raising your arm, the muscles tense ever so slightly. That's why they have the helmet on you—to check what's going on. If the muscles in your, uh, lower back are showing, um, *coordinated movement*, it means you're not only watching, but *doing* something down there."

"I miss feeling things when I'm back there. I see and hear—but nothing else."

"Don't let them kid you. Sometimes you can feel, too. It happens."

She stretches and closes her eyes. "Maybe it's because when I'm back there I can actually see myself with my boyfriend in my dresser mirror, it—um—makes it easier to get into. Pretty soon, I can feel the bed sheets against my back, and how cool they are—and I can feel my hands on him—feel his skin. After awhile, it's like I'm there. Taking my own place. You ever done anything like that?"

"You mean, on my trips to the past?"

"No, in the real world." She turns to face me, her bare legs no more than a few inches from mine, the hem of her dress resting gently against her skin. "You ever do it in a farmhouse with the window open—and the breeze blowing the curtains?"

"No, but in my senior year at college I took my girlfriend to a motel in Kansas City."

"How very romantic," she says drily. "Did you bring a pocketful of quarters for the vibrating bed?"

"Hey, it *was* romantic. We brought along some grapes—rye bread with real butter. Okay. Maybe it was margarine. But we had real Swiss cheese and wine with two glasses."

"That doesn't sound too bad," she nods. "I'll give you a B plus."

"My girlfriend and I would go around the motel and look at the windows—to see which ones were steamed up. We figured *something* was going on."

"That's pretty funny. When I first met you I thought you'd be real businesslike. You know—wear a watch to bed or something."

I move closer and she moves her legs slightly. "I'll take my watch off."

"No," she says, brushing her lips against mine. "Let me do it."

In the distance, I hear a helicopter. Probably the police, searching the rooftops for anything unusual. Couples making out, for example.

"What if someone comes up here?"

"Nobody will," she says, taking my hand. "It's just us."

15

Entrainment

The voice is familiar.

"It's been a long time since I've had a philosophy course, but if you need a paper by next Friday, I'll do what I can. Who did you say the philosophers are?"

"Hume, Kant and somebody else."

"Schopenhauer."

I'm sitting at a kitchen table. The room is dark except for the pale yellow flicker from a small incandescent wall lamp. In the corner, near the refrigerator is a stuffed pink bunny and a variety of toy soldiers. Smoke from a cigarette wafts up and forms a gray haze near the ceiling.

Bob Dominic gives the pack a quick shake and three white filtertips appear. "Cigarette?"

"I quit. Too expensive."

"Yeah. It's up to a quarter a pack. I remember when it was only fifteen cents. How about another cup of coffee?"

As he pours hot water into the cup, I notice a hairline crack that curves around the rim, then disappears into the ceramic surface half-way to the base.

"I'd write the paper for you and you could pay me, but there's two problems. You're a college student, short on cash, and I'm not a writer. So I guess you'll have to knuckle down and do it."

"I like college, but I never thought I'd have to write so many reports." I glance at the coffee. There is a light brown foam on the surface.

"College is a lot of fun, but it's like marriage. There's a humiliative effect."

"Don't you mean cumulative effect?"

"No, humiliative. It gets more humiliating as it goes along." He takes a drag from the cigarette, then stubs it in the ashtray. "You know, if you need a philosophy topic for your paper, you could write about *mentalism*."

"What's that?"

"Mentalism was the theory that everything is in the mind. For example, because everything is up *here*, I can't really be sure you're sitting there, looking like you're ready to fall asleep. What if it's only my imagination?"

It occurs to me this is a remarkable event. An image of someone I once knew is casting doubt about *my* existence. It's dark outside and very late, so I'm probably staying overnight. I see a blanket and a pillow on the couch. Probably where I slept when I visited them.

"But I *know* you have to be here," Bob Dominic continues, "I see you acting rationally: You're not drinking this bad coffee."

"The coffee's fine," I tell him. "Really it is."

"Rachael said you don't drink coffee, so I know you're just trying to be nice. Listen. We've got Vess Cola. Had it a week. Bradley left the cap off and the fizz is all gone, but it's still probably all right."

"Tell me more about this mentalism stuff."

"To tell the truth, it's been years since I studied it, but it's the old problem—how do you know what's real? I mean, I can only suppose you're real. You avoid my bad coffee, you're going with my daughter— at least I know she's got *somebody's* class ring and it has your name on it—so I guess you're real." He pauses to tap another Salem from the pack onto the table.

I look around at the yellowed wallpaper in the small rectangular kitchen, blue wallpaper in the living room. A green sofa with blankets and a pillow next to a dark, rectangular hi-fidelity set. I concentrate on the wood laminate cabinet, hovering like a dark icon at the edge of my peripheral vision. It's been years since I've seen one of these things.

Now someone is standing in the doorway. A young girl wearing a long white tee-shirt that barely reaches her knees. Her dark hair is a forest of pink rollers. A thought surfaces unexpectedly: There is rarely a time when Rachael is without her rollers.

"That light is keeping me awake. Are you two gonna talk all night?"

"We were planning on it," Bob says. "Care to join us?"

"No."

"Want some coffee?"

"No. I won't be able to sleep."

"You can't sleep anyway," Bob says. "Might as well have a coffee with us."

I see her now, a lone image in a darkened kitchen—inside my own mind.

"If you're going to talk," she says, "at least turn out the light. I'm going back to bed—and don't try to get me up in the morning, 'cause I'm sleeping *late*."

"One thing you have to know about Rachael," Bob says. "She won't talk philosophy. She's practical, like her mother."

He taps an ash from his cigarette. I watch this movie, dark and sepia-toned like an old print. I know why people like sepia so well. It's the color of memory.

The ash freezes in mid-air, a gravity-instant in time. With a blink, the world changes to become dark purple with the light of early morning. Rachael wakes up, rubs her eyes, gives me a quick kiss. The rollers are gone.

Her face is near mine, her head on my shoulder. Her lips are shiny with—what was it she used? Didn't I call it Slicker? I have a strange thought: In my past life, the life years ago, I tasted those lips and then forgot them. Lying in bed with her now, I wonder how I could have ever forgotten this.

"Back in a minute," she whispers.

I watch her climb out of bed. She pads across the hardwood floor in her bare feet and steps through the bedroom door into the hallway. More steps, and now I hear the bathroom door close.

She's wearing the blue-and-black striped nightshirt I bought for her in Kansas City. Suddenly the images pour in: The store was Maillairds at Metcalf South Plaza. It cost thirteen dollars and fifty cents. Another image, as crisp and clear as last week: I'm handing a young clerk a twenty-dollar bill. He returns with the change and the shopping bag. I push the receipt into my jeans pocket, then leave the store. I walk to the parking lot on a cold, brisk early December day. Was this memory waiting for me here?

Now, I'm staring at the ceiling in this place, watching the images drift through my mind: the drive back from Kansas City, walking into the front door and hearing Mrs. Dominic tell me that Rachael is home from the hospital—

The hospital?

The sound of running water—she's brushing her teeth. Outside the window, a truck scratches by. She comes back to bed and, in a quick motion, slips in next to me between the sheet and blankets.

"Now. Gimme another kiss—and take more time with it." I brush her lips with mine, feel their softness. A quick kiss on the bow of her upper lip, followed by a lingering graze to the corner of her mouth. Then, back to touch the full, sweet curve of her lower lip. She tilts her head slightly and our lips meet again at the middle, forming a perfect X. She retreats for an instant, then returns for a quick bite at my lower lip followed by a brush back and forth. She is like an artist putting the finishing touches on a painting. Outside, the indigo light of morning is washed with lighter blue.

How could I have forgotten *any* of this?

"Mmm, now *that's*—" she stops mid-sentence, then moves in for another grazing pass. I feel her tongue flick my lower lip, as her bare foot curls behind my ankle "—a *kiss.*"

A blink in time and suddenly I'm in darkness again.

A shadow dances across the floor. There is movement in the hall. I sit up. The door to the hall is open only a crack.

Outside, the wind picks up, spattering the window with rain.

The door opens, and someone enters the room.

As I sit up, the scene stops, then fades to black.

In this darkness between worlds, I hear a voice:

Always remember.

But I can't. With no anchors to hold them, the scenes drift and fade and finally become like old photographs—kitchens and bridges and trains and a bed and someone in a nightshirt. Someone I once knew. Pictures at the bottom of the well. In a moment they are gone.

I open my eyes to an unfamiliar room. Here the curtains are drawn across the window; only a thin streak of light shows through. And the sheets smell different. I'm in Gail's room. In *her* bed.

She turns to me, drawing me near. In the half-light, I see my wedding ring is still intact. Still there.

"Mike-mmmm." She says something to me in sleep. When I fail to answer, she rolls to her right side. Her breathing becomes rhythmic again. Perhaps she's having a dream of the roof. I look for a clock and find it, a little square travel model resting near the window sill. Good grief: It's 1:00 p.m.

But it's the weekend.

Gail shifts slightly, touching my leg with the soles of her feet. She's waking up. I wonder what Linda is doing now.

·····◆·····

Tuesday. 9:45 a.m.

I'm sitting in the induction chair in my green surgical scrubs, watching Leonard go through the final checks on the equipment. A few minutes ago, Zey and one of the nurses came in to position the theta detectors on my scalp just behind my hairline and attach EKG leads on my chest.

"What about the cuff?" I ask the nurse, a tall, pretty woman with a round face.

"Oh, on these extended sessions we usually wait to attach the blood pressure and oxygen probes after you induce...unless you want them on now." She smiles. "You didn't drink anything this morning after you got up, did you?"

"Uh, nope..."

"If you did, we can put a catheter on you.

"That's fine. I really don't think I'll need it."

"You're going to be out six hours—" she injects a syringe into a small bottle and extracts the clear liquid, "—and there's no need to be uncomfortable. I'm going to give you a little shot of muscle relaxant. Would you like it in the arm or the hip?"

"Arm."

"I usually like mine in the hip," she says, rubbing my left arm with an alcohol swab. "It doesn't sting quite so much. Okay. Say 'ouch, Terri, that hurts.'"

She injects the clear liquid into my arm, then retracts the needle, leaving a dull, throbbing ache behind. "If that injection site still bothers you when it's time to go under, tell me. We'll give you something for it."

"I'll let you know." I rub my arm, trying to knead away the pain.

"Of course, we don't give tranqs on these extended runs—" she pauses to drop the used needle into a red plastic box, "—the vocal cords relax so much they don't work properly. Then nobody knows what you guys are trying to tell us from down there."

"Actually, it's a translator problem," Leonard says. "Normally, the vox translator circuit can figure out what you're trying to say. But if the input is less than optimal, the vox goes to a lookup table for the closest translation. When there's nothing in the lookup table, the circuit starts Markov Chaining—reads back what the dreamer said before, plugs in the grammer rules and vocab, and just starts *riffing*. Before you know it, we're not talking to the dreamer, we're talking to our robot. Actually, a *conversation-bot*. We had a schoolteacher in here once that got hosed on too much liquid sleep and started broadcasting from hyperspace. Real collision in the hash tables. The translator circuit decided she was reading us out in Southern Puget Salish."

"*Was* she?" the nurse asks.

"Well, Terri," Leonard says, "only three people in the world speak Southern Puget Salish, and they're men. So judge for yourself. Personally, I'd say the computer was faking it."

"I've never heard Salish. I'll have to listen to that tape sometime." The nurse places the helmet on my head. "Be careful you don't move around too much, we don't want you to pull these little t-7 leads loose."

"The t-7's don't work anyway," Leonard says. "Just another Defense Department–inspired gonkulator. Feeping creaturitis."

"Oh, Leonard—" the nurse pulls the visor down over my eyes. "Okay, Mike, tell me if you see two little green lights."

"Yes."

"Good. Close your eyes and look up. Look down. Look left. Look right."

"Think of your aunt Nancy naked," Leonard says through my headset. "Thank you. Nice pupillary response."

"Isn't he terrible?" I hear the nurse's voice.

"Terri, that phrase works with *everybody*," Leonard says. "Except women of course...Mike, give me a count on mind radio."

I think the numbers ten to one and hear the voxbox respond.

"Yeah, input is optimal. You're okay," Leonard says. "Machine induction this time?"

Sure.

"Arm still hurt?" Leonard asks.

Nope.

"Let's do it then."

The chirping sounds begin—then the choir of angels.

"Entrainment."

I hear the chime, a deep resonating pulse of sound that unframes my mind from my body, letting me drop through the surface of the chair and submerge in the ocean of stars.

There below me is my life. And I have six hours to explore it. Where will I go? To some soft, hazy time in childhood. No responsibilities, no problems. I could use that now.

I head for the point of light furthest back. The furthest stop on my highway.

As the light begins to form around me, I feel motion toward a cloudy, gray afternoon. Rachael is hugging her family—now, she's in the car with me and the white lines of the highway rush toward us. It's a Sunday afternoon and we're returning her to her grandmother's home in Corinth. From there, I'll travel on to college in Kirksville. These were always boring drives for me. Why did I land here now? Was it random? Probably.

Passing north through Weslayan, the sky darkens noticeably and the drizzle turns into a steady rain. Up ahead, ragged gray clouds scrape east across the horizon. Rachael points them out, telling me they look like her mother's dishrags. "You have to understand she never throws towels away. When they get too ragged, she uses them as a dishrag. By then, they're really nothing but pieces. That's what the sky looks like right now. Dishrags."

I listen to her, think to myself—what would she say if I told her I'm from the future? A ridiculous thought—she's nothing but an image in my mind. Still, the question persists. Would her image disappear? Would I instantly go somewhere else—to some other part of my past? Or would my mind create some kind of fake response that never happened? I decide it will have to remain a mystery. Still, the situation is not unlike being with a girl you've liked for years but were afraid to tell her for fear she would leave. You don't know what to say, so you say nothing.

A fragile relationship I have with myself—fearful of making contact with my own memories. The memory that can be real is not the true memory. *The dream that is real is not the true dream.* Who said that? Leonard, probably.

Midway to Corinth, the rain stops and the clouds change from ragged gray to huge flat boards pulled along by the rushing river of wind.

"Look," Rachael says. "Cold weather clouds—they're dark on the bottom and bright on top."

A gust of wind hits the car. Above us, the sky is fragmented. As we pass through the central Missouri town of Columbia, we see a stoplight swinging in the wind.

The pinging in the engine increases and my eyes flash to the gauges—scanning from idiot light to idiot light. No needle gauges back then. Back now.

The pinging stops. Absently, I lock and scan the passing cars. Here, a red and white 1957 Ford, there a blue 1963 Chevy Malibu.

As we drive, I listen to Rachael and look down the highway, scan the texture of the road surface, each crack that spreads and turns black at the edges—count each white dash as it disappears beneath us, scan the yellow lines as they race alongside and then vanish.

I look around at the trees along the hillsides, soft brushes in the cold wind. The landscape is muted and fuzzy, like a rough brown blanket with dark fringes. By now, it's twilight and the clouds are pearl-like, with lavender edges. Directly above, a slab of cloud stretches from east to west, a slowly moving river of dark ice.

Night falls, and I turn on the headlights. As we pass through the darkness, I see the incandescent lights of the isolated farmhouses. The headlights illuminate a tree near the highway. I lock/scan it, counting the branches down to each filament. I'm amazed how precise the memory is—how can all this information be stored? Yet it must be.

I unlock and the tree blurs past.

I hear a rattle—probably something serious—a ball joint maybe. Probably will fail soon. No. It must have failed thirty or so years ago. I keep forgetting that none of what I see exists anymore.

"Michael, your tire jack is rattling," Rachael says to me. "If you want it to stop, open the trunk and lay it the other way. One direction, it'll rattle at 70 miles an hour, the other, it'll rattle at 60."

"Why is that?"

"I don't know," she says. "But that's what it does."

I slow the car from 70 to 65, and the rattling stops.

We pass near a town. For a brief instant, the reflections of the buildings appear as thick columns of light supporting the roof of the sky. I blink my eyes; the beams vanish and a ridge that was the ceiling is replaced by stars and a wonderful gauzy blanket of cloud.

Rachael turns up the radio and a song fills the car, "Happenings Ten Years Time Ago," by the Yardbirds. No need to call Leonard, I know where I am. I think of the first time I heard that song—I was with Rachael. I wonder if this was that night. Probably.

Night. On each side I see the dimly lighted villages with their 25 miles per hour speed limits, MFA OIL signs and cops. Little spots of neon in the darkness. Finally, I pull into Corinth, my home town.

After dropping Rachael off at her grandmother's house, I drive to see my folks, amazed at how much time I've been able to spend here. Hours, it seems. I step through the front door to greet my mother and father. In the introductory sessions, Poundstone had suggested against visiting one's parents while in the past. The emotions involved were often simply too strong and usually resulted in a premature wakeup. Now, with them at this island in my past, I feel those emotions, as well as one that was unexpected: guilt. Seeing my father's lined face I now understand how hard he worked to put me through school, how much he and my mother cared for me, their remaining son.

An hour later, I'm climbing into the car for the drive to college.

"Come by when you can stay longer, Son," my father says. I hear myself promise to spend the summer working in Corinth.

If only I had.

I twist the key and hear a gentle, rhythmic roar. I see a splash, then four small figures drop to the bottom of the lake—drowned. No. They're still alive, fighting their way back to the surface, around the churning undersea landscape of shirts and underwear.

They're at the side of the tub—now, back into the water. But this time the surface is covered with foam. Who knows what's below the surface? Jeans. Work clothes. Towels.

"Don't lose your toys in there," my mother says. "You don't want them to go through the wringer." She pauses to wipe the steam from her glasses, brushes the hair from her face, then with a determined look starts a line of white sheet through the wringer.

"I'll be careful, Mom."

On the side of the ivory-colored machine I see a nameplate: Maytag—and beneath it, a plunger-style gadget with a red plastic handle. What's it for? Who knows, but it's *neat*. The world could use more things like this. More plungers and casters and machines that get your hands wet. Of course, I would think that now. I'm a kid.

Looking around, I can almost smell the dampness of the basement, feel the cool wet cement floor beneath my bare feet. And I'm sure they are bare—there was never a summer back then that I didn't go barefoot.

I look up through the basement window to see the sheets on the line, full in the stiff summer breeze—sheets, pillow cases, dresses, workclothes, blue jeans, shirts. Perfect. Not a bad place to come to, I'll have to remember this.

As my mother pulls the sheet through to the basket, I return my toys to the rinse tub, watch them sink to the bottom again. Then I hear something.

"Michael—"

I recognize the voice.

Lock. I scan the scene. My mother is still here, the washing machine, the basement, the time is still here. Yet something is pulling me away from this place—pulling me back into the river.

"I think it was the potato salad."

It's Rachael.

She's lying on the couch, her head hanging over a half-filled pan of something.

Vomit.

She's wearing a white cotton pajama top with little hearts printed across the front. Beneath the hem I see a strip of red fabric: gym shorts.

I remember this evil night. The Dominics still lived in Cherokee, and Bob and Wanda were with the kids at the Weslayan Drive-In, twenty minutes away.

"Rache, I'm gonna call the doctor."

"This town doesn't have a doctor. I'll just have to get over it. I'll—" she pauses to throw up into the pan. I wipe her mouth with a damp face cloth. "Jeeeez. I gotta get some sleep. I wanna die."

There is no sensation of touch, but somehow the room looks *cold*. I hear my own mind racing—where are Bob and Wanda?

"Look. In the medicine cabinet is another bottle of mom's morning sickness pills. Get 'em, okay?"

"Sure."

The picture moves from the couch to the hall and into the rectangular tile-covered bathroom. I'm looking in the medicine cabinet. Perhaps I'm nervous, but the scene is wavy, gray at the top. Like a television picture that needs adjusting. I watch as I rummage through the cabinet.

Should I lock the scene? After all, this happened more than thirty years ago.

No. Rache is sick. I watch my hands fumble over squeezed tubes of Crest toothpaste, baby aspirin, a few loose bars of Zest, looking for pills. Or something.

"Rachael, they aren't here."

"Sure they are. Just a minute." I turn to see her wobble into the bathroom, her face absolutely white. "I'll find 'em—ah. Here they are."

The scene begins to ripple, then become hazy. Am I leaving already? I lock the scene.

"Leonard?"

"Yeah. How's it going down there?"

"Were you trying to bring me back?"

"No. If I wanted you back, you'd be back. What's going on?"

"Nothing. I'll talk to you later."

As I unlock, the room whirls into chaos. From the lower border of my vision, I see a viscous greenish stream flow toward the commode.

Was I sick that night too?

"Rache—?" She's gone.

I flush the commode, throw some water on my face and weave back into the living room. She's pale, curled up in a fetal position, her eyes closed. Out like a light. At least she's sleeping.

Another trip to the bathroom.

This is not fun. Perhaps I can leave, go back to the basement with my mother washing clothes—or to that nifty street dance where I first heard live rock and roll. Maybe sit with my folks on the back porch. Maybe a nice family dinner—

No.

"Mike, you okay down there? Your blood pressure's sliding. What's going on?"

"I'm okay. I'm trying to bridge out of here. I'll get back in a minute—"

Lock. I see nothing but a blurred commode. More slosh coming from my gut. What the hell is going on? I think back to the breakfast I consumed before getting in the chair. What was it? Some kind of Mexican breakfast—God, what if it was contaminated too? If I get sick up there, it's sayonara. I'll probably puke into the helmet.

Lock. Unlock. Doesn't matter. I'm getting sick watching all this. *Where is Rache?*

The scene jumps. I'm in the living room sitting in a chair oppo-site her. She hasn't moved, and I apparently haven't thrown up within the last few minutes. Perhaps the pills worked. I try to remember: Did I take them too?

Watching this, it occurs to me things are getting dim—as though a short-circuit is forming between the me that is here and the me that is back there. I see a brown bottle on the floor near the couch. Pick-ing it up, I see the cap is gone and the bottle is empty. As the light dims, I turn the bottle in my hand until the label comes into view. Robt.A.Dominic. *Seconal 100 mg. Take one at bedtime.*

I lock the scene. Dim, losing light. Rache is in a fetal position on the couch. Not moving. Did she take them so she'd sleep?

Mike. Leonard here. Your heart rate is getting nontrivial. If it goes past a hundred, I'll have to reel you in.

Wait! No! I have to call, have to get those out of her—

I feel the electricity pour into me, lifting me up like a ferris wheel. Up and back, away from Rachael.

No!

I try to lock the scene. Call the operator. Call the operator and have her call the ambulance...102 Main, Cherokee...

Then the wheel brings me up. To somewhere else.

And now I'm in a lounge chair, sitting by a pool. Overhead is a crisp blue sky with patches of blue and gold clouds. Nearby, a road crew rips apart a city street.

I know where I am—summer, 1974.

Linda is still in our room, splayed out under a thin sheet, one bare leg uncovered, toes pointing to an empty wine bottle. Taylor's New York. On her left hand is the diamond I gave her last night.

A jet thunders overhead. We're near the airport. Am I able to search my memory here? I see an image of the night before—in our car parked on a hill overlooking the runway, watching the jets come in.

I look down at my notebook, and see it—Lightning Wife—an old poem I'd written in the army. More images: Linda reading it, then walking to the sink to brush her teeth. I'm surprised how slim and perfect her legs are.

She turns on the faucet and squeezes Crest onto the brush. "It's a very good poem, Mike—you should have been an English major."

"I'll stick with history."

"Let me show it around the department. Everyone would love it—especially Henry. You'd probably get an A." She looks in the mirror, scrubs her teeth furiously for a few seconds, turns to me, foam in her mouth. "Henry is very big on death, you know."

I've got to get *back*.

I *must*.

The room—the bed, the floor, the walls, Linda with the foam on her mouth, everything—stretches like plastic film, collapses into a point. For a brief instant, I'm at the top of the wheel, and now it begins to move.

Back.

And down—right into chaos.

We're in the bathroom. Rache is doubled over, I'm holding her above the commode, her feet tripping over each other. We stagger, fall. More chaos.

"Did you throw up?"

"No—Lemme sleep."

I pick her up, hold her over the toilet again. I see an old image from years before: my mother holding me face-down over the bowl until I rid myself of whatever was making me sick.

"Lemme go," Rachael says, her voice barely audible. "I can't throw up anymore. I *hurt*."

"Please."

"I *hurt*. Lemme go."

"No! Rache! Think of the potato salad."

She dips her head for the commode and opens her mouth, but nothing comes out. I turn, run the pink plastic tumbler full of water from the bathroom tap.

"Drink this!"

"I don't wanna throw up. I *can't*."

"Please."

She spits the water onto my shirt. I run more and make her drink it. Then I place her over the commode. "Rache. I gotta tell you. I got that water from the toilet."

"Arghhhhh." She aims her elbow squarely at my field of vision.

A round yellow flash full of red spider webs. Then nothing but red and green spots of light. When Rachael's bathroom reappears, everything looks blurred and double. Almost simultaneously, she sprays the commode, the wall, me with a voluminous blast of yellow vomit. More than I'd suspected was there.

"What's going on here?" I turn. Bob and Wanda, the little kids—the entire rest of the family, all in the doorway, their mouths open in horror.

"Rache and I are sick—I think we took some pills."

"Oh, good Lord." Bob's eyes widen. "How many?"

"I don't know. The bottle's on the floor."

"Hold her there."

"Bob," Wanda commands, "run some cold water in the tub. Bradley, bring Daddy all the ice trays. We have to keep her awake. Bob, you call the ambulance."

"I already called them," I tell her. "There was no answer."

Bob steps over me, turns on the faucet, then lifts the limp girl from my arms and places her in the tub, vomit-stained clothes and all. There is also a trace of red.

Blood.

I look down and see a dark stain on my shirt, about the size of my hand. What the hell is this?

"How's your nose?" Bob allows himself the faintest smile. "It looks swelled."

"I think it's broke."

"Can you breathe through it?"

"Yes."

"Then it's probably just bruised." Bob turns to splash water onto the groggy Rachael. "I always tell everybody my nose was broken, but the fact is, I was born this way. It just *looks* broken."

Wanda appears. "Bob, the line is busy."

"The nearest hospital is in Weslayan. Let's go."

Minutes later, the tires squeal out of the Dominic driveway as Bob aims the Pontiac down the hilly blacktop toward the Community Hospital in Weslayan. In the front seat, the three little ones sit perfectly still, facing straight ahead, while in the back seat Wanda and I support Rachael between us. I try to steady her against the bumps and still keep the ice-wet cloth pressed to the bridge of my nose.

I count the hills. Eight of them, and four near-right-angle turns.

Bob takes them all with the needle lying far to the right. In minutes we screech through the intersection to Highway 13. Minutes later, we approach the outskirts of town—a service station, a hamburger stand. All closed.

A stoplight. Red.

Bob runs the light, leaning on the horn all the way.

Another and another, all red. Bob accelerates through them, and within minutes, there is a police car following us. Bob rolls down the car window and motions him to follow. Thankfully, there are no other vehicles on the road. I tighten my arm around Rache as we turn into the hospital's emergency entrance.

The doors swing wide as I carry her into the white corridor. Seconds later, an orderly takes her from me.

I watch the clock tick. Second by second. Is that how we record time in our minds? *Every* damn second? How long have I been here? I look at my wrist. My watch is encrusted with dried vomit and blood. I detect a trace of what appears to be a bit of potato. Or maybe an onion. I resolve never to eat potato salad again, either now, *or* in the past.

Or future.

"Reverend Dominic, I'm Doctor Brian Walker." The physician is medium height with short blond hair and very tired eyes. "We flushed out your daughter's stomach and didn't really find anything. Your bottle of Seconal was labeled June of '62, and it was only for five days. That's a maximum of five caps." He looks at me. "Did you happen to take any, young man?"

"I don't think so."

"*Don't you know?*" The doctor gives me an exasperated look.

"I mean, no I didn't take any."

"Do you feel sleepy?"

"I feel sick."

"Want your stomach pumped too?"

"No."

He flashes a slight, perplexed smile and turns to Bob and Wanda. "Your daughter's running a slight temp so it looks to me like either the flu or food poisoning. And she apparently mistook the secobarbital for antinausea medication. I think she got it all out of her, but she's very dehydrated, so I'd like to keep her overnight. We're building her fluids back up..." He looks at me. "Sure you don't want me to look you over?"

"I'm fine. I think I threw up everything."

"Do you know what it was?"

"Potato salad."

"Yeah," the doctor nods. "That'll do it, all right—that and turkey. You should have seen this place the weekend after Thanksgiving. The whole *town* was sick. We call it turkey flu."

"I'd like to stay with her," I say. "If it's okay with everybody."

The doctor looks at Mr. Dominic.

"Sure. Fine with us," Bob says, then he turns to me. "Wanda and I will go on home—put the kids to bed and bring you a change of clothes. I've got some pants that'll probably fit you."

I sit in the darkness of the hospital room watching her in the bed, watching her chest move with each breath. I notice the IV bottle is the old kind, glass. Of course. There were no plastic IV bags in 1966.

Despite where I am, I feel a sense of fatigue. As though I'd actually been through this again. And yet, it seemed like it was the first time.

I look down at my shirt—a short-sleeved white cotton job with a little pocket protector. Courtesy of Bob Dominic. The white cotton jeans—if that's what they once were—are lying in a pile near the corner, replaced by a pair of loose-fitting surgical scrubs.

I sit here in the darkness with my swollen nose, watching this girl on the bed. Watch the IV drip into the tube. Watch her sleep.

And now, I'm watching it again. All over again. This girl from my past, now lying pale and still in a darkened hospital room, a thousand miles away and decades from where I am.

I wonder: If I fall asleep here, will I wake on the other side?

I'll take the chance.

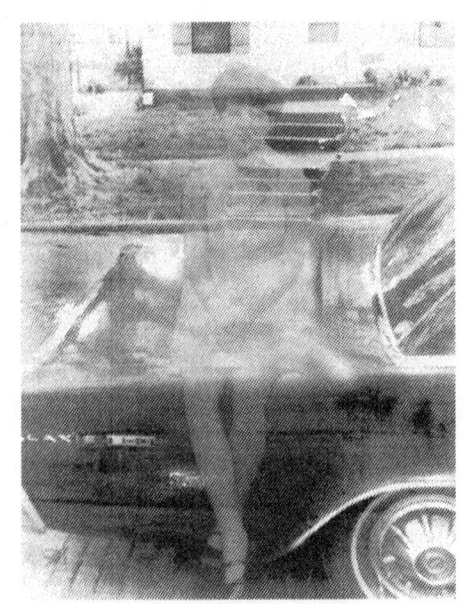

Part III

16

December, 1966

It's morning in my memories. Amazingly, I'm still here—after a cramped night in a metal hospital chair. If I dreamed, I can't remember. Perhaps I had visions of the future. Perhaps I skipped the dream altogether and went for unconsciousness.

Regardless, the nice thing was waking up and seeing Rachael smiling gamely at me from the bed—to hear her voice the first thing this morning.

"Hi. You spent the night, didn't you?" Her speech is slower. Like she has all the time in the world.

"Yeah. I stayed." I yawn, stretch, rub my eyes. "I don't think I got much sleep, though."

"You're wearing Dad's shirt."

"We're the same size, believe it or not."

"I thought you would be. There's a resemblance." She leans on one elbow and looks at me. "Same height, both of you have black hair."

"I guess."

"Michael, I want you to know something—" her voice is soft, almost a whisper. "I really, really like seeing you the first thing in the morning. Even if I did throw up the night before."

"Thanks, Rache. I feel the same way"

Shortly after that, Wanda and Bob stop by with a freshly washed pair of jeans, shirt, socks and underwear. I quickly lock and scan the scene. The jeans are pale blue cotton Levi's, the shirt a light blue oxford, the socks blue and brown argyles and the underwear white Kerry

Knit. Nothing I could take back to the future, nothing I'd want to.

At 8:30 another doctor arrives. He's a short man with brown hair and a bland disposition. We leave the room and return a few minutes later. "She's running a slight fever. Probably nothing to be concerned about, but I'd like to keep her here one more day. Just to be on the safe side."

Disappointment.

Returning to the room, Rachael complains about the hospital gown, then is quiet. Moments later, her eyes close and she's asleep. Maybe keeping her here was a good idea. I look at the gown. Open at the front, I can see a swath of bare skin from her neck to her stomach. It occurs to me that she is wearing her hospital gown backwards.

Later in the morning, after returning to Dominic's in Cherokee for an early lunch of fish sticks, bologna sandwiches and Vess cola, I head the car down highway 50 toward Kansas City. Watching the scenery race past I try to remember why I'm driving away. I try to listen to my mind, but all I hear is the sound of the radio. The station is playing something from 1966—which makes sense, because that's exactly where I am. It's a song by the Four Tops: "Reach Out."

Didn't I recommend that song to a giant—*company*—once? I can't remember. It's sometimes hard to remember the future from back here. It's like the memories associated with *this* time and place crowd the others out. Makes sense, though: the river of my life is made of memory. And right now, since I happen to be immersed in 1966, most of what I know at this instant in time is from this place.

It's an interesting phenomenon. I'll tell someone about it when I get back, only I'm not sure who it would be.

I settle in and scan the scenery: The eastern edge of Kansas City seems to begin at the town of Lees Summit. Here, beneath a high, thin cirrus, I see rows of commercial buildings, car dealerships and highway restaurants. Another few miles and I cross the hill to see the jagged gray outline of the city. Though the grass along the side of the road is still green, most of it is covered by brown leaves. The closer I get to the city, the chillier the day becomes.

I punch in the second button on the car radio and turn up the volume. The song is "Good Thing," a new release by Paul Revere and the Raiders. Immediately after it is Jimmy Ruffin's "I've Passed This Way Before." It's ironic and funny but I'm not sure why. My logic processes seem to be an odd, unwieldy combination of those from the future and those from this place. My volition, my senses, are directed by the 'me' living in the world of 1966, while the inner conversation with myself seems to be purely from the me located in the real world of the future. And yet, there is a part of me that seems to be a combination of the two, probably the result of simple confusion. Probably from spending so much time back here.

I notice another thing: Contrary to my expectations, most of the experiences back here are *not* accompanied by a sense of deja-vu. But when it does occur, the feeling is remarkably intense. Listening to that song, watching the scenery roll past on this blue early winter day, it seems I can almost see the events just seconds away in the future.

But no, I'm wrong. Here at the wheel of my cranky, droning 1964 Ford Fairlane, on this winter day in 1966, the future rolls away ahead of me, opaque as it ever was, and seconds out of reach. Just like in the real world.

Continuing west, I pass by the Art Museum, several hamburger restaurants, a wonderfully baroque fountain, and finally come upon The Plaza, Kansas City's first shopping center. It's a surprise, covered in ornate tile roofs with Spanish-style ornamentation. In the cool pale light of early December, it's another world.

I coast through, narrowly avoiding the shoppers. Several miles later, I pass State Line Road. Now I'm in Kansas. I lock the scene: the cars here are bigger, more *squarish* than in Missouri. Is it my teenager's perception at work, or simply because people over here can afford bigger, newer automobiles?

Another thing—here on the eastern edge of Kansas, the sun has a much grayer cast. A line of high, dense altocumulus has drifted in from the west to darken and chill the day. Cold air from the sparse brown plains of western Kansas. I slide the chrome heater control all the way to the right, turn on the fan, and steer the car toward a stand of brown brick buildings. I see a sign: Metcalf Mall. I'm in the suburb of Prairie Village.

I park the car, zip up my coat and walk toward the shopping center. I'll know it when I see it. And there it is, in a store window. Perfect.

And now I'm inside, reaching for my billfold. It's a men's clothing store and the object is a blue and black striped nightshirt, a cotton pullover with wide horizontal stripes. It has half-length sleeves and two clear plastic buttons at the collar. Apparently my teenage mind believes Rachael would love it. Something in me agrees. I pay the clerk, a tall pinstripe-suited college student, $13.56 and watch him wrap the nightshirt in rough brown paper, then put it in a sack marked Mailliard's: 22 On The Mall. Walking from the store, I stuff the change in my pocket and head for the parking lot.

A voice drifts in from the static: "Now she can wear something besides that stupid hospital gown."

On the way back to Cherokee, it suddenly occurs to me that in the clothing store I had an excellent opportunity to log in design data. There were walking canes, suspenders, paisley ties, vests, driving caps, gloves and scattered bottles of Brut, British Sterling, Canoe, By George, Russian Leather and Jade East. The best of fashion forward circa December 3, 1966. And I didn't lock the scene once. But why should I lock the scene at all?

As I drive east on Highway 50, I listen to my memory for nearby scenes—those experienced only a few weeks or months before. At first, there is nothing. Then, suddenly I see Rachael and I driving somewhere in the rain. See her place the lethal bowl of potato salad on the back seat, next to her green plastic overnight case. I feel her snuggle against me as the darkness falls, listen as she complains that her front teeth are too big and that she looks like a chipmunk.

I tell her I think she's beautiful and perfect.

The memory dissolves and I'm alone in the car, turning south at the Weslayan exit—the Weslayan of winter, 1966—blue and cold in the dying light with small houses lining the main road. At the intersection of Market and the main road through town, I see the KuKu Hamburger Restaurant, a fat square glass box glowing brightly in the middle of an asphalt parking lot. It's Rache's favorite restaurant. Twenty minutes later, by the time I turn west on State Road 2 toward Cherokee, the clouds have become dense and dark with snow.

Negotiating a winding curve, I see the first soft white flakes hit the windshield. I count the hills on the winding two-lane blacktop—eight in all, one winding around to the south past three prominent grain bins. By now, the road is covered with a thin layer of snow. But it's all right: I'm only two miles from Cherokee.

A gust of wind smacks the car as I turn left onto the gravel road to her house. And there it is, a small clapboard house nestled between the water tower and the church on the dark, lonely eastern edge of town. In a few moments I'm walking up the cracked cement path to the front door. Perhaps I'll load the family into the Ford and take them to the hospital tonight to see Rachael.

Even before I reach the front steps, the door opens and Wanda welcomes me inside. "Michael, we were worried about you," she says. "Afraid you got lost in Kansas City. Bob'll probably be at Safeway until late. He has to stock oranges again...so there's nobody here but us mice." I hear a nervous lilt in her voice. Is Rache okay? I look past her to see Amy and Brad playing on the living room floor with their toys. In the kitchen, seven-year-old Stacie, her long blonde hair askew and both hands encased in oversize oven mitts, is peering intently at the range. Something inside the oven is obviously not doing what she wants it to.

"Michael," Wanda says, taking my jacket. "Stacie is making fish sticks. You like fish sticks?"

"Ah. My favorite."

"And we have spinach and vinegar—with bologna sandwiches." Stacie nods gravely. "In case the fish sticks don't work out."

Wanda turns to me, smiling brightly. "Michael, I've got a surprise,"

"Yeah," four-year-old Amy looks up from her trio of identical Barbies, "Rachael's home."

"She called us about two this afternoon," Wanda says. "Said she felt fine and wanted to know where you were. I told her you went to Kansas City and she said she wanted to come home—right then." She turns and leads me through the narrow hallway to Rachael's room. "The doctor finally said it was okay. I think she wore him down."

I step inside the darkened room, around the pile of clothes to the bed. "Rache—?"

"Hi, Michael." Her voice comes from far away. "I've been waiting *all afternoon* for you." As my eyes adjust to the darkness, I can see that her hair is matted and her eyes are puffy. "I really feel miserable, but I'm better now."

"The doctor said it was acute gastritis and to keep her on liquids for a few days," Wanda says.

"Yeah, that potato salad really poached my egg," Rachael mumbles. "Mom and Day says you can stay in here tonight."

"Here?" I glance back at Rachael's mother. "You mean *in this room?*"

"We'd like you to keep an eye on her," Wanda says. "Her dad and I didn't think she was well enough to come home, but once Rachael gets something in her head, you can't change her mind."

"They made me wear this stupid see-through gown and everybody could see my boobs," Rachael said. "Not that there was all that much to see, but it was embarrassing."

"That's because you were wearing it *backwards*, Hon,"Wanda said.

"Well, I wanted to come home. That way I could wear what I always wear. Pajamas or a t-shirt."

"Michael,"Wanda says, "Bob won't be home until after one, and he'll be bone-tired. And Amy's acting like she's coming down with another sore throat so I'll be busy with her. Do you know how to take a temp?"

"Well, yes—"

"Good." Wanda hands me a glass thermometer. "Just shake it down, get all the mercury into the bulb, then put it right under her arm. If she gets up above 102 you just come and wake us up. And if she starts to get sick to her stomach again, you wake us up. All you have to do is knock on the door, we're light sleepers. There's a pan in the bathroom, but try to get her in there to throw up, if you can."

"Sure, but—"

"I'll put down a quilt on the floor, and you can use the pillow from the couch,"Wanda says. "And if you get cold, there's some extra blankets in the hall closet. Probably be more comfortable than sleeping on that old couch anyway."

"Um, probably. Thanks." I turn to Rachael. "Are you sure you're okay?"

"I feel awful." Rachael looks queasy. "My stomach's been cramping like I'm having my period, only a zillion times worse."

"I think you should have stayed in the hospital."

"Yeah? After you've come all this way to see me? Your college is almost two hundred miles from here. Did you know that?"

"No, I didn't know that."

Stacie appears at the door next to her mother. "Fish sticks are about ready. Rache—you want tartar sauce on yours?"

"Get it outta my sight," she pulls the covers up. "I don't even want to *think* about tartar sauce."

"C'mon Sissy." Wanda pats Stacie on the shoulder. "You can get the ice for the Cokes."

I hand Rachael the package. "I thought you were still going to be in the hospital, so I got you this."

"Oboy!" She sits up. "A present." After some fumbling with the paper, she retrieves the article from the bag. "I love it." A pause. "Okay. What *is* it?"

"It's a nightshirt. You sleep in it."

"Sleep in it, huh?"

"Yep," I tell her. "I was going to give it to you to wear in the hospital."

"Why, Michael, that's so sweet." She smiles. "Want me to put it on right now? Over my tee-shirt, that is."

"Sure. Go right ahead."

As she wriggles into the blue nightshirt, I hear a thin howl of wind followed by a creaking noise from outside. Tree branches scraping against the house. Limbs against limbs in the chill darkness of early December, 1966.

"There," she says, holding her arms out. "How do I look?"

"Perfect," I tell her. "Absolutely perfect."

Some time later, after fishsticks, spinach, and instant coffee with Wanda and the kids, and hours of talking in the dark with Rachael, I take off my boots and socks and slide to the floor. I close my eyes and the world goes away.

When I open my eyes again, the blankets are massed in a huge soft ball midway between my chest and feet. Approximately five inches from my face is my boot. Nearby, a small stuffed elephant eyes me warily from a mound of clothing. Scanning my visual field, I'm amazed at the forest of objects surrounding my position—only a few identifiable in the darkness: a pair of girl's white boots, a jewelry box, a transistor radio, a sewing kit. Directly across from me, I scan the underside of the bed. I guess that the darkness harbors a coven of shoes.

There's music, a muffled "Hazy Shade of Winter." I hear the squeak of bedsprings as someone turns. Then a whisper: "Hey. Michael. You awake?"

"I'm awake, Rache. How do you feel?"

"Still got a headache. And my stomach still hurts. Of course, it might just be my period. I have terrible periods. I practically *live* on Midol."

I lean on my elbow. "Want me to get you anything? Glass of water, maybe?"

"Yeah. Glass of water would be nice."

I get up and stumble out of the room. I watch my feet find their way from the carpet of the hallway to the linoleum surface of the kitchen. I'm barefoot in white t-shirt and light blue cotton jeans.

I open the cabinet, extract a glass, run the tap, then return to the bed-room.

Rachael sits up in bed to take the glass. She's still wearing the blue and black striped nightshirt. She's also wearing a gold chain around her neck. Is my ring suspended on it? Probably, but I can't tell.

"I really hate this western Missouri water. They get it from some-where in the ground." She takes a sip and then makes a face. Did you happen to notice this water is actually *white*? Stacie says Cherokee, Missouri water tastes like Zest smells. Care for a drink?"

"No."

As she reaches over and sets the glass down on the nightstand, I see that under the nightshirt she's wearing a t-shirt and her pajama bottoms. White, with tiny red hearts. The same ones she wore when she first got sick.

"I guess I'll go back to the floor—"

"You can sit here and talk." She pats the bed. "If you don't talk too loud. My folks are real light sleepers."

"Okay. If it isn't gonna cause a problem." I sit down on the edge of the bed.

"I don't think it will. My folks trust you. They think you saved my life by making me throw up that pill. Besides, you've been sleep-ing down there on the floor *for the last three nights* and you haven't tried anything. They know you're safe."

I lock the scene, but all I get is a dark gray with outlines. Three nights? I must have jumped ahead. I think about what I've missed—lost time with Rachael. I resolve to come back someday to retrieve it.

Unlock.

"Your folks think I'm safe, huh?" I lean over and give her a kiss.

"*Real* safe," she smiles. "I bet they'd let us sleep together if we wanted—if we kept our clothes on, that is. I'd probably want to wear my red gym shorts." She looks at me. "Are you comfortable sleeping in those jeans?"

"Sure. I've spent a lot of time sleeping in jeans. When I was in Boy Scouts, we had a camporee in April one year when the temperature got down to twenty. I went three days without taking my jeans off once."

"Must have been uncomfortable. Didn't you have to go to the bathroom?"

"Well, not counting *that*."

"It must be awful to go to the bathroom out in the woods. My friend Jeannie Collins went camping with her cousins once and she said the bathroom was the worst part—there wasn't any."

"How's your headache?" I brush the hair back from her eyes.

"I'll get over it. Mostly my stomach hurts."

I stand up and look at her, a girl surrounded by quilts and covers. "Well, Rache—"

"Did I tell you they missed the vein and my arm swelled up?" She shows me her arm. "It's fine, but they said it could have caused nerve damage."

"I'm gonna go back to the floor."

"Michael—"

"Yeah?"

"I really don't think they would say anything. If you sleep up here on the bed, I mean."

"Rache—" I look at her. "I really like you a lot. And I like your folks—"

"They like you too."

"I don't want them getting mad at me for *any* reason. I'll sleep on the floor." I kiss her again, then step around the bed to my quilt next to the wall.

"Michael—"

"Yeah?"

"Goodnight."

"G'night, Rache."

I listen to the radio. It's playing an obscure song, "What Becomes of The Broken-Hearted." I'd call Leonard and ask him the stats, but if I go to sleep, I'll probably see him in a few minutes anyway. It *does* seem like I've been here for days. And I was only scheduled for how many hours? Six? I think back to what Gail had told me once about a drug that dilates time. Maybe they're putting that in the IV up there.

"Michael," Rachael whispers. "What if I go in and *ask* 'em?"

"Ask them what?"

"Ask 'em if it's okay for you to sleep with me on the bed. If you wear your jeans. And a shirt, of course. And maybe even a *jacket*, if you want."

"I don't know. I don't know if we should—"

Suddenly, it occurs to me I'm hearing someone else—from somewhere inside. My thoughts back then?

I lock the scene and listen.

Yes, they're here: Little sensate *beings* drifting up from some deep place, coalescing near the surface to agree first on the thoughts, then the words. Echoes of my own thoughts from thirty years ago.

In the stillness of the full lock, I listen, fascinated: *"I've never slept with a girl overnight. Never. What will it be like? What will I say to her folks in the morning? I don't know if I can do this—"*

Then, the voices fade and are gone, leaving me only silence. Like a birder who had only briefly caught sight of a flock of cranes, I examine the void for an echo of what I'd heard.

Nothing.

An improbable question: If I'm inside my own memory, why is it so rarely that I hear my thoughts from then—from now? Is it because they aren't really a part of this place after all? Maybe thoughts are like migrating birds flying high above the landscape of time.

If so, where do they call home?   Maybe someday I'll try to find out.

Unlock

"Look," Rachael says. "You've been sleeping on that hard floor ever since I came home from the hospital. It's like Daddy said—if we were gonna do anything, we would have done it already. So I think I oughta' ask em."

"I don't think you should. Okay?"

"Okay." She pauses a minute, then throws the covers off and climbs out of bed."

"Where are you going?"

"To the bathroom. It was that glass of water you gave me." She closes the bedroom door behind her. I hear another door open. Then the sound of running water. I close my eyes. The radio plays a rare oldie from late 1966, "It's Now Winter's Day."

Gone is the green grass, the trees have turned brown—
The sky has gone gray, it's now winter's day—

About five minutes later, she returns. "Guess what!" she whispers. "They said it was okay!"

"What? You asked both of them?"

"Both of them. Daddy said 'yeah, it's fine. Go back to sleep.' Mama said I gotta put some gym shorts on underneath this nightshirt. So close your eyes—okay?"

"Okay." Darkness descends. I hear a drawer open, then some shuffling of clothes.

"All right." I hear the bedsprings squeak. "You can get off the floor now."

I lift the covers and slide in beside her. I can almost feel her putting her leg over mine, feel her curl up next to me. "I can't believe you talked them into it."

"They were real sleepy. They'd agree to anything when they're sleepy. Besides, I told 'em if you couldn't sleep on the bed, I'd sleep on the floor with you. Gimme a kiss g'night."

We kiss, then she curls under my arm. A second later, she's asleep. I begin to close my eyes, but all I see are sparks.

Lightning.

Is it the future calling? Maybe only a storm—

"Mike, this is Leonard."

"I'm here." I feel my heart sink.

"Sorry I haven't gotten back to you earlier. Our theta detectors went off the trolley again and I've been fooling with that all afternoon. Looks like they're no-op. I'll have to bring you up."

"Sure. But can you wait a few more minutes—"

"Sorry. Poundstone's coming down for a look-see. Hang on."

I open my eyes. It's 4:00 p.m. Real World time.

17

Coltrane

Five p.m. I'm in my room and the phone has been ringing for at least a minute. I wonder: Should I answer? It's probably Gail, wanting to meet for dinner. I don't have an objection to that, but still—

The ringing stops. I settle back on the bed and close my eyes, trying to recapture some part—any part of the place I've just been.

The phone begins ringing again.

I pick it up.

"Mitch? It's Jerry. How're ya doin? Security said you're in your room, but you won't answer the phone. So I figured you were asleep. Or in the shower or something."

"Jerry." I collapse back onto the bed. "How are things?"

"Mitch, they are not going very well. I expected a call from you yesterday telling me when your plane would be coming in. You know what I got? I got bupkis. You didn't call me, Mitch. Can you tell me why you didn't call me?"

"I was thinking it over, Jer. That's why I didn't call you."

"Mitch, I told the staff this morning—you know what I told them? I said, listen, I've known Mike Mitchell since I was a college student. I'm the godfather to his little son Paul. I stood up at his daughter's weddings—both of 'em. I *know* this man. He's a decent, caring, *responsible* man. And I know he won't let us down. When the Japs come to hand us their wallet, Mike Mitchell will *be* here to accept it from them."

"Jerry, I'm not gonna do it."

"You *dick!* Why the fuck not?"

"I've decided to stay at the Institute until the end of August. And maybe longer."

"You rat's ass! You're gonna sink our company!"

"I'm not going to sink anything. *You* talk to them."

"You putz, I'm forty-two years old. I start talking real old time rock and roll they'll laugh in my face!"

"Go a couple of days without sleep. Put a little gray in your hair. Anyone can look older if they work at it."

"Mitch, *please!*"

"Tell them you took acid at Woodstock. Tell them anything. But don't tell them I'll be at the meeting, because *it isn't going to happen.*"

"Mitch. I'm your *partner*. We've known each other *a long time*. We can work this out. How about if I tell 'em you're meeting them down there in San Angelo?"

"I'm in San *Antonio*."

"Angelo, Antonio. *Whichever*. Look. Maybe you can talk 'em into getting together at a coffeeshop or something. Take the day off and show 'em around. Find some camera stores or some kind of amusement park. They really go nuts for cameras and amusement parks. Then send 'em back to Boston so we can get that contract."

"I'll let you know."

"Tomorrow. You gotta call and confirm by tomorrow."

"I'll let you know."

I hang up the phone and look out the window. It seems the sky has become a malevolent, intense blue.

Hours later, I'm in my jeans sitting cross-legged on Gail's bed. The sun has gone down and the blinds are open, revealing a deepening purple sky.

Gail pushes the plate of cheese cubes over to me, then gets up from the bed. She's wearing a pair of bleached, ragged cutoff jeans—the shortest I have ever seen, even counting the ones I happened to see in 1966. The top hem crosses her stomach well below her navel, and the rear view exposes at least an inch of tan, perfect derriere. The hem of her plain white t-shirt falls just above her lowest ribs, exposing a smooth stomach and perfectly round navel. The shirt itself is tight enough to outline her breasts—no bra, of course.

With her long, smooth legs and hair tied back she could easily pass for a thirty-something perfect wife and sex partner. The thought of spending time in bed with her should be an exciting prospect. For some reason, it's something less than the sum of its parts.

"Guess you heard," she says from the kitchen, "Keller's back."

"He is? How is he feeling?"

"Better. Seems Kapp got it all wrong. What happened was some widget shorted out and broke the connection."

"So he didn't go flatline after all."

"That's the company line, anyway."

"You think they're telling the truth?"

"Well, just from what Kapp said, *something* obviously happened to Keller." She pauses to uncork a bottle of wine, then reaches into the cabinet for some glasses. "Maybe it was just a scram, I don't know. I'll tell you this, though," a pause to pour the wine. "I'd *love* to see what his chart looks like."

She returns with two glasses of wine. "Now, are you gonna tell me where *you* went?"

I look up at her.

"Fair's fair. I told *you*." She sets the glasses on the nightstand and climbs onto the bed next to me. "Did you fool around any?"

"No," I tell her. "I went back to 1966. A friend of mine—okay, a girlfriend I once had—ate something that made her sick. We had to take her to the hospital."

"Sounds interesting. What possessed you to travel to that particular place in your life?"

"Oh, I've been traveling back to see her before—"

"Really?" Gail's eyes brighten. "This sounds serious. Tell me more. What was her name? What'd she look like—was she cute?"

"Rachael. Rachael Dominic. She was about five-four, had black hair. She was always complaining about her acne. She thought she was ugly and her breasts were too small. She said her stomach stuck out. The last time I went back she told me she looked like a chipmunk."

"Sounds like a normal girl to me," Gail says. "Was she pretty?"

"At the time, I thought she was the most beautiful girl in the universe."

"Now *that's* a serious crush," she laughs. "Was she?"

"Was she what?" I look at Gail.

"The most beautiful girl in the universe." Gail is motionless, waiting. She really wants to know the answer to the question.

"Well, in *my* universe, she was."

"You mean the universe you've been visiting?" Gail crosses her legs. "The one where you're nineteen or twenty or something?"

"Let me tell you a story. Years later, in 1974, when I was in a motel with my perfect fiancee, Linda, I would have given anything to trade her for Rache. Would have done it then and there. No contest. Not even close."

"Why didn't you marry this girl?"

"She broke up with me."

"Why?"

"She thought I was seeing someone else."

"Were you?"

"In a way. I was in my freshman year of college, Rache thought she was pregnant, and I thought I was looking at serious real life. No question, my running around days were over. So sometime in the late spring of 1967, I got a call from an old girlfriend who had recently transferred to my school. She told me she heard I was engaged and she wanted to wish me the best."

"Yeah, right." Gail smiles. "She just wants to talk."

"Well, yes. But that's all we did. Spent all of twenty minutes sitting in my car talking about which professors graded high, which ones to avoid. Then, out of the blue, she started hammering me for wanting to marry Rachael. Said I would be spending the rest of my life digging ditches or something, and she wasn't going to let that happen."

"Was she serious?" Gail asks.

"Serious as a heart attack. When I dropped her at her dorm room, she called Rachael and told her that we were seeing each other again. It was a lie, but I actually made it worse. I denied even seeing her. I promised Rachael I'd never lie to her—and then I did."

"And—?"

"And then, I felt guilty for lying to her, so I told her that, yes, I had seen Brenda Lacey again. In fact she was attending my college." I pause at the thought. "I hadn't told Rache any of that before, I just didn't think it was important. Well, of course, it was, to Rache. That Friday when I drove down to see her, I knew I was headed for trouble."

"I'd say."

"Actually, it was catastrophic. One Saturday morning in the spring we were in her room talking about our wedding, our life, the kids we would have—and then, she told me this old girlfriend of mine had called. Told her about the date. She just reached down—took the engagement ring off her finger and handed it back to me."

"Ouch."

"She gave everything back—my ring, some old fireworks, an old nightshirt—everything. My world came to an end that morning. It was like somebody reached up and turned out the lights." I take a deep breath. "I made a deal with myself to forget everything about Rachael Dominic from the time I met her to the time we—well, to the present. I just closed the door, walked away into a new life and did everything I could to forget the old one. I once told a drill sergeant that my wife had died. What I probably meant was that part of my *life* had died."

"Sounds like a big chunk of your life to try to forget."

"Well, I was doing a pretty good job of it." I look at her.

"Until now."

"Until now. It's crazy, really. I take up a profession that analyzes the past down to the finest detail and somehow I'm this big success. Stockholders are happy. My business partner is usually happy. My wife *used* to be happy."

"Are you happy?"

"It doesn't matter. What's important is that I'm down here, suited up with wires and throat microphones and IVs and I'm swimming around in my own memories. And one of those memories is going to get me."

"Where she gave you your ring back?"

"That's the one. The place where my world changed. I'm not looking forward to visiting that place again. Mostly because it leads directly to where I am today."

Gail pats my arm. "Hey, Sport. They're just a bunch of memories, that's all. And maybe they're tired of being repressed. Maybe it's time to confront them and get over it."

"I don't know what their problem is, but I'm almost sorry I went back there at all. I don't want to go through that time again. Once is enough."

"Then simply *don't go there*," Gail says. "Can't you control where you visit?"

"On my extended run yesterday, I found myself in the bathroom throwing up my guts. That should give you an idea about my navigation skills."

"I don't always find myself with Eric either—I've been to some bad times, too. I just try to forget them as soon as I can."

"Eric, huh? Was he your lawn-mower friend?"

"Yeah," she smiles. "My little Michigan yard stud," she rolls onto her back and looks at the ceiling. "Eric DeWayne Fenster Jr. Great name, huh? It's supposed to be Scandinavian."

"Fenster means window in German, doesn't it?"

"That's appropriate," she closes her eyes. "Yeah. It fits. Eric DeWayne Fenster Jr. sure opened *my* windows," she chuckles softly. "Actually, you might say he *cleaned* them for me. Let me see the possibilities—see what I'd been missing."

"Whatever happened to him?"

"Oh, he went home to Michigan. We wrote letters and counted the days until we could get back together. By the time May rolled around I was impossible. I wrote him this big long letter describing everything I wanted to do with him in extremely lurid detail." She smiles sheepishly. "His mother read it—then called my folks and read it to them. I felt like one of those guys at the Watergate hearings—what did you do and when did you do it?"

"Did you ever see him again?"

"Yeah. We wrote letters to each other all through high school. Most were confiscated by our families, but some got through. We dated other people, but it never seemed right somehow. It seemed as if Gail Lynn had found her one perfect person." She sighs. "Then I went to college, met Phil at a frat party, got pregnant and got married."

"And Eric?"

"I wrote him about it. Told him how I was sorry. Told him how I felt about him. About a month later I got the letter back, stamped 'Moved, no forwarding address.' It *killed* me. Hammered me right into the dirt. For years I wanted to know what happened to him. Wanted to tell him how I felt. I even spent a couple thousand bucks on a private investigator, looked through all the search engines for his email—but got nowhere. Finally I gave up on it."

"Why don't you ask Leonard?"

She looks at me. "Leonard?"

"Listen, he can do anything with that jukebox. He can probably find Eric the Scandinavian."

She smiles. "He's probably fat and bald."

"Would it matter?"

"Are you kidding?" She laughs. "Do you *really* think Leonard can find him? I mean, you've got me thinking about this now—"

"Doesn't hurt to ask." I reach into the chips. "Of course, you might have to deal with a few things—like marriage for instance."

"Oh, *my* marriage, I can deal with." She loses her smile. "In fact, I'm a real expert at dealing with it. Say—" she pauses for a drink of wine, "you want to hear Banks' Rules on how you can tell if your husband is fooling around?"

"Sure."

"Okay. Rule number one—if you think they are, they probably are...and rule number two—if you absolutely know they're *not* having an affair, they *definitely* are."

"Is there rule number three?"

"Yeah. Rule number three—when you catch them at it, they always accuse you for driving them to it. And here's number four—they always, *always* start out by complaining about your cooking."

"Always?"

"Invariably." She nods her head. "What's going on, of course, is some bimbo is feeding him steak by candlelight, then screwing his eyes out. Which leads to rule number five—sooner or later, he'll be too tired for sex." She pauses at the thought. "I have considered writing a book about this. Or in the very least, starting a website."

"Is this from personal experience?"

"Afraid so." She nods. "Phil was incorrigible, even when I was pregnant. There was always somebody. Always." She looks into the glass. "I'd spend a little time, collect the information, get the name...then I'd lay it all on the table. 'Here it is, Phil. What's the excuse this time?'"

"What'd he say?"

"Sometimes he'd get real aggressive. Sometimes he'd cry. Usually he'd try a plea bargain—he'd quit the floozy if I'd quit all my friends and family. 'Cause the reason for the affair, you see, is because I was spending too much time with them—and not being a good wife and mother. Circular argument stuff."

"So if you didn't isolate yourself, he'd continue the affair."

"I actually went along with it once. I quit all my friends, didn't see my family, devoted myself to the house—and he found *another* floozy. This time, he said I wasn't fun to be with anymore—all I cared about was housework. Took me awhile to figure that one out."

"So how would a guy know if his wife is having an affair?"

"Michael," Gail laughs. "This is *not* rocket science. If you want to find out if your spouse is having an affair, your best friend is the phone. I used to check the redial every day. Half the time some bimbo would answer. Once it was a friend of mine."

"You really *should* write a book."

"Two summers ago, when I was in Seattle with the kids, Phil asked me to phone him back home in Bridgeport every night. So I did it— called home every night and he'd always be there, nice as could be— telling me what shows were on television, telling me the guy across the street was mowing his lawn. You know, minutiae, but it gave me the impression that he was at home."

"So? It sounds perfect."

"Well, it was *too* perfect," she says. "On a hunch, I called the phone company and just asked where the calls to home my number were being forwarded to. Sure enough, the operator gave me the number that was the fax line in his secretary's apartment. You almost had to admire him. His capacity to cheat was phenomenal."

"Was?"

"Okay. Probably still is. I don't care anymore. This kind of thing wears on you. Each time you get the goods on somebody like that— what have you got? It's like spending all this time to prove your home is worth less than what you paid for it. Anymore, I ignore it." She looks at the ceiling. "I thought about having affairs myself, but it'd never work. I'd feel worse about myself. Other than Phil, you're the first guy I've slept with in years."

"Look, why don't you try to find your old Scandinavian window cleaner."

She looks at me for a long moment. "Do you think Leonard could—?"

"Find Eric Fenster?" I look at her. "Sure. And I think it would be a great idea."

She looks at me a moment. "You know, you really are a nice guy."

"Nice guys finish last," I tell her, taking a drink of wine.

"And *that*," she says, pulling her t-shirt up over her head, "is what is so nice about them."

The clock reads eleven-fifteen. Gail is lying a few inches away, asleep after a round of lovemaking. Did she know she called me Eric? Perhaps I should tell her before she returns to her husband.

He wouldn't appreciate a mistake like that.

I look down at her body, thin and smooth with perfect, round breasts. In a way, her body is a lot like Linda's. And she makes love like Linda did years ago.

I look at the ceiling. I am having what could probably be termed a revenge affair—a once-a-day sex and comparison session. "I really like that. Phil *never* asks what I like...does your wife like it this way? No? I can't imagine why anyone wouldn't."

Making love with Gail, I feel a sense of goofy desperation— like the health geeks at the gym who have to try out each piece of equipment at least once. "The new electronic rowing machine is okay, but have you tried the torso-twister? It's right next to the lat-shaper."

And now, having tried them all, I'm lying here, worn out and ready for the showers. Tomorrow it'll be the same gym. Different equipment maybe, but the same gym. I could do without this right now, I really could.

I close my eyes and drift into a fitful sleep.

I hear a familiar voice. "So tell me again what the future is like, Scout."

It's Earl, propped up on his bed, a magazine in his hand. On the nightstand is a tray with a tall Pepsi and a half-eaten sandwich. "Do I die young?"

"Yeah, you do, Earl."

He grins. "Probably in a barroom brawl over some skinny little woman. Right?"

"You die in a plane crash. Just after Kennedy gets shot."

"*Who* gets shot?"

"Kennedy. He gets elected in 1960. And he gets killed in 1963. The same day your plane goes down."

He stubs his cigarette out in the ashtray. "Is it in a jet?"

"It's a Piper Cub. You're taking flight lessons and something happens to the engine. Dad says it was probably carburetor ice. You crash in a field on the Thompson farm. Near the river."

"I die in a Piper Cub crash—*in Fred Tompson's back forty?*" He shakes his head, then looks up. "Jeez. You'd think I'd do better than that. Now, what's this about somebody getting shot—"

"John Kennedy. He's a senator from Massachusetts. He runs against Richard Nixon and wins."

"Little brothers...whoo-ee." He takes a bite of the sandwich.

In the background I hear a chorus singing *double-you-ell-esssss*—
Chicaaago—followed by "No One Knows," a song by Dion and The
Belmonts. When did it come out?

I can't recall.

I'm in the dark. There's someone in the hallway.

I hear a whisper: "Don't worry. It's only Stacie getting a drink of
water."

I turn to see Rachael, propped on her left elbow, looking at me,
her face illuminated by the yellow light from the bedroom window.
"What were you saying about your brother?"

"It's weird. It's like I just talked to him."

"But wasn't he killed in that plane crash four years ago?"

"He was. But I just talked to him. Sort of."

"Michael, this is really *so* weird." She sits up in bed. "Why can't
you tell me what's going on?"

"I can't. It's complicated."

"Okay. Lemme guess." She brightens. "*I know!*"

I look at her.

"You're really *making all this up*. That's it, isn't it? You're playing
another trick on poor, sweet, gullible Rachael. Like the time you told
me you weren't coming down from college, but you came anyway, and
then hid in the closet? Or the time you started this long joke on the
phone, but it was really a tape recorder? And here I was, listening to
you on the phone, but you were really at the front door? I swear, between you and Daddy with *his* dumb practical jokes—"

"*No*, Rache—"

I open my eyes.

It's way past midnight. Somehow I was able to slide out of bed
without waking Gail and now I'm walking the streets alone—or in this
case, the dark, empty corridors in the top floors of this building.

Taking a deep breath, I inhale the solvent smells of the walls and
carpet, then kick off my shoes to feel the rough fibers beneath my feet.
I pause at a window to look outside. Yet another storm is brewing over
San Antonio, probably the fourth since I came here.

Though it's summertime outside, the window glass is cold to
the touch. But at least I can feel it. After nine o'clock tomorrow
I'll get in the chair and drop into the past. And for many days—
perhaps months—afterward, the only sensations I'll experience

are sight and sound. Taste, touch and smell will be buried in a cloud of warm cotton—the perfect container for a disembodied soul exploring his past.

At an intersection, I look left down the corridor and see a steel door with a red bar across it. A silent alarm. Go through and I go back to the real world—and leave the Institute forever. No more trips to the past. No more visits with family and friends. No more Rachael and no more runaway train headed for that wall in the spring of 1967.

I look straight ahead and see the hallway curve to the right. At the end of this corridor is the skybox lounge with its wall-to-wall view of the city. I look at my watch: 1:00 a.m. sharp. I'll be the only one here.

As I near the skybox, I see bolts of lightning arcing across the sky. I step inside the darkened lounge and take a seat at the window to watch the fireworks.

"Walkin' after midnight. Isn't that a Patsy Cline song?"

Startled, I look behind me. A tall figure dressed in denim shirt and jeans ambles in and takes a seat near me. A sheet of red heat lightning flickers from his round rimless glasses and illuminates his rough angular features. "Hey, Russell, what brings you up here at this hour?"

"Same as you," he smiles. "Came to watch the storm."

"I'm doing a long run tomorrow. I guess I wanted to take in this place before I leave it again."

"Yeah. I know what you mean," he nods. "It kinda' grows on you— boy!" He points to the sky, "that's a *fine* thunderhead out there. Bet *that* one packs some wind."

"Are there storms like this where you come from?"

"Does it storm in Wyoming? I'll tell you a story." He folds his arms and leans back in the chair. "Before I moved to Thermopolis, I had a little cabin outside of Cody. A tornado took it out in '56. I was riding the fence line and saw it comin' from across the road. I smacked the horse on the rump and we both headed for the ditch. Tornado went right overhead, probably twenty or thirty yards across. Ripped the shirt off my back, cut me up some. The horse managed to stay on the ground, I don't know how. But when I got back to my cabin, it wasn't there anymore."

He looks at the lightning for a moment, then continues.

"Now, my neighbor up there was an old Hopi named Gus Kwa. The 'Kwa' was short for *Kwamahongnewa*. Anyhow, I said, Gus, that tornado blew away my house. And he said 'Coltrane—that cabin isn't gone— it just not happening right now.' I said, 'well, Gus, when's it gonna *start* happening again?' He told me as long as I didn't accept that my house was gone, all the possibilities were open."

"I like that philosophy," I tell him.

Coltrane glances at me over his glasses. "Now, 'ol Gus would pull your leg if you let him. But I heard he was once a medicine man in Arizona, and I was young and ready to believe anything—so I figured what the heck. I'll wait a few days and see what happens. See if my cabin'd come back."

"Did it?"

"Nope," Coltrane shakes his head. "So I sold out, and got me a job at the oil refinery."

A bolt of lightning branches across the sky, illuminating Coltrane's smile.

"I heard you've gone on some long runs here."

"Yeah. I've done 'em. Got another one in two days."

"I hear there's problems associated with them. Like coming up with multiple personalities."

"What's the problem with that?" Coltrane grins slyly. "Sometimes you can get a lot more accomplished when you're working as a team."

"I'm not much of a team player." I decide to change the subject. "You know, I still have a few questions about this whole dreamer thing."

"Such as?"

"Well, I've done a few trips, none of them long. But I always seem to end up around the same time."

"Must be a reason. Is a woman involved?"

"Maybe. I had a little girlfriend back then. I guess she meant a lot to me."

"That's probably it," he nods. "Some women have real magic. They'll draw you back from wherever you are. My wife's like that." He clasps his hands across his chest. "We have a little ranch a coupla' miles south of Thermopolis. I go there every chance I get."

"She's taking care of the ranch by herself?"

"No," Coltrane takes a deep breath. "As Gus would say, she quit happening in the spring of '85. So I go back to see her before that."

"I'm sorry."

"No, it's all right—it works," Coltrane says. "Where is it you generally go?"

"Mostly the sixties. In fact, I came here as a business exercise to get data on that time period." I shake my head. "A month here and I'm reliving a lot of stuff that I'd thought I had put aside a long time ago."

A lightning flash illuminates Coltrane's face. "Like I said, maybe it's for a reason."

"I think about it a lot." I look at him. "It's almost like I'm seeing my life back there for the very first time. I don't know how else to describe it. Like every detail means something."

"A life *always* means something," Coltrane says. "No matter who you are—or *when* you are."

"Yeah, but it was more fun for me then. I wish that when I go back, I could taste the hamburgers, smell the burning leaves, feel—" I pause for a moment, reining in my thoughts, "—feel what it's like. Or what it was like *once*."

"First, you have to understand that what's back there is as real as anything that you see here." He pauses to let that sink in. "And when you accept all those times in your life are real—then those times will accept you."

"Russell, I have no idea what you're talking about," I tell him. "But it sounds great."

"Well, he says, getting up from the couch. "Guess I better turn in. If I don't see you tomorrow have a nice time. Say hi to your little girl-friend for me," he smiles. "If you remember, that is."

As Coltrane leaves, clouds drop over the city, obscuring the streets below in a torrent of rain.

I slide into the induction chair with the practiced ease of a seasoned traveler and sit quietly as the nurse attaches the sensors to my scalp.

"Since you'll be out for awhile, we have a little something to keep you from getting thirsty." She pulls the stand holding the intravenous bag next to the chair.

"Is the IV necessary?" I ask. It sounds like a whine.

"Yes. Forty-eight hours is a long time to go without food. Be-sides—" she ties a rubber band around my arm, "we want to keep your electrolytes stable. Make a fist."

I comply and a needle stick later, I'm plugged into my food and water supply.

"We like using the IV on long runs," she says brightly. "If the doctor wants to administer anything, we don't have to inject—we just add it to the fluid already going into your arm. Neat, huh?"

"Neat." I briefly wonder what they would put in there while I'm asleep. Of course, I've already signed a blanket authorization, so it probably wouldn't do any good to concern myself. Still— "Okay. Administer what kinds of things?"

"Oh," she says, attaching an EKG probe to my ankle, "some people lock up on long runs and need a muscle relaxant. If your experience down there is less than wonderful, so we could give you a mild tran-quilizer—" she pauses to attach a set of metal discs to my chest, "if your heart rate gets too high we can add a beta blocker. If you stop breath-ing or go into arrest, we can give you—"

"Okay, I get the picture."

"All *kinds* of things," she says, turning the dial on the EKG monitor.

"Terri likes excitement," Leonard says. "She used to work at the San Antonio Trauma Center."

"You know, I think it'd be fun to go back to the past sometime." She pauses. "Of course, I'd probably wonder if everything back there was real and everything *up here* was the dream."

"Terri often confuses San Antonio with Dallas," Leonard observes. "The truth is, this is a top-secret Defense Department experiment. And none of what you saw back there is real—not even this. Somebody's merely giving you LSD."

"Oh, Leonard—" Terri says. "I saw that movie. It was the 'Man-churian Candidate.' Where they hypnotize this guy to kill somebody for the CIA. Right?" She smiles at me. "We wouldn't do that *here*."

"Not enough imagination," Leonard pauses. "The EKG's on the screen, Terri. Signal looks good."

"Uh, guys," I ask. "Are you sure no one has ever flatlined on a long run?"

"Not on my shift," Leonard says.

"Oh," Terri says, "Mr. Coltrane had us scared once, but I think it was a computer problem. The sensors weren't picking up his signals properly. I think the same thing happened with Mr. Keller."

"It was a gonkulator misfire," Leonard shrugs. "That old dinosaur in Lab 10 just quit barking for awhile and the thetas lost the signal. Over there, the casters-up stories have the highest cred."

"What would have caused it?"

"I dunno. Sunspots. Neutrino rust. Bogon attacks. High anomalon flux." He pushes his glasses up. "Maybe some suit tripped over the power cable. Whatever, it was a showstopper."

"So, nobody came back with any problems, huh?"

"You mean did they come back shredded?" Leonard asks. "Nah. But we had a suit in here from the State Department that went multiple bigtime. Came back like Los Angeles at rush hour."

"Leonard, that guy didn't go multiple," Terri says. "I've never heard of anyone doing that."

"Okay," Leonard says. "But he definitely came back with his core dumped. It was like there was code missing."

"I saw that movie, too, Leonard," Terri says irritably. "When I was *six years old*." She removes a white paper package from the cabinet. "Mr. Mitchell, you want to wait for the catheter until after you're out?"

"That would be nice."

"Most people want me to wait," she says, placing the package on the counter top. "The only one who wants to put the catheter on *before* the induction is Otto."

"I'd guess that."

"He's such a nice man. He's going to start a 72-hour run tomorrow in Lab 12. Three days down. Isn't that something? Probably going to visit his wife again." She takes a step back. "Well, Mr. Mitchell, it looks like you're all wired up and ready to go. If you experience any unpleasantness, just call and we can install a midazolam drip."

"Wait. Isn't that—"

"An amnestic," Terri says. "It's the drug of choice for ablation of the remembered event."

"Yeah," Leonard says. "If a particular decade is annoying you, Terri can fix that."

"Oh, Leonard," she shoots him a quick glance. "Midazolam is very safe. Practically no side effects. You just don't remember anything from your session."

"*Ever*," Leonard interjects. "I've used it to erase my entire freshman year in high school."

"Isn't he *awful*?" Terri shakes her head. "Would you like me to put on your helmet and throat mike now?"

"I don't think I'll need anything *special*," I tell them, my eyes on the plastic IV bottle. Is this what Poundstone meant when he said they could *ablate* the experience? The thought that they have the power to erase my past has suddenly become overwhelming. I notice the room feels warm. Hot.

"Goodness, Mr. Mitchell, your heart rate is over a hundred. Would you like to cancel?"

"No. No, I'm okay. Let's go." As the helmet slides down over my head, I can feel my heart rate begin to slow back down.

"He's okay, Terri," I hear Leonard say. "Mike's one of our cool ones. That heart rate never gets over one-ten."

He's right. I'm a cool guy. I feel the reassuring chill of the ceramic microphone against my throat. What did she call that stuff? An amnestic? Funny name for something like that. I decide to give them *no* reason to use strange drugs on me from up there. None whatsoever.

Darkness. Then the twin green lights wink on.

"You know the drill," Leonard says. "With your eyes closed, look left, right, up, down—your Aunt Nancy naked—"

"Leonard—" the nurse growls. "You are gonna *get it*—"

"Showing a good pupil response there, Mike. Think of a blue circle, yellow square, count backwards by sevens from a hundred—thank you, thank you and thank you. All processors go. Vital functions go. Big Iron is up and running and Terri's waiting with the catheter. You want a countdown?"

Sure.

"Ten, nine—" The sound begins, a chorus of angels arriving to take me back to my life.

"Eight, seven—" As they get nearer, my body becomes lighter. Or is it my mind that's becoming lighter?

"Six, five, four—" The vibration begins as the angels pick me up, shake me loose. Inside my mind I hear a bell.

"Entrainment—three—" I can almost feel the wind from their wings, as they lift me away from the earth.

"Two—one—zero. Have a *nice dream.*"

I float downward, toward the stars.

18

Window

I descend toward a row of pictures, lined up inside the dim yellow days of winter, 1966-67, segmented by bands of dark and light. Days? Probably. I look at the photos one by one and see the spare interior of my dorm room—a stack of books in the corner, my blue Royal portable typewriter with a black ribbon lying nearby on the desk. Jack, my roommate is carefully poring over something. Nearby is a book: *Debate Tactics*.

From here, Jack appears grainy—I can barely make out his light brown flattop, horn-rimmed glasses, intense expression as he sorts though a stack of index cards.

Closer, though, and he takes on substance. He's wearing light-colored slacks and, improbably for the time of year, a green short-sleeved shirt.

The phone rings, and Jack answers it.

"S'for you, Mitchell." He hands me the phone, then returns to his desk.

"Hi. This is me."

At first, I hardly recognize the voice. Over the long distance lines she sounds impossibly young.

"Hi, Rachael. How are you?"

"I'm fine," she says. "I gained back all the weight I lost, but it's all going to my hips. Can you believe it?"

"I'll bet you look great."

"Listen. Daddy found a two-story house in Weslayan and the

movers are comin' Wednesday. It has two bathrooms, which is real handy with six people in the house. Anyhow, my bedroom window is right across from a street light, so I get to see what's going on out front."

"Sounds nice." I turn to look at Jack, with his new stack of debate notes.

"So you better come down this weekend, 'cause it'll be your last chance to see Cherokee."

"I dunno, Rache—I promised my folks I'd have dinner with them Friday night. I might be able to drive down Saturday morning—"

"You should have dinner with your parents, but I want to see you too. Hey, you know what else? I asked Mom and Dad if you could wear your shorts—you know—cutoffs—to bed with me and they said yes, *if* I promise to wear shorts and a t-shirt. We've also gotta promise we won't do anything. Until we get married, of course. Isn't that something? I think they're resigned to the fact that you're part of the family. Whattaya think of that?"

"I think that's really great."

I lift up from the scene, leave it etched on the fabric of space. Scanning ahead, I drift into Friday afternoon, see my father working on the Fairlane's trouble-prone generator, watch him as he fixes it with a sliver of cardboard and a paperclip. It's evening and I see my mother and grandmother set the table, watch my own attempts at frying chicken. The television news comes on—fighting continues in Vietnam with heavy casualties.

My father turns up the television, glances at me, then looks away. I want to tell him not to worry—it will be three years before the army has me. And I make it out alive.

I look at the terrain of this stretch of my life—see the time with my folks, then the long drive ahead to Cherokee tomorrow morning; see the time spent with Rache and her family—going on and on—all the way to the horizon.

I decide to land my mind-ship here on Friday night—settling in between these images at the dinner table—waiting for the fit, the gentle bump that tells me I am inside the scene. Inside this *now*.

There is movement. My mother's voice comes in mid-speech. "—I don't see why you have to get married now." She looks at me. "Rachael's not—you know—?"

"No. She's not pregnant."

"Are you sure? When she was here before Christmas she looked like she was putting on weight." Mom turns to my grandmother. "Didn't you think so, Grace?"

"Oh, I don't know," my grandmother says. "I thought her pants looked a little tight, but that's the way the kids dress nowadays. I heard they put their jeans on, then get in the bathtub so's they shrink."

"Actually, Rachael'd lost weight when you saw her," I say after a moment. "The doctor says she lost eight pounds. Rache says she's putting it back on and now thinks she's overweight again—"

"It's probably the scales," my dad says, pouring gravy over his chicken. "I've never seen two scales read the same."

"It was the potato salad." I reach for a crisp brown chicken leg. "She ate potato salad from the band picnic and got food poisoning."

"Bad potato salad. That'll do it all right," my grandmother says soberly, picking up the bowl of cranberry sauce. Then she looks at me over the top of her glasses. "Michael—"

"Yes, Grandma?"

"This girl *does* know how to cook, doesn't she?"

"I think so. She's fixes fish sticks with vinegar all the time."

My father cracks a smile. "Heh. Sounds like you've got an interesting life ahead of you, Mike."

"Didn't Rachael work down at the Dairy Queen?" my mom says. "Maybe she can make you a hamburger. I can't imagine fish sticks with vinegar—"

"Mike," my grandmother says, "if you're driving down there tomorrow, maybe I ought to pack a lunch for you. We can send some cold chicken. Probably be enough to last you the weekend."

"Thanks, Grandma, but I'll be fine."

"I've always liked Rachael," my mother says after a few minutes. "When she came over here this last summer and Mike was out with Brenda, Rachael just looked so *pitiful*. I felt sorry for her." She turns to me. "Michael, you didn't do that girl right."

"Mom, I'm asking her to marry me."

"You *still* didn't do her right," Mom says. "I think she should have broke up with you."

"But I wasn't going with her then. I was going with Brenda Lacey before I started going with Rachael."

"You mean you were going with *both* of them?" My grandmother looks up. "Did I miss something here?"

"I thought Brenda was nice," my mother says. "She's real polite, always says 'hi' to me..."

I listen to my mother and watch the images pass by: the Saturday mornings in April watching Brenda at the piano playing "Cast Your Fate To The Wind," the walks in Corinth park, the summer nights in her pool, floating on the air mattresses and looking up at the stars. The night she swam topless, then completely nude.

"Rachael's nice too," my mother says. "But she's so *quiet*."

The images of Brenda vanish, replaced by Rachael—Rachael planting her bare feet on my windshield; illegally driving her grandmother's Comet all over town; setting off skyrockets in the town square to celebrate our going steady—and recently, in that hospital bed, weak, pale and frightened.

"—I notice every time you bring her by, she just sits there—doesn't say a word." My mother shakes her head.

"Maybe she doesn't feel like talking," my grandmother volunteers. "Some people are like that."

"That's the way she is." I pause, looking around the table. "She's *reserved*. Very, very *reserved*."

19

Replay

I'm standing at the jewelry counter. Behind the salesman is a sign: Winsler's Jewelry: Finest Diamonds. Nearby is an illustration of an impossibly beautiful Brenda Lacey type in an impossibly long bridal gown. Not too much different than the ads today. In the future.

Whenever.

"Could I take a look at it?"

"Sure." The man goes to the back and returns with a little square blue box. He opens it and I look at the gold ring, a size six. The diamond is supported by four tiny prongs. On the box I see in tiny lettering: Orange Blossom.

"Only $35.80 to go," the man smiles.

"Okay. I got it." I open my billfold and lay two twenties on the counter. An hour later, I'm driving south toward Weslayan. The temperature must be holding steady under the January sun—the car window is open and my coat is unbuttoned. I glance in the mirror to see my long hair flying straight back—a kid straight out of the sixties.

As I stop at the main intersection of Brunswick, a small town in the Missouri River bottom, I watch the wind kick up dust, leaves and scraps of paper. Walking along the sidewalk are groups of children dressed in winter clothes. Along the street is a cluster of 1960-vintage Fords and Chevies.

The light changes, I release the clutch and continue on. As I leave town, I watch the dull red speedometer needle swing toward the 70 mark. The wind picks up and I turn on the radio. A commercial for a used-car dealership in St. Louis followed by a song, "Too Much To Dream Last Night." When did it come out? I try to think but can't. Should I call Leonard?

No. Instead, I listen to the music. Even though I'm on the machine, floating behind my eyes, I can almost feel the wind against my face—almost detect the hard plastic of the wheel on my hand as I turn it left, following the road south toward the Missouri River bridge.

I look around inside this dream, see the changing January landscape move toward the edge of my vision and disappear—an endless array of browns, yellows and tans beneath a milky sky. South of the river, the geography changes from flat river bottom to limestone and granite hills. The sun is closer to the horizon when I turn onto the interstate. I swing the sun visor down to shield my eyes.

As I follow the interstate west into the glare, I wonder—where is this place exactly? There can be no question it's real—I experience it—even if only in sight and sound.

Of course, the universe is always more complicated than it appears. What if everything I see is just a series of static events—pictures separated by infinitesimal segments of space? By stepping through the events, one after another, I create the time myself: a series of snapshots, pictures of thought, all strung together, that turns into a film. The very same ones I saw more than thirty years ago, and now am visiting again.

Yet I also crossed this same exact path over thirty years ago. Does the universe—does God—allow events to happen more than once? Is He also here in the past, watching me replay this scene again? How would a God of 1966 view this intruder from the present? More to the point, does God reside in the archives of my past? Or am I in a place where nothing happens except what was *supposed* to happen? Now, I know why I have no volition back here, why I'm present only as an observer. I am in a dead zone where nothing ever changes. This place exists in my mind as an unalterable film. Just as the present would be to someone from the future.

And yet, I have this feeling that somehow, *someone* is with me, watching me drive my car through this series of images. Is someone from the future watching me now? Do the inhabitants of this dead world know I'm not one of them?

A Plymouth Valiant accelerates around my Ford, and takes its place ahead of me. Behind the wheel is a blonde smoking a cigarette.

A thought occurs—what if there's a person from the future float-ing behind the blonde's eyes, stepping through the endless series of instants that make up a segment of her life in this world of 1966?

Am I the only one re-experiencing my world? Or are there *others* here? Are they calling in, as I do, to someone from their own time, relaying information about songs on the radio, and automobiles and weather?

If there were other travelers here, would I recognize them?

Would it matter if I could?

No. Because all I see is from inside my own mind. A glorified, high-definition, sixteen-million polygons per second instant replay. I'm inside my own digital disc. And that's all.

I turn off the interstate and head south toward my last weekend in Cherokee.

Unexpectedly, as if someone threw a switch, the lights go out and I jump a track to some other time and place. I look down and see two parallel lines dissolving into the darkness. Ahead of me are two fig-ures, their flashlights casting perfect yellow circles on the dead brush and brown cinders of the track bed. I know where I am—that warm February night in 1959 when Evan, his sister Pammie and I almost got hit by a train.

The shorter of the two figures aims a flashlight skyward. I look up and see a gray oval of light on a ceiling perhaps a hundred feet above our heads. "Mitch, would you look at that!" Pammie says. "The sky's coming down!"

She's right. The sky is descending to earth.

Her brother pulls off his light jacket and balls it under his arm. "Aren't you guys hot? I'm burning up out here." I remember: An-other mile and he would have to sit down, exhausted, burning with a fever. Then, amid the deepening gloom, Pammie would go for help, leaving me with Evan and the approaching train.

Another blink and Pammie and Evan are gone.

Yet it's still night. Someone beside me points to the sky and I look up at a sliver of crescent moon surrounded by soft feathers of cirrus, fronting a black, star-filled sky. As I watch the cirrus feathers curl at the front to resemble the runner of a sleigh—a stream of ice crystals high above the earth. Another feather of pale cirrus crosses in front of the moon, and I see the faint bands of red, green and yellow. A rain-bow at night.

"See that star?" Rachael is aiming her mitten at something directly overhead. "That's Jupiter. And I think Saturn's around here somewhere."

Another time shift.

Though I can't feel anything, I hear teeth rattling, sense muscles tighten. It must be cold out here. Wherever *here* is.

"Look Rache, when are we going back home? I'm freezing to death. And my car's heater doesn't work."

"Michael, that's *the sky* up there. Don't you think the sky is *important?*" She gives me a look of perplexed irritation. "I promised when we started going together that I would learn something about science. Now, you act like you're all bored."

"If my battery freezes, we'll get stranded in the middle of nowhere."

"Michael, you are such a baby. This isn't the middle of nowhere. It's a missile silo. And I told Daddy we'd be here. If we're not in by midnight, he'll come looking for us."

I can see her breath in the night air. It *is* cold tonight.

"Rache, it's almost eleven. I gotta get up early tomorrow and drive back to school."

"We'll go in a minute. I was just gonna show you the dog star. It's up there somewhere. Probably near a tree. Ha!"

"Yes, yes. I see it. I can even hear it bark. Rachael, I am really, really cold."

"Michael, you know what I don't?"

"What?"

"*Care.* Learning about the stars is important. You don't want me to be a *stupe,* do you? I mean, last summer you were always telling me how Brenda Lacey was going to college to take art and chemistry and—"

Lock. It's time I called home.

"Leonard. Are you there?"

"Sure, Mike. How's the vacation?"

"A little jumbled up lately. You probably want to know where I am, right?"

"As always. The pupillometer tells me it's either night down there or you're very interested in something."

"It's night. I'm standing on a country road—five miles south of Weslayan, Missouri. It's definitely winter. We're—uh—I'm wearing a coat."

"*That's probably appropriate. Wouldn't want you to come back with the flu. Any music playing?*"

"No. But I've got an astronomy fix. Jupiter's in the east and Saturn's in the west. And there's a crescent moon in the southwest."

"*You give me Jupiter, Saturn and a crescent moon? Given the lat-long of Weslayan, I can tell you with confidence that it's late at night sometime in late winter, 1967. Plus or minus a season.*"

"Is that the best you can do?"

"*Mike, the technology has its limits.*"

"Okay. I'm going back to school in the morning, so it must be Sunday night."

"*That's better. Okay. The envelope please. Your mystery date is. . .January 15, 1967. If I'm right, you should keep your coat buttoned, because it'll get down to 19 above zero where you are. You're probably seeing some cirrus clouds, too, because there's a front moving in.*"

"Thanks."

"*Hey Mike, remember that Beatle song, 'Day in the Life?'*"

"Of course."

"*They're recording it next Wednesday—in your time zone, of course. See you in a millifortnight.*"

Minutes later, I'm following the white glare of my headlights down a brown dirt road, trying to keep the tires centered between the frozen tire tracks. Rachael, bundled up so only her face is visible, is glued to my side. For some reason, my side window is rolled down, probably to keep the frost from inside the windshield. I'd forgotten what it was like to have a car with a nonfunctional defroster. I put my arm around her and she leans against me, shivering in the cold air.

We turn onto a gravel road, cross a one-lane bridge, then return to the gravel. The hands on the wheel clench and the car accelerates around a turn.

I turn back to the road ahead and see Bob Dominic.

Lock.

"Leonard!"

"*Back so soon? That was quick. What are your coordinates this evening?*"

"I don't know. I'm jumping from year to year and hour to hour. It's like a roller coaster down here"

"*Sounds like it. Probably drank too much coffee. Try the decaffeinated next time.*"

"I think I'm getting whiplash. I wanted to know if this is normal."

"What's normal anymore? Your memories are either stored together for some reason or they have similar access codes. Call me if you get timesick. Out."

I unlock the scene. The haze clears. Bob Dominic is sitting at a dining room table with a bottle of Vess cola. He's in his standard short-sleeved white shirt and grey slacks. In his hand is a cigarette. Sitting next to him and across from me is his wife, Wanda, her brown hair cut short, wearing a denim shirt. She seems to be studying a road map.

I briefly lock the scene to check out the room: light tan paint on the walls, hardwood floor with a yellow rug, a painting of the Last Supper. We're definitely in their new house in Weslayan. Though I can't see it, directly behind me, facing the front door, is the stairs. And the short walk to Rachael's room.

One thing for sure: I'm in 1967. But which month? I scan my peripheral vision to the window—the blinds are closed. I could be anywhere within a six-month radius. I unlock the scene.

"...Well, I started out in radio back when all they played was country and western," Bob Dominic says.

"How Much Is That Doggie In The Window," Wanda croons. "Remember that one, Honey?"

"That's not country and western." Bob takes a drag from the cigarette.

"Sure it is. I remember you used to spin that record all the time for me."

"That's 'cause you used to call the station and pester me until I did. Then, I'd play it and everybody else in town would call and complain." He leans back in his chair and smiles. "Those were the days."

"Remember the preacher's wife, hon?" Wanda says, still looking at the map. "The one that wanted you to play 'Sixty Minute Man'?"

"I don't remember that," Bob says.

"Oh, sure you do, Bob." Wanda looks up at him. "Don't you lie."

"Mama here's got my whole life story." He looks at me. "Knows more about the things I've done than I know myself." He takes a long drag on the cigarette and puts it in the ashtray. "I enjoyed radio, but I liked working for the newspaper even more. Went from want ads to obituaries to editorial in six months. Of course, we only had a circulation of ten thousand."

"Honey, you weren't happy on that newspaper." Wanda says, tracing a route on the map with her finger.

"It was the editorials, that's the reason I quit." He looks at me. "I couldn't bring myself to write 'em unless I'd had a few drinks first. Pretty soon, I needed a drink before I did the want ads. The doc told me I had 'no more than *a thin sliver of hepatic cells left to perform the detoxifying functions.*' That scared me enough I quit the newspaper and haven't taken a drink since. That was when I first got into preaching."

"There are things that are more important than money," Wanda says, drawing a little line on the map.

"That's right," Bob says. "As that great poet, W.T. Grant said, 'feeling is first.'"

"Hon, I think you mean e.e. cummings. W.T. Grant is a department store."

"W.T. Grant must have said *something* important," Bob looks at her. "Maybe 'sales is first.'"

"You know—" Wanda pushes the map toward the center of the table. "If Michael takes this route here back to Kirksville, he can probably save an hour." She looks at me. "If your class starts 8:30, you could leave here at 6:30 Monday morning and make it."

"Are you sure?" I hear myself ask.

"Sure!" Wanda points to the map. "Instead of taking the interstate, turn north at Concordia—then on up to highway eleven. Takes you right into Kirksville."

"And remember," Bob smiles, "no state cops. You can drive as fast as you want."

"Bob—" Wanda glares at him. "We don't want him driving too fast—"

"He's young," Bob says. "Got good eyes. He can handle it. Drive ten miles over the speed limit and you'll make your class and have time for a cup of coffee."

I lock the scene.

"Leonard. How's things up there?"

"I'm bored out of my brain. How are things inside yours?"

"I'm still in 1967. The place is Weslayan, Missouri. What's the shortest, quickest route to Kirksville, Missouri from here? Is it highway eleven?"

"Justaminute...okay. Lessee...Mike?"

"Yes?"

"Forget highway eleven. The interstate is better."

"Are you sure?"

"*I'm sure. In the sixties, you could drive 80 on the interstate without getting tagged. But if you tried that on those crummy state blacktops, you'd have wound up in a ditch with an engine sitting on your face.*"

"They tell me it's a better route."

"*They? Listen, Mike. I am here with a very modern, sophisticated routing algorithm. I've had my second Jolt cola and I am extremely alert. Bored, but alert. And awake. You, by contrast, are lying on your back fast asleep listening to dream people. Case closed.*"

"Give me the stats."

"*Okay. It's 192 miles on I-70 versus 182 miles in the backwoods. However, those 182 miles are over some very interesting road. I think someone down there is trying to kill you. Excuse me, someone in your past tried to kill you. You want some pizza when you get out of there? You've only got another forty-one hours.*"

"No. I'm fine. I'll get back later."

Unlock. Bob Dominic leans back in his chair.

"...I used to drive this road all the time when I preached at Novenger. There's a few hills and curves, so you've got to be careful. All you gotta do is remember to crank the wheel a little when you go over the top. That way, you can make the curve on the other side. It's a little tricky, but you'll get the hang of it. Here, take this map with you."

"I think I'll take the interstate."

"Suit yourself." Bob gets up from the chair. "It's midnight and I've got an early service tomorrow—" he looks around. "Did Rache go to bed already?"

"She's up taking a shower," Wanda says. "I'll leave this map here, in case you want to take the short cut."

"Thanks."

Wait. Something's not right.

I lock the scene. Bob is halfway out of his chair. Wanda apparently is in the process of blinking; her eyes are closed. The room looks the same. Everything looks like a normal, standard, clear memory—

But still—

I unlock the scene and the image vanishes.

20

Horizon

I open my eyes to soft brown darkness and the sound of water running. I'm alone in the small bed—Rache is probably in the bathroom. I lock and survey the scene. Filtered by the window's lace curtain, a yellow rectangle of light stretches across the floor—probably from a streetlamp outside the window. Along one wall is the outline of a dresser and a simple round mirror; while across from the bed, in the opposite corner of the room, I see the door to the hallway. It's slightly ajar and the light from the hallway pours across the floor in a gentle spray.

Unlock.

I kick the covers loose and raise one knee into the yellow beam from the streetlight. Just as I thought—I'm wearing a J.C. Penny's white terry t-shirt with light blue cutoffs. Probably Levi's Sta-Prest with a thirty-inch waist. After all, I was fifteen pounds lighter then. Now.

Whenever.

The water stops. On the floor, hazy shadows of tree limbs move gently through the yellow light, pushed by a brisk southern breeze. I recall seeing the news on television—a high pressure area is expected to bring warmer temperatures with wind.

"Let's watch the weatherman with the fake toupee," she had said, then clicked through the channels until she found him, along with his areas of high pressure over Missouri and Kansas.

I hear the bathroom door open and close, followed by the decisive padding of feet up the hall. The bedroom door opens.

"Here I am," she says, jumping on the bed. "Gimme a kiss."

I kiss her quickly, then follow by slowly brushing my lips against hers. The sudden darkness means I've closed my teenager's eyes, leaving me with only the sound of her soft breathing.

"Justaminute."

I open my eyes to see the back of her nightshirt, a study in wide, horizontal stripes. The nightshirt from December, 1966.

A click and the radio comes on—midway through a Johnny Rivers song, "Baby I Need Your Lovin."

> *Every night I call your name*
> *Sometimes I wonder, girl, will I ever be the same...*

"There," she turns back to me, snuggling close. "Now, where were we?"

I lock the scene before my eyes close again. At the deep periphery of my vision, I see a star of light on her ring finger. Orange Blossom? Yes, that was it.

Unlock and the scene goes dark again. I listen for her breath against my ear. "Michael, I've wanted to tell you something now for a long time."

I open my eyes, kiss her cheek. "Then tell me."

"You know, I think some people are perfect for each other. Don't you think so? Some people look like they were born to be together. Other people can tell."

"*Most* of them can tell. At least I hope they can."

"And I figure the way to tell if you've found that perfect someone— is to look in their eyes."

"That right?"

"You really have to look sometimes, but if they're the one, you'll *know*."

I look across at her, inches away—look at her small mouth, slightly open, the smooth skin of her high cheekbones, her black hair cut in a ragged line inches above the dark curves of her eyebrows. I look into her eyes, feel myself being drawn into their depths, into her soul.

No, into *our* soul.

And now I'm afraid—as though I'm about to follow these photos of my past to a place I'm not ready for. I draw back. In a flicker I'm ahead in time. A minute? An hour?

Rachael is talking, her voice soft, deliberate, as if patiently explaining the secrets of the universe to a ten-year-old: "So when two people make a baby, they send a little message out and everyone can hear it. They may not know it, but some part of them does. That's why you can always tell when someone's pregnant."

"You can?"

"Yes! There was this girl in my class at school. And from the minute it happened I just *knew*."

"From the minute?"

"Well," she smiles, "from the day. I mean, you know, I wasn't actually there with 'em, but I knew. And when we get pregnant, I'm sure there'll be people who know it. The instant that baby happens inside me, there'll be people who'll know. My mom, for example. I bet your folks'll know too."

"I'm sure they will." My voice has a dolorous quality. "They've been expecting it ever since we got engaged."

"Michael—" she looks at me, her eyes glistening with the reflection from the window, "I'm really looking forward to it. I want you to know that."

She snuggles closer, her cheek next to my mine. I hear her breath in my ear, hear the words of the song shimmer into the room:

"...*You are my winter, the days and the nights*—"

Suddenly, there is something else shimmering—this one visible, just at the periphery of my vision. As I watch, the image forms, floating up from the depths. An outline of my room, years before. I see the walls, grainy and indistinct, the bed in the far corner with smoke curling from the ashtray.

The image flickers and becomes real. It's my brother, Earl. He smiles, removes the cigarette from the tray, takes a quick drag, then blows a thin stream of smoke into the air. After an eternity, he looks across at me. "You getting this down, Scout?"

"I don't know yet."

"Remember, if you tell yourself a lie, and you come to believe it, you can hurt your whole life.'" Earl looks at me for a moment, then is gone, leaving only the smoke from the cigarette. I watch it curl up and through the wooden slats of the venetian blinds, out into the cold winter night.

"Hey, get up." Rache pushes me. "You've got two hours to make it to Kirksville."

"My class starts late today. Lemme sleep."

"Michael, get *up!*"

Another push and I'm sitting up. Minutes later, I'm in the bathroom, brushing my teeth, staring blearily at the mirror. A brief lock and scan: I definitely look younger: thinner, for one thing. A lot more hair on my head, for another. And of course, the acne—one horrible red spot on my nose. And minimal hair on my chest.

Oh well.

Unlock and into the shower.

I step out of the shower, wrap a towel around my waist and reach for the comb. There's a knock at the door, followed by a click. Without warning, the door opens and Rachael squeezes into the bathroom with me.

"Just had to give ya a kiss—here."

I can almost feel her lips against mine.

The door closes and she's gone.

Twenty minutes later, I'm aiming the Fairlane north toward Kirksville. I pass a lone tractor-trailer rig as the first light of dawn sifts into the eastern horizon. The sky at this hour looks robin's-egg blue with watercolor swatches of yellow and salmon.

I drive down a hill, then back up on the ridge of the road. Looking to the east, I see that the fields are still blanketed in ground fog in anticipation of the sun. In fact, the fog is everywhere—in the valleys, floating above ponds, hanging above the small creeks, drifting scant feet above the road. Driving beneath a patch of gray, I see a delicate network of dark lines, the internal framework of a cloud.

The fog drifts through a line of trees, obscuring their branches momentarily, then moves on, pushed by some infinitesimal morning breeze. As I watch, the bright winter sun rises above the hills to the east.

I stop the car at an intersection to wait for the traffic light. As I wait, I lock and scan the nearby field—scan the frost on the grass, more dense on the western side, thinner where the light brightens it. The stoplight shifts to green and I continue on.

The sun is now an orange balloon on the horizon and the fog has become luminous. Above me, the colors cascade across the vault of sky from east to west—from orange to yellow in the east to robins-egg blue at the zenith to a darker blue in the west. Looking to the western horizon, I imagine the bright line of the advancing dawn, racing across the brown grasslands of Kansas and eastern Colorado.

It occurs to me that a sunset appears in precise strokes—certain clouds light up while others don't. The sun*rise*, however, is painted with a broad brush. The entire sky glows with blocks of clouds taking on color, coming in from the high levels, ultraviolet to yellow to red. Dropping from the top of the spectrum instead of rising from the bottom.

Did I see this dawn the same way years ago? Surely I did, my eyes are the same, the images are here. The photos exist.

The sun is well into the sky when I steer the car off the interstate and onto the blacktop shortcut. As I cross the Missouri River bridge into the west-central Missouri plains, I see an immense stream of cloud blanketing the entire valley and spilling up over the banks into the flat, empty fields on either side of the road.

Further north, I accelerate to 85 mph and pass beneath a shelf of high cloud, its underside resembling a dense, thick mattress. I notice that the puddles on either side of the road are coated with a glassy crust of ice.

Two hours into the trip north, the sky has taken on the milky cast of impending snow. Now I enter rugged far north Missouri, a corrugated landscape of steep, narrow ridges and valleys. I accelerate to 95 mph and the momentum carries the Fairlane over the tops of the hills, two wheels off the pavement. Is this feeling of acceleration in my mind? No, it's real.

The wheels hit the pavement—*Kabang!* Following Bob's advice, I turn the wheel to the left, steering the car around the curve to the next hill. By now, granules of snow are hitting the windshield and the horizon is hidden in gray. The defroster has failed and I slow to 80 mph to wipe the windshield with the sleeve of my coat.

Fifteen minutes later, with ice already forming on the rear window, I pull the car to a stop near my dormitory.

The week passes in a fast-forward blur, a series of quick jumps starting with my second class of the day, then the chem lab, then jump to World History, then to the horrendous cafeteria food.

Study? Fast forward.

A walk to the drug store for the latest Playboy? Blur it.

Playing football with the guys in the dorm? Okay. A few minutes, then forward to Tuesday—where I rocket through the whole day, slow briefly for a phone call home, then wait for the Tuesday night call from Rache.

As always, my roommate Jack gets to the phone first: "Mitchell, it's for you."

I take the phone, then press the receiver to my ear, trying to bring her voice as close to me as I can.

"Michael, I want to tell you something really funny. You know nosy Mrs. Langston up the street? She was over yesterday collecting for the heart fund and she asked Mama who you were. Actually wanted to know if you slept on the couch while you stayed here."

"And?"

"While they were talking, I came downstairs and I had two towels wrapped around my waist, up under my blouse. Looked like I was four months along. Her jaw dropped right to the floor! Ha! Are you coming down this weekend?"

"I don't know—I have a history test next week—"

"You know what I don't?"

"What?"

"*Care*. Listen, Michael, you could come down if you really wanted to. In fact, why don't you just *move* down here? Transfer to the college in Weslayan and be done with it. Think of all the money you'd save living here."

"You'd get pregnant."

"We'd be married, so it'd be okay. In fact, I'd try to get pregnant. Wouldn't that be fun? I mean, we'd have to try every other night. Maybe even in the daytime…"

"I don't know, Rache—getting married so soon—"

"Michael, you've come this far, you may as well come the rest of the way. Please come to Weslayan this weekend, I'll be here waiting for you."

I hang up the phone and step into Wednesday, then Thursday. And, finally, Friday—slowing down to savor the moment I leave this place for Weslayan. From Monday to Friday in one minute and thirty seconds, plus phone calls to my folks and Rachael. With practice, I'll do even better.

A minute later and I've covered four hours of driving time. Now, I pull into the Dominic's driveway. Time to slow down. How many minutes do I have left in this world? I'm afraid to call and ask.

The bedroom door closes, the light goes out, the radio comes on. She climbs into bed, her hair, longer now, flows over the pillow.

"Remember when I picked you up after you got off work at the Dairy Queen?" I tell her. "You always smelled like a hamburger."

"I can't eat 'em any more. Enough was enough...remember when you said you weren't coming down and then Dad sneaked you in and you hid in my closet? I about fainted."

"It wasn't that much of a surprise, was it?"

"Are you kidding——?"

I wrap my arms around her and close my eyes, knowing I may wake to face the other side.

But maybe not.

Maybe there is a place where I can dream from within my dream. Maybe instead of going up I can go further down. Deeper into my mind, into my universe.

So, instead of stepping down, I step *to the side*.

Suddenly I find myself inside a dusky room filled with objects from my earliest memories—a small red tricycle, my stuffed teddy bear, a high chair. In the background I hear soft music from a distant choir. As I watch, remnants of thoughts float down from above like dust through rafters to settle in this place. Memory shards.

Through a window I see dunes, pyramids, planets—perhaps from some discarded dream. I step outside and watch the clouds float past, huge mountains of fog against an indigo sky.

Nearby, the bright orb of my consciousness rises past, oblivious of me, toward this immense, vast ceiling. Across the vault of my own heavens, the moon rolls by, leaving its sandy track. Parts of me are here. Parts of my universe discarded in childhood, unused. I'm in the back storage room of my soul, searching through hazy meanings for the one true meaning. To the east, I see a door. I know where it leads.

Someday I must go there. But not now. Not yet.

I hear someone speaking. Softly, from across space and time.

"I can't get to sleep. Talk to me."

"What?" I open my eyes to see Rachael's face, inches from mine.

"Talk to me. I mean, tell me a story or something. Tell me one of your long jokes that goes on forever. Tell me the one about the sleeve job. That'll put me to sleep."

"I was dreaming."

"Yeah. I know."

"I mean, I was having a dream—inside my own memory. And I

saw this, I dunno, something. And I knew what was inside it."

"Lemme guess what was inside it—me," she places her leg over mine.

"I don't think so—it was different, that's all."

"Hey, I know." She rolls on top of me. "Maybe it was an angel inside. And the angel was talking to you. Did you ever think of that?"

"Angels?"

"Sure. Angels talk to you when you're asleep. What do you think dreams are all about? That's when the angels talk to you—or at least, they talk to the part of you that's an angel too."

"I really don't think I'm part angel, Rache."

"Sure you are," she gives me a quick kiss. "We're all angels. Part of us, anyway—and it's a part we don't always see. But it's there. How do you think we got together?"

"I wonder about that all the time."

"Me too, but there's a part of us that knows. I really believe that." She puts her head on my chest. "Hey, I kinda' like this. Mind if I sleep up here tonight?"

"No," I put my arms around her. "That would be fine."

21

Heat Lightning

Today the wind is roaring across the small airfield west of Weslayan. The dry weeds across the fence from the landing strip are nearly flat against the ground, forming a sand-colored surface broken by dark undulating waves.

"I don't see how you can fly in this wind, Bob."

"We'll have to see what my flight instructor says. If he isn't too scared to take it up, we'll go."

Bob parks the Pontiac at the hanger and glances at the windsock. It is sticking straight out, resembling a hard orange cone. "It's not a crosswind, so there's no problem getting in the air." He stubs a Salem into the ashtray. "It's no fun to fly when you have to aim the plane sideways to take off."

I follow him into the flight center, a small, cramped room with papers and maps pinned to the wall. I notice a stack of yellow teletype paper has spilled from a desk and onto the floor. On the wall is a Playboy foldout, a pretty blonde with a ponytail tied in black ribbon. She is in profile, her back to the camera. Next to the pinup is a calendar, February, 1967.

A short, balding man appears, flashing a smile. "Reverend, I thought you'd be preaching today."

"Did the early morning service," Bob says. "Marshall, this is Mike. He's down from Kirksville and I'm grooming him as a potential son-in-law."

"Howdy," Marshall grabs my hand. "Bob you gonna make him a

bush pilot?"

"Nah," Bob says, glancing outside at the planes. "He's got other plans on his mind. What's the wind like out there?"

"Oh, it's a little breezy," Marshall says, "gusts to forty-five, but it's right down the runway. You can take Oh-three-Lima, shouldn't have a problem."

"Gusts to forty-five huh?" Bob scratches his head. "And right down the runway? That might get interesting."

"Well, Lima's gassed and ready to go if you want. Just don't try any spins without caging that gyrocompass. You know what happened last time."

"Yeah, sorry about that." Bob turns to me. "Marshall here won't ever let me forget that. And I *paid* for it, too. Cost me ninety dollars."

We leave the building and I follow Bob toward the airplanes, rocking in the wind. Though I can't feel the temperature, I notice Bob's sheepskin jacket is open. I'm wearing a yellow London Fog windbreaker. It must be warm for winter. Perhaps the low sixties.

Living in the Northeast for the last twenty years I'd forgotten how changeable the weather is in western Missouri, especially in late winter. There would be weeks of bone-chilling cold followed by sunny stretches of warm, dry weather. And there would be wind, great waves of wind whistling and screaming across the brown grassy hills, kicking up dust and paper and loose twigs. In late winter, the Missouri landscape *moves*.

Bob heads toward a high-wing Cessna 172, but stops at a little yellow plane parked nearby. "Now, *here's* a plane," he says, patting the fuselage. "Put a 145 horse engine in this and you could take it over the Sierra Madres."

I watch him pat the wing, look beneath it to check the cotter pins. He pauses to inspect a small, finger-size hole in the wing. "They probably ought to patch this. Wouldn't want to have it rip open at ten thousand feet."

"No..."

Bob pauses to look at the wind sock. "Let's see. The wind is forty-five knots down the runway. You know, if we did a power-on stall, I'll bet we could fly backwards."

"Maybe some other time," I tell him.

"How about tomorrow?" Bob says. "My flight physical is due next month and I'd like to get some hours in before then. The doctor's getting real picky lately."

"That right?"

"Yeah," he looks around at the planes. "With my luck, I'll probably need new glasses and I don't have the money to spend on 'em."

Seeing him standing there next to the little yellow airplane, his jacket open, his black hair blowing in the wind, I know he would have made a good bush pilot. From the far end of the runway, a thick-bodied Luscombe Silvaire whines into the air like a huge metal pelican. Bob tracks it with his eyes, watching until it disappears into the bright yellow haze of the western sky. After a moment, he turns back to me. "Your dad has his pilot's license, doesn't he?"

"Yeah. But he quit flying when my brother was killed."

"I remember when that happened—remember reading about it," Bob says. "I never knew your brother but that stuck with me."

"Happened the same day Kennedy was killed," I tell him.

Bob nods. "You have some time in the air too, don't you?"

"Yeah. Earl always talked about getting a plane and flying through the clouds, looking for the places where the Elk Fork river began. He never got a chance to do much of that. I figured I owed it to him." I look out across the runway, at the waves of wind flowing across the brown grass. "So—after I solo'd last spring, the first thing I did was find the source of that river."

"That right?" Bob smiles. "Where was it?"

"It starts in a little ditch along a side road west of highway 24. Goes to a branch that crosses under the highway. From there, it cuts across a field into a creek. And the creek turns into the river."

"And I guess the river runs into the ocean," Bob says.

"Eventually." I look at him. "That's the idea, anyway."

"I'm glad you know how to fly," Bob smiles. "After I'm too old to fly I can ride with you."

"Any time."

"You know," he says, "from that first time Rachael met you—that's all we heard about—*Michael this, Michael that*. She probably dated every boy in her class—but it never lasted more than a week. After the second or third month of *Michael, Michael, Michael*, we figured it was special."

"I really care about her." I look at him. "'Course, I guess you know that."

"Yeah, I know. I can tell there's something special there." He pulls a pack of Salems from his shirt pocket. "Wanda and I are kind of like that. First time I saw her, I was working at a little grocery store down in Corinth. She walked in the front door and asked me where the laundry detergent was. I think she wanted Tide. I took her back and showed her which aisle it was on. Right then, something said, 'Bob, there's your future.'" He lights the cigarette. "And then, when I was telling Del, my boss about her, how cute she was, and how I was probably gonna marry her—he said, 'well, she'd probably like to hear that—you're the reason she's been coming in here.' Turned out Wanda was Del's youngest daughter."

"Love at first sight, huh?"

"Well, Wanda claims that she'd been coming in for about a week, asking where things were, just to get my attention. But I only remember that one time. After we got married, I found out that before Del hired me, he had Wanda stock all the shelves. She'd been doing that ever since she turned sixteen. Knew the store better than anybody."

"How old were you when you got married?"

"I was eighteen and Wanda had just turned seventeen. Army wouldn't take me, said I had some kind of heart problem, so there we were. Back in '51, nobody was thinking about college, and the economy was pretty good. Just after the war and all—"

"Our college prof says that war is good for the economy."

"Well, he's right. With the war in Vietnam, business down at the supermarket is going like gangbusters. Last night I stocked the biggest load of oranges I'd ever seen. Fifty boxes." He takes a drag on the cigarette. "I could probably land you a job down there. Two hours a night, $1.60 an hour. Dollar-ninety on weekends."

"I'd have to move down from Kirksville."

"Well, the whole family's been expecting *that*." He smiles. "The college here is a state university, so it's cheap. The married students housing on campus is real reasonable. You could get a nice little apartment, work and go to school. Of course, Rache would probably want to quit her job at the Ku-Ku, so you'd have to think about maybe two jobs."

"Two jobs? And go to school too?"

"I know the manager over at the radio station. You could do what I did—spin records on the late shift. Put on a long-play, turn off the microphone and ask the engineer to wake you when the record is over. That's what I used to do. I'd work four hours and sleep two. Then, I'd go to the Safeway and work another two. A person really doesn't need as much sleep as he thinks."

"I don't know. What if I don't wake up in time and the record just keeps clicking or something?"

"Nobody but Rache and her Mama listens to that station anyway. It only has about ten watts. I wouldn't worry about it."

"It's such a big change, getting married and all. Gotta get all these jobs, find a place to live—"

"If you can keep Rachael from getting pregnant you two will do fine." He laughs. "If she's like her Mama, you tell her a dirty joke and she'll get pregnant. She loves having babies. Been bothering me to have another one, and I told her four is plenty. Besides, I'm working all the time as it is."

"I just don't see how you do it."

"The Dominics have never needed much sleep. After you and Rachael get married, you'll probably find that out. Just something you get used to." He stubs the cigarette out on the ground, then looks at me. "Most of the boys Rachael has dated weren't exactly the pick of the crop. Back when she first told us about you, I thought she'd made a mistake. You didn't smoke, drink beer, ride a motorcycle. Never been arrested for speeding. Came from a good family. Was planning to go to college—"

"I did get stopped for speeding once."

"Yeah, but that was just last week, so it doesn't count," Bob smiles. "Anyhow, you were the first boyfriend who never fell asleep in my sermons. To a small-town preacher, that means a lot. Wanda and I figured you were it. Of course, when Rachael has her mind made up, you just can't change it. So we didn't try."

I lock the scene to study Bob's face for clues to his feelings. Is he happy with my plans for Rachael's future? Resigned? I don't know. I decide that I'll *never* know.

After a moment, I unlock the scene and watch as he lights another Salem, then blows a thin stream of smoke into the wind. Then he looks at me. "The thing is, I love my daughter—and I like you. And I think you both have a lot going for you. If things didn't work out financially, I probably couldn't help you much—except give you a temporary place to live and a whole lot of moral support."

"There's always the army," I say. "They'll probably get me anyway. If I make it out, I'll have the GI bill to finish college—and if I stay in, then I guess I'll have a guaranteed job."

"Contending with both Rachael *and* the military for the rest of your life——" Bob looks at me, "is that something you think you could do?"

"I could do that *easy*."

He pats my shoulder. "And if you get a post near Weslayan, you could babysit for us if Mama gets pregnant again."

"No problem."

"And maybe I could get you to substitute preach for me on alternate Sundays."

"I wouldn't know what to talk about," I say. "The last time I read the Bible I was ten or eleven."

"It'll come back to you. Besides, you can use my notes. The thing to remember is, a good sermon consists of three points, and a poem." He ticks each off on his fingers. "And if you have the shortest sermon in the world, you can suggest long hymns, then have the congregation sing all four verses rather than just two out of four. Pauses add up, too. You can get five good minutes out of pauses alone."

"I'll try to remember all that."

"If you're game, so are the Dominics." Bob extends his hand. "For what it's worth—welcome to the family."

Two hours later, we're huddled in the corner of the Kuku, the large white-and-red glass-and-tile hamburger joint on Weslayan's main drag. Bob, cigarette in his hand, is halfway through a fish sandwich and a tall cola. From my position here in the future, I notice his eyes are red and tired, see a trace of gray in his thick black hair. He looks much older than his thirty-four years. He's telling me what life with Rachael will probably be like.

"——it won't always be easy." He finishes the cigarette, then stubs it out in the ashtray. "She's a little like her mother—you get only *one* chance. And once she gets her mind set on something, it's impossible to change it. So you might have to admit you're wrong even when you're not. Just to keep the peace."

"I can probably do that."

"On the positive side, she's absolutely loyal. She'll stick with you through thick and thin——" He pauses to open another pack of Salems. "And the way the world is, you might get more than your share of *thin*."

He lights another cigarette, blows a stream of smoke, then taps the ash into the foil ashtray. I scan down and slow the scene, watching the ash tumble into the tray and dissolve there. Looking outside, I see children pull their collars against the chill wind as a high, gray stratus obscures the sky. In a few short hours it will be dark.

Twenty minutes later Bob pulls the Pontiac into their driveway. From here, I can see through the kitchen window. Wanda stands at the counter, working at something, while Rachael moves back and forth across the field of view. No doubt setting the table. In the living room, the kids are probably watching television. It's a Monday night.

As I catch Rachael's movement behind the window, I lock the scene—her hair is in disarray. She's wearing her favorite red sweatshirt, turned inside out. And even though it's still winter she's in her denim shorts. I see her face, her eyes. This is her world, her time.

As I study this perfect, real-life image, I think of what my dad used to tell me: "Son, when you know, you *know*."

Right now, I *know*. I also know how this will all turn out. Will I be able to face losing Rachael a second time? If I had any sense, I'd bail out now. Call Leonard to pull me back.

I unlock the scene and she vanishes past the window.

Bob turns off the ignition and places the keys in his pocket. Then he hands me a stick of Doublemint gum. "Rachael is probably helping Wanda with dinner. If our breath smells like Kuku french fries, we'll never hear the end of it."

I step out of the car, close the door, and walk around to the front of the house. On the old wooden porch swing, someone has lined up a platoon of plastic soldiers. Bradley, no doubt. He'll probably grow up and join the military.

Through the dining room window I see Rachael run to the front door. Bob walks a step ahead—she'll give him a hug first. I'll get the kiss and a quick "Love you—where ya been?" Everything seems real. It occurs to me that this simply *can not* be just a film playing in my mind—some dusty reel from the events of my early life.

I see that Wanda is wearing something white on her left hand. A bandage. Of course. The weekend before, she had cut her finger on a broken glass in the kitchen sink. I remember driving to the emergency room, steering with one hand and squeezing Wanda's bleeding hand with the other. The song on the radio: "My Back Pages." I remember the police car following us to the hospital and getting my first speeding ticket.

It's all flooding back. I take a deep breath and feel my lungs fill with the air, feel the night breeze on my face.

"That's the night wind," Rache had told me once. "Comes through here at five-thirty every night. Without fail. It's supposed to bring good luck."

Something flashes in the sky. I lock the scene, scan toward the edge of my vision. More flashes, even in lock mode. Something is going on.

"Mike, this is Leonard. Can you hear me?"

Something is wrong.

"Yes, I hear you."

I've got to bring you up. Tell you why in a minute.

"Leonard, wait."

"On the count of ten——."

Unlock. My foot touches the front step.

"Nine—eight——"

I'm on the porch as Rachael opens the door for us. "Where you guys been? Supper's almost ready."

"Seven—six——"

"We stopped for a coke," Bob turns to me. "But we're both starved, right, Mike?"

"Absolutely."

"Five—four——"

She hugs her father, then takes a step toward me. "C'mere."

"Three—two—one——"

Inches away, I hold her here, those beautiful eyes, that smile, her arms out, her touch only inches away. "Love you——"

A lightning flash and I'm in a train pulling away from a station. Rachael becomes a photograph. The photo recedes into the distance. And now she's gone.

"You okay, Mike? Let's get this stuff off him, Terri——" I hear Leonard nearby. Vaguely, I feel someone tugging at my scalp.

"Why—ouch!" In the darkness behind my visor I feel a sharp stab as wires are pulled from my skin.

"I got it." Terri's voice. "Theta's off—EKG's off—catheter's already out—IV is out. He's clear."

Someone lifts the helmet from my head and the green dots of light slide up. I look around at the sterile lab, the machine, the chair. "Leonard, I wasn't ready to come back."

"Yeah, I know. Sorry. What's the square root of 144?"

"Twelve——"

"What's today's date?"

"I have no idea. I've been out of town, dammit—what's going on?"

"Anything unusual happen down there just before I brought you back?"

"I saw a little lightning. That was all. Was it you doing that? Did you scram me?"

"No. If I did, your eyes'd be rolled back in your head. Here, let me help you up—" He pulls me to a sitting position.

"What happened—?"

"I don't know yet," Leonard says, wiping perspiration from his forehead. "One minute your trace was okay and the next thing I knew, the theta alarm went off. The t-4 wave from your right temporal lobe gave a couple of quick blips, then went to east hyperspace."

"What?"

"Vanished. *Supposedly*, you see that sort of thing on the screen right before the dreamer goes flatline. I'm not going to have you circling the drain on my shift. Very career-limiting move." He turns. "Terri, can we get a printout of that trace, please? We'll have to send that up to Poundstone."

"What's going on?" I feel my heart begin to pound.

"I don't know," Leonard says. "I don't do the diagnosing around here. I'm not that high on the food chain."

"Leonard, it's not coming up," Terri says, tapping the keyboard. "Nothing's happening."

"Read the famous manual, Terri," he says irritably. "First hit the F-5 key—"

"Everything's locked." She looks at Leonard, then at me. "I think Mr. Mitchell scrammed your computer."

22

Observer

I'm standing inside the door to Gail's room, telling her what had happened. As usual, she's in t-shirt, shorts and no shoes.

"Let me get this right—" she laughs. "You—Mike Mitchell—actually scrammed the Big Iron? That's great. That is *so* great."

"Leonard didn't think so. He called Zey and Poundstone. We all spent about an hour talking about it." I run my hand across my sandpaper-beard face. "They finally decided it was a computer glitch. Leonard's trying to track it down."

"Computer glitch, huh?" She grins. "I *love* it."

"Yeah, for a minute I thought it was all over. But Poundstone authorized me for another run in two days. Once they get the computer up." I pause, my fatigued brain trying to collect its thoughts. "How's Coltrane. Has he come up yet?"

"He came to breakfast this morning with a beard like yours. Otto's due back from his trip any minute now. I haven't heard anything, so he's probably okay."

"That's good." I look at the floor, then up at her.

She chews her lip. "Look, if you want to use a shower, c'mon in. And if you want to get rid of that sexy beard, I even have a safety razor—"

"Thanks for the offer, but I think I'll go to my room and crash for awhile—it's been 48 hours here, but down there it's been about two weeks."

"Hey, guess what?" Her smile brightens almost to breaking. "I took the plunge and asked Leonard to look up Eric."

"And Leonard found him, didn't he?"

"It took less than a minute. Now I know where he lives," she says. "I even know his American Express card number."

"Okay." I lean against the wall. "Fill me in."

"Well-l-l," she says, "he used to be a reporter for a Detroit newspaper, and quit to teach high school in the Milwaukee, Wisconsin school system...he's won four national awards for excellence."

"The important stuff, Banks," I laugh. "Is he married?"

"He has three children—all boys—"

"And?"

"He's divorced—" she says, her voice pitched high like a schoolgirl's, "and he's flying down to see me next weekend!"

"Congratulations." I reach out to give her a hug. I notice her eyes are glistening. Has she been crying?

"Mike, I called him and he knew who it was! It was like he'd been waiting all this time—" she quickly brushes the back of her hand against her eyes— "this is so stupid. I feel like a high school girl going on her first date." She looks up at me. "Do I look okay? I'm not too skinny am I? Do my eyes look—you know—too *old*?"

"Yes, no, and no," I tell her. "You look terrific—I'd do something about that zit on your nose, though."

"Omigod! You're not serious!" She claps her hand over her face.

"You're right. I'm not. See you at dinner tonight." I turn to leave.

"Mike—" She touches my shoulder. "Is it all right if we don't sleep together anymore?"

I look at her for a minute, my fatigued brain searching for the right words. "I'll miss it, that's for sure...but I understand. It was nice while it lasted. *Will* I see you at dinner tonight?"

"Sure." Gail stands in the door, her dark blonde hair down around her shoulders, eyes red with tears, while I walk the long stretch of hallway back to my room.

·····✦·····

It's 6:30. I'm sitting in the cafeteria picking my way through an unexceptional Caesar salad. Across from me, Otto and Keller are engaged in a quiet discussion—probably about some science concept, while nearby, Lowell and Leonard are pointing at a stack of computer readout, arguing about someone named Joe Code.

Gail hasn't showed up. In a way, I didn't expect her to come down, given the conversation earlier today. She's probably in her room thinking hard about her next moves in life. And I don't blame her. It's not every day someone gets a second chance like that.

I consider the salad. While I've been sitting here brooding about the past, some part of me has neatly arranged the olives into a line along the side of the plate. Across from them, the boiled egg slices are stacked neatly next to the carrot sticks.

Someone in here is trying to be an engineer. If my life isn't so orderly, maybe my salad can be.

My mind shifts to Rachael—to the wonderful times I've been having with her and the impending disaster waiting only weeks ahead.

When did we break up? Was it June, 1967—or was it much earlier? I can't remember. Having purged it from my memory banks years before, I can't access it now that I need it.

I feel like I'm on a train heading for a brick wall, but I don't remember exactly where the brick wall *is*. One month away? Or three? Will I come back while I'm on my date with Brenda—or will it be when Rachael confronts me, tears in her eyes? Maybe it will be those horrible days I spent in the hospital after the accident. Did I cross that traffic divider on purpose? Some part of me already knows; now the rest of me will find out.

One thing I know for sure, the moment is up ahead. And I'm approaching it at record speed.

"Mind if I sit down?" I hear a voice and look up.

It's Coltrane.

Eleven-thirty. Nearly midnight.

I'm in the skybox lounge in jeans and t-shirt, sock feet resting on a fake marble table. Coltrane is sitting at the other end of the couch in essentially the same configuration, one boot on the table, the other on the floor.

We've been here for the past hour and haven't said twenty words between us. Instead, we sit here in the dark and look out the window—at tourists lost on the streets below, at the occasional bus threading its way through the city, at the lonely jets arriving at the airport to the north.

We don't talk. We just watch and think. Right now, I'm thinking about what it all means. At dinner, after Leonard went back to the lab, Lowell and Keller got into a discussion about the nature of the mind. Lowell claimed that one particular part of our personality oversees everything and views our life from somewhere outside of time. More- over, it makes decisions for us based on what is best for our entire life— start to finish. "It explains coincidence anyway," Lowell had said with great finality.

Keller, for his part, argued that Lowell's position was only half- right. *Obviously*, we were *all* part of one greater thing and *It* made all the decisions in our lives. And, It also decided what parts of the past to visit. Otto said he expected something like that from Keller, who had once attended a Jesuit college.

Gail had said nothing. Her own beliefs were intact—all she did was smile and eat her fruit salad. She seemed truly happy—perhaps for the first time here. She believed there was one perfect person for her. And in a few days—after years of waiting—she would be with him again. Nothing else mattered. I felt good for her.

Seeing Gail, I considered asking Leonard to locate Rachael too. But would I be prepared for who I'd find? Right now she's probably living somewhere in the midwest, a great wife to somebody and a caring mother to her children. Solid and territorial—protective of her life and those around her. I saw that in her even in our first months to- gether.

Yet nothing is certain. We all change. What if I found someone different—what if the hidden part of her that was supposed to watch over her life didn't do so well—what if it let her down, took away her smile, hurt her life?

Earlier tonight, I had asked Coltrane if I should even be going back to that time—should I even see Rachael again, knowing what the fu- ture held. His answer was typical—strange and convoluted. But it made perfect sense. "That time is part of your life, Mitchell," he said. "It will always be there for you. *If* it's what you want."

I look out the window at the dark, endless sky. *Is* that what I want?

There's no answer. It's midnight and the door to the philosophy class is closed and locked. The light is out and the only sound from inside is the ticking of the clock.

Nine a.m.

I take a deep breath and settle into the induction chair, feel it envelop me. Nearby, Terri is attaching the temporal sensors to the right side of my scalp. "You know, I've always thought we should shave a little spot on your scalp here—then it wouldn't hurt so much when we pulled it loose—what do you think, Mr. Mitchell?"

"C'mon, Terri," Leonard says. "Nobody wants little spots shaved on their scalp."

"It'd probably catch on somewhere," I tell her.

"There," she presses the sensor on. "Now be good and don't lose your t-4 signal again," she smiles brightly, "or we'll have to bring you back."

"I promise."

"Here's your lunch wagon," she says, bringing the IV rack.

"Mike," Leonard says, "you want some Japanese bean crackers? Last real food for 48 hours."

"Thanks, but I've got a dinner of fish sticks and spinach waiting for me down there."

"Fish sticks and spinach?" Terri says, tying the rubber constriction band around my arm. "That sounds good. I'm jealous…make a fist, please."

I wince as the IV needle goes into my arm, then close my eyes. Will I return to the same place I left—inches away from her? Probably not. My chances of hitting that exact second are remote. The past is a big place.

"EKG's up—oxygen saturation—temporal leads good. General signal strength okay. All right Terri, let's squid him and cap him."

Terri places the ceramic microphone cylinder against my throat, then looks at me with her big blue eyes. "'Squid him and cap him.' Have you ever heard of such a thing? I don't know where he gets that stuff." She turns. "Just a minute, Leonard. Okay, I got it. Here's your crash helmet, Mr. Mitchell. Have a nice dream."

"And drive safely," Leonard says.

"I'll try." I fit the helmet onto my head.

The visor comes down and I'm all alone.

But not for long.

Part IV

23

Morning, 1967

The hallway is filled with college students. In the background music is playing. Across the room, opposite the phones, a group of people are watching television: "Batman." It's probably some Thursday night in early spring, 1967. I guess middle or late February.

I pick up the phone, wait for the operator, deposit fifty cents and dial the number.

"Hello?"

"Rache? This is Mike."

"*Hi!* Am I gonna see you this weekend?"

"Yeah. I'm driving down tomorrow after my last afternoon class."

"Listen. There's a teachers' conference and I don't have to go to school tomorrow."

"Rache—I have a night class at six, but I should be out by eight-thirty or nine. And I can skip my classes tomorrow. Maybe I can come down tonight." It occurs to me I'm listening to one reason I never made straight A's in college.

"Tonight? *Could* you?"

"It'll be late. Is that all right?"

"I don't care if it's three in the morning. I'll be waiting for you."

As I pull into Weslayan, the town is deserted—quiet, except for the clicking of the stoplights. A scrap of paper kites up the street in advance of the storm. I vaguely remember the hours preceding this:

The teacher droning until 9:30 p.m., then another half-hour looking for my cutoff jeans.

Then a gas fill-up—28 cents a gallon—and four hours of counting white hyphens against the brown pavement. Between were irregular bursts of headlights, a string of semitrailers lumbering along the two-lane road, the occasional microwave tower. But mostly there was darkness. Somewhere along the road, I rolled down the window and let the night stream in.

To the west, paralleling the highway, I could see an intermittent display of lightning signalling an approaching late winter cold front. Somewhere near the town of Renick, was a benign blue-gray mountain of fog, floating five hundred feet above the ground, it's diaphanous edges illuminated pale yellow by the full moon.

A half-hour later, the scud had moved in and the windshield was spattered with rain. The radio produced only static. At some point, I switched it off.

A right turn onto the interstate, then half an hour later, across a Missouri River bridge illuminated by lightning. Then, at Blackwater, the darkness turned white as sheets of rain slammed into the windshield.

I pass cars, pulled off along the road. I remember thinking about earlier trips down this road, Rache illegally at the wheel, peering intensely at the road. Drinking bottles of ginger ale. Depleting bags of potato chips.

On one trip, completely bored, she threatened to remove her blouse, then her bra, then "stick George and Charlie up against the window."

It never happened.

Instead, we traded places—she scooting beneath me to take the wheel while I sat nervously watching for the highway patrol, planning what we would say to them if caught: "Yes, sir. She has a license to drive...no, I don't think she brought it with her...yes, we're married. *Newly* married. Last week. Her dad performed the ceremony, you can call him."

The rain let up as I reached the exit to Weslayan. Ten more miles of absolute quiet. No cars. Nearly midnight.

By the time I reached town, the temperature had dropped ten degrees, yet the streets were dry. Had the storm reached here yet? No.

I have to decide: Should I call or not? No. Too late. It would only wake everyone up. And they knew I was on the way. I told them I'd be here.

I steer the car down toward the Safeway store. Perhaps Bob is working there tonight, restocking supplies. Maybe I could help.

No. The store parking lot is completely deserted.

I turn on the radio and hear the Four Tops singing "Bernadette." I pass the Harrison Street church, then, after two quick turns in succession, I'm at the Dominics.

I switch off the engine and look at my watch: It's 1:55 am. Inside, there appears to be a light on in the kitchen. A memory: Some weeks ago, my car ran out of gas on the way down from college. As a result, I was three hours late and had to sleep in the Fairlane until morning. When I awoke, Stacie and Amy were peering through the car windows, laughing at the grubby, desheveled college student lying in the front seat. The next day Wanda sliced open her finger on a broken glass in the sink.

Exhausted, I walk to the front porch. Should I knock on the door at this late hour?

"Hey, Sport." I turn. It's Rache, sitting in the wooden porch swing. Dressed in her nightshirt, no shoes, and with the ubiquitous rollers in her hair.

A hug, then a kiss. She takes my hand and leads me to the kitchen where I find a plate of bologna sandwiches, potato chips and a large bottle of Vess Cola.

I look at the rollers. "You hear any stations with that antenna?"

"You'd be surprised what I can get with this." She gives me a another quick kiss, then hands me a plastic tumbler brimming with iced cola. "I know you don't like this stuff, but it's all I could find, sorry."

After I use the bathroom and splash water on my face, I return to the kitchen. The light is out and there is a small, lighted candle in the middle of the table. "I bought the candle today after you called," she says, pouring me a glass of cola. "I figured it be more romantic."

"It looks really nice."

She sits on my lap. "Notice anything different?"

"No, what?"

"I've got my nightshirt on—"

"I can see that."

"And I'm not wearing my shorts. Only my underpants."

"Are you going to bed with me this way?"

"Sure—if you don't try anything. I got tired of wearing those shorts. They were just too uncomfortable." She jumps off my lap, then pads around to sit down at the table opposite me. "Let's pretend we're married and I'm fixing you a late dinner."

"Real late dinner." I bite into the sandwich. Strangely, wonderfully, from up here in the future—I can almost taste it. Bologna and mayonnaise with a pickle.

"Did I tell ya I got my old job back?"

"No, where?"

"The Kuku. Can you believe it? I walked in and asked if they wanted to hire me again and they said yes—" she pauses to take a bite of sandwich—"anyhow, they asked me if I remembered how to grill a hamburger and of course, I did. Next Friday when you come I'll be working."

"I remember when you worked at the Dairy Queen in Corinth. You smelled like a hamburger and onions."

"And it made ya hungry, didn't it?"

"I think I'm falling to sleep. Can we go to bed now?"

"Soon as you finish your dinner. And don't forget the chips. And you gotta drink all your Vess cola. I mean, I *worked* putting this together."

"Great meal." I return to the bologna. "I love it."

"Michael," she looks at me across the candlelight. "I really like this. Sitting here at the table, just you and me. I hope this is what it's like when we're married."

"It'll probably be that way. I'll have to work three jobs like your dad. And come home late."

"I gotta tell ya what Mom said." She leans forward. "She said she wished we'd wait to get married until I finish high school—" a pause, "—but if we didn't, we could live here with them. Until you can apply for college down here and get into the married students housing." She leans forward and whispers, "*Good plan, huh?*"

"That's really nice of them. Maybe I can transfer to the college down here in Weslayan and work three jobs. And then I'll be too tired to pass my army induction physical."

"After we get married, I promise you'll be too tired to pass your physical. I plan to keep you real busy." A sly smile. "Well, for the first *year* anyway."

"I'm really falling asleep." I push the plate away. "Let's go to bed."

"Okay," she gets up from the table, then sits down on my lap. "But just because we're pretending to be married down here in the kitchen doesn't mean we're married upstairs. So ya gotta promise not to do anything. I'm trusting you now."

"I promise I won't do anything—I'm too tired." Then, I stop, my eyes focused on her nightshirt.

"What." Her eyes narrow.

"No t-shirt underneath?"

"No."

"Let me see."

"For*get* it," she jumps off. "It'd make you worse than you already are." She picks up the plate and takes it into the kitchen. "Anyway, George and Charlie are too tiny to fool with. In fact, if I could gain about five pounds up here—I'd be okay."

"I think you're probably fine—" My gaze drifts from Rachael's chest to her hips, then to her legs, finally to the kitchen floor. And stays there. "I think I want to sleep, now."

"The school nurse at Cherokee said if you want big boobs you have to eat Graham crackers and bananas. I tried it, but, as you can see, it didn't work." She runs water into the kitchen sink. "I don't know if I told you—there was a girl in my class who massaged her boobs to make them bigger—but it only made 'em *longer*. Ha!"

"Probably massaged them the wrong way or something—should have asked her boyfriend how to do it."

"I'm sure *you* could have given her some good advice. But it's too late for that, 'cause *I've* got you now." She takes my hand. "C'mon."

I open my eyes to a bright yellow morning in Weslayan. The sun is streaming in through the venetian blinds, washing the opposite wall and dresser in long, horizontal bars of light.

My right arm is around Rachael. Though it's cold outside, the room is probably warm—I see her leg on top of the covers, bent over mine. Beginning at her toes curled down in sleep, my eyes trace the soft line of her bare leg up past her dimpled knee, then down to the smooth perfect curve of her thigh. I pause there and study the yellow light pouring across her leg, like a gentle ridge facing the morning sun— bright on one side, darker in the valleys.

My eyes move up to the top of her thigh, where it meets the hem of her nightshirt. From there, I trace the edge of dark blue fabric as it travels and ripples across her body, finally meeting with the shaded white surface of the blanket.

Is she cold? I pull the blanket over her leg, leaving only her foot exposed to the cool air in the room. I study her small, gentle form for a moment, then pull her closer to me. In response, her toes curl momentarily, then her foot disappears beneath a fold of the white flannel sheet. Somewhere in 1967, I can almost feel her legs against mine.

Two hundred miles away in Kirksville, my class is probably starting up and my Semantics professor is marking me absent. I didn't care then, I don't care now.

Next to me I hear a sigh.

"Rache, you awake?"

"Um-hm." She snuggles closer, pressing her body next to mine.

"You're sure you're awake?"

"Yep." The blanket moves as she curls her leg over my body. "Mmm. Y'know what?" She asks in a soft whisper.

"What?" I turn to face her, her lips inches from mine.

"There's no school today," she opens her eyes, heavy, dreamy with sleep. "Isn't that great?" A stretch, a sigh. "I think we should stay here all day."

"Along about six tonight, you're folks would start to worry."

"Listen," she smiles. "They worry if we're not up and out by sunrise."

"Yeah." I give her a long, slow kiss. "I could spend the day with you like this."

"Um-hm." She looks at me from across the pillow. "You know, Michael, when two people love each other—I mean really love each other—I like to think they should have a special place they can go where it's them and nobody else. What do you think?"

"I think that's a pretty nice idea."

"If we had a special place," she pauses to share a quick kiss, "what would you want it to be like?"

"I'd like a place outdoors," I tell her. "Like on top of a grassy hill."

"Yeah. And it's spring," she says. "The sky is just a perfect blue. With great big puffy clouds and the wind blowing. I just *love* the wind."

"Me too."

"And there'll be a little country church nearby—where we can finally get married. That'll be our place, okay?

"Okay."

"Forever and ever. Just ours. And I'll make sure."

"Deal." I give her another kiss. Downstairs I hear the sound of pans clanking on the range. "Hear that?"

"Yeah. Mom's up. Pretty soon everyone else will be too, so if you wanna use the bathroom, you better get to it."

"No, go ahead."

"Thanks. I've got dragon-mouth." Rachael pulls the blanket back and slowly climbs from bed. I watch her walk across the bedroom in her nightshirt, watch her hips undulating beneath the blue cloth. I notice the line of underwear is missing. Perhaps the shirt is all she had on last night. My eyes then travel up her back to her neck, past the thin gold chain, then up to her hair, thick and black and in disarray from the night before. As she opens the door, she scratches her head, then quickly bends to attack a spot on her right leg. It is the fluid, quick motion of the natural athlete.

As she disappears into the hallway, I try to arrange the bedcovers.

"Hey Michael," she says from the hallway. "C'mere."

I push the covers back and follow Rachael to the hallway. She's standing at the window, shivering, her arms folded tight.

"Look at that. Isn't it beautiful? I never thought we'd see something like this."

The skyline of trees behind the house has become white with frost, shimmering in the early spring sunlight. As we watch, a sparrow lights on a small, high branch, sending a feathery, sparkling cloud of crystals to the ground.

I know from my general science class that what I see is the result of a precise combination of fog, temperature and perfectly still air. I also know that the phenomenon is supremely local—not likely to be recorded on any databases. Like so many things in our lives, it's a small, bright island of wonder in the gray stream of time—accessible only by memory.

"We gotta take a walk," she says. "That's all there is to it."

"What about staying in bed?"

"With something like that out there? *Forget it.* I get the bathroom first. Then you." She closes the bathroom door behind her, and I'm alone in the hallway.

I knock on the bathroom door. "Rache. Tell you what. I'll brush my teeth while you take your shower."

"Nope. You can't see my shower-suit until after we're married."

I hear the sound of the faucet, then, a flush of the toilet. More running water and the sound of furious toothbrushing. "Okay." The door swings open. "Your turn. Don't stay in there too long."

I close the bathroom door behind me. For some reason, this place seems more sixty-ish to me than anyplace else I have been: a half-melted bar of Zest soap on the sink, a line of blue-green goo running into the drain. Elsewhere in the bathroom: a half-squeezed capless tube of Crest; an open bottle of fingernail polish, its contents dried to a red crust; a tube of Noxema; a box of Stri-dex Medicated Pads. A bottle of Micrin mouthwash. A bottle of Prell.

"Hurry up in there. This ice is already started to melt off the trees."

I brush my teeth faster. Glancing up, I see a young, thin face, short black hair, pimples near the corner of an uncertain mouth. Spitting the last of the Crest into the sink, I remove my cutoffs, then my underwear: white Kerry-Knit briefs. Where did I buy those things?

Inside the shower, I carefully adjust the shower curtain so that it's inside the tub. The first time here—during the first week in January—I had left the curtain outside, leaving an inch of water on the floor.

I adjust the faucet and check the flow for the right temperature, then reach down and pull up on the shower knob. After a quick gurgle the shower head produces a dense stream of warm water. Perfect. Like a rainstorm in the summer. I can almost feel it—

Suddenly the curtain snaps back and Rachael jumps inside the tub with me. "You were taking all day and I couldn't wait. And I've got my eyes closed so I can't see you. So move over! Hurry up!"

She's wearing a shower cap and a pair of underpants, with her arms folded over her breasts. "Quick, gimme the soap," she says, her eyes squeezed shut. "Not the Zest. The face soap. There's a bar in the corner." I hand it to her and she backs away and quickly covers her face in a layer of white lather. "Okay. Lemme have the shower. Hold your horses, this'll only take a minute…hey, did you ever notice Prell smells like a new car?"

"I never knew that."

"Well, it does." Her eyes still squeezed shut, she nudges past me again, sticking her face into the stream of water. After a few seconds, she backs away from the shower, and I see that the soap is gone, along with all traces of makeup. "You can have it back, now. Thanks."

The curtains part and she is gone. Turning off the shower I hear the snap of elastic as she removes her wet underwear, then the rustle of a towel. "I'm gonna dry my hair now, and all I've got on is this towel. *So don't look.*"

"The water is getting cold."

"Michael, you are *such* a liar. We've got the biggest water heater in Weslayan. You'll have to wait until I get my hair dry."

Amazingly, I don't look. Instead, I scan the inside of the shower, surveying the pink faux-porcelain tile inside the shower. I see that the faucet handles don't appear to match. Halfway to the floor of the tub is a huge white rubber drain stopper hanging from the faucet by a beaded metal chain.

Suddenly, Rachael's voice. "Allright. My hair's dry. Now, if you don't hurry up in there, we'll miss the frost."

I wait for a second, then hear the door slam. Only a few months to go and then I've lost her forever.

Again.

24

Skyline

It's late Friday afternoon. The weather is unusually warm for late February—well into the fifties. I'm sitting in my car wearing my blue windbreaker over a sweater and jeans. Rache is wearing new jeans and a fuzzy pink sweatshirt with a hood. Somewhere in the car is her windbreaker, probably folded neatly into a square, then placed on the floorboard.

As I turn on the ignition, Rachael opens the door and climbs inside the car, pausing to toss something into the back seat. "Mama fixed us a snack in case watching airplanes makes us hungry."

I shift the car into reverse, but before I can move my car, Bob taps on my side window. I roll it down. "You want to come with us to watch the jets, Bob?"

"No, I've got to be down at the school this evening. Listen, if you two are going to the city, you better take Sam along." He hands me a large metal object.

"Oh, Daddy, we're not gonna need *that*," Rachael whines.

"It's a Colt .45 caliber service automatic. Model 1911A1." Bob smiles at the weapon. "Got it when I worked for the sheriff's department in Grain Valley. I never used it, but I always took it along."

"Okay...let me see it." Rachael reaches across and takes the gun, then quickly thumbs a release on the left side of the grip. The clip obediently slides from the bottom of the grip into her hand.

"Remember," Bob says, "there's a grip safety and a thumb safety over here on the left side of the frame..."

"Yeah, I see it." Rachael turns the weapon to the side, the barrel pointing in my general direction.

"If it looks like you're gonna have to use it," Bob reaches across me to take the gun, "—just trip the thumb safety *like this* and squeeze the grip safety with your hand as you pull the trigger. Clip holds seven rounds plus one in the chamber. Here." He hands the gun back to his daughter.

"Gotcha." *Klatch*. Rachael pops the clip back into the gun with the heel of her hand, then twirls the huge weapon on her index finger.

"Don't do that, Rachael," Bob says sternly. "You might shoot your foot off."

"Or my boob," she says, without cracking a smile. "Of course, there's nothing there anyway—"

"Don't be smart now, or I won't let you take it," Bob says. "Put it in the glovebox and don't show it unless it looks like trouble."

"Right." Rachael opens the glovebox and tosses the gun inside—barrel pointing my way. "Now, let's go to the airport."

Two hours later, we're at the park on the corner of Eighth and Patterson in Kansas City. Perched at the top of a bluff, the park overlooks the Kansas City Municipal Airport, which is nestled in a curve of the Missouri River. From this vantage point we—and the other couples parked here—can watch huge commercial jets roar across the sky, passing us at eye level only a few miles away.

Perfect. Finally some good information. I decide to take a chance and call in. *Lock.*

"Leonard."

"Lampman Monitoring System, Leonard speaking. How are things down there?"

"Great. I'm in Kansas City at the corner of Eighth and Patterson streets. It's a little place where people come to watch jets land at the airport."

"Wasn't there television in Kansas City back then? Movies?"

"Very funny. Want some data?"

"Sure. Let's give the search engines a workout. Tell me what you see."

"Well, I see a '62 Chevy Bel-Aire station wagon, a red Corvair Monza, a new Olds 442 and parked next to us is a Chevy Impala. Probably a 1963 model, but I can't tell."

"Okay. A love-wagon, a deathtrap, and a muscle car. What was the last one?"

"Chevy Impala. Probably a '63."

"Okay. List on that was $3849. So now that we have the love-wagon survey, is there anything else interesting? Anything on the radio?"

"It's turned off. But I think I heard 'For What Its Worth' on the way over here. And we're wearing light jackets. Temperature's probably in the low sixties with an overcast."

"Okay. From the song, you're between late February and May, '67. Give me a call when you get another song or two and I'll narrow it for you."

Unlock.

"Let's turn on the radio," I hear myself say.

"I got a better idea. Let's get closer to the airport. It's too crowded up here."

Moments later, we're driving parallel to the high ridge separating the airport from the river. To our left is a carnival of blue and red runway lights. As the car goes over a slight rise, I see a sign: *Watch for Low Flying Aircraft.* I park the Ford near a row of other cars.

A quick lock, and I'm able to identify a white 1960 Ford Galaxy, a Chevy Nova and a 1961 Plymouth Fury, its four headlights staring angrily out from beneath its angled "eyebrows." All great cars. Good retro design.

Whatever that means.

Unlock. We park the car next to the Fury and turn off the engine. In the car I can see five people—two adults and three children. It doesn't look like the kind of place where a gun will be necessary.

"Sure you don't want to listen to the radio?"

"Turn it on. Either the K's or the W's are fine."

I turn on the radio and come in halfway through an Elvis song: "Can't Help Falling In Love With You."

"Hey! It's Elvis," Rachael says. "My Mama just adores Elvis, but Dad can't stand him. He likes Nat King Cole—say, I'll bet you didn't know this: Elvis is actually singing this song to his cat, Shirley."

"Shirley—?"

"Shirley," Rachael nods. "And if you listen real close you can hear it. Listen. It goes, 'like a river flows—*meeowwww*—Shirley, to the sea—*meeowwww*—'"

"That's not a cat making that sound. That's a steel guitar."

"Have you ever seen it?" She narrows her eyes.

"No."

"Then *you don't know*, do you?"

Suddenly Elvis and his cat are drowned out by an ear-splitting roar.

"Look!" Rachael sticks her head out the window.

I look up and all I can see are the lights and undercarriage of a Boeing 707. It thunders overhead, then drifts down to the runway a few hundred yards away. An instant later I hear the distinct "sktch" of rubber hitting concrete.

"Wooaaah!" Rache says. "When's the next one?"

"I don't know." On the radio, I hear another song, one by Neil Diamond song, "You Got To Me." I relay it to Leonard.

"Okay. That narrows it a little. It was released January 28 and was on the chart exactly eight weeks. I'd say you're in the last week of February, 1967. The weather data matches anyway. See any more interesting vehicles down there?"

"A few. I'll tell you in debrief. Say, would you happen to have the airline schedule for Kansas City in February, 1967?"

"Ha. What do you think I am? The Smithsonian?"

"Sorry. I only wanted to know when the next plane would be coming over."

"Maybe I can check some stats. I'll just open up the Jukebox and fire up the search engine. Hm. This thing is really slow tonight—okay, here we are. In the mid-sixties the busiest airport was O'Hare—with a plane arriving every three seconds. Kansas City Municipal was way down at the end of the ramp. Looks like an average of one plane every five minutes. Does that help?"

"Thanks."

I turn off the radio and turn to Rache. "You want to take a walk? I want to show you something really neat."

"Yeah. I'm gettin' bored."

I lock the car, then take her hand and head for the asphalt road behind the parking area.

"Where are we going?" she asks. "Maybe I should take the gun. I don't wanna get robbed out here."

"We'll be okay." We cross the road, then squeeze through a break in the hurricane fence separating the airport from the hill surrounding it. After a few minutes of climbing through tall weeds we're at the top. A hundred feet beneath us is the Missouri River, running black and cold. Across the river are the lights of the city. Leonard said *five minutes* between landings. It took us maybe three minutes to get up here.

"Isn't this nice?" I ask her. "See the city over there across the river?"

"Yeah. But I still think I shoulda' brought the gun. You know any karate in case we get mugged?"

"No." For an instant, I think I feel mist against my face. Then, it's gone. *Two minutes left.*

"I guess you'll have to take care of 'em while I run for help," she looks around warily. "Kick 'em in the balls or something." She looks over the edge of the hill down toward the river. "Wonder why there's no planes?"

"Don't know." It's quiet. All I hear is the sound of cars on the interstate a few miles away. That and the gentle whistle of wind. A whistle that increases in pitch.

One minute.

A red light blinks. Something is moving on the horizon. Something big. And it's at eye level.

"Rache—" I point straight out. "Take a look."

At that instant, night becomes day as the sky explodes in a bank of high-intensity landing lights, illuminating our hill and moving directly toward us.

The darkness contracts to show the enormous object behind the lights—the hawklike superstructure of a triple-engine jet airliner. The hill shakes with the din. Rachael is holding her ears, screaming.

The massive undercarriage completely fills the sky, rows of lights and tubes and metal panels and rubber tires, perhaps fifty feet overhead. Then the wind hits us, hot and laden with debris, blowing our jackets and hair. After rubbing the weed dust from my eyes, I turn to see the huge metal bird gently settle to the concrete runway.

Sktch—*sktch.*

I turn around and see Rachael standing next to me, her sweatshirt covered in weed stems and thistle burrs, her hair blown straight back. After a second, she shakes her head, then begins methodically picking the burrs, weeds and grass particles from her sweatshirt, then from her pants.

"All right, then," she says, smoothing her hair down. "Exactly what was it that you wanted to show me?"

"The jet."

"I saw it," she nods soberly. "It was about one inch over my head. And, I'll have you know, I probably wet my pants. You may take me home now."

25

Return

I wake up in bed—alone. Am I back in San Antonio? I open my eyes and see Rachael at the dresser, peering into a drawer.

Good. I'm still here. In Weslayan. I close my eyes and try to think: When I came it was Thursday...and yesterday was a Sunday...

It must be Monday. Then how come I'm not back in Kirksville? Is must be spring break.

I hear another drawer open. "Oh, rats."

"What?" I open my eyes again. Rachael, dressed in her black and blue striped nightshirt, is rummaging through the drawer. I look for the outline of her shorts. Not there. Did she wear them last night?

"All I've got is pink underwear. And it's Monday. Every time I wear pink on a Monday, something stupid happens. I forget my lunch card or I leave my purse somewhere. Or it rains."

"I didn't think you had school today."

"I don't. But I still gotta find the right color underwear. I gotta find yellow. Yellow is okay for Mondays."

"Gonna wear a yellow bra too?"

"All my bras are white. It's the under*pants* that are different. I wish I knew where that yellow one was. Did I wear it yesterday?"

"Mind if I take a shower first?" I push the covers back. As usual, I'm wearing my blue cutoffs and terrycloth t-shirt.

"Yeah, go ahead—" she mumbles. "Lessee—I wore the white ones with the little valentine Saturday. And another pair of pink ones yesterday. Oh, I'll just wear the blue ones." She digs into the drawer.

I climb out of bed and give her a kiss on the cheek. "I'll be out in a few minutes."

"Okay," she pushes the drawer closed. "If you go out with the wrong color underwear you're just *asking* for trouble."

After a shower, I pull on my jeans and come downstairs to find Bob at the kitchen table—cigarette in the corner of his mouth, a cup of coffee nearby—scribbling into a notebook. At the opposite end of the table are four used bowls of breakfast cereal. Wanda and the kids are already gone, leaving Bob to struggle here with some arcane mental task.

I lock the scene momentarily and notice that his face has a hard, pale cast, and his eyes are like small black coals—concentration against all odds. There is a noticeable shake in the pen. It occurs to me he's wearing the same clothes I saw him in last night—wrinkled slacks and short-sleeved white shirt. On the table is an open Bible. I unlock and take a step into the kitchen.

"Hey, Mike." He looks up wearily. "You know anything about Second Corinthians, chapter 12, second verse?"

"Nope. Sorry."

"That's okay. I've got to give a talk at the fellowship dinner tonight and I don't want to use a canned speech. Just fishing around for ideas." His voice trails off as he stares at the page. I lock the scene again. Looking into his eyes, I sense painful desperation. The notebook page is covered in scribbles and crossed-out lines. On the floor next to his chair is a pile of crumpled notepaper.

Unlock.

I walk to the refrigerator and open the door. "Want some orange juice?"

"Thanks, but it would probably upset my stomach."

"How long have you been up?" I ask, joining him at the table.

"Altogether?" He takes a deep drag from the cigarette and grins sheepishly. "Thirty-six hours. Unless you count the ten minutes sleep I got on a bag of potatoes at Safeway last night. I think it's starting to affect my concentration." He pushes the sheet of scribbles toward me. "I've been here since five this morning and in two hours all I've got is Second Corinthians. That's why I thought you might have some ideas. I'm all out."

"Sorry. Wish I could help."

"I wish you could too." He opens up the battered notebook and leafs through the pages. "Guess I'd better to go with a canned talk after all. Three points and a poem—they won't know the difference. You want some coffee?"

"No, thanks." I hear the shower stop upstairs. Rachael will be down in a few minutes. Good.

"Lessee." Bob stops at a page and rubs his eyes. "Yeah. Here's one I could use—huh?"

I look up. "What is it?"

"I'm trying to read. And you know, the print seems to be falling off the page—" His face has a perplexed, confused look.

"What do you mean?"

"The print's sliding off the page." He chuckles. "That's what it's doing all right—it's moving down and falling off the page." He turns the notebook toward me. "Don't you see it too—or am I imagining it?"

"It looks fine to me—*Bob, are you okay?*"

"Probably got into some chemicals at Safeway last night. Maybe they sprayed the oranges with something—" He tries to stand up, then quickly sits back down. The smile is gone, replaced with a look of irritation. Clearly, something in his world isn't working the way it should.

Lock. Did this ever happen? It must have, but I don't remember it. Probably it turned out to be nothing. Yet—

"Leonard."

"GrandWizard here. How are things in dreamland?"

"What are the symptoms of stroke?"

"You think you're having one?"

"No. Someone else might be, though."

"Justaminute. Lemme check the medical—okay—stroke—cerebral hemor-rhage. Whoa. Sudden headache, dizziness, visual or auditory disturbances—"

"Thanks. I'll be back in a minute."

"What's going on down there?"

"Keep an eye on my vitals, but don't bring me back, okay?"

"You visit some interesting places. I'm here if you need me."

I wheel and head up the stairs to Rachael's room, covering the distance as quickly as I can. "Rache!" I open the door.

"Hey—" She is standing at the bed, wearing two towels—one

around her waist and the other wrapped around her wet hair. "Darn it, Michael, I'm not dressed—"

"*Get* dressed! Your dad's sick. We gotta get him to the hospital."

"Omigod." She throws the towels to the floor and quickly steps into a pair of faded blue jeans. "Gimme my shirt. It's on the chair—"

Within a minute, I return to the kitchen, Rache a step behind me. Bob is seated at the table, his glazed eyes staring at a point on the opposite wall. As Rachael grabs his legs, I put my arms under his. Together we carry him to the front door.

"Look, I'll get him into the car, you call the hospital."

"Gotcha." Rachael leaves us and grabs the phone.

Seconds later, with Bob across the back seat of the Pontiac, I jump behind the wheel and close the door. No keys.

"Keys are here, under the floor mat," Rachael says, jumping into the car. "The emergency room said to bring him in *right now*."

I start the car, shift into reverse, and hammer the accelerator. The Pontiac roars backward, missing my car by inches.

Five minutes and three red lights later, we're at the hospital.

Twelve hours later, we're still here—Stacie and Brad with me—Amy wedged between Wanda and Rachael. By now, the children are asleep and I've read everything in the waiting room—four 1965-vintage *Good Housekeeping*, two old issues of *Life* and an assortment of used coloring books. On the intercom, I hear a full orchestra version of "Moon River" for the fourth time.

I look at my watch—7:00 p.m.—then glance around the room—first at the spare white walls, the orange carpet, the Danish modern couches filled with worried people and sleeping children. I search for the familiar feeling of deja vu—the sense of replay that occasionally accompanies these trips to the past. Yet the only memories I can jog are the ones that occurred when Rachael was sick four months before. This truly seems to be happening for the first time.

It *had* to have happened before, but I can recall no specific incident that brought Bob to the emergency room.

Yet, here we are—Brad reading a magazine, Stacie curled under my arm asleep, Wanda, her face drawn, getting up to talk to a nurse. Rachael, her eyes closed in silent prayer.

The emergency room physician walks in, a tall man with thinning brown hair and wearing green surgical scrubs. "Mrs. Dominic?"

A half-hour later, Rachael, the kids and I are sitting in the Pontiac, waiting for Wanda. For the past hour Rachael has been sitting in a bundle next to the door, staring straight out across the hospital parking lot.

"That doctor was really mad," Bradley murmurs from the rear seat. "He yelled at us."

"He wasn't mad at *us*, Bradley," Stacie tells him. "He was mad at Daddy for not getting enough sleep. He said no human being on earth can go without sleep."

Rachael looks at me. "Michael, why did God let this happen?"

"The doctor said it was probably exhaustion. But it's a good thing we brought him in. Anyway—I got a chance to see your shower-suit."

"Michael saw Rache in her show-er suit," Amy sings. To my horror, I realize the term isn't only Rachael's—it's family-wide.

"That means she was *naked*," Bradley grins. "That's how they sleep together."

Rachael lunges across the seat, "Bradley Allen! That is *not true*! Michael and I wear our clothes to bed and *you know it*! Any of you repeat that *anywhere*, and it'll be your *butts*! That's between me and Michael and the family—and nobody else! *Got it?*"

"Got it," Bradley mumbles.

"Yeah," Stacie mumbles. "I got it, too."

"With Daddy sick and all, nobody knows what's gonna happen. We don't need any more—" she pauses, her voice softens, "—*trouble*. Okay?"

"Sorry, Rache," Bradley murmurs. "Sorry, Mike."

Rachael returns to her place on the far side of the car, her knees curled up to her chest—protection against a world that has become bleak and uncertain.

Lock. On the floorboard, her tennis shoes lie amid a pile of KuKu hamburger wrappers and soft drink cups. Even though it's not particularly cold in the car, I can tell she's shivering. I see a tear in mid-slide down her cheek.

Unlock.

"Hey. C'mere." I reach across the seat and grab her arm. "We're going for a walk."

"Ouch. No—lemme get my shoes—"

"No, here." In a second, I'm carrying her across to the wet grass.

"Michael—what—"

"Listen to me, Rache—your dad is going to be all right. It's only exhaustion. He'll be fine. He lives for a long, long time."

"How can you know that?" She looks at me, her face inches from mine.

"Because I *remember*. I was here once before. Years ago." I feel the chill in the air, the dampness of the grass. It occurs to me I'm barefoot. Feeling—pure feeling—washes over me in waves, trying for the connection. As though the waves of this beautiful time were trying to find me all these years. And now they have.

I feel Rachael's warmth through her cotton shirt, feel the rough fabric of her jeans. Feel her quick warm breath against my face.

And, I'm *here*. Totally and completely *here*.

"What are you talking about—'remember'?" She narrows her eyes.

"Rachael, I want to tell you something—" I feel the cold air enter my lungs, smell the scent of her perfume—*Occur*, isn't it? Taste the faint trace of her lipstick. Holding her in this dark, cold damp night I'm overwhelmed by the sensations.

"What? What are you gonna tell me?" She has a tentative smile.

"I want to tell you that—I'm *here*."

"Are you *sure*?" She gives me a suspicious look.

"I want to let you know something, Rachael Dominic—" I look in her eyes. "I want to tell you you're the best thing that ever happened to me, and I've missed you all my life."

"All nineteen years of it, huh?" She says. "Well, that's long enough. Gimme a kiss." I feel her lips, then her face against mine, feel the wetness of her cheek. Then she pulls back and looks at me hard. "Are you sure about Daddy being all right? Don't say it just to make me feel better—"

"He'll be fine. *I remember*."

She looks at me, her eyes wet with tears. "Do we still get married?"

"We still get married."

"When!"

"How about—now?"

"*Now?*" She looks at me. "*Right* now?"

"Or as soon as we can get a church. And if your parents okay it—"

"Yes! Oh, yesyesyesyesyes!" She grabs and squeezes my neck. "Daddy can even do the wedding! We can do it as soon as he gets home—before he can think about it too much. And before you can change your mind!"

"This weekend?"

"Sure! Daddy can perform the ceremony, Mama can play the piano and Stacie can be the bridesmaid. We'll get married at home in our living room, and and then we can get married later in a real church. That way, if I'm pregnant it won't matter."

The world of February, 1967 is flooding me, washing through me like waves in a storm. Cold air, frost on the grass, a blustery wind blowing her hair into my eyes. I spin her around, feel the pressure on my muscles, in my back, in my knees. Feel my body adjust to the grass, feel her in my arms.

"Listen, Michael," she says. "I'm serious about this. I want to get married tonight, or if not tonight, then real soon. Like tomorrow or the next day. And I want to get pregnant and have a baby. Is it okay?"

I stand here with her, my face inches from hers. "Yes. It's absolutely okay. The sooner, the better."

She looks at me, tears running down her face. "Michael, I really— *coconut cream pie* you."

"What?"

"I want to say something more than I love you, so I thought of my absolute favorite food. Coconut cream pie."

"Rache, I—uh—"

"Any main food group will do," she says.

"Okay. Cherry pie. I *cherry pie* you." I look into her eyes. "And I'll never leave you. *Ever*."

She smiles. "That's what I've wanted all along."

"Rachael, listen, I've got to tell you something—"

She puts her finger on my lips. "Tell me later. Tonight, maybe. Okay?"

"Sure. Tonight." I look into her eyes, bright in the lights of the parking lot.

Something has happened.

Somehow, I'm *here*. Captured by the waves and the vibrations and the feelings of a February night in 1967. Somewhere, somewhere in the back of my mind, overwhelmed by the sensations of this instant in time, I feel another memory fade. A memory of another life in a city somewhere. And people I used to know.

But now, like a car's tail lights on a dark night, it recedes into the distance.

And is gone.

It's early morning now. Rachael is lying in my arms, one leg thrown over mine. Outside, I hear the first drops of rain against the window. A cool front has come in. By mid-week, there'll be snow. It's a good thing I'm on spring break—I'd hate to drive back to Kirksville in this kind of weather.

Rachael shivers slightly and I pull the blanket over her. Outside, I hear a car drive by, its tires hissing on the wet cobblestone street. Did I leave my car too far out in the street?

I slide my arm from beneath Rache, then sit up and look through the window. My car, its hood wet and glistening with rain, seems to be intact.

I look around the room, the walls illuminated by the streetlamp. I wonder if Wanda and the kids are asleep. Probably not. Amy is always awake until three or four. I lie down again, sliding my arm under Rachael. In response, she snuggles closer.

I look at her, think of the last few hours—coming home from the hospital to catch the last few minutes of the Monkees—then fish sticks, bologna sandwiches and Vess. I think of the song that ended the Monkees show and how it fit: "You Just May Be The One." At ten, we took our showers and came to bed.

And now, we lie here, amid the smells of Brut and Occur and Zest soap and the taste of Crest toothpaste and Frost lipstick. I feel her hand beneath my shirt, on my chest; her bare legs against mine.

"Michael?"

"Yes, Hon?"

"Would you take off your t-shirt?"

I pull it over my head and lay it next to the wall. Without a word, she pulls the nightshirt up over her head and tosses it to the end of the bed. I look at her in the darkness, beautiful and perfect.

"Come here," she says, "I want you to hold me."

I put my arms around her and bring her to me—feel her small, soft breasts against my chest, touch the bare skin of her back. We're face to face and I brush my lips across hers. Lightly at first, beginning at the corner of her mouth and moving to the other side. Then back. And in the middle I pause at the bow of her upper lip, touching it with the tip of my tongue.

I taste toothpaste and lipstick and cola, but mostly I taste Rachael, taste her lips and tongue and the tips of her front teeth as they bite into my lip. I kiss her face, her eyes, her neck, and her collarbone, moving across to her bare shoulders. And from there, my lips trace a line to the cleft of her elbow, down to her wrist, to the palm of her hand, between each finger. And then back to her collarbone and the small triangle of her throat.

I hear her breathing increase, feel her breath against my face. "Michael—"

I move my fingers from the nape of her neck, down her back, feeling each bump, each muscle until I reach her waist, then back her neck again. And then return.

Beneath the sheets I feel the inside of her foot against the calf of my leg. My hand reaches down and I run my fingers along her toes, up to the sole of her foot, up to her knee, then to the smooth skin of her thigh, and then to her waist. I stop.

"Rache—where's your underwear?"

"I'm not wearing any." She looks at me, our faces separated by only inches.

"You're completely naked?"

"Shhhh. Yeah. I'm completely naked."

I move my hand from her waist to her back.

"But what if your mom—?"

"She never comes in. And Amy's fast asleep. I checked."

"I don't know. What if you get pregnant?"

"What if I do? We're getting married in a few days anyway."

I look at her in the darkness, her face inches from mine. Then, without a word I unbutton my cutoffs, unzip them slowly and finally slide them down and off. I feel the cool sheet against my body. For an instant, I feel vulnerable, alone. Then I feel her hands on my back, pulling me toward her, feel our bodies touch for the first time. And now her legs soft and cool at first, slide against mine, become warm. I sense her breath on my face, feel her breasts soft against my chest. Suddenly, I feel safe, secure. Enveloped in love. This instant of time I will remember for all eternity.

Outside, there is a flash of lightning. Then another. And another. And now everything is like a movie. And now like a snapshot.

No sound of rain, no breathing. Things have *stopped*.

And I can't feel Rachael against me anymore!

"*...Lessee—if the Monkees had that song on their television show, then you're probably in February 27 or the morning of the 28th.*"

"I locked the scene earlier. Looks like it's raining outside."

"*Okay. Then it's between two and three in the morning. Weslayan, Missouri gets about a tenth of an inch. Hope you didn't go outside, the temp is only forty-one degrees.*"

"I didn't know it was that cold. The radio isn't on, but earlier I heard 'You Got To Me' and 'For What It's Worth.'"

Now there's a radio playing inside my head. Is this a nightmare? *It has to be a nightmare.* But I'm awake!

"*On this minute in time, Mike, the Beatles are rehearsing 'Lucy In The Sky With Diamonds.' And Elvis is putting on another five pounds.*"

Maybe my fillings are picking up the signal. I read about that happening once. But why has everything stopped?

"*...and if you didn't have that layer of rain cloud at 7500 feet, you could see Regulus is in the southern sky, Procyon is in the west and Arcturus is almost directly overhead.*"

"Thanks for the info."

"*Is everything okay?*"

"So far."

"*We're starting to get a little interference in your temporal leads again. Just like the last time. You sure there's no problem down there?*"

"I'm sure. Everything is fine."

"*I really don't like the way this t-4 is looking. I'd feel better if I reeled you in, now.*"

The voices are familiar. I've heard them before. Maybe in a movie I saw once. But why should I be hearing it now? Am I going crazy? Doesn't craziness show up early? In your late teens?

"Leonard, I'm hearing something that I can't make out, but it's probably just some random thoughts from this place. I'm okay. Really."

"*Fasten your seatbelt, Mike. You've got ten seconds.*"

"No, Leonard! I'll call you back."

I see Rachael next to me in the darkness, her eyes closed, her face inches from mine.

Nine. Eight. Seven—

I want to kiss her. Tell her I love her. Tell her I would never hurt her. Ever.

Six. Five. Four.

Tell her—

Three. Two. One.

I would never leave—

26

Congregation

A wet towel wrapped around my waist, I stand at my window looking out over San Antonio. The late afternoon sky is almost free of clouds and the temperature on the streets below probably is in the high nineties. Exactly two hours ago in this world it was 3:30 p.m., 1999. Two hours ago in my mind was a little after 3:00 am, February 28, 1967. Caught between two worlds—one surrounding me of which I'm not a real part—and one inside my mind—which is a part of me.

While in the shower, washing the accumulated grime from two days in the chair, I considered all my options. By the time I turned off the water, only the sensible one remained—pack up my bags, drop out of the program and return to Boston. The alternative would be to spend the rest of my life inside my past, rummaging around in it like a fool obsessed with his attic.

Of course, I could try Gail's route—find out what happened to Rache—if only to know she's okay. But who am I kidding? Having been with her these last few weeks, these last six months, I would probably want to write her, phone her, see her. *Remember me? I'm the guy who let you down. Who gave our lives away.*

What a great way to continue a relationship. Of course, it would all be a moot point if she was married. Which she no doubt is. Was it today or yesterday she told me she wanted five kids? Oh yes. Almost two nights back and thirty-two years ago.

And what about Linda? After all, I *am* still married and have my own responsibilities and obligations. Certainly no time to fall headlong for an old flame from the past. Wouldn't be fair to anyone—least of all Rache.

And yet, I think about what Coltrane had said, about that time back there being part of my life, as real as now. I had come here to cruise my past, to avoid all the bad places and to stripmine everything else for saleable songs and minutiae. Instead, something had brought me back to the very places I'd tried to forget. As Leonard might say, they were the places I had diked off but had neglected to nuke.

In effect, my past had stripmined *me.*

When I get to the lab, Leonard is sitting at his desk reading a Japanese comic book, something called Kirara, his feet resting on an abandoned computer cabinet.

"Yo, Mike," he says, putting the book aside.

"Leonard, I need a favor."

"Sure," he adjusts his glasses. "If it doesn't take too much random access memory."

"I need to find someone. In the present."

"Sorry. I already took heat for finding Banks' little buddy. One more and Poundstone would scram me."

"I want to find Rachael Dominic. You've heard me talk about her. You know who she is."

"Rachael Dominic, huh?" Leonard squints one eye at me and cocks his head to the side. It's a gesture I'd seen Evan Carswell do a million times.

"It's important."

"Allow me to explain," Leonard swivels his chair around to face me. "My *confidential little favor* to Banks resulted in her new squeeze getting an *extremely* unauthorized, guided tour of the facility."

"I know, but—"

"Plus, the Institute has been getting spammed with threatening email from a certain someone in Connecticut. All of which makes me very unpopular with the suits downstairs."

"Sorry to hear that."

"Glad you understand. If they find out I let you into the database too, they'll go fireworks mode—whiiiich means my job will be in *casters-up mode.* Very career-limiting. Sorry."

"It's either that or *I'll* go fireworks mode."

"Beg pardon?" Leonard looks at me over the tops of his glasses.

"Leonard," I place my hands on a nearby chair. "I like you. I genuinely do. But unless you help me find Rachael Dominic *starting right now*, I plan to begin picking up big heavy things and throwing them at the Big Iron, just to see if it makes dents. How would you like to have roached equipment and a casters-up dreamer on your hands?"

"Dents?" Leonard glances at the chair I'm holding, a heavy oak model with a metal arm-desk.

"Dents. *Big* ones." I lift the chair. "Try explaining *that* to the suits downstairs."

"Yes. Of course. Dents." Leonard nods, swiveling around to the keyboard. "Ahem. Let's take a look at the database, shall we? Just the high bit, please."

"The name is Rachael Dominic. Spell the Rachael with an 'e'."

"That helps." Leonard keys in the name. "By the way, Mike—"

"What?"

"Remember, you don't *roach* hardware. That's what you do to software. Hardware, you *toast*. Everything else you got right."

"Thanks."

"No prob. I'm here to help." He peers at the screen. "Hm. Okay. Nothing. When was she born?"

"May 9, 1952. Corinth, Missouri—on Locust street—her parents are—Robert and Wanda Dominic—"

"Ah. Okay. Maybe this is it. Rachael Sara Dominic. Family left Weslayan in 1968, moved to Blue Springs, Missouri. From there to Novenger, Missouri in 1970. Attended Northeast Missouri State from '72 to '73. No degree. Married Jackie V. Warden in '73. Good credit rating. Bought a house. One car, one truck, one child."

"She had her baby."

"Looks like it. Then they moved from Novenger."

"Go on?"

"That's it. The record just stops. All we have is blank space."

"What about her folks? Maybe we could find them—"

"Justaminute." He types on the keyboard. "There's nothing here on them either. Maybe they all left the country. What were they, CIA?"

"Hardly. Nothing on the brothers or sisters? There was Amy, Stacie, Bradley—"

"Here we go. Here's a Bradley Allen Dominic—born in 1958— that about right?"

"Pretty close."

"It says here he's picked up a degree in computer science and spent time at the Princeton Quadrangle. The trail ends in 1985. No address, no phone. And there's nothing on anyone else. The computer geek—er, *specialist*—probably told the rest of the family how to firewall their privacy."

"Thanks, Leonard. I appreciate it."

"No prob. Look, the Juke is only a preliminary search engine. There are other sources I can check. You want me to call you if I find anything?"

"Yeah. That would be great."

I close the door to the lab and head back to my room.

At least she got to have her child.

I open the door to my room. The bed is made, the wallspeaker is playing something slow by Beethoven. The curtains are drawn back, showing the orange lights of the city. I compare the image to the ones I remember from the sixties. City lights were blue and white then, not orange. And there was often the smell of burning leaves and grass, even in the early spring. And there seemed to be more rain.

Of course, if I had grown up in San Antonio, I would have different memories. But then, I would be someone else and it would be a different universe. One that would have never included Rachael.

My life is my life—it's the one I own. The one that owns me.

There's a knock at the door. I open it to see Gail, smiling. She's with someone. "Mike, I want you to meet someone—this is Eric Fenster."

She introduces me to a medium-sized, muscular man with short blond hair and a shy smile. It's a face right out of Scandinavia—somewhat weathered skin with crinkles at the corners of sharp, blue eyes. His handshake is firm, solid. And he *looks* like a high school teacher.

"Eric came in this morning," Gail says. "He drove straight from the airport. Hasn't even looked at the Alamo or the River Walk—"

"That wasn't what I came here to see," he smiles at her. His voice is soft, but assured. And there's something else—something I also hear in Gail's voice—a definite *giddiness*.

"Eric will come back when I finish the program," Gail says. "And then we're going to see San Antonio together. Isn't that great?"

"Absolutely." I look at them and think of something Rachael said once—about when two people belong together, everyone can tell. With Gail and her old friend, it shows.

"Mike—" Gail says. "Thanks."

"Hey—I'm here to help."

"And you understand." She reaches up to kiss me on the cheek. And then she takes Eric's hand and walks with him back down the hallway.

I close the door, look around my own room. I see the khakis, ironed and stacked neatly on the desk—suits in the closet with their odd assortment of ties, pinstripe shirts, tab collars, Rockports—all waiting for the trip back to Boston in a few short weeks.

No evidence of life here.

No evidence of Penny's Sta-Prest cutoffs with terry t-shirts, no evidence of blue striped nightshirts smelling of *Occur* and *Brut*. No *Zest* or *Micrin*. No fish sticks with vinegar—bologna sandwiches and Vess cola. And no Rachael.

All that belongs in a different time, a different place—a different country. And you can't get there from here.

I collapse on the bed and stare at the ceiling until it becomes hazy, then gray. Then I close my eyes and try to remember what Coltrane had told me: "It will always be there for you—if that's what you want."

Rachael, it's what I want. It's what I want more than anything. Where are you now? Are you married, do you have your five children? I hope you can hear me now. If I can't come for you, then come for me.

"Remember what happened at the Alamo?" A voice.

Inside my dream I see a young girl wearing a knit top, jeans and tennis shoes. Her long dark hair is pulled back in a ponytail. She holds up a small tree branch. "If you're gonna stay, you gotta cross the line."

She looks up at me. It's a knowing look. And suddenly I feel new. Not new-er, but *new*. It's not that I've traded my old body in for a new one, but this is my own body again when *it* was new. It's not autumn anymore, it's spring. It's April forever and it's the spring of my own time.

Rachael is sitting on the bed, wearing only a t-shirt and underwear, a new ring on her hand.

I touch her face. She smiles and reaches for me. The light goes out. She pulls the covers back. Then I'm under the cool sheets just inches from her. Then closer—and I feel the warmth of her small body.

Feel the softness of her breasts against my chest, her legs against mine.

Outside it is raining. I can hear the radio playing a new song—one I've never heard before.

I kiss her lips, her face, her shoulders, feel her muscles tense, her arms tight around me. The talk between those who haven't spent much time on the earth:

"Hold me tight. Never let me go."

"I never will."

"I *more* than love you. I just wish I could tell you. I really, really wish I could—"

The scene dissolves and now I'm standing at the door of a small country church high on a hill. It's a Sunday in early March and the wind zephyrs ripple through the tall grass like waves on a lake.

Above, great volumes of cloud curl through the blue sky; their shadows race across the wheat fields and high grass, past the church and on toward the eastern horizon.

I turn to see Rachael standing beside me.

And now, we're inside and the congregation is standing, singing the first verse of a hymn I'd heard years ago.

I know these people—I've always known them. People from my childhood, from my life—

All my lives.

Inside, as the choir begins the second verse, the light pours in through the arched stained glass windows, creating columns of light as strong and solid as the pillars supporting the walls.

We're part of another—

And now, as the choir begins the third verse, I see the light from the church reaching out—out through the stained glass windows and walls, back up to the sky.

One with each other—

As the choir begins the fourth verse, I hear the sound of bells. Coming from outside. From all around. Angels.

I look at the hymnal, someone is holding it with me.

Rachael.

"Michael—" She looks at me. "This is our special place. It's where we belong."

A phone rings.

I sit up in the darkness.

Another ring. I pick up the receiver. "Yeah?"

"Mike, this is Leonard. Hope I didn't wake you."

"Yeah. I mean, no. What is it?"

"I finally located your friend Rachael Dominic. You want to come to the lab?"

"Sure. Sure, I'll be right down."

27

Pilot Wave

I'm sitting in the darkened lab looking at the computer screen. Minutes earlier, Leonard had explained how he located the information, querying the Internet, digging through various databases until he finally found her.

I swallow hard, trying to force the hurt down from my throat.

"There it is," Leonard says, pointing to the screen. *Jan 2 1975: A truck driven by Jackson Virgil Warden, 26, of Novenger, Missouri—*

I read the lines over and over until they become mere marks on the screen. Then the marks dissolve into a blur. All I can think about is the little girl with the tree branch, drawing the line across the gravel. *—was involved in a two-car head-on collision—*

I see her face, her eyes, hear her laugh.

"I was born on Locust street. How would *you* like to be born on a street named after an insect?"

—on Missouri 65, two miles north of Sedalia yesterday morning at 2:00 AM. Killed in the collision was Warden's wife—

"I really—coconut cream pie you."

—Rachael S. Warden, 24. Mr. Warden is listed in serious condition with multiple fractures. The driver of the other vehicle, a minor whose name was not released, was listed in serious but stable condition—

I feel numb. The world has gone flat. "Leonard, are you sure it was her?"

"It was her. I made a cross-match through the insurance files."

"What about the child? Didn't she leave a baby?"

"No record. Probably went to live with relatives. If you want me to look into this—"

"I don't know. Let me think about it."

"Sorry, Mike." Leonard pats my shoulder. "Real bummer."

3:20 a.m. The hour of failure. I'm sitting on the couch in the skybox lounge with my socks against the window, watching as the vapor outlines their shapes on the glass. Didn't Rachael used to do that to my windshield? Yes.

I'm real territorial. Did I tell you that? If some other girl looks on your windshield, they'll know I've been here.

Across the couch, Russell Coltrane sits with me in the darkness, his weathered face a terrain of lines and shadows. One of his boots is planted on the floor, the other on the table. On the horizon is the subtle flicker of heat lightning.

"I really appreciate you coming up here tonight, Russell."

"Sure," Coltrane shrugs. "I know what you're goin' through. I've spent a lot of nights up here myself, looking out this window."

"Tonight, after the regression, I had a dream about Rachael—two of them, actually."

Coltrane turns to look at me. In the reflection from the window, his spectacles are twin discs of yellow light.

"I was in bed with her—and I noticed that on her finger was a second gold ring—next to the orange blossom diamond. I knew our wedding had just been that day."

"Sounds like a pretty nice dream."

"But there was another dream—one that came before. We were at a church. People were singing and I felt I belonged there. Maybe that was where the wedding took place, I don't know. All I know is, it was the most beautiful place in the world. It was there I saw the possibilities with her that never happened."

"Was the dream real?"

"We broke up before we got married."

"That's not what I asked," Coltrane says softly. "I asked *was it real?*"

I look at him. "More real than anything I've ever known."

"Then it must have happened," he smiles, "*somewhere* in your life."

"Not in the one I remember." I take a deep breath. "The one I remember isn't like that at all."

"Let me tell you a story." Coltrane sits up on the couch. "I first met my lovely wife while I was working at a little refinery outside of Lovell, Wyoming. She was an English teacher at the school there—but she was also a full-blood Shoshone and she wanted to go back to the reservation and teach. I thought that was fine, so we bought us a little shotgun house in Thermopolis. We were gonna find work and buy us a ranch in the Wind River." He pauses for a moment.

"I remember we'd sit up nights talking about all the things we'd have—goats, sheep. Cattle. And it would be right outside the reservation, so she could drive it every day. Even drew it out on paper—what kind of bedroom it'd have, what was gonna be in the kitchen. Where the fireplace'd be."

"Sounds nice," I tell him.

"It never worked out," he says quietly. "I couldn't find a good job. We were never able to buy that little ranch. And after a few years, she ran into health trouble and couldn't teach anymore. There'd be times, though, we'd sit together and talk about our ranch. Just like it was real.

"There toward the end, she told me, '—Russell, we really do have our ranch. It's real and it's ours and we're there. And one of these days you'll know it.'" He looks at me. "It's taken me a lot of years, but I know she was right. I know, because part of me is there right now."

"But Russell, that place isn't in the real world—it's—"

"Mike," he leans forward, "if I tried to look for that place that *you* go back to, I'd be looking for a long, long time. But you know *just* where it is, don't you?"

"I know what you're trying to say, but—"

"Don't you believe in it anymore?" He looks at me intently. "Don't you believe in your *own life?*"

"Of course, I do, but—"

"Then, it's always gonna be there for you."

"Yeah." I flash a weak smile at the obvious. "Memory," I say to myself. *"It's all in the mind."*

"Maybe. And maybe not."

Four a.m. The hour of decision.

I'm in my room, alone. The curtains have been drawn and I'm lying on my bed, eyes fixed on the ceiling. Can I do this?

I close my eyes and the darkness surrounds me like a dense, protective cloud.

The appearance of multiple personalities has happened on occasion. After all, we are different people at different stages of our lives—

And begin the waves of tension and relaxation—

—but there's one core personality that guides the rest of them through—

And now my body becomes heavier. Like iron, like lead, sinking down.

—because for every physical interaction involving light, there must be two waves—one traveling into the future and one traveling into the past—

I have become mercury, slipping through the fabric of the bed, through the floor, into space and through the door of time—

—pilot waves crossing spacetime to sample events, in all their probabilities—

I am falling into the sky, while below me, is the river of my life.

"We only have to follow those waves to see the real worlds existing beside us—"

I visualize an elevator and one appears.

"The path is within us all. It is called memory."

I open my eyes to the darkness of my room. I know where I must go. One last time.

3:45 p.m. The afternoon sun paints the walls of my room with brilliant yellow light. It's my last day in San Antonio. Everything has been taken care of. The meetings, the goodbyes, the plane reservations. Only a few more things to do.

I put down the phone, then draw the blinds.

Now, I pick up the phone again and place another call.

"Lisa? This is Mike Mitchell. Is Jerry in? Good. Could you get him for me please?"

"Mitch? Is that you? Where are you?"

"San Antonio."

"Omigod, you're still there. Damn! I knew it. Mitch, the Japanese are coming in tomorrow afternoon and they want to meet with you. Nobody else. Not me, not the President of the United States, not Elvis. You. Listen to this—hear this? I'm getting on my knees—tell him Lisa—"

"He's on his knees, Mike. He's really on his knees."

"See? See? I'm begging you. I'm walking around this office on my knees *begging you* to get your ass back up and save the company—"

"Jer, I'll be back tomorrow at noon."

"I—*what?*"

"I've already bought the plane tickets. I'm taking one more trip to get some sixties information and right after that, I catch a plane for Boston. I'm leaving San Antonio at nine tonight."

Silence. Then, "Mitch. Thank you. From the bottom of my heart, thank you. I'll get a caterer, bring in lots of hamburgers. Maybe we can all comb our hair into DAs. Real sixties stuff."

"Thanks, Jer, but I don't have that much to comb. Just wear nice clothes and have their names on my desk when I get in. And Jer—"

"Yeah?"

"DAs were popular in the *fifties*."

I hang up the phone, then dial it again.

"Henderson, Cobham, Mitchell, Lambert."

"Hi, Kazy, this is Mike Mitchell. Is Linda in?"

"I don't think she's in yet. Would you like me to take a message?"

"Tell her I'll see her tonight."

"Oh. One minute—"

"Mike. This is Linda. What's going on?"

"I'm coming home. My flight will arrive at Logan tomorrow morning at 1:15."

"I—that's really—I didn't expect you back *tonight*. Uh—"

"Will you be home?"

"I—uh—listen, Mike—there's something I have to tell you—"

"I'm sure there is. And I'll be looking forward to hearing every word. Also, I'd appreciate it if you switched the call forwarding back to the house *before* I get home. Your friend must be getting awfully tired of all those extra calls."

Silence.

"Linda, I know you're there. I can hear you breathing."

"I really would like an opportunity to explain—"

"I'll be there to listen. See you soon, Linda."

I hang up the phone and scan the room. This is it. Goodbye, San Antonio. I know what I have to do. One more call. One more goodbye.

"Leonard? This is Mike. Everything ready?"

"Ready. Come on down."

I place the helmet on my head, attach the ceramic throat microphone. Hear Leonard run through the procedures.

"Okay, Mike. Give me a count…thank you. Loud and clear. Full body signal. Thank you. EKG looks good…how'd Poundstone take the news of your leaving?"

"He was real nice. Welcomed me back anytime."

Actually, Poundstone seemed disappointed. I couldn't give him the real reason I'm quitting; it would just confuse everything. Make things infinitely more complicated. Better he doesn't know. I take a deep breath and close the visor. The green lights wink on.

I listen to Leonard's voice in my headset. "Look left, right. Look up, down. Think of a blue square…thank you…"

Will I miss this place, the people here? Of course. Gail, Coltrane, and Leonard. Especially Leonard. I'll miss that strange, funny voice in my mind, telling me about the minutiae in my past.

"—Okay, Mike. Square root of 144—that's such an easy one. Thank you. Your aunt Terri naked. *Very* good signal in the frontal lobes, and of course I don't blame you."

But mostly, I think about where I'm going—and who I'll see for the very last time.

"You're getting an echo on your t-4 temporal lead. Probably the equipment. Looks like no scrams on the agenda this evening."

Gail gave me a hug, told me about her plans with Eric—and for Phil. Good for her. She seems truly happy here. She really lucked out.

"Well, Mike. Looks like the elevator's here. Seat belt fastened?"

Yes.

I hear the whirring sound of the machine followed by the chirping in the headsets. Finally, the choir of angels.

"We have theta…and…entrainment."

I drop into the sky above my life.

I drift downward toward a light. The walls coalesce around me. It's Rachael's bedroom on a Saturday morning—probably the month we broke up. If I've reached the right time, then I've already had my date with Brenda. And she's already called Rache to tell her. If so, I'm falling right into the one hour I've always tried to forget. And that hour would be my last with Rachael. Ever.

The light becomes solid and I'm here.

The house is quiet. Bob is either at school working on a lecture or at church prepping for a sermon. Wanda has probably taken the kids to the store with her. I sit in a chair and watch the sunlight run through the squares, skipping over, under, through the venetian blind to form a brilliant pattern on the bed sheets.

I'm wearing my jeans, a blue shirt and my green nylon jacket. My sock feet are propped on the bed. I must have driven in from college this morning.

Rachael is sitting on the half-made bed sewing a button on her shirt. She's dressed in a pair of blue denim shorts, a birthday present from me, maybe a month earlier. She's also wearing a white blouse. Unbuttoned. My class ring, held by the gold chain around her neck, bounces gently against her bare skin. She doesn't seem to notice, but she's unusually quiet. Does she know? Has she received the phone call yet?

I scan my memory for images of Brenda. Of the hour at the Student Union cafeteria—

"You know, Michael, when we talked about the church wedding, I could only think about one place—" Rachael looks at her sewing. "It was that little place up near Novenger near where Daddy used to preach." She looks up at me. "A little church on a hill, about halfway to the clouds. Really pretty. Daddy's always talked of moving the family up there, you know."

I search for the image of my time with Brenda, and now I find it— close by—we're standing in front of her dorm and she's screaming at me—telling me I'm crazy to stay with Rachael— "you marry that little brat and you can forget your future—you'll be digging ditches the rest of your life—*and I won't let you do that!*" Then the door slams and I'm alone on a Friday night—last night.

And while I drove back to Corinth, Brenda was calling Rache— telling her that she'd been with me.

No question: The machine has dropped me into the worst day of my life.

"Mama and I spent all last week looking at apartments," Rache is saying, her voice quiet. "We decided they cost way too much. She even said it'd be better if we lived here for awhile."

"Rache, do you still think you're pregnant?"

She looks up. "I started my period this morning." There's a sadness in her eyes. "I really thought I was pregnant. I felt them—"

"Felt what?"

She looks down at her sewing. "Remember I told you it's like a leaf falling into a pool of water—and you get these ripples? I felt the ripples. I really felt 'em. It was so nice."

I see the hurt in her eyes that I'd missed before. Over the last thirty years I had only remembered my own pain—and forgotten how much she had lost too.

I look around the room to see the texture of what I'll miss—blue wallpaper, a white bedspread, blue pillowcase, blue sheet with little flowers on it—there's a dresser with a bottle of *Occur*, a cork-covered bottle of *Tropical Lime* cologne, a stuffed pink bunny, a stack of magazines—looks like *Sixteen*. In the corner is a row of toys—probably Amy's. I would always trip over them in the darkness. I'll miss them all, but most of all, I'll miss my beautiful Rachael.

"You know, Mama and Daddy liked you from the start." She studies the thread, then returns the needle to the little red tomato-shaped pincushion. "Daddy actually called some people at the radio station and told them he knew this disc jockey." She looks up.

"Is that right?"

"Uh-huh. And when he told me about it..." she looks down again at the button. "I dreamed how it'd be. I'd be here with the baby and maybe call in requests. I'd say, Michael, I wanna hear 'Summer In The City' for Mike and Rache and the baby. And you'd play it, wouldn't you?"

"Yeah. I'd do that."

"And you'd play anything by The Righteous Brothers or The Ronettes. And 'It's Now Winters Day,' and 'Sweet Pea.' And that new one, 'Love Eyes.' I really like it," she looks up.

I lock the scene. *Love Eyes*. How could I have forgotten that song?

"Leonard. Do you have anything on a song called 'Love Eyes?'"

"Sure. I'll just key it in. Okay. 'Love Eyes.' Nancy Sinatra. Charted from March 25 to May 25. Are you listening to it now?"

"No. I was just wondering."

"Better hurry up, Mike. I hate to tell you, but you've got a plane to catch."

"I'll be just a few more minutes."

I unlock the scene.

She looks up at me. "Brenda Lacey called last night."

"I know. I went to see her."

"That's what she told me." Rachael touches her engagement ring. Is this where she removes it? Gives it back to me? Have I come all this way just to live this moment again?

"Time's running out, Mike."

"I'll be there, Leonard. I just have to get through this."

Rachael suddenly looks up at me. "*No*, Michael."

"No—?"

"Tell him you're not going back."

"Mike, are you okay? Your heart rate just jumped ten points."

I stare at Rachael. "What did you say?"

"To wherever it is you go. To the future—*someplace.*"

"What makes you think that?"

"Little things," she says evenly. "Things you don't think I see, but I do. Knowing what songs will play on the radio. You knew exactly when that jet would come in." She smiles. "And you're always talking to some guy named *Leonard.*"

"Mike, your temporal lead is behaving randomly. Is everything okay down there?"

Rachael looks directly at me. "I know who you are, Michael."

"Rachael, I— "

"And I know why you came back..."

Everything in her room seems the same, but the light has taken on a different cast. Dark, like in the minutes before a storm.

"It's because I called for you."

"Holy cow, Mike, your entire t-wave just went to hyperspace! Hold on, I'm bringing you up!"

"Not this time, Leonard," Rachael says. "This time he *stays.*"

Suddenly the sky explodes into the room. The walls, floor and ceiling flicker, then vanish abruptly into an endless dark blue distance. High overhead, cirrus clouds rush across the vault of black sky and disappear behind a bright, distant horizon.

And below, stretching into the distance, is the landscape of my life. At the center I see the bright green and yellow paths of my childhood, see them turn into roads, then highways. Further toward the horizon, I see my life in Corinth, my college years, my time with Linda in Boston. Boarding a plane to San Antonio. My instant in time here.

And now I see more—the other paths I took. Other places I saw. Places where Evan was killed, the ones where he lived, the ones where Earl lived, got married, started a family. I see the paths where my own life ended, the ones where I married, started a family, stayed in Corinth. The one where I lost my arm at the factory—each path, *each life* extending toward a bright, distant horizon.

And I see something else: the lives that are Rachael's. Her birth in Corinth, her early years in Mexico, her childhood in Missouri, her first date, that time she died in the hospital, the times she lived.

Her life in north Missouri, the ones in Nebraska, New York, California, her life with the young man from Novenger—

And her life with me.

Now, the circle contracts, and I'm standing on a hill with the wind rippling through the tall grass. The horizon is obscured by the dense, dark clouds of a storm. I know that storm. I've seen it before.

"Rachael, I have a life back there."

She steps towards me. "Michael, we both have lives back there—and in each of those lives, we're apart. Except for *just one*."

The lightning draws near.

"Let the other Michael go back. He has his own life—let him live it."

"I can *do* that?"

"You can do anything you want."

A line courses through the tall, rippling grass—it's a border separating my old life from the one I almost had.

The one I have.

Somewhere.

"All you have to do, Michael, is step across this line."

The storm is upon us—there can be no other choice.

This time, I take the step.

28

Darkness.

Somewhere far away, someone is waking up in a beautiful bedroom in a huge house—driving to work in a new car. Meeting with people from far away. Working hard, being successful, rebuilding his life.

In here there is only darkness surrounding me like a warm blanket. In the distance there is music, and voices, spoken softly as in sleep.

Now I see the door open, the light spreading across space, across the floor. Someone is here. Someone I've known all my life.

"Mommy, can I sleep with you and Daddy tonight?"

"Sure, Honey, you can sleep between us."

Rachael pulls the covers back. "Now, you gotta promise not to kick."

As our little girl climbs into the bed, Rachael turns to me and gives me a quick kiss.

I put my arms around them both, and pull the covers up tight to protect them from the darkness.

Then, listening to their soft breathing next to me, and the rain outside our window, I fall gently to sleep.

www.ingramcontent.com/pod-product-compliance
Lightning Source LLC
Chambersburg PA
CBHW050551260626
47157CB00002B/516